Praise for CAROLYN HART and
GHOST AT WORK

"[A] charming new sleuth. . . . Bailey Ruth and Wiggins
will delight readers."
Boston Globe

"Carolyn Hart is one of the best at writing the cozy
mystery and this one has everything needed to make it
successful—humor, suspense, and great characters. . . .
Ghost at Work is a novel all mystery fans will want
to add to their reading list.
American Chronicle

"The intriguing first of a new series. . . . Hart blends
an enjoyable fantasy with realistic characters
and an engrossing plot that's sure to charm
even ardent materialists."
Publishers Weekly (* Starred Review *)

"Nobody does it better than Hart, whose plotting
skills rival those of Britain's Agatha Christie."
Cleveland Plain Dealer

"Bailey Ruth is a lively, original heroine and a pleasure to
read. Hart gets to design heaven and indulges herself in
celestial fantasies. . . . A master at constructing a mystery,
she builds this one with finesse, suspense, and humor."
The Oklahoman (Oklahoma City)

By Carolyn Hart

Death on Demand
DEATH ON DEMAND • DESIGN FOR MURDER
SOMETHING WICKED • HONEYMOON WITH MURDER
A LITTLE CLASS ON MURDER • DEADLY VALENTINE
THE CHRISTIE CAPER • SOUTHERN GHOST
MINT JULEP MURDER • YANKEE DOODLE DEAD
WHITE ELEPHANT DEAD • SUGARPLUM DEAD
APRIL FOOL DEAD • ENGAGED TO DIE
MURDER WALKS THE PLANK
DEATH OF THE PARTY • DEAD DAYS OF SUMMER
DEATH WALKED IN • DARE TO DIE

Henrie O
DEAD MAN'S ISLAND • SCANDAL IN FAIR HAVEN
DEATH IN LOVER'S LANE • DEATH IN PARADISE
DEATH ON THE RIVER WALK • RESORT TO MURDER
SET SAIL FOR MURDER

Bailey Ruth
GHOST AT WORK
MERRY, MERRY GHOST

GHOST
AT WORK

A BAILEY RUTH MYSTERY

CAROLYN HART

A V O N
An Imprint of HarperCollins*Publishers*

AVON BOOKS
An Imprint of HarperCollins*Publishers*
10 East 53rd Street
New York, New York 10022-5299

Copyright © 2008 by Carolyn Hart
Excerpt from *Merry, Merry Ghost* copyright © 2009 by Carolyn Hart
ISBN 978-0-06-174534-8
www.avonmystery.com

First Avon Books paperback printing: November 2009
First William Morrow hardcover printing: November 2008

Avon Trademark Reg. U.S. Pat. Off. and in Other Countries, Marca Registrada, Hecho en U.S.A.
HarperCollins® is a registered trademark of HarperCollins Publishers.

Printed in the U.S.A.

10 9 8 7 6 5 4

To Phil—"Side by Side" has been our song since that sunny summer of 1957

GHOST AT WORK

CHAPTER 1

Incandescent dashes of pink and gold spangled the fluffy white clouds that arched over the entrance to the Department of Good Intentions. The opening was wide and welcoming. Heaven doesn't run to doors. No one is shut in. Or shut out.

If I entered, I was committing myself to an unknown adventure. Possibly. Or possibly not. Perhaps I wouldn't be considered a worthy candidate. My natural effervescence immediately bubbled, banishing that negative thought. Of course I was a worthy candidate. I love to go and do and hold out a helping hand. I was a superb candidate.

I hurried forward even though I didn't know what to expect. Unctuous solemnity? Goody Two-shoes stuffiness? Earnest exhortations? That hadn't been my experience of Heaven. Surely the Department of Good Intentions was filled with kindred spirits eager to offer a boost up to those in need.

A wash of golden light spilled out, beckoning, encouraging, welcoming. I was drawn by the warmth, yet wary of the unknown. I had felt the same conflict of anticipation and reluctance when I was a kid at the swimming hole a few miles outside of Adelaide. I remembered the dammed-up pool with shivery delight, the water deep and cold, shaded by majestic oaks. We clambered up the rope ladder to the top of a huge red rock, teetered on the sloping surface, scared yet eager, and took a flying leap. That plunge through air was as near to weightlessness as I ever knew. Until now, of course. The first jump was always the hardest. The shock of the icy water took your breath, turned your skin cold as ice. The thrill was worth the scare.

Could I, Bailey Ruth Raeburn, late of Adelaide, Oklahoma, take the plunge now? Certainly, if I ever, within an eon or two, intended to offer my services, it was time and time past. Time and age do not exist in Heaven, but I had the sense that Bobby Mac and I had been here quite awhile. Our cabin cruiser went down in a sudden August storm in the Gulf of Mexico. I expected much had changed since we departed the earth. If I hoped to be helpful, possibly I should volunteer while I still had some memory of earthly ways.

Our arrival here had been precipitous, but, as Scripture warns, the householder knows not the appointed hour. Dark clouds had scudded toward us. Blinding rain pelted our struggling boat. Thunder crashed, lightning blazed. *Serendipity,* our small but sturdy cabin cruiser, capsized beneath a thirty-foot wave. I'd chosen our cruiser's name. I always felt that I was in the right place at the right time, even then. Now, that's a funny thing. I'd come close to being lost at sea when I was seven. I'd been visiting my California cousins and we'd taken the excursion boat to Catalina. Ever a daredevil, I'd scooted behind a lifeboat and hung over the edge. I lost my balance and tumbled overboard. Happily for me, a brawny seaman saw me fall and raced to the railing and climbed to the top to jump after me. I'd flailed to the surface, choked and stunned. The excursion boat faded in the distance. Happily, perhaps fatefully, the sailor kept me afloat, and not long after a sailboat ran near enough to find us. I doubt I would have survived on my own.

Maybe it was full circle that Bobby Mac and I were lost at sea. Of course, our daughter, Dil, was furious with her dad and even more furious with me for tagging along. There had been warnings of a coming storm, but Bobby Mac had lost a big tarpon the day before and he was determined to go after him again. That man was what they call a fishing fool. Still is, and he's thrilled that the tarpon have never been bigger than here in Heaven. Dear Bobby Mac, built like a bull rider with coal-black hair, flashing dark eyes, and a rollicking grin. I smiled, grateful for love that had spanned our years together and flourished still. We two were as youthful in Heaven as on the day we'd met at Adelaide's famous rodeo, Bobby Mac dust-streaked and swaggering after his event, but blessed as well in Heaven with the glorious depth of all we'd known and shared together, happiness, passion, sorrow, tears, and, always, laughter.

From my watery adventure off the coast of California to the *Serendipity*'s demise in the Gulf of Mexico, I was convinced I'd led a charmed life, thanks to the brave sailor on the excursion boat. Now I wanted to do my bit for someone in trouble. As I understood it, the Department of Good Intentions specialized in lending a hand to those in tight spots.

I strode under the arch of clouds, as much as an ethereal figure who isn't terribly tall can stride. I'm not small, but then again I'm not large. Five foot five on a good day in slingback pumps. I glimpsed my reflection in a shining crystal wall, curly red hair, a skinny face with curious green eyes, lots of freckles. I remembered a Polaroid picture Bobby Mac had taken when I was twenty-seven at a church picnic. That's how I looked now! Heaven is full of wonderful surprises and perhaps one of the sweetest was knowing that others see me always at my best, my brightest, my happiest. Age doesn't matter. There is no old, no young. The dear children who left the earth too soon are what they were meant to be in full flower and the aged who are worn and bent and frail at death once again blossom. It was such a thrill for me to see Mama in a glittery, beaded flapper's dress, with a little tilted red hat and high heels, her beautiful face shining with love. In Heaven, your essence determines your appearance. You are the best you ever were and yet nothing is lost of your lifetime.

My image was crisp in the glittering crystal. I must admit I paused for an instant to admire—certainly not in a prideful manner because we all know what pride goeth before—my charming seersucker jacket and slacks and comfortable white sandals. Heaven is simply heaven-sent for fashion. Picture what you want to wear and you are wearing it. It's that easy and never a concern about sizes. We are all a very good size, whatever it is.

I gave my reflection a two-finger salute, a remnant of my days as a Cub Scout mom, and felt a thrill as I swung around the soft cumulus corner. Suddenly I was confident. I hurried, passing a cool rushing stream and tall pines.

Ahead of me, nestled against a green hill, was a little red-brick country train station. A train whistle sounded in the distance. I smelled coal smoke, saw a dark spiral curling into the sky, and heard the clack of great iron wheels.

Was I going in the right direction?

Not more than a half dozen feet away, a small white arrow pointed toward the steps. On the arrow was painted BAILEY RUTH. Oh, I was expected. I took the steps two at a time and laughed aloud as I reached the platform. Wooden carts were lined up against the wall, filled with luggage of all sorts, the kind that speaks of faraway places, satchels and grips and great leather trunks, tagged and plastered with travel stickers. I was already eager. Maybe I would get a ticket to adventure, always keeping in mind, of course, that the objective was to help someone in travail, not to provide me with excitement. Certainly I understood that.

I rubbed my hand along the top of a leather trunk. Mama and Daddy had owned a trunk just like that one.

Suddenly a florid-faced man with a huge walrus mustache appeared directly in front of me. He wore a high-collared white shirt. Substantial suspenders and a wide black belt with a heavy silver buckle combined to hold up gray flannel trousers above sturdy black shoes. Arm garters between his elbow and shoulder pulled his shirt cuffs up a trifle. Pencils poked from his shirt pocket. He looked in charge, the man I was meant to see. Heaven is like that. People appear. Who and when depends upon what you are seeking.

A stiff dark cap topped his curly brown hair. His round face was made heavier by his mustache and thick muttonchop whiskers. Penetrating brown eyes seemed to look into my soul. "Bailey Ruth, I've been waiting for you. I'm Wiggins." He reached out both hands to fold mine in a warm clasp.

"For me?" I wished now I'd not tarried. But, as Wiggins well knew, Heaven offers so much. The wondrous glory of God and His angels permeates every thought with love. There are people to cherish, books to read, plays to see, songs to sing, colors and nuances and beauty to absorb, God and all God's creations to adore.

He beamed at me. "I knew you'd come."

The train whistle sounded nearer. The acrid smell of coal smoke tickled my nose. I looked around the platform. "I wasn't expecting a train station for the Department of Good Intentions, Mr. Wiggins."

"Simply Wiggins, please. As for my station, isn't it beautiful?" He gazed around with innocent joy. "Since my section of the department could be whatever I wanted it to be, I chose a station just like mine used to be. I was the station agent.

I helped people travel, make the right connections. When I got to Heaven, I felt right at home when I was asked if I'd like to keep on helping. There are many other sections and they are all different. But we know that you love to travel. So, here you are." His smile was avuncular. I don't suppose I'd ever had a proper use for the word, but it suited him. He was jolly and made me feel jolly. I smiled in return.

"I'm glad to see a smile on your pretty face and glad that you've come. However." He dropped the word like a boulder and peered at me from under thick beetling brows, his gaze questioning. "Am I correct in understanding that you want to go back to earth?"

I tried to look properly solemn, though I could have tap-danced with excitement. "That's right. I want to help someone in big trouble."

"Admirable. Sterling. Inspiring." He was nodding, his walrus mustache quivering. "Right this way." His hand was on my arm and he shepherded me into the main waiting room with its great wooden benches. We passed through to an office with STATION AGENT above the lintel.

He waved me to a seat on the hard wooden bench to the right of his desk. He carefully hung his hat on a coat tree, replaced it with a green eyeshade, and settled behind the huge oak desk. The stacks of paper and folders on top of the desk were geometrically aligned. A telegraph key was fastened to the right side of the desk next to a sounder to amplify the sound of incoming messages.

The desk sat in a big bay window that overlooked the platform. From his seat, Wiggins could look out and see the track in both directions. The windowpanes showed not even a trace of grime despite the inevitable soot from coal-burning trains. The left side of the office faced the waiting room and had a ticket window. Blank tickets rested in a slotted rack. A clutch of rubber stamps hung on the wall.

He sat comfortably in his four-legged oak chair, tapped a folder. "I know a bit about you." He tugged at his mustache, eyes intent. "You grew up in Adelaide, Oklahoma. Your daddy, Paul, had the drugstore on Main Street. Your mama, Kate, kept you rascally kids—"

Four of us, all redheaded as a woodpecker—Sammy, Joe, Kitty, and me. We were rambunctious as colts and got into our share of scrapes.

"—bright as new pennies and in church every Sunday. You were the liveliest of them all." His gaze was searching. "Inquisitive." It was a pronouncement.

I nodded. After all, how else would I ever know what was going on?

His gaze was thoughtful. "Impulsive."

I'd been known for responding first, quick as a lightning strike, thinking later. Mama had often urged me, "Bailey Ruth, honey, *think* before you speak."

Wiggins placed his fingers in a tepee.

I was afraid I understood the direction he was going. I tried for a bland smile. "I've changed a lot since I arrived here. After all, Heaven encourages grace in all matters. I'm much more reflective." I hoped I didn't sound defensive. I repeated with assurance, "Reflective." Such a dignified word, though I suppose no one would ever think of me as dignified. I almost told him I'd recently reread *Walden*. It was our book-club selection. We have a lovely book club, but that is not germane at the moment.

"Rash." He wasn't talking about measles or poison ivy.

I waved a deprecating hand, hoped my nail polish wasn't too vivid. I wanted him to take me seriously. "Such a long time ago." My tone invited him to join me in rueful dismissal of impulsive behavior. I wondered if he was thinking about the time I lost my temper at a faculty meeting and told the principal he was an idiot. Of course I had justification. Of course I lost my job. It all turned out well. I got a job as the mayor's secretary. The principal had put Bubba, the mayor's oldest son, on probation and Bubba missed his chance to be quarterback at the state championships. I loved being in city hall. Nothing happened in Adelaide that I didn't know about.

He flipped to another page. "Forthright."

We gazed at each other with complete understanding. All right, so I called a spade a spade. I liked forthright better than tactless.

"Daring." He shut the folder.

"I would hope"—I tried to sound judicious—"that a willingness to take chances might be just what the department is seeking. In appropriate circumstances."

"Mmm. That is always a possibility." Wiggins dropped his hands to his desk, reached for a pipe from a rack. As he tamped sweet-smelling tobacco, he looked thoughtful. "A good-hearted emissary is always prized. No doubt you are offering your services for the best of reasons. It wouldn't do to send someone seeking adventure."

I tried to banish all thoughts of adventure from my mind. Adventure? Of course not. I gazed at him sincerely, eyes wide, expression soulful, an approach I'd always found very effective when I'd explained to Bobby Mac that the latest crumpled fender was an utter mystery to me, that certainly I thought I'd had plenty of room to back out. "I truly want to be of help to someone in dire straits." My pronouncement had a nice ring to it and I hoped *dire straits* conjured up a vision of a hapless victim stalked by an Alfred Hitchcock villain.

He nodded, his green eyeshade glistening in a golden glow. "Very well." Now he was businesslike. "Where do you want to go?"

When fresh out of college, Bobby Mac and I had spent a summer hitchhiking through Europe. It was the most glorious impecunious ragtag holiday that could be imagined. I'd loved Montmartre. What fun it would be to return, to see the street artists, drink coffee in an outdoor café, visit the Moulin Rouge . . .

"Possibly Paris." My shrug was casual.

The pause might have been described as pregnant. "Paris," he said finally.

"Paris." I clasped my hands together to keep from wriggling on the bench.

He plucked a pencil from his shirt pocket, tapped it on the desktop. "How's your French?"

"Oh." I looked into chiding brown eyes. "I'd thought it would be like here." In Heaven, everyone is understood, always, whether they speak Urdu, Cherokee, Yiddish, Welsh, Hindi, or any of the world's 6,800 languages.

"Ah"—he waggled an admonitory yet gentle finger—"that is the crux of the situation. There is not here."

I suspected this was more profound than I could manage. I'm bright enough, but I have my limits. Deep thoughts remain precisely that, deep thoughts, and I don't have a shovel.

"Once in the world again, some"—Wiggins didn't name names, such as Bailey Ruth—"might find it a struggle not to revert."

"I see." This useful phrase had seen me through many puzzling moments on earth. Revert to what?

"So"—now he was brisk—"should we enlist you—"

Was I going to be given rank and serial number?

"—it will be with the clear understanding that your mission is for others, not yourself. Moreover, we will go over the Precepts before you depart. Now, where would you like to go?" His brown eyes were sharp.

I had a moment of inspiration. "Where would you like to send me?"

"Bailey Ruth"—approval radiated from him—"that reflects a splendid understanding of our program." Wiggins reached for another folder.

I basked in a glow of rectitude. Certainly I was not in this for myself. I felt noble. I would charge forth and do my best wherever I might be sent. I bade a silent, regretful farewell to visions of Paris. London, perhaps?

"We've given some thought to the matter." He was thumbing through several sheets that looked to be densely typewritten. "It seems quite likely that for your first task you would feel more comfortable in familiar surroundings. We are sending you to Adelaide." He was as pleased as if he'd presented me with a beribboned box of Whitman's Samplers. Whitman's Samplers were always a favorite in Daddy's drugstore. I wondered if the store was still there . . .

Even though Adelaide, Oklahoma, pop. 16,236, was a long way from Paris or London, I smiled and felt a quiver of anticipation. I loved Adelaide and its rolling hills and soft-voiced people, Mississippi kites making watchful circles in a hot August sky, sleet crackling against windowpanes in February. It wasn't Paris or London, but I'd do my best. Would I know anyone? Of course, my daughter, Dil, lives there. It would be such fun to pop in on Dil—

"First, however"—his tone was emphatic—"you must master the Precepts." He waggled a roll of parchment. "After you have familiarized yourself with them, we'll have another visit and I'll give you your specific assignment." He bent his head forward, looked at me sternly. "You will be on probation as you undertake your first task."

I almost whipped back a quick "Not to worry," but decided upon looking into his serious brown eyes that he might not appreciate snappy retorts. Instead I simply repeated approvingly, "On probation."

The tension eased from his face. "That's the right attitude. You will find that attitude is everything, Bailey Ruth."

I couldn't have agreed more. It was my job to be sure he had the right attitude about me. I nodded soberly.

"If you successfully complete this assignment, we will welcome you as a full-fledged emissary." He pushed up the rim of his eyeshade, looking perplexed. "I suppose . . ." The words trailed off. He gave a shake of his head, his mustache quivering. "I scarcely like to bring this up. I find the topic distasteful." He looked pained.

I attempted to look pained as well, though I had no idea what dreadful behavior we were contemplating.

"Ghosts." He pursed his lips in disapproval. "I deplore that characterization of a Heavenly resident dispatched to be of service."

I offered quickly, "We aren't ghosts." I tried to keep the hint of a query from my voice.

He thumped a great fist on his desk and folders bounced. "Precisely. Never. Stories of apparitions and rattling chains foment the most inaccurate imaginings on earth. It is of foremost importance that you do not, in the pursuit of your duties, create situations that will further these mistaken beliefs."

"Oh." I was fervent. "I would never do that."

"Subtlety is the key." Wiggins appeared troubled.

I wondered if he was remembering unfortunate episodes with previous emissaries or if he feared I might be lacking in that quality.

"Subtlety, of course." I was as world-weary and wise as Barbara Stanwyck. Turner Classic Movies had given me a whole new world to emulate. Actually, here in Heaven she's quite approachable.

The flush faded from his face. He nodded benignly. "I will take that as a solemn pledge."

I raised my right hand. If the man wanted a pledge, I was ready.

"Very well. We won't talk of ghosts." His nose wrinkled

in distaste. He glanced down at his papers, thumbed through a stack. "Oh yes. I should mention that we sometimes have missions that do not succeed. Not"—he spoke quickly to preclude any misunderstanding—"that we would ever characterize any volunteer as a failure. Oh, Heavens no. But"— and he clapped his hands together—"there is a foolproof means of achieving success."

My expectant look was a model of the pupil eager to hear the master's declaration.

"Adhere to the Precepts." His nod was emphatic.

I was fascinated by the quiver of his walrus mustache.

"For example"—his look was stern—"there is an absolute stricture prohibiting casual contact with family members, such as your daughter, Dillon. We do not want the living preoccupied with the dead. It simply doesn't do."

"Of course not." I was righteously indignant. Besides, I felt quite close to Dil without making a special trip to earth. One of the lovely aspects of Heaven is that whenever anyone on earth thinks of you, you are there with them for that instant. Why, Dil had thought of me just this morning. She was driving too fast and clipped a hedge as she came around a curve. As her husband cringed, hearing the scrape on the fender, she'd grinned. "If it had been Mama, she would have leveled that bush. Hold on, Mike, we're late."

I didn't share this with Wiggins.

"However, there will be a special familial aspect to your first visit. As for the other Precepts, I'll give you this copy"—he unrolled the parchment and slid toward me a cream-colored sheet embossed with gold letters—"which you can study while we prepare the materials for your visit. The most important Precept—"

I leaned forward, ready and alert. It looked as though I might make the grade. As for the Precepts, I was good at following rules.

Well, usually . . .

Except when I forgot.

"—is this: You will be *on* the earth," an emphatic pause, "not *of* the earth."

My, Wiggins certainly felt strongly about this rather simple concept. Where was the problem? I was quite sure I wouldn't have any difficulty.

. . . on the earth, not of the earth . . .

Simplicity itself.

Wiggins tone was solemn. "If, after studying and mastering the Precepts, you still feel that this is the right path for you, you can come back—"

Just then, a staccato *dot dot dot* erupted from the telegraph sounder on his desk.

Wiggins listened, quickly tapped a response.

A rapid *clack clack* erupted.

He pulled a pad of paper near, wrote furiously, his face creased in concern. The minute the message ended, he was on his feet, gesturing to me. "Bailey Ruth, there is no time to delay. You must be dispatched immediately."

He moved hurriedly to the ticket window, grabbed a ticket, found a stamp, slapped it to the cardboard slip. "Here." He thrust the ticket at me, then yanked at a lever on the wall. "I'm dropping the signal arm on the pole outside. The Rescue Express will stop long enough for you to board. Quickly, now. You'll have to make a run for it."

A rumble announced the train's arrival. I glanced at my ticket, which had a corner nicked off, but I could read *delaide, Oklahoma* stamped in bright red. I jumped to my feet and raced toward the platform. The Rescue Express slid to a stop. A conductor leaned out to help me board.

Suddenly heavy footsteps sounded behind me. Wiggins caught up, breathing fast. He thrust another ticket at me. "Your ticket's torn. That will never do. Here's a proper one."

Clutching my new and perfect ticket, I clasped a strong hand and swung aboard.

A stentorian shout sounded from the platform. "The rector's wife is in dire straits. Do your best for Kathleen Abbott."

CHAPTER 2

rrr. I hadn't been cold in a long time. A gusting wind fluttered autumn leaves from a big maple and a sweet gum. Daylight was almost gone, though enough dusk remained to emphasize the stark shadows thrown by the evergreens that fringed one side of the yard. I was standing near a puddle, shivering and wishing for a nice warm coat . . . Oh. How nice. I smoothed the arm of a thick woolen jacket. It had been one of my favorites, red-and-black plaid. I remembered it well.

I looked at the back of a rambling two-story frame house with excited recognition. "Ohhh . . . " My voice was soft. Wiggins could not have pleased me more. I'd been here many times. The sweeping backyard was one of the glories of the rectory. I'd enjoyed croquet and watermelon socials and volleyball games here, especially when we had that very athletic priest, Father Meadows. He had been quite hearty, with a penchant for mountain climbing, so he'd jumped at an invitation to lead a church in Colorado.

A dim light shone above the back steps to the screened-in porch. I moved forward eagerly. I came around the old stone well and stopped, breathless and shocked. My heart pounded.

Bulbous red eyes glowed in a huge rounded body with four great striped legs that arched to the ground. A moaning sound issued from the huge creature's orange lips. A few feet away, a skeleton lounged in a lawn chair, bony hands holding a book, one leg folded over the other. A witch on a broomstick poked from the woodpile. Her dark cloak streamed in the wind.

Gradually my gasping breaths eased. Obviously, it was near Halloween. The monstrous spider was eerily realistic. I hoped this wasn't Wiggins's idea of a joke. Was there really a Kathleen Abbott in dire straits or had some Halloween mischief gotten out of hand?

I was uncertain whether to call out for Kathleen. Perhaps if I went inside, I'd find her. As I came nearer the rectory, I became aware of a dimly visible young woman standing rigidly on the back porch.

I wafted through the door. Her frozen posture was understandable. She gazed down at a dead man lying on the worn wooden planks, a dead man with a small bullet wound in his left temple.

"Oh my, oh my." She wavered unsteadily on her feet, lifted a shaking hand to her lips. Frantically, she looked around. She stepped toward the back door, peered into the yard. She took another stumbling step forward. A series of unmistakable expressions flitted over her face—shock, apprehension, panic.

If she hadn't been terrified, she would have been pretty. Curly dark hair framed a long face with deep-set brown eyes, a high-bridged nose, and a generous mouth.

I admired her cardigan, multicolored, with swaths of violet, purple, and blue in some kind of fuzzy material. Very attractive and the material was quite new to me, rather reminiscent of angora. She was trim in a black turtleneck and slim-fitting dark pants.

"He's dead!" Her voice was a whisper. "What am I going to do?"

"Call the police." I clapped my fingers to my mouth. I hadn't intended to speak.

"I can't." It was a moan. The moan turned into a strangled gasp. She looked wildly about. "Who's there? Where are you?" Skirting the body, she hurried to the back door, flung it open, clattered down the steps. In an instant she returned to the porch, dashed to the rectory back door, yanked it open, seeking the source of the voice.

I felt a pang of remorse, knowing I'd made a big mistake. Wiggins had worried that I might be impulsive. I supposed his worst fears were realized. But it had seemed natural to speak up. After all, the woman had her duty as a citizen. However, would I have been dispatched, especially in such a hurry, if the solution were as simple as picking up the phone and alerting the authorities?

She struggled for breath and looked as though she might faint. I had to do something, though I was afraid one of the Precepts dealt with appropriate moments to actually be of the world. From Wiggins's dour discourse about ghosts (Heaven forbid), I suspected he favored as few manifestations as possible. If I'd had time to study the Precepts, I'd've known the protocol. Since I wasn't sure, I had to use my best judgment.

I willed myself present.

Kathleen tottered back, a hand pressed to her lips.

"Don't scream! I'm here to help." I spoke gently but firmly as though to a frightened child. "You're Kathleen Abbott, the rector's wife?"

Her yes was scarcely above a whisper.

"I was sent because you're in trouble."

"How did you know? Who are you?" Her voice wobbled.

"That doesn't matter now. It's rather complicated to explain." I glanced at the dead man. "What happened?"

"I don't know. I just found him. How could you possibly know I needed help?" She looked past me as if fearful others might arrive. "Where did you come from? You don't belong in Adelaide."

I was indignant. "Of course I do! I grew up here, my dear, and I know where the bodies are buried."

She made a choking sound and took a step back.

I waved my hand. "Simply in a manner of speaking. Now, I've arrived to lend you a hand. I gather you don't wish to call the police?"

"I can't call the police." Her voice was desperate. "I'll be in terrible trouble if he's found here."

I looked down at the body, a man in his forties who had likely been rather attractive when alive, thick brown hair, a trim mustache, regular features. "Why?"

"Because—" She choked back a sob. "Oh, I don't have time to explain. The women's Thursday-night Bible study is here tonight." She gestured frantically toward the backyard and the drive. "They'll park there and come in this way. Any minute now somebody may drop in to bring a dessert or leave a note for Bill. Oh," she moaned, "what am I going to do?"

I understood. Parishioners consider the rectory to be an extension of their own living room. "That would be awkward." I glanced outside. Mercifully, no one was approaching, but Kathleen was right. We might be joined at any moment.

"Awkward?" Her voice rose in despair. "They'll put me in jail."

"We can't let that happen. Let's move him." I didn't consider this to be a rash suggestion. My mission was to help Kathleen Abbott. Clearly, if the presence of a murdered man

on the screened-in back porch of the rectory put her in jeopardy, he had to go.

"Move him?" She stared at me in horror. "How? Where?"

I pointed out the back door. "Outside, of course." I looked at the body, wished the light were better. He was tallish, around six feet. In the dim glow from the porch light, one hand was oddly distinct. Manicured nails. Bobby Mac had no use for men with manicured nails. The dead man's navy woolen sweater was expensive and so were his black loafers. Slacks of fine worsted wool. I frowned as I studied him. "He wasn't killed here."

"He wasn't?" Her gaze was suddenly sharp and suspicious. "How do you know?"

I patted her arm, tried not to notice that she jumped at the touch. Was my hand cold? "You didn't grow up in Adelaide."

She plunged fingers through her hair, tangling the curls. "This is crazy. First you say he wasn't killed here, then you want to talk about where I grew up." Her voice was rising. "That's part of my problem here. Everybody knows I'm from Chicago and they say I'm nice but awfully worldly for a rector's wife."

I understood. Episcopal Church Women (ECW) do have opinions and the vestry expects so much of a rector's wife. "Chicago is lovely. Bobby Mac and I went to Wrigley every chance we got. Don't worry about being from Chicago. But you don't know anything about hunting. I've heard almost as many hunting stories as fish tales. I'm one Adelaide girl who knows about guns and"—I looked down, made a careful effort to phrase my sentence with delicacy—"people who've been shot." A tracery of blood streaked from the crusted circular entry wound, but no blood or tissue surrounded his head. "Unless I'm very much mistaken, Mr. . . ." I looked at her encouragingly.

"Murdoch. Daryl Murdoch." She spoke the name with concentrated loathing.

". . . Murdoch was shot somewhere else and brought here."

"Oh." She looked startled. "You mean somebody brought him here?" Her voice wavered. "That's dreadful. That means somebody knew I'd be in trouble if he was found here. Somebody knows—" She broke off, apparently stricken by the enormity of the murderer's knowledge.

"First things first." It was time to get to the matter at hand. "Is the toolshed still behind the weeping willow?"

"Yes, but it's locked, and the sexton keeps the keys." Once again her gaze was suspicious. "How do you know about the toolshed?"

"My dear"—and I spoke with a lilt—"there isn't much I don't know about St. Mildred's Episcopal Church and the church property." I'd been directress of the Altar Guild three times. "Back in a flash." With that—and I suppose I should have prepared her for it but didn't—I disappeared. I didn't intend to startle her. I felt apologetic when I heard her gasp.

I was too elated with my discovery of ghostly movement to spare time for Kathleen's travail. I went from there—the back porch—to here—the shed—in an instant. I had no need to tramp through the backyard. How exciting! In the future I would think of a destination and a graceful zoom later, there I would be. And, of course, no door was a barrier to me.

Inside the shed, I turned on the light and found the wheelbarrow. It was no problem to unlock the door from the inside. I wheeled out the barrow, turned off the light, but left the door ajar. I was glad for the golden glow of the porch light because it was truly dark now, the trees and bushes black shapes in the night.

I trundled the barrow up the flagstone walk, frowning because the front wheel squealed like a banshee, not the happiest of sounds when planning to transport a body.

I parked the barrow next to a ramp at the end of the porch. That was an addition since my days. How useful. When I once again stood by the body, I thought for a moment that Kathleen had left and then I saw a kneeling figure feverishly unrolling a tarp.

"Excellent, Kathleen. Couldn't be better." We definitely needed a means of pulling him to the ramp.

She rocked back on her heels. "I've lost my mind." Her voice was ragged with despair. "That's all there is to it. I'm delusional. I hear voices and no one's here. I imagine this woman and I talk to her and then she disappears and now that hideous voice—"

Hideous? Not a generous description, but I had to be charitable. I'd always thought my voice rather attractive, a trifle husky perhaps, but cheerful. I debated reappearing. However, I wanted to follow the Precepts. I must study them as soon as possible, but it seemed to me that I was truly encouraged to remain invisible.

In the world, not of the world . . .

I decided instead to have a frank talk. "Kathleen, let's straighten things out."

She looked wildly around. "Where are you? Come out! You're driving me crazy."

"Deep breath, Kathleen," I barked. "Suck it in, let it out. One, two, three, four . . ." I tried to sound as authoritative as the tartar who'd directed the ladies' morning exercise class at the Y when I was in my exercise years, the earnest years of push-pull-shove-away-dessert until the realization came that chocolate made me happy and happiness was a virtue.

Kathleen breathed in, breathed out. Then, with an anguished cry, she flailed her hands, jumped to her feet, and backed toward the doorway into the kitchen.

"Stop right there." I tried to remember how Humphrey Bogart cowed opposition. I'd watched *Casablanca,* my all-time favorite movie, not too long ago. "Get a grip, sweetheart." Maybe I'd missed my calling. I had a knack for this. "I'm here, but you can't see me right now. It isn't appropriate for me to be present in the flesh at the moment"—she could mull that over—"and we don't have time to waste. I'm going to help you move him. Let's take him to the cemetery."

The cemetery was on the other side of the church from the rectory. As I recalled, a graveled path through oaks and willows curved from the backyard of the rectory behind the church to the cemetery. "Now, are you in or out?"

She cowered by the door, frozen in a crouch. "In." It was scarcely a breath.

I flowed past her, grabbed the tarp, pulled it briskly across the floor.

Kathleen watched the moving canvas with the same horror she would have accorded the progress of a cobra.

I tried to distract her. "Hop to it. We'll ease him onto the tarp." I spread the canvas out beside him. "Take—oh, wait." Forensic matters had never been a consuming interest of mine, but I dimly recalled that cloth could hold fingerprints. Of course it depended upon the coarseness and weave of the material, but it would be best if Kathleen had no close contact with the deceased. "Fingerprints. Hmm."

"Fingerprints." She was struggling not to hyperventilate.

"Deep breaths. In. Out." The advice was a bit perfunctory. Perhaps I could scare up some backbone pills for Kathleen. Fingerprints . . . Ah. I spotted a pair of gardening gloves lying on the counter near a sink. I picked them up, moved toward her. "Better put these on."

She scrambled backward.

Before I could toss the gloves to her, a girl's voice called from inside. "Mom . . . Hey, Mom, where are you?"

Kathleen clutched at her throat, tried to speak, couldn't make a sound.

Footsteps clattered in the kitchen. A girl's voice carried through the open back door. "I've got to ask Mom first. Maybe she's over at the church. Come on, Lucinda."

I swooped to the body and pulled the tarp over him.

The screen door banged open. "Hey, Mom, what are you doing out here in the dark?" A flick and a hundred-and-fifty-watt bulb blazed above us, throwing the furnishings of the porch into sharp relief, the counter with an old-fashioned sink, a rattan table and three chairs, a shiny galvanized tub, two bags of apples, a pair of muddy work boots, a mound of pumpkins, several large bulging black trash bags, stacked newspapers, a heap of old coats.

And the shiny black tip of a shoe peeking from beneath the tarp.

Kathleen saw the shoe, wavered on her feet, moved in front of the body. "Bayroo, stop there." Kathleen's voice was scratchy.

Bayroo. What a curious name.

A skinny red-haired girl, all arms and legs like a wobbly colt, balanced on one foot, throwing her arms wide. "Mom, you won't believe it." She was a bundle of excitement, energy, and vibrant personality.

I felt an instant liking for her and an immediate sense of companionship. I was enchanted by her golden red curls and green eyes and the intelligent, questing look on her narrow face. She was eleven or possibly twelve, almost ready to slip into her teen years, angular now where she would soon be slender. And lovely.

Behind her, a plump girl with dark hair in braids, gold-rimmed glasses, and prominent braces echoed, "You won't believe it, Mrs. Abbott!" She bounced up and down in excitement.

Kathleen's daughter clapped her hands. "Mom, Travis Calhoun's here in town! We actually saw him at Wal-Mart and he's staying with his aunt Margaret. You know, Mrs. Calhoun up the street. I invited him to come to the Spook Bash Saturday and asked him if he'd judge the painted pumpkins and told him how great it would be for everyone who's worked so hard for the bash to raise money for the food pantry and, Mom"—it was an unashamed squeal—"he said he'd come. Isn't that great?"

"Great. Wonderful. Lucinda, why don't you stay for supper with Bayroo. The stew's ready. There are oatmeal cookies in the cookie jar." Kathleen waved a shaking hand toward the kitchen.

"Mom." Meals were for ordinary times. "Travis Calhoun! Besides, we're going over to Lucinda's for pizza. The committee's meeting and will they be excited when they hear about Travis!"

"Golly, they won't believe what happened!" Lucinda's voice rose in a squeal. "Bayroo is so brave. We would have missed him if she hadn't hidden and then she heard noises and got scared but—"

Bayroo reached out and clapped a hand over Lucinda's lips.

Kathleen kept glancing down at the tarp, then away. "That's wonderful, honey." She gestured toward the screen door. "You'd better hurry over to Lucinda's if the committee's coming."

Lucinda was staring toward me. She couldn't see me, of course. What could she possibly . . . Oh. I still held the gloves. I released my grip. The gloves floated gracefully toward the floor.

Lucinda tugged on the red-haired girl's arm. "Bayroo," she hissed.

"Anyway, Mom, Lucinda and I are going over to her house—"

"Bayroo." Lucinda's whisper was piercing. "Where did those gloves come from? They were like, up here." She held a hand to her chest. "Now they're down there. How were they up in the air all by themselves?" She pointed at the gloves just as they reached the floor.

Bayroo turned toward me. Our eyes met. She smiled, a quick, engaging, hello-we-haven't-met, I'd-like-to-be-friends smile.

Oh dear. Bayroo saw me. I couldn't explain it. Sometimes the young have eyes to see what no one else sees. Bayroo saw me. Lucinda did not.

Bayroo asked quickly, "Mom, who's—"

I held a finger to my lips, shook my head, then smiled and turned my hands as if I were shooing chickens.

Bayroo's lips parted in surprise, then she grinned and gave me a tiny conspiratorial nod. She removed Lucinda's arm. "Oh, those gloves." Her tone dismissed levitating gloves as unworthy of notice. "It happens sometimes when the fan's turned on." She gestured toward the ceiling fan.

Lucinda looked up at the still blades, her face serious and thoughtful. "The fan isn't turned on."

"Well, I guess it was. C'mon, Lucinda. We've got to hurry. We can tell everyone about Travis. Mom, I'll do my homework later." With that, the girls turned toward the back door, Bayroo in the lead.

Lucinda's head swung back for a last puzzled glance at the ceiling fan and her left foot caught the tip of the dead man's shoe. She staggered forward. "Whoops."

Bayroo held the screen door open. "Don't kick the dummy. He's going to sit on top of the magic maze at the

Spook Bash. C'mon, Lucinda, let's hurry. They're not going to believe . . ."

As their voices faded, lost in the soughing of the branches and the keening of the wind, Kathleen reached out to cling to the counter. "What am I going to do?"

"Buck up." I was getting exasperated, although I did understand how draining the girls' arrival had been. Even I had felt an icy qualm when Lucinda stumbled over the tip of the dead man's shoe.

Kathleen jumped. "Please. Don't talk."

I didn't bother to answer, merely scooped up the gloves and thrust them toward her.

Kathleen shuddered, but pulled them on.

"All right. I'm here." I tugged at his shoulder. "You take his ankles."

As her face stretched in a gargoyle grimace, Kathleen gingerly grabbed the dead man's ankles with her gloved hands, shuddered again, and pulled.

"One, two, three."

Daryl Murdoch slid onto the tarp. In the sharp light from the overhead bulb, I could see there was no muss on the wooden flooring. Decidedly, he had met his fate elsewhere. Perhaps when we knew that, we would know who shot him.

The thought bobbed in my mind and I realized I was concerned about justice. I felt no scruples about removing the murdered man from the rectory's back porch. After all, someone had brought him there with no good intentions. Other thoughts bobbed. What connection did Kathleen have with the dead man? Why had the murderer assumed Kathleen would be implicated if Daryl Murdoch were found here? There was much I needed to know to complete my mission. I hoped I was off to a good start. If I did well, I wouldn't be on probation. I would be officially attached to the Department of Good Intentions. Perhaps I'd be awarded a ribbon or badge.

As we passed the switch near the door to the kitchen, Kathleen turned off the overhead light.

"Hustle." I tugged on the tarp.

Kathleen again gave that odd little moan from deep in her throat, but she hurried forward.

As we maneuvered the tarp across the porch floor toward the ramp, Kathleen muttered, "It's shock. That's all. I'm in shock. That's why I'm strong enough to move him. Adrenaline. Memory lapses. I'm doing things and I don't remember them. That's what's happening." She looked almost cheerful as the tarp slid down the ramp. Then she saw the wheelbarrow. "How did I get it out of the shed? The shed's locked. Maybe it was unlocked. That's it. I just don't remember . . ."

Poor dear. She would have to come to grips with reality— me—sooner or later. Later would suffice. I concentrated on easing our burden from the ramp into the wheelbarrow. Daryl's feet dangled over the back.

Kathleen, looking squeamish, pulled a corner of the tarp down to cover his shoes.

I was glad to see she was thinking ahead. "Good job."

"In case we see—" She stopped, shook her head, grabbed the handles. "I have to stop talking to myself," she muttered. "I am not carrying on a conversation with anyone. I am not."

She stopped after a few feet, struggling to catch her breath. "I never knew a wheelbarrow was so heavy."

I doubted she'd ever moved one before. Especially not a wheelbarrow laden with a body. I slipped in front of Kathleen and placed my hands in front of hers. Fortunately, I didn't have to worry about muscle strain. The wheelbarrow moved with noticeably more speed, though still lurching and squealing. The flagstone path ended.

It was harder going through the grass. Kathleen breathed in quick gasps. We reached the edge of the rectory yard and stood in the shadow of a pine. The always-present, ever-vigorous Oklahoma wind whipped the branches, buffeted us.

Even with my warm wool jacket, I was cold. I was exhilarated. In Heaven you choose your surroundings, the ultimate in climate control. Bobby Mac and I love the seashore. Other climes are also available. Amundsen, for example, spends most of his time on an ice cap. Sarah Bernhardt exults on a stage with the velvet curtains parting. To each his own. Yet now I was in the world and must cope with weather.

I wasn't surprised at the bite of the wind, the plummeting temperature. Halloween in Oklahoma was often synonymous with the arrival of a blue norther. It may have been seventy-five degrees earlier in the day, but if Halloween was imminent, so was cold weather. Weather in Oklahoma is an adventure, in the twenties one day, nudging seventy the next.

I wished we'd thought to bring a flashlight. We wheeled onto the graveled path, which added a crackling sound to the screech of the wheel. The path curved around a stand of pines. Ahead were blazing lights. I admired the brightly lit paved parking lot behind the church. My goodness, that was a change. A half-dozen cars were parked near the side entrance.

Kathleen stopped. To reach the west gate to the cemetery required crossing the far end of the lot. The wheelbarrow and, of course, Kathleen would be in full view of anyone leaving the church or looking out of the parish hall.

Despite the circumstances, I took pleasure in a swift survey of my beloved St. Mildred's, a graceful church built of limestone. A latticed wall and limestone arches enclosed

a cloister between the church and the L-shaped wing with the Sunday school rooms and church offices. The parish hall was between the church and the wing.

Kathleen crouched.

I divined her intent just in time and pushed down the handles of the barrow as she was pulling up, preparatory to dumping our burden.

I was firm. "We can't leave him here."

She jumped back from the barrow, pointed at the starkly illuminated parking lot. "Don't you see?" She shuddered. "Of course you don't see. You aren't here."

I stamped my foot.

She looked down at the stick that crunched.

"Quickly, Kathleen." He who hesitates . . .

She pushed back a lock of dark hair, looked fearfully toward the church. "If anyone looks out, they'll see us. Me."

"We'll run." It was a straight shot.

She dropped her hands from the shafts. "He can stay here." Her sigh of relief rivaled the whoosh of the wind in the pines. She turned to go.

I grabbed her arm, hung on, rocked back on my heels for leverage. "Don't be silly. The barrow might be traced back to the rectory. Look, we're really close. You take one shaft, I'll take the other and run like . . ." I remembered to be of the world, not in the world. After all, one doesn't want to trifle with Hell. ". . . fast." I firmly fastened her hands on the right shaft. "Go."

We pelted across the blacktop, the barrow rocking from side to side, wheel rasping, Daryl's shoes thumping. I'm sure it seemed a lifetime to Kathleen, but in only a few seconds we plunged through the open gate into the cemetery, leaving behind the light. The gently rolling, heavily treed cemetery was dark as a root cellar.

Kathleen stumbled to a stop. "I can't see a thing."

I have excellent night vision and saw that the graveled path picked up again. "Straight ahead, then veer around the clump of willows." I gave Kathleen an encouraging pat, ignored her recoil. "We'll leave him near the Pritchard mausoleum." It was a showpiece of the cemetery, white marble with Corinthian columns. The marble tombs within were crowned with a sculpture of a greyhound on Maurice's tomb and an Abyssinian cat on Hannah's. He loved dog races and she loved cats and they were rich enough to indulge their whims.

Locals who visit the cemetery make it a point to swing by the mausoleum and stop to pat the greyhound's head and stroke the cat's whiskers for luck. The custom assured that Mr. Murdoch's remains would be found tomorrow. He was due that courtesy, not that cold wind and darkness were a trouble to him now.

The barrow wheel continued its grating screech. We came around the curve, brushed by the dangling tendrils of a weeping willow. The Pritchard mausoleum stood only feet away on a small rise. There was a clinking sound. A darting beam of a light danced within the mausoleum.

CHAPTER 3

The wheelbarrow squealed as Kathleen jolted to a stop.

"What's that screeching noise?" A young voice quavered. "Buzzy, somebody's out there."

"Haven't you ever heard an owl?" Buzzy's equally youthful, but more forceful voice dripped disdain. "That's why they're called screech owls."

"Yeah. Well, I don't like it here." The words came in uneven spurts, likely a product of struggling breaths. "This is a lousy idea. Everybody around is dead. Let's get out of here."

I wafted inside the mausoleum.

A tall skinny boy pulled at the crowbar jammed beneath the edge of the greyhound's pedestal. "What's the matter, Marvin? You scared?" Plaster crackled, drifted down toward the floor.

Marvin held the flashlight trained on Maurice's tomb. "Who, me? No way. But this is a stupid bet, and if anybody finds us we'll end up in jail and Mom will yank my car keys for the rest of my life. Anyway, that dog's probably too heavy to move even if we get him free."

I flew into action. I don't know how many times I'd

brought flowers to graves and I always stopped at the Pritchard mausoleum to smooth the dog's head and run my fingers over the cat's whiskers. I was furious. Halloween fun was one thing, say draping the statues with plastic leis, even a touch of washable paint. But defacing a tomb . . .

I grabbed the crowbar away from Buzzy and flung it out into the darkness, where it clattered down the steps.

Buzzy stared at his empty hands. "How'd you do that, Marvin?"

Marvin, eyes wide as saucers, tried to speak, couldn't.

Outside, the wheelbarrow screeched. Where was Kathleen going?

Marvin's head jerked, seeking the source of the shrill whine. "Something's out there. And something weird's going on in here." He began to edge toward the exit.

"That wasn't funny, Marvin." Buzzy's straight dark brows drew down in a frown. "Go get the crowbar. I can't get the dog loose without it."

I marched over to Marvin, yanked the flashlight from his hand, twirled it in a circle. Light swung disco-quick around the walls of the mausoleum.

Marvin yelped, flung himself toward the entrance. Buzzy outran him.

I followed, sweeping the flashlight high and low. That turned out to be a mistake. I intended to scare them sufficiently to discourage a return, but the light swept over Daryl Murdoch lying on his back a few feet from the steps into the mausoleum.

Marvin flailed his hands in panic, then broke into a lumbering run, trying to catch up with Buzzy.

I turned off the flashlight and it was dark.

Excited shouts, the thud of running feet, and grunts marked the teenagers' progress as they careened around headstones. When silence once again cloaked the cemetery, I turned on the light.

"Kathleen?" I called softly. No answer. I'd not expected one. That high rasp of the wheelbarrow when I was inside the mausoleum must have signaled her departure.

Murdoch was lying on his back near the first step. The tarp was gone as well as the wheelbarrow. I hoped Kathleen shook the tarp well and put it in its customary place and returned the wheelbarrow to the shed. Perhaps I'd better check with her before I departed, though I doubted she would be pleased to see me. Or not see me.

Now I felt a need to make amends to Daryl Murdoch. I placed the flashlight on the top step. The beam illuminated him and perhaps five feet or so beyond. I folded his hands on his chest and straightened his legs. He looked quite peaceful, though I wondered how pleasant his face had been in life. But I mustn't make assumptions just because Kathleen didn't like him. There was a lovely bouquet of artificial chrysanthemums in a nearby vase. I selected a bright yellow bloom and placed it in his hands, then said a prayer to speed him on his way and for his family's comfort.

Sirens wailed in the distance. I lifted my head, listened. At least two sirens rose and fell. The wail increased in volume. I smiled. The boys were good citizens despite their Halloween prank. I must move quickly.

I dropped to one knee beside the body. The ground was cold. I shivered as the frosty wind whistled around me. I was reaching for his wallet when a ding-dong bell sounded very near. I stared at the body. The sound, which reminded me of long-ago cartoon music, emanated from his jacket pocket. How odd.

I reached in the pocket and brought out a small hard plastic oblong not much larger than a fancy compact. The musical tones sounded three more times, then cut off. How curious. I shrugged, replaced the object, and focused on my task. Once I had the wallet out of his pocket, I flipped through it. His driver's license gave his address as 1906 Laurel Lane, not an address I knew.

The sirens were loud enough now to wake the dead. The quip was irresistible. Red lights flashed. One police car, then a second jolted to a stop on the paved road about fifty yards south of the mausoleum. Car doors opened, interior lights flashing.

A woman's voice shouted, "Police. Don't move. Put your hands up. Police." A low murmur ensued and two dark shapes moved cautiously toward the mausoleum, flashlights sweeping back and forth.

I replaced the wallet. As I stood, one of the lights swept near me and I saw the track of the wheelbarrow in soft dirt near the path. Heavens, I should have checked the area first. Now there was no time to lose or the police might track the wheelbarrow back to the rectory. I scooped up Marvin's flashlight. I had no choice but to turn it on.

The police officers both called out. "Halt, there. Police."

I swooped to a nearby grave, plucked a large evergreen wreath from the marker, returned to that revealing trail. I took a good look, turned off the light. One of the perks of being a ghost was the ability to propel myself high, low, or in between. I moved a few inches above the ground—picture a glider—pulling the bristly wreath over the track of the barrow.

A stunningly brilliant light swept toward me, illuminating the wreath and the flashlight I'd borrowed from Marvin. Both were several inches above the ground. I came to my feet, the flashlight and wreath rising, too, and flung them into the darkness.

In the stark light from her huge flashlight, a slender

young woman stared in disbelief as the flashlight spun out of sight behind a clump of shrubbery. The wreath plopped into a puddle. "Jake, did you see that?" Her pleasant contralto voice was matter-of-fact, but her blue eyes were startled.

A stocky young man growled, "Who's the joker? You kids better—Oh hey, Anita, look. By God, that call was for real." He, too, held an oversize flashlight and his bright beam centered on the body. "Hey, that looks like Daryl Murdoch."

Her light joined his. "He looks dead." Her voice sounded strange. "We've got to get the EMT. Call the dispatcher. I'll check for a pulse." She crossed to Murdoch, taking care to walk on the paved area in front of the mausoleum. She knelt, turned that blazing light down, and lifted Daryl's wrist.

Jake held a small plastic oblong to his face, spoke fast. "Car Seven. Officer Harmon. Suspected murder victim, St. Mildred's cemetery. Send ambulance and fire truck. Notify the M.E. Contact the chief and Detective Sergeant Price." As he spoke, brown eyes darted in every direction.

"No pulse." Anita rose, reached for her gun. "Somebody was here. We'd better check around."

"Wait a minute. You get a look at the perp?" Jake stared at the wreath in the puddle.

"No." She shook her head. The wind stirred her short honeycomb-blonde hair. "Did you?"

Jake peered at the tombstones, his bony face wary, eyes searching. "I don't see how they got away without making a sound, especially without any light. They must be hunkered down, crouching behind something." He reached for his gun.

She glanced at the tombstones, some large, some weathered and crumbling. Everything beyond the radius of the flashlights lay in dense darkness. "Listen up, Jake. No shooting unless somebody shoots at us. I know we got a body, but that call came from a kid. He said they'd found a dead man,

not killed somebody. The corpse felt cool. He's been dead
for a while. I don't think it was the perp we almost caught."

I thought her declaration a trifle extravagant. I definitely
had not almost been caught.

"Call dispatch back. Better let them know we think the
victim is Daryl Murdoch." She stood and once again swung
the light in a slow careful circle. Light streaked over graves
and stones, probing the shadows beneath towering sycamores.

Jake held a plastic oblong similar to the one I'd found in
Murdoch's pocket, spoke into it. I wafted to him and peered
over his shoulder, close enough to smell a piney aftershave
scent.

"Dispatch." Jake tried to sound cool, but excitement lifted
his voice. "The DOA in the cemetery next to St. Mildred's
looks like Daryl Murdoch, the businessman. Somebody got
away just as we arrived. We're looking around."

I scooted in front of him. He was talking—somehow—
into that object. Curiosity overcame caution. I reached out,
seized the shining metal object so similar in size to a compact
though oblong, not circular. I stared at the hinged lid, which
contained a small screen and a lower surface with numbers
on it, then held it up to my ear as Jake had done.

I heard a brisk voice. "Chief says to secure the scene.
He and Detective Sergeant Price and the crime lab are en
route."

I realized I held a small radio of some kind. How amazing!

Jake's young face creased in astonishment. He stared at
the now silent object hovering a half foot from him.

I placed the object in his hand.

He jumped as though it radiated static electricity, then
once again held it to his ear. "Damn." He punched one of the

numbers. "Yeah, dispatch. We got cut off." His breathing was rapid. "Sure. I'm right here. We won't touch a thing." He clicked a button, then swung his flashlight in a circle. "Anita?"

Leaves crackled. She came from behind the mausoleum. "Nada. Have you looked that way?" She speared a beam of light behind him.

Jake turned. "Just got off the horn. I'll look around."

As she waited, she swept her light back and forth near the mausoleum.

In a moment Jake returned. "I don't see anything out there. We need more light to check everything. Anyway, the chief's on his way." He glanced at the metal object he still held in one hand. "Hey, Anita. Funny thing about my phone . . ."

Phone! I had expected changes from my day to now, but I never thought I would see a phone without wires that worked in the middle of a cemetery. Why, Bobby Mac would have been in hog heaven out on one of his drilling rigs with a phone.

"Phone?" She stared down at the dead man, her attractive face pulled into a puzzled frown.

"Yeah. It kind of got away from me." His tone was bewildered. "And it hung in the air like for a minute."

She turned toward him and I knew she was recalling the wreath and flashlight that I heaved away. She opened her mouth, closed it.

He hunched his shoulders. "Kind of strange."

"Yeah." Her tone was thoughtful. "Kind of."

He shivered. "Spooky place for a guy to get killed. What do you suppose he was doing here?"

Anita scanned the ground. "Don't know. I guess the chief'll find out."

Jake looked nervously toward the mausoleum, spoke loudly. "Bet there's a hell of a story behind it. Isn't he the guy you liked to hassle?"

Anita folded her arms. "I enforce traffic laws. So far as I'm concerned, that isn't hassling. Murdoch thought the rules didn't apply to him. He drove like he was special. I tried to teach him he wasn't special." Her young face was stern. She stared down at the body without a glimmer of pity.

Jake's bark of laughter sounded odd in the cemetery. "So you gave him enough tickets to—" Sirens sounded. "Here they come." His relief was obvious.

Anita turned toward the road, walked swiftly toward a tall man in a brown suit. He swung a huge flashlight from side to side.

I was tempted to remain. I'd never seen the beginning of a crime investigation, but I knew there wasn't much to be learned here. I hoped relocating the body didn't pose a special problem for the authorities. Still, the detectives might as well start from this false location as from the equally false location on the back porch of the rectory.

I wondered if my task was done. If so, it had been a rather short adventure. I hastily recast my thoughts. I was not adventuring, definitely not. A rather short mission was a much more appropriate description.

If I would soon be boarding the Rescue Express for my return to Heaven, there were two stops I couldn't resist making.

Broad windows on either side of a huge limestone fireplace overlooked a patio bordered by Bradford pears. Dancing flames crackled in the fireplace. Comfortable sofas and easy chairs, a game table, two walls of bookshelves, and shining pegged wooden planks created a warm and lovely room.

However, I was startled when I saw the woman sitting

near the fire. For an instant I felt confused. I was here, so how could I be there? She was speaking into one of those curious telephones. Even her voice seemed like mine ". . . be glad to help with the chili supper except Mike and I will be out of town that weekend . . ."

Of course. Dil and Mike. I remembered their wedding as if it were only yesterday. She was always young in my memory and now as she talked and laughed, occasionally smoothing back a golden red curl, I realized she was on the sassy side of forty-five. I hoped she hadn't minded becoming so much like her mother.

I wafted near, bent, touched my lips to her hair.

Dil broke off. In a moment she spoke again. "Sorry, Ellen, I missed what you said. Oh, do I sound odd? No, nothing's wrong. I had the strangest feeling my mom was here. No." Her eyes moved to a picture of me and Bobby Mac on the *Serendipity*. "No, she died a long time ago. You would have liked her . . ."

The thump of the small black ball caroming around the walls combined with hoarse grunts and the scrape of athletic shoes on the floor.

Rob's thatch of flaming red hair had thinned. He was a little portly but he'd always been built like his dad. His dark eyes slitted in concentration. Muscles tensed as he swung.

My face creased in concern. Rob (Robert MacNeill Raeburn III) was truly a dear boy and a kind man, but he couldn't help himself when he engaged in a sport. He revved up his motor and gave it his all.

The score was called. I was never too quick about numbers but I gathered the handball game was tied, Rob was serving, and if he prevailed, the match would be over.

His face was frightfully red.

In a flash, I darted into the court, timed my swing and

scooped up a ball a scant inch from the floor, and drilled it into the corner, barely escaping Rob's tardy lunge.

Rob blinked, glanced at his hand, which had missed by half a foot. "Game."

His opponent blinked, too, then shrugged. "Good shot, Rob." He stared at the corner. "Kind of miraculous, actually." He shrugged again, grinned. "Spot you to a brew."

I decided it would only be proper to check on Kathleen. She was my responsibility until I felt she was no longer in peril. That done, I might immediately be on my way back to Heaven if my assignment was completed. Should there be more for me to do, I must return to earthly ways and have a moment's respite. After all, when *on* earth even though not *of* the earth, I was affected by temporal realities. I'd had a momentary lift from my glimpse of Dil and Rob, but I was tired, hungry, and thirsty from the excitements of my arrival at the rectory and that challenging trip to the cemetery.

I wondered if Lulu's was still on Main Street next door to the bank. Lulu's was a single storefront wide and twenty feet deep, with a counter that ran the length of the grill and room for a half-dozen booths. Onion burgers were her specialty, topped by grated longhorn cheese and chili. Mmm. A burger and fries with a frosty root beer would lift my spirit.

But, duty first.

CHAPTER 4

A cuckoo clock warbled the quarter hour. No wonder I was hungry. Bobby Mac expected his supper at six-thirty sharp and it was past seven. He groused when we had to go out to dinner. As far as he was concerned, dinner at eight was more than late, it was an offense to the natural order. Bobby Mac was big on the natural order. I grinned and hoped the tarpon was giving him a majestic battle. I wouldn't tell him I'd given Rob's handball a slight bit of assistance. Men are so sticky about rules.

I adored the new color scheme in the rectory kitchen, lots of orange and yellow and tomato red. A golden oak table overlooked the windows to the back porch. Chairs at either end and two on each side afforded plenty of space. I felt at home when I saw Fiesta dinnerware. Two azure plates topped by butter-yellow soup bowls sat on red woven cotton place mats. The napkins were white and red gingham.

I especially liked the vivid painting of the Grand Canyon on the wall where our rector's wife had placed a shaggy macramé in tones of beige, brown, and gray.

The flooring was new, no longer wood planks that had a distressing tendency to slope in one corner. Instead, beige tiles were interspersed with blocks of smaller red, yellow, and orange tiles in a pyramid pattern. Instead of avocado green, the refrigerator was a shiny steel color with two vertical doors, one small and one large. A pot bubbled on a flat surface with concentric rings where the stove had sat.

I wafted nearer, drawn both by the savory aroma and my interest in the gleaming surface with the coils. My, what a lot of controls. We had a gas stove. You turned it on, lit the flame, and cooked.

I found a hot pad, lifted the lid. Mmm. Brunswick stew. A light glowed in the oven. I opened the door, welcomed a rush of heat, and sighed in happiness at the old-fashioned heavy iron skillet with cornbread batter, one of my sister Kitty's specialities.

Steps sounded from the central hallway. Slow steps. I heard a voice, but couldn't distinguish words. Kathleen entered the kitchen. She looked younger in the bright overhead light. Her dark curls were freshly brushed. She'd applied fresh makeup and changed into a berry-red turtleneck sweater and a long paisley skirt that swirled as she walked. Ah, she was talking into one of those new phones.

". . . don't know if the candles have arrived or not . . . Certainly the rector keeps track of orders, but he hasn't mentioned it to me. I'll let him know of your concern, Mrs. Harris." Her voice was pleasant, but Kathleen surely wouldn't want her face to freeze into a mask with those icy eyes and grim frown. "Certainly, Mrs. Harris. I know the ECW luncheon will be especially meaningful to everyone who is new to Adelaide. I will be there." She whirled and stalked toward the stove.

Nimbly, I moved aside. She might be startled to bump into what seemed to be air. The thought caught me by surprise. I puzzled over the physics of it. I was invisible, but I knew I existed in space since I had no difficulty gripping the handles of the wheelbarrow, yet I was able to move through the solid medium of a door. Probably there was an equation that explained everything, but I'd never been good at math.

Kathleen held the phone over the stove and punched a button. A grating buzz sounded. She pulled the phone back. "That's the timer! Excuse me, I have to run. Thanks for calling." She punched a button, apparently ending the call. She turned off the timer and, mercifully, the noise ended.

"Clever." Oh dear, there I went again.

Kathleen stiffened. Her eyes shifted nervously around the kitchen.

I didn't hesitate. Wiggins would have to understand. As I appeared, Kathleen's mouth opened, but no words came. My arrival was reflected in the mirror over the sink, and I had some understanding of her distress. At first, I wasn't there. Suddenly colors misted and swirled, resolving into me, red curls damp from the misty night, green eyes glistening with eagerness, a friendly smile on my face. The red-and-black plaid jacket looked as new as the day I'd bought it. It did look a trifle unseasonable hanging over seersucker.

Since the kitchen was toasty, I slipped out of the jacket, tossed it to a straight chair near the door. I nodded approval. I've always loved seersucker, though I would have to think about winter clothes if I was going to be here very long. I glanced again at Kathleen. Perhaps a white turtleneck and a crimson wool skirt and black pumps would be better.

Kathleen gasped. "How did you do that?"

I checked the mirror. I must remember that the thought is mother to the deed. I managed not to preen. But honestly, and speaking without pride because we all know what pride goeth before, the combination was striking. I studied my reflection judiciously. Possibly a crimson scarf might add an accent.

Kathleen moaned and backed away, apparently an unfortunate habit of hers. She held up shaking hands. "You aren't here. It's all in my mind."

It was time to set her straight. "I am here. At least, I am here for the moment. Don't be frightened. I want to help you." I couldn't resist a small complaint. "I had rather thought you'd stay long enough to assist me in the cemetery."

Her eyes were huge. "There was a light in the mausoleum and voices and I was scared. I didn't think you were there."

I understood she might have felt abandoned. "Some boys on a Halloween prank. I couldn't let them take Maurice's greyhound."

She watched me uneasily. "You sound as though you knew him. Maurice, not the dog."

"Everyone knew Maurice and Hannah." I wouldn't claim intimacy. The Pritchards were one of the first families of Adelaide.

"Sure. Of course." She spoke soothingly, as if to a child describing an encounter with martians. "Right."

I almost took issue, but time would prove my claim and Kathleen would offer a suitable apology for doubting me. "All's well that ends well." I was willing to be charitable. "Did you put the wheelbarrow in the shed?"

Kathleen shuddered. "I put it up and pushed the button inside to lock the door. I folded up the tarp and put it out there." She bent her head toward the porch. "I'll never use it again. Never—"

"Steady." I reached out to pat her arm, but she moved away.

"All right." Her tone was resigned. "You know everything, so you must really be here." She still faced me with her hands raised, palms out. Not a welcoming gesture. "If you're here, who are you?"

That was a reasonable question. A woman has every right to know the identity of a guest—especially an unexpected guest—in her kitchen. The difficulty was in knowing how much to say. Whip quick, I decided a long-winded explanation of my history and connection to Adelaide was surely unimportant. I matter-of-factly announced, "I'm Bailey Ruth Raeburn."

The effect was amazing. Kathleen's eyes widened. She appeared to be having difficulty breathing.

I put my hands on my hips, possibly in a confrontational manner. "For Heaven's sake, what's wrong with you now?"

She struggled for breath. The words came in uneven spurts. ". . . crazy . . . has to be all in my mind . . . she's dead . . . that's Grandmother's sister . . ." Then, angrily, "Why are you impersonating my grandmother's sister?"

I flung myself toward her, wrapped my arms around stiff shoulders. "You're Kitty's granddaughter? How wonderful." Finally I loosed my embrace of her rigid body. "Kathleen, your grandmama would be mighty upset to know you were treating me this way."

"You're too young." Her tone was accusing.

What sweet words. "I'm me. As I was." And will always be. Odd to think that on earth though wrinkles had come and a sprinkling of silver in my hair and an occasional pang that our time here was fleeting, I'd still, deep within, been fresh and new. Now that was the me Kathleen saw. I wondered how the world would be if no one judged anyone else on the basis of age. Perhaps I could write a letter to the editor . . . Oh, Wiggins would deplore a public statement. I'd have to mull this over, but for now Kathleen must be persuaded. "My dear, take my word for it. You see, Heaven has no calendar for anyone."

She squinted at me. "You do look like an old picture of Grandmother's sister." Kathleen looked wily. "How did you die?"

"A storm in the Gulf. Bobby Mac and I went down in the *Serendipity*."

She folded her arms. "You could have looked that up somewhere."

"My dear, you have such a suspicious nature. If you have any doubt about who I am, Kitty always had a cat named Spoofer. It didn't matter whether that cat was black or white or tortoiseshell, that cat was Spoofer. I don't know where anyone would look *that* up."

Kathleen swallowed, said jerkily, "Spoofer."

"The last Spoofer"—I was emphatic—"was all black except she had white whiskers and a white throat and tummy and four white paws. And she bit."

Suddenly there was a thump. I looked on the table. A huge black cat walked majestically toward us, yellow eyes gleaming.

Kathleen waved weakly. "Get down, Spoofer."

I laughed aloud.

Kathleen didn't join in. Instead she walked unsteadily to the kitchen table, pulled out a chair, and sank into it.

I followed, settling on the opposite side of the table. How dear of Wiggins to send me to help Kitty's granddaughter. I hoped I was scheduled to stay for a while. Since I was still here, there must be more for me to do. Perhaps I was expected to offer reassurance, though so far my appearance had not appeared to afford Kathleen any pleasure. "We're family. Now—"

The phone rang.

Kathleen popped up and grabbed the little phone. She glanced at the tiny window and smiled. She was genuinely pretty when she looked happy. She answered with a lilt. "Bill." As she listened, the smile fled. "Sure. I know. Of course. Try to grab something to eat." Her shoulders sagged. She walked back to the chair, dropped into it. "Sure. See you." She clicked off the phone, set it on the table. "Whenever." She buried her face in her hands. Her body sagged in sad resignation.

"What's wrong?" I would have liked to give her a hug, but I didn't want to see her cringe.

She dropped her hands, pulled a Kleenex from her pocket, swiped away tears. "I wouldn't cry except everything's so awful. And I can't even tell him—"

I scooted forward in my chair. "Who's Bill?"

"How can you know all about Grandmother and not know who Bill is?" Her eyes glinted with suspicion.

I took a deep breath and launched into my narrative. I tried to be cogent, though she looked bewildered about Wiggins and the Rescue Express, but finally she seemed to understand.

Huge brown eyes stared at me. "You're a ghost."

"Shh." I looked warily around. Wiggins would not be pleased. In fact, I had the strangest feeling that he was quite near, his walrus mustache quivering in indignation. That was absurd. I mustn't get nervy. Perhaps Kathleen's uneasiness was affecting me.

Kathleen hunched in her chair, her eyes huge. "I don't believe in ghosts. Huh-uh."

"I am an emissary." That was Wiggins's line, and I was stuck with it.

"If you're dead and you're here"—Kathleen thumped the table—"you are a ghost."

"All right, ghost it is." I spoke soothingly. "It doesn't matter whether I'm a ghost or emissary." Why did I feel a sudden chill? "The point is that I am here to rescue you from an almighty mess."

Kathleen rubbed her face with the tissue. "Mess. That's what it is. A great big mess. Your Wiggins had it right when he said I was in dire straits. I am definitely in dire straits even if it sounds like an episode from *The Perils of Pauline.*"

I clapped my hands. "Mama loved Pearl White. Mama said she had the most expressive eyes and great grace and style. Mama showed us pictures. I loved the hairstyles then, those soft puffy curls. Pauline was so daring. I hope I can do half as well."

Kathleen closed her eyes for a moment, opened them, shook her head. "Spoofer and *The Perils of Pauline* and a body on the back porch." Her smile was strained, though she tried to be gracious. "I appreciate your good intentions, Bailey Ruth, but maybe . . ." She looked yearningly at the back door. "Maybe you can go on back to wherever you came from now. Everything will be all right now that Daryl's gone." She pressed fingers against her cheeks. "Except somebody brought him here. That scares me. What if they know—" She broke off, her expression distraught.

I began to suspect my task wasn't done. What could be known about Kathleen and a man whose body had been dumped on her back porch? "Know what?" I didn't have two red-haired children to no avail. Anybody who can survive the teenage travails of two redheads can worm the truth out of anyone. I fixed a commanding eye on Kathleen.

I saw the desire to jump and run, and I saw her shoulders slump. I doubt she quite articulated her thought, but, clearly, wherever she went, I could go and no doubt would.

She drew a ragged breath. "—about me and Daryl Murdoch at his lake cabin Wednesday. Or about Raoul. What if Daryl wrote something down? It would be just like him. I don't care what I say, nobody will ever believe nothing happened. Bill would be so hurt. I wouldn't have had anything to do with Raoul except it's always the same old story." She pointed at the phone. "Bill calls and he can't come home for dinner. Tonight he's at the hospital. Old Mr. Worsham is dying and he's with the family. I understand. But if it isn't the hospital, it's a vestry meeting or the finance committee or a Lions Club dinner or somebody who needs counseling or . . ." Tears trickled down pale cheeks. "It's always something for somebody and never for me. I know it's wonderful he can be rector of such a fine old church—"

Of course. Bill was the rector of St. Mildred's. That made everything clear.

"—but he never has a free minute. He spends more time with other people's kids than he ever does with Bayroo—"

I had to interrupt. "That's such an interesting name. What is its origin?"

"Oh, that's funny." She was laughing and crying at the same time. "Bayroo is Bailey Ruth. After you. She was born on your birthday, and when Grandmother heard she had red hair, she asked me please to name her after you. Bayroo couldn't say Bailey Ruth when she was little, just the beginnings of both names. She'd say 'Bai Ru,' and we started calling her Bayroo."

"And it stuck." I tried not to sound too proud. No wonder I felt such empathy with Bayroo. And here was her mama, Kitty's granddaughter, in about the direst straits possible. Obviously, I had my work cut out for me. "Bayroo looks like a happy girl."

Kathleen used both hands to wipe her cheeks. She sat up straight. "So why am I such a mess?"

I was crisp. "Don't take everything personally."

She flared right back. "I didn't know 'for better or worse' meant always taking second place to the church. Bill's wonderful. He's good and kind and funny and sweet. That's why I fell in love with him. But he never takes time for himself and that means he never takes time for me."

I looked at her kindly. "Which brings us, I expect, to Daryl and Raoul." I fervently hoped there had not been a romantic

entanglement with Daryl Murdoch. I remembered that Errol
Flynn mustache. Surely Kathleen had better taste. As yet, I
knew nothing about Raoul, though I had some suspicions.

Her mobile lips drooped. "I felt up to here"—she chopped
the edge of her hand at her throat—"with the ECW and the
Altar Guild and Winifred Harris, though I know she's a
nasty exception. Most of them are old dears who are as
kind as can be. Sweet Mrs. Douglas keeps bringing me
cherry pies. She knows I'm blue and she thinks a cherry pie
solves everything. Sadie Marrs brings by the nicest clothes
from her shop"—she touched her turtleneck—"in exactly
my size and insists they were used in a style show so of
course she can't sell them and they are as good as new
and of course they are new and she knows we don't have a
dime and she thinks pretty outfits will get Bill's attention.
Sometimes I think everybody in town knows I'm a church
widow. If I were a golf widow, I could learn to play the
game, but what can I do about the church?"

I understood. The rector of a small church has to do prac-
tically everything himself and works from dawn to midnight. His wife is always onstage. As for Mrs. Harris, I knew
the type. I'd dealt with a few overbearing ladies in my years
at the church. I remembered, with a distinct lack of charity, Jolene Baker, who never thought anyone could iron the
linens as well as she and didn't mind saying so.

Kathleen looked forlorn. "Bayroo's busy as can be. That's
what I want for her, but the house is empty now most of the
time. She's in the choir and she plays tennis and soccer and
half the time she's having dinner with Lucinda, then going
to the Baptist church because they have the biggest youth
group in town. Friday night they're having a Halloween skating party at the roller rink in their gym and tonight Bayroo's
at Lucinda's helping plan our Spook Bash. It's on Saturday
from four to eight. Last night she went to the youth meeting

with Lucinda. There are some on the vestry who don't like the idea of the rector's daughter going to the Baptist youth group on Wednesday nights.

"Bill stood up to them and said he was glad Bayroo wanted to go and learn Scripture verses, and if they played games in the Baptist youth group and had fun, too, so much the better. He pointed out how he'd proposed building a youth center and the vestry hadn't agreed. Daryl Murdoch was the main obstacle, insisting the church couldn't afford that kind of expenditure even if the Goddard family was willing to put up the major portion of the cost."

The Goddards. That was an old name in Adelaide dating back to the time when the first oil field was discovered. How nice that some of the family still lived here and still served as patrons of the church. But we were getting rather far afield from Daryl and Raoul. Or Raoul and Daryl. "You were fed up. What did you do?"

"I decided to take Spanish at the college—"

One of Adelaide's charms is Goddard, the four-year college established shortly after the city was founded, the land donated by the Goddard family. The campus is in the historic part of town not far from the rectory. Adelaide is hilly and Goddard's ivy-twined, red-brick buildings spread over three hills.

"—and Raoul Chavez was my teacher. He seemed to like me and I was one of the best students and we got into the habit of having coffee in the union."

"Handsome?" I pictured the young Anthony Quinn I'd seen in Turner Classic Movie reruns.

She nodded. "He has a wonderful laugh."

"Single?" Did I need to ask?

Another nod. "He told me he'd never met the right woman." She bit her lip. "Until he met me."

I wished I could place my hands on each shoulder and

give Kathleen a gentle shake. Or maybe I should get her a primer: *Single Men Who Flirt with Married Women Are Up to No Good.* "All of the fun and none of the bother."

She looked at me blankly.

Kathleen was definitely naive for a girl who grew up in Chicago. "Of course he liked you. You were married and obviously at loose ends or why else take Spanish, and you probably had long soulful conversations over coffee about life, love, meaning, the universe, and his hand brushed yours and there were looks."

She was genuinely impressed. "Were you there?"

I was startled when I realized she was serious. "No. I've just now been dispatched here. Had I been there, I would have spoken to you about the primrose path."

She blinked.

The allusion didn't register. I said gently, "Beware a stranger bearing gifts."

Her face crinkled in thought.

I put it baldly. "He had designs on your virtue from the moment you walked into class. Flattering, of course."

She gasped. "But I thought—he was so reluctant—he said he knew we had no future—"

Except, of course, for idyllic sweet-sorrow assignations at his apartment and no danger of entanglement.

"—and he knew he'd always love me and we might have just a brief moment together—"

"He invited you to his apartment one rainy afternoon, and when you came . . ."

Her cheeks turned rosy red. "I walked in and looked at him and all I saw was Bill and Bayroo and I turned around and walked out."

"You felt cruel, leaving his wounded heart behind you, and you didn't go back to class and dropped the course. But somehow Daryl Murdoch found out."

She was astonished. "How do you know this?"

It wasn't the moment to explain that I, too, had once been young and naive. I still had interesting memories and I'd learned to dance a dramatic tango. Ah, Latin men. I settled for a dictum: "A married woman must never trust a single man." Or married ones, for that matter, but we couldn't cover all the bases tonight.

"I never will again. Oh, damn, I don't know how I got into so much trouble."

The buzzer sounded on the oven. "The cornbread's done." She looked at the clock and abruptly jumped up, "I've got to eat something. The Bible study class will be here in about twenty minutes. The stew's ready. But there's nobody here to care."

"Not so." To me, the succulent stew was a matter of great interest. "I'd love to have a bowl." I thought under the circumstances I wasn't being too forward to invite myself to dinner, though Mama had always been strict with us: "Don't let me ever catch you kids asking for food at someone's house. Wait till it's offered."

Kathleen looked surprised. "Do you eat?"

"When invited." I grinned at her.

She managed a smile. "I'll move Bill's plate—" She stopped, her face suddenly stricken, one hand holding the lid from the pot, as she stared at the table.

I stared, too. All I saw were the place settings and, of course, that cunning small telephone.

Emotions rippled over her face, recollection, shock, panic. "Daryl's cell!"

I was bewildered. Cell? Did he have monastic interests? Surely she'd not visited him in a cell. Was she confusing the mausoleum with a cell?

She banged the lid back on the pot, whirled, and started for the back door. "I've got to get it. He took pictures of me when I was at the cabin, and if they find it and see, I'll be in a terrible mess."

I plunged after her, grabbed her arm as she tugged at the door handle. "Cell? He isn't in a cell."

She tried to wriggle free. "His cell phone. His cell takes pictures."

I made the connection. I'd heard the ring and even picked it up. How amazing. A little phone could take pictures? But it must be so. Nothing but the hideous reality of images captured in the phone would explain her panic.

"Let go." She yanked her arm free. "I have to get that phone or I'm ruined."

As the door banged open, I grabbed her hand. "The police are there."

She stumbled to a stop, her face despairing. "The police are there? Already? They've found him?"

I explained about Marvin and Buzzy's good citizenship. I glanced at the clock. "The police have been there a good twenty minutes now. The chief had just arrived when I left. They were expecting someone else." I couldn't remember. "Something about a laboratory."

She leaned against the wall, unable to move.

"Daryl's phone has pictures of you?" I wanted to be sure I understood.

"He laughed, asked me if I wanted him to put them on the church Web site. I knew he wouldn't because of his wife. But there they are, in his phone. The police—oh, what am I going to tell them? What am I going to tell Bill? He knows I loathed Daryl and wouldn't have gone to his cabin unless I had to."

Web site? That conjured up an odd and ominous picture of a gauzy web. I didn't have time to ask for an explanation. "You stay here. I'll go to the cemetery and see what I can do."

Obviously, I didn't intend to walk. Time was clearly of the essence. I disappeared. Kathleen shuddered. Poor Kathleen. She should be getting the hang of it. I was.

I landed on a tree above the body. I shivered and and wished I'd brought the red-and-black plaid jacket. Oh, how nice. I welcomed its warmth. I buttoned the front, felt much more comfortable.

Now, where was Daryl's cell phone and how was I going to get it?

CHAPTER 5

I sat on the branch of a cottonwood and watched the scene below in fascination. Bobby Mac would be impressed when I told him. The activity under way was as taut with suspense as any battle with a tarpon. Brilliant spotlights arranged in a square illuminated Daryl Murdoch's resting place. Yellow tape fluttered from poles jammed into the ground. A slender man in a French-blue uniform stood on the mausoleum steps. He held a camera and slowly panned the area.

Just inside the fluttering tape, a big man with grizzled black hair stared down at the body. He stood with hands jammed in the pockets of his crumpled brown suit. His hairline receded from a rounded forehead, now creased in concentration. His eyes were deep set in a heavy face with a large nose large and blunt chin.

I studied him, trying to recall . . . Oh yes. He reminded me strongly of Broderick Crawford in *All the King's Men,* the same open countenance and burly build, the same aura of power. A man to be reckoned with.

A rustle sounded in the bushes. An officer stepped toward the man in the brown suit. "Hey, Chief. Take a look at this."

The police chief strode near. "What you got?"

The officer pointed a flashlight beam toward the ground. "Crowbar. No rust. Doesn't look like it's been here long."

The chief frowned. "Get pics. Measure. Bag it up."

I supposed many extraneous objects were gathered up in the search of a crime scene. I turned back to the body. As far as I could tell, it had not been moved. Did that mean the picture mechanism was still in his pocket? Kathleen had called it his cell phone, which was certainly a curious use of the word. A walkabout telephone that took pictures seemed quite remarkable to me.

A half-dozen cars were parked on the road on the other side of the Pritchard mausoleum. Most had their lights on and the beams illuminated trees with thinned leaves and old tombstones. A yellow convertible with the top down pulled up behind a white van. The driver's door opened. A young-ish man in a navy pullover sweater, faded jeans, and tennis shoes swung out. He shaded his eyes. "A cadaver in the cemetery? You guys pulling my leg, putting on a special Halloween party for me?"

The chief glanced down at the body. "Not even for you, Doc, would we go to this much trouble. We got a body. Daryl Murdoch." He spoke the name without pleasure.

The young man gave a whistle. He jumped lightly over the tape, but he took care to land on the sidewalk. "Daryl the mighty? Has the dancing begun?" As he spoke, he moved to the body, knelt. For a long moment he observed. "Somebody have second thoughts?" He pointed at the bouquet I'd placed in those lax hands.

The chief nodded. "Yeah. We'd noticed. Odd."

The doctor scanned the ground nearby. "You find a gun?"

"Nope." The big man reached in his suit-jacket pocket, pulled out a package of spearmint.

I wafted close, sniffed. Some things never change, the smell of spearmint, the way leaves crackle underfoot in winter, the need to handle harsh reality with nonchalance. And, of course, the incredible intimacy of a small town. Everybody didn't know everybody, but if you had any prominence at all, you were known. Even more important was the fact that someone always saw you. It was that simple. No matter where you were or what time or with whom or why, somebody saw you.

Kathleen didn't understand how anyone had been privy to her visit to the bachelor professor's apartment. She was the rector's wife. She was known. Perhaps the apartment manager saw her. Or the postman. Or Raoul's next-door neighbor. Or a bicyclist. Or . . .

The big man sighed heavily. "Already got a call from the *Gazette* and from the Oklahoma City paper and a couple of TV stations." He sounded aggrieved. "What can I tell 'em, Doc?"

"DOA." A chortle.

There was no answering smile. "Yeah. And?"

The doctor pulled a tubular flashlight from his pocket, trained it on the small crusted circular wound in Murdoch's left temple. A fine red line had trickled and dried from the wound to his cheekbone. "It isn't official until I do the autopsy, but you can say preliminary examination suggests he was shot to death by a small-caliber weapon." He turned the grayish face to one side. "No sign of an exit wound. Probably means it was a twenty-two and the bullet lodged in the skull. That's all I can tell you for now, Chief."

The chief snapped his gum. "Killed here?"

The doctor shrugged. "Can't say. No rigor yet, so he probably died within the last couple of hours, which means there won't be any lividity. The blood pattern on the cheek would be more consistent with the body lying on its left side, not the back. Might have died here, but he could have been moved."

Another heavy sigh. "On TV the doc can tell you he was

sitting up when he was shot and he fell down on his left side, and from the way the blood settled, he was moved twice."

The young doctor bounced to his feet. "Go watch TV. It's always good for a laugh." He jerked a thumb at the corpse. "Send him along." He was thudding toward his car when the chief called after him. "Suicide?"

The doctor stopped, looked around. "Thought you didn't find a gun."

"Right." The chief moved out of the way as the slender man who had taken pictures stepped past him. Now he held a sketch pad. I craned to look. The camera rested on one of the mausoleum steps. I'd have liked to get a close look at his camera. Bobby Mac loved to film the family, but our camera had been huge in comparison.

The chief unwrapped another stick of gum. "The squeal came from a kid. Maybe he heisted the gun. Cool souvenir."

The doctor was skeptical. "I played tennis with Daryl. He cheated on line calls." A cool glance at the dead man. "Anyway, he was right-handed. It's a challenge for a right-handed person to shoot himself in the left side of the head." He trotted back to Daryl, squatted on his heels. "Doesn't look like the slug went in on a slant. I'll check it out." He came to his feet, headed for his car. He called over his shoulder, "Since you didn't find a gun, it's probably homicide."

I wafted back to my branch, rocked by what I'd learned. My initial assumption may have been absolutely wrong. I'd decided Murdoch had died elsewhere because there was no blood and mess on Kathleen's porch. That may not have been the case. He may have been shot on the rectory porch, the bullet remaining in his skull.

If Murdoch was shot on the porch, it suggested the un-pleasant possibility that the murderer accompanied Murdoch to the rectory and shot him there for the express purpose of

ensnaring Kathleen. The rectory seemed an unlikely place
for a spontaneous quarrel and attack.

Did Kathleen have a bitter enemy? Or was she simply an
attractive candidate for suspect number one?

The doctor strolled toward his car, whistling through his
teeth. The slender man continued to sketch on his pad. Every
so often, Anita, one of the first police personnel to arrive,
called out information to her fellow patrol officer. ". . . four
feet nine inches south of the steps . . ." I was impressed by
the meticulous record that was being made.

However, this record was irrelevant. Oh dear. What had
I wrought? Words danced in my mind. It was almost as if
Wiggins were at my elbow, reciting: impulsive, rash . . .

Well, what was done was done and I had to focus on what
I should do to rectify my possible error. At this point, only
I—and, of course, Kathleen—knew the investigation was
beginning from the wrong place.

Oh yes, someone else knew. The murderer.

I didn't see any way to point the authorities to the true
locale of the crime without involving Kathleen. Yet if the investigation went in the wrong direction, there was no one to
blame but me. That made it my solemn responsibility to provide aid and encouragement to these hardworking officials.

I can only stress my absorption in the shouldering of this
task to defend myself from responsibility in what followed.
I was, in fact, so consumed with concern that it took a long
moment for the ripple of music to register.

When it did, I gasped aloud. Fortunately, no one heard
me. I suppose a puff of sound from a tree branch wasn't noticeable in the creaking of limbs in the wind and the crunch
of leaves underfoot on the periphery of the scene.

I realized perhaps an instant before the chief that Daryl's
phone was ringing. Of course I'd heard it before and even
held it in my hand. Panic swept me. Inchoate thoughts

bounced in my mind, unruly as flung marbles: . . . *got to get it . . . Kathleen's picture . . . mustn't be seen . . . if I'd paid attention to business . . .*

I reached the body at the same time as the chief. He pulled on plastic gloves of some sort as he knelt.

I plunged my hand into Daryl's jacket pocket. As I did, the pocket visibly moved.

The chief's hand stopped inches away. He had the air of a man who refuses to accept what his eyes are telling him.

I edged out the phone.

He shook his head, blinked, grabbed for it.

The chief's hand closed around mine.

I held tight.

The chief grunted, tightening his grip around my hand. "Funny shape to this damn thing."

My fingers crunched against metal. "Ouch."

He shot a startled glance at the young policewoman standing near. "Was that you, Anita? Something wrong?" He didn't ease the pressure on my hand.

"Chief?" She stepped closer, her face attentive.

"You hurt yourself?" He looked up in concern.

"Not me. Jake?"

Jake strode forward, bent toward the chief. "Anything wrong, sir?"

I dug my heels into the ground, but I was losing the battle. There was only one solution. With my left hand, I gave the chief's fanny a big pinch.

Startled, he let go of the phone and my hand and shot to his feet like a man poked by a pitchfork. "What the heck!" His exclamation brought everyone to a standstill. All eyes focused on him.

He looked around, frowning. "Something poked me in the rear. I guess a bug or something got me." He gave Jake, who was nearest him, an odd glance.

By this time I was once again on my tree limb. My heart raced. Obtaining the phone had been touch and go. I held tight to it, but I was far from home free. What if it rang again? All eyes would swing up. Probably there was a means of forestalling that occurrence, but I didn't have any idea what it might be. I couldn't simply secrete it up here in the tree. The ding-dong ring would reveal its hiding place immediately.

"Jake, did you jab me with something sharp?"

Jake looked shocked. "No, sir. There was nothing close to you. Absolutely nothing."

The chief shrugged. "Doesn't matter. Let's see. Oh yeah, that phone."

I worried about taking the phone to the rectory. If it were found there, Kathleen would be in direr straits than she'd ever imagined. However, I had no expertise with the cunning little machine and I needed Kathleen's help. Wafting through the air with the phone in hand posed a danger. Even though it was dark, someone might glimpse an airborne object in the glare of a passing headlight or in the radiance of a streetlamp. That would cause comment.

I had an instant's qualm. Had I undertaken a task beyond my capabilities? Sternly, I quelled my misgivings. I was on a mission. If there were unfortunate repercussions, odd incidents that would go down in Adelaide folklore as the peculiar occurrences attendant upon the discovery of Daryl Murdoch's body in the cemetery one wind-whipped night shortly before Halloween, so be it.

Below, flashlights crisscrossed the ground. The chief knelt again by the body. "The damn phone has to be here. Everybody stay where you are. Jake, grab me a Maglite."

All eyes were on the ground. I made my move.

I was learning more and more about my invisible state. When unencumbered by objects, if I were in one spot and desired to be in another, I promptly found myself there. Material possessions required passage through the material world. That is to say, when I was on the branch and resolved that, whatever the risk, I must confer with Kathleen, I did not make an instantaneous leap to the rectory kitchen as I had from the rectory kitchen to the crime scene. Instead I swooped from the branch to the rectory and, in consequence, passed over the church parking lot.

Below me two elderly women were progressing slowly toward a large white car. One leaned on a cane. The other bobbed beside her, speaking in a club woman's clarion voice. "Absolutely a disgrace that the rector—"

The ding-dong bell of Daryl's phone pealed, its shrillness emphasized in the quiet of the parking lot.

The woman with the cane jolted to a stop. She looked up, startled. "Look, Maisie." She pointed her cane at the sky.

The smaller woman's gaze rose, but, fortunately, I was beyond the bright circle from the light pole. "What?" The voice was loud.

The older woman bellowed, "Maisie, don't you have your hearing aid turned on? There was a bell and something flew by right up there." She gestured with the cane. "It sounded like a cell phone. It looked like a cell phone. Up there all by itself!"

Maisie looked huffy. Her voice had the loudness of the hard of hearing. "I declare, Virginia, you don't need to try and fool me with any Halloween nonsense just to make me turn on that fool hearing aid that makes me feel like I'm inside a washing machine. And—Virginia, look over there. All those lights in the cemetery. Oh, my goodness, something's happened. We'd better go see." Maisie headed for the path to the cemetery.

Virginia couldn't keep up with her short plump friend. Her progress was also slowed because she kept pausing to look back, her face a study in bewilderment tinged by shock.

I wished I could reassure Virginia. Obviously, she was a woman who knew what she had seen. But I had problems of my own. I waited in the darkness near the trunk of the big sweet gum behind the rectory. At all costs, I hoped to prevent anyone else from glimpsing the phone. I was tempted to appear so I could slip the thing in my pocket. I started to appear, changed my mind. It would be just as detrimental for me to be seen as for the airborne phone. Adelaide was a small town. I would immediately be noted as a stranger and, once seen, an interesting subject for discussion.

I could imagine the conversations now: "Who was that redheaded woman in the backyard of the rectory Thursday night?" "She was there and then she seemed to disappear. Do you suppose she was visiting Kathleen?" "Did you ask her name?" "I was hurrying toward her and then she was gone."

I know small towns. I was positive calls had already begun, spreading word of Daryl Murdoch's demise to almost every household in Adelaide. Virginia and Maisie wouldn't waste an instant in sharing the exciting news about a body in the cemetery.

I dared not appear where I might be glimpsed by anyone other than Kathleen. The best I could do was lurk in deep shadow until I could slip unremarked into the rectory and find her. I was beginning to feel frazzled.

Suddenly a deep voice boomed, "Bailey Ruth."

I shrieked.

"Bailey Ruth, please."

I felt instant empathy with Kathleen. I would be more understanding in the future if she exhibited distress at an unexpected voice apparently coming from nowhere. I looked frantically around, struggling to breathe without hiccuping.

I saw only shifting shadows made more ominous by the moan of the wind.

"Wiggins?" My voice wobbled.

He cleared his throat. "Forgive me for catching you unaware, but you've been dashing about." He sounded plaintive. "In and out. Here and there."

I wanted to add "up and down" in a lilting voice, but as Mama often warned, "Smart alecks always get their comeuppance, Bailey Ruth."

Indeed, I had covered a lot of ground. I swiftly reviewed the evening's activities—making contact with Kathleen, moving the body to the cemetery, retrieving the cell phone. I'd packed quite a bit of action into a short period. I doubted Wiggins's usual emissaries achieved this much this early. Perhaps he'd come to commend me.

"Wiggins." I almost had my breathing under control. "How nice of you to come." I wondered if it would be impolite to ask that in the future he somehow let me know of his presence before shouting my name. It would be even nicer, more comfortable, if we both appeared and I'd see him in his stiff cap and crisp white shirt and gray flannel trousers. That would be much jollier than voices unattached to bodies. Clearly, we would see each other if we were in Heaven, yet such was not the case on earth. That required becoming visible, not a state Wiggins viewed with favor. I supposed he'd located me by following the suspended cell phone.

There was a rumble. It sounded like distant thunder, then I realized Wiggins had cleared his throat.

"It is imperative that we speak." His tone was heavy, dour as a high school principal discussing a panty raid with the chief raider. (A true-life experience for one Rob Raeburn many years ago. His daddy thought the entire episode was funny.)

I tried to lighten the moment. "Speaking with you is

always a pleasure, Wiggins." Was fudging the truth a misdemeanor or a felony at the Department of Good Intentions? "You've caught me at a bad time. I'm working hard to extricate Kathleen from a truly difficult situation."

"Bailey Ruth, there must be no more departures from the Precepts. I understand you are new at this, but rules are rules. Already"—he held up a hand, ticked off my offenses one by one—"you have encouraged the popular misconception about"—he shuddered, forced out the word—"ghosts by becoming visible. Moreover, you have attracted unwarranted attention at the mausoleum, pinched the police chief, stolen that contraption, and displayed it above the church parking lot. These incidents will combine"—horror lifted his voice—"to suggest the cemetery is haunted."

Twigs crackled nearby.

I feared Wiggins was pacing.

A heavy sigh sounded. "You have done all of this in the space of less than two hours earthly time."

"Oh." I was not to be commended. "Kathleen's not in jail." My voice was small.

There was such a long silence I wondered if he had left. Then I thought—perhaps I dreamed it—I heard a faint chuckle.

"Well put." His tone had warmed. "We do not subscribe to the belief that the ends justify the means, but I agree that so far you have executed your duties as capably as possible."

I brightened.

Another sigh. "For you. There's the difficulty. You may well not be suited to serve as an emissary—"

I interrupted swiftly or I suspect I might have been handed a return ticket on the Rescue Express. Did I smell coal smoke? "Trust me, Wiggins. I'll be a model of subtlety from now on."

Headlights swept over the sweet gum as a car turned into

the rectory drive. Two more cars arrived. Doors banged. Loud cries of greeting ensued. There was the enthusiasm of friends gathering who had likely not seen one another for all of a day and a half.

Abruptly I realized I was alone below the sweet gum. Faintly I heard an admonitory order: "Follow the Precepts." A pause, and fainter still, "Please."

Oh, sweet Heaven. I was still here. I had another chance to do my best. Wiggins would be proud of me. I could be subtle. Certainly I could.

The chattering group moved toward the rectory back door. I smiled. Adelaide's church ladies hadn't changed a whit since the days when I came for fellowship, bringing a plate of cookies or a casserole. I edged to the far side of the trunk, the phone well out of sight, and watched as seven— no, eight women surged onto the porch and into the house, chattering and laughing. Kathleen would be off-limits to me for an hour or so. After the lesson and discussion, there would be dessert and coffee.

Dessert . . . I was ravenous. I waited five minutes. No more cars arrived. I reached the door to the back porch and once again was reminded of my burdened state. There would be no slipping through the door without opening it. I reached for the handle, stopped, looked at the phone. It dangled inches from the entrance, its luminous window glowing sea green.

Despite my hunger, I knew my duty. It took only a moment to waft up to the roof. Once there, I squinted to see and struggled to keep from zooming into space. The night sky was a black pit without a hint of moonlight. The lights from the church lot afforded no illumination here. A fitful wind gusted out of the north, a harbinger of winter.

I moved close to the rooftop, up and over a peak to the central chimney. I tucked the phone next to the base of the chimney on the lee side. I was pleased. No one would find the phone there. The ring wouldn't be heard over the rustle of branches and the keening of the wind. Now I go could inside.

I was in the kitchen when I heard a clatter at the back door. Bayroo's high clear voice carried well. "Mom made some oatmeal cookies. We'll have a snack, then go up and do our homework."

I was back on the roof in a flash. Bayroo would see me at once and I certainly couldn't have dinner while she and Lucinda were at the kitchen table. I sighed. I felt that I'd spent a good deal more time on the roof than Santa's reindeer. Then I smiled. It wouldn't take the girls long to eat their cookies and meanwhile I would explore my surroundings, set up a base camp. I wondered if the guest bedroom was available.

Indeed it was. I turned on the light, welcoming the warmth within. I clapped my hands in appreciation of the burl-walnut bed topped by a snowy chenille spread. Puffy pillows looked extremely comfortable. A cozy nook held matching Egyptian Revival chairs with Sphinx-head armrests. The Herter wardrobe glistened with inlays of mother-of-pearl. I suspected a church patron had provided the beautiful Victorian furnishings so appropriate for the rectory.

This was a perfect spot for me. I was tempted to become present, but perhaps I should remain as I was until I'd studied the Precepts. My lips curved upward. I wondered if this interlude had been arranged by Wiggins to provide me with a moment to chart my future on, of course, the basis of the Precepts.

I settled into one of the easy chairs. Hmm. Not the most comfortable of resting places. I plucked a downy pillow from the bed, placed it on the seat, sank comfortably down, and unfurled the shining parchment scroll that appeared as I thought of it.

PRECEPTS FOR EARTHLY VISITATION

1. Avoid public notice.
2. No consorting with other departed spirits.
3. Work behind the scenes without making your presence known.
4. Become visible only when absolutely essential.
5. Do not succumb to the temptation to confound those who appear to oppose you.
6. Make every effort not to alarm earthly creatures.
7. Information about Heaven is not yours to impart. Simply smile and say, "Time will tell."

I understood. What I knew wasn't to be shared. Heavenly realities are confined to those in residence.

8. Remember always that you are on the earth, not . . .

"Got it." Oops. I'd spoken aloud. I must remember that in my present situation silence was golden, always a difficult concept for me. And, I think, for most redheads.

It was deflating to realize, as Wiggins had pointed out, that I'd already broken four of the eight Precepts. I'd do better tomorrow. I patted a Sphinx head for emphasis.

A high squeal in the hallway heralded the arrival of Bayroo and Lucinda on the second floor. I refurled the parchment and, out of mind, it disappeared. Now I could have dinner.

I thought and, presto, I was in the kitchen. Perhaps someday Wiggins would explain the dynamics to me. I moved toward the stove and felt bitter disappointment. No pot. Had Kathleen forgotten that she'd invited me to dinner? The cuckoo chimed the quarter hour. Oh, it was almost nine o'clock. The engaging author of *The Egg and I,* Betty Mac-Donald, proclaimed that to dine at nine was divine. I was in fundamental disagreement. Seven is Heaven, but I would admit that delay had definitely enhanced my appetite.

A kitchen is a kitchen. In only a moment I had plucked the covered bowl from the refrigerator and poured a substantial portion of stew into a saucepan. It was a bit of trial and error, but I managed to turn on the stove top. Fortunately, the cornbread was still in the skillet. I cut a generous wedge, added a chunk of butter. I carried a bowl of steaming stew and a small plate with cornbread to the table.

It is more cheerful to say grace with a full table, but I nodded my head and murmured a favorite . . . "Bless this food to my use and me to your service . . ." The first spoonful was grand. Kathleen was a good cook. The stew was savory and the cornbread a twin of Kitty's recipe. In fact, I was certain it was Kitty's recipe, with buttermilk and a dollop of bacon grease. I enjoyed every mouthful, though my thoughts swirled uneasily.

If murder had occurred on the rectory back porch, where was Kathleen at the time? I don't have a good head for puzzles. In school the very words *thought problem* made my head throb and my hands sweaty. Moreover, it was a matter of supreme indifference to me how long it took someone rowing four miles an hour to go six miles upstream against a three-mile-an-hour current.

Unfortunately, what had happened and when and where to Daryl Murdoch was very near to being a thought problem. The examining doctor said Daryl had been dead for a couple of hours. I worked backward, trying to estimate times. When I'd first arrived to find Kathleen discovering the body, it was dark and blustery from the heavy clouds, but there was a glow on the horizon from the setting sun. Kathleen and I discussed the situation and I located the wheelbarrow. That took at least fifteen minutes. I spooned a particularly delicious chunk of beef. I added another fifteen minutes to load him up and reach the mausoleum. How long had it taken for me to rout the boys and their crowbar? Five minutes, perhaps. I hadn't remained long after they fled. Perhaps another five minutes. I arrived in the rectory kitchen at a quarter past seven. The times were approximate, but I figured that Kathleen found Daryl between six and six-thirty.

I was pleased with my calculations. Once I'd discovered what time he arrived at the rectory . . . Oh. That might be difficult. If he was shot on the porch, likely he was in the company of the murderer. I doubted the murderer would cheerfully reveal times to me. If he was shot here—

The swinging door into the kitchen opened. As Kathleen stepped inside, she stopped, flat-footed. Her eyes widened. She executed an awkward turn to block the doorway. "Elise, I'll see about the dishes. Listen, there's a special gift I think we should present to Miriam."

I listened with interest and scraped the last spoonful from my bowl. Kathleen sounded stressed. I was concerned for her. Tonight was not a good time for her to appear distraught. I would encourage her. Be of good cheer when others are near. Perhaps that could be her mantra. Everyone had had mantras in the sixties. Bobby Mac would stand at the top of the stairs and trumpet, "I am the tarpon man." My mantra. I blushed. Perhaps that was better left to posterity.

A high sweet voice sounded puzzled. "Gift? I thought we were going to cut the cake."

Cake? I looked around, saw a silver cake stand with a cover on the counter near the mixer. I wafted to it, lifted the lid. Burnt sugar, Kitty's signature cake. I felt the same mixture of elation and delight I'd enjoyed as a girl when I received a new Nancy Drew. I resisted the impulse to edge just the tiniest taste of the delectable icing onto my finger.

"Upstairs." Kathleen was gesturing wildly. "Please, Elise, go up to the sewing room. There's—"

Silence stretched. I don't want to claim that I am immediately empathetic. Yet I knew that poor dear Kathleen not only didn't have a gift upstairs, but was frantically trying to think of some object for Elise to retrieve. I was at her side at once. I whispered into her ear. "Pincushion." The sewing room at the rectory always had a plethora of pincushions.

A jolt of electricity couldn't have startled Kathleen more. She managed to convert a yelp into the cry, "Pincushion."

Elise stood with one hand on the doorjamb. Tall and thin, she stared at Kathleen with puzzled dark eyes. "Pincushion?"

"Yes. The red one." Kathleen managed a smile. It was strained, but it was a smile. "It will be perfect for Miriam. I hadn't had a chance to wrap it. There are paper and ribbons in the bottom drawer of the chest in the closet. Please wrap it. I'll take care of the cake and coffee and you can bring it in and we'll present it to Miriam."

Kathleen sounded frantic. Almost feverish. Perhaps I should remove my dishes from the table. It wouldn't take a moment to wash up, put everything in order. I was surprised that a few dishes on the table upset her. There are women who must always have their kitchens in perfect order, especially when there are guests. I wouldn't have thought Kathleen was that particular. I was at the sink when the kitchen door closed. Suddenly Kathleen was beside me. In fact, she bumped into me, recoiled, then grabbed the soup bowl, hissing, "You've got to stop doing things like this."

I relinquished the bowl. "My dear, you are under too much stress. I was simply cleaning up—"

"What if Elise looked toward the table and saw a piece of cornbread move through the air and disappear? What if she saw the bowl and plate flying across the kitchen all by themselves?" Kathleen shot a hunted glance toward the door. "What if she comes back and hears me talking to no one?" She moved closer to the sink, automatically rinsed my dishes and silverware.

Oh. How could I have forgotten? However, it is difficult to remember I'm not here when I am. "I'm sorry." I must be more careful. That reminded me of my perilous journey with the phone. "Kathleen, you'll be pleased to know I was able to retrieve Daryl's phone." Considering her present discomfiture, I thought it best not to mention that moment above the church parking lot.

"Where—"

The hall door swung in. Elise bustled toward the table, a tomato-red pincushion shaped like a teapot in one hand, pink wrapping paper, scissors, and tape in the other. My tête-à-tête with Kathleen would have to wait.

Elise deftly wrapped the pincushion, chattering all the while. "I thought tonight's discussion of Saint Philip Neri was excellent. I agree with his insistence that rigorism keeps Heaven empty."

When Elise fluttered paper, I used the crackling sound as cover and leaned near Kathleen to whisper, "We'll talk in the morning. The phone's safe for now."

I wished my whispers didn't have such a galvanizing effect on Kathleen. Her eyes flared, her mouth opened, her hands opened and closed spasmodically.

As she used the scissors to curl a strip of ribbon, Elise turned toward Kathleen. "And I love Saint Teresa's—" Elise broke off, staring. The scissors snapped shut, cutting the ribbon in half. "Are you all right?"

"Just"—Kathleen gulped for breath—"scalded my hand."

"Cutting the cake?" Elise looked toward the cake stand with its cover in place.

"The cake knife." Kathleen whirled and moved to a drawer.

Elise looked at the stack of plates on the corner of the counter. The plates contained no cake. "Why did you put the knife up? You haven't cut the cake yet."

"It was so hot. The water, you know." Kathleen yanked open a cutlery drawer, drew out a serrated knife.

Elise unwound another long strip of ribbon. "You'd better check the hot water heater. It's extremely dangerous . . ."

I passed through the swinging door into the hall. Literally and with pleasure. It was such a bore to have to open and shut doors. I wanted to take a peek around the rectory before I slipped upstairs to my lovely guest room. My duties were done for the moment. Kathleen seemed to be safe. The police investigation was under way. In the morning, I would confer with Kathleen. For now, I was free to relax and consider my rather breathtaking day.

I was mindful that it behooved me to commit the Precepts to memory. Surely Wiggins understood that the opportunity for thoughtful consideration had so far eluded me due to circumstances utterly beyond my control. I pushed away the memory of his doleful voice. Hopefully, he had returned to the Department of Good Intentions. Perhaps another gh— emissary might benefit from consultation. I would redouble my efforts to remain unnoticed.

In the hallway, I gave a sigh of sheer delight. I might have been transported as an eight-year-old to my Grandmother Shaw's stately home in Fort Worth. Since my time the rectory had been restored to its Victorian glory. An ornately carved walnut Renaissance Revival étagère held a collection of Bristol glass, three vases, a mortar and pestle, and a fan holder. A pink porcelain clock on a center shelf was gilded with bronze. The hallway was papered in Delft blue with a golden medallion pattern.

The flooring was now custom redwood, the entryway runner a fine Oriental in pale shades of rose and gold. One of the church patrons must have made possible the restoration of the rectory to Victorian glory. Clearly Kathleen and Father Bill wouldn't have the funds.

I heard the chirp of women's voices in the living room. I lingered by the étagère. I picked up one of the fans, flared it open. It reminded me of stories I'd heard from the era when my grandparents were young. Ah, those romantic days when a young woman might flick a wrist, flutter a fan, and send a seductive sidelong glance to a sideburned gentleman tipping a white straw hat.

I was caught up in my fancies when the front door rattled with a brusque knock. Quickly, mindful of Kathleen's concerns in the kitchen, I replaced the fan and slipped to one side of the étagère as a patrician woman stepped through the archway from the living room into the hall. Short-cut silver hair glistened in the shower of light from the chandelier. She was tall and slender, with a confident carriage.

The kitchen door swung out. Elise held it open as Kathleen entered with a serving tray.

"I'll get the door, Kathleen." The newcomer spoke with a brisk assumption of authority. The directress of the Altar Guild no doubt. As to the manor born, she strode to the door, flicked on the porch light, and opened the door. "Hello, Sam." There was the faintest edge of surprise in her voice.

The police chief squinted in the sudden glare. He straightened the baggy coat of his suit and cleared his throat. "H'lo, Rose. The reverend here?"

"Father Abbott isn't here." Rose emphasized the title.

It was the old chasm between the evangelical brethren and the Episcopal congregation. The police chief, likely a stalwart Baptist, wasn't about to call any man Father.

"Come on in, Sam. We're just finishing our Thursday-night Bible study." Rose held the door and turned toward Kathleen. "Chief Cobb is looking for Father Bill."

The chief stepped inside, looking exceedingly masculine and large. His leathery complexion reflected years of too much sun. Another fisherman, I decided. Bobby Mac would have liked him. Cobb's gaze was steady. His broad mouth looked like it could curl into a big grin as well as straighten into toughness.

Fortunately, my gaze also encompassed Kathleen. I reached her just as the tray began to tip. I steadied it. This time I tried to keep my whisper gentle, but to the point. "Look lively. No one knows. Find out what he wants. Act normal."

Elise's head swiveled back and forth, seeking the source of the soft murmur.

Kathleen thrust the tray toward Elise, walked to the door as if facing the guillotine. What was I going to do with her! I flowed alongside and breathed in her ear. "Relax. Smile."

Kathleen looked up at the police chief. She managed a tight smile. "Bill's not here right now. He's at the hospital. I can give you his cell number."

The chief's big head bent forward. He looked uncomfortable. "You can help me, Mrs. Abbott, same as him. Thing is, we've had a crime in the cemetery. The body of Daryl Murdoch—"

Shocked cries rose.

"—was discovered near the Pritchard mausoleum."

Rose stepped forward. "Sam, what happened?"

The chief was brisk. "He was found dead with a bullet wound. We've been attempting to contact family members but haven't had any success."

Rose looked at Elise. "Do you have Judith Murdoch's cell number?"

Elise pointed toward the living room. "I'll get my purse, check my address book."

I perched on the hideously uncomfortable red plush chair next to the étagère.

I heard a click and looked down. Spoofer moved purpose-fully across the floor toward me. Some insist that cats' claws always retract and can't click on a hard surface. That is not true of all cats and Spoofer proved my point. He looked up at me, flowed through the air, and settled on my lap. I gave him a swift hug. Heaven knows that cats are God's most elegant creatures.

Chief Cobb nodded. "That would be helpful. However, I'm here because we got an anonymous call that a weapon was hidden on the back porch of the rectory. I know it's Hal-loween and crank calls can happen, but this one sure came fast. If you wouldn't mind, I'd like to—"

I came to my feet. Spoofer twisted in surprise, but landed on his feet. He gave me a reproachful glance, but I wasn't there.

Once on the porch, I turned on the brilliant overhead light. Kathleen might be puzzled, but that didn't matter. I doubted I had much time and I must be able to see. The anonymous call proved how fast word travels in a small town. The mur-derer had heard that Daryl was found in the cemetery and knew immediately that the body had been moved. That must have caused consternation, but the murderer was resourceful and determined. Obviously, the gun was hidden somewhere on the porch. Had Kathleen called the police to report the murder, a search would have ensued and the gun would have been found. Now the murderer was taking Daryl's removal and turning it to his or her advantage. Everyone with access to the rectory would be under suspicion if the gun was found here.

Kathleen and I hadn't made a search. We'd simply noted there was no gun near the body. Now I looked carefully.

The porch ran the length of the house. The counter and sink were handy to the kitchen door. I knelt to peer underneath, noted with approval that the pipes were wrapped for winter. I poked a hand in a dark corner, not an exercise I would have undertaken had it been a hand of flesh. Brown recluse spiders do not take kindly to trespassers.

I scrambled past the sink and counter, ran my hand behind the rolled-up tarp. Nothing. The gun was not behind the stack of garden pots or tucked in a mélange of rubber boots or nestling in the drawers of a dilapidated desk or wedged among the pumpkins. I sped to the other end of the porch.

Voices sounded and the kitchen door swung out. "Sure appreciate your cooperation, Mrs. Abbott." The chief looked back at the gaggle of women surrounding the kitchen door. "Ladies, if you'll stay in the kitchen, I'd appreciate it. This will only take a minute." He tugged a pair of plastic gloves from his pocket, pulled them on, then turned to his left, the portion of the porch I'd already checked.

I don't know what I would have done if he'd turned toward me. Another pinch? Three bulging black garbage sacks were clumped against the south wall. I loosed a tie to peer inside the first one. Unfortunately, I might as well have picked one up and spilled out the contents. The cans banged and clanged. I was almost startled into my skin. I tried frantically to quiet the surging metal. Heaven knows I applaud conservation, but the collection of empty soda-pop cans might be my undoing.

Chief Cobb swung around. "Nobody's supposed to touch—" He broke off.

Of course nobody had.

He gazed at the south end of the porch, the quivering sack and cascading cans, his face puzzled.

Kathleen bent down, picked up Spoofer, who was edging

past her ankle. She held up the wriggling, offended cat. "He hates it when garbage bags are closed."

Elise bent forward. "But the cat wasn't—"

Kathleen's voice rose, drowning out Elise. "He probably heard a mouse. That's what it was. Mice. Come on, Spoofer." She hurried across the porch, opened the door, and put him out. She turned back toward the kitchen door, one hand behind her, waggling frantically.

I understood it was some kind of warning to me, but I didn't have time to figure it out. The chief was moving purposefully along the counter, stopping to check beneath with a flashlight he'd pulled from his suit coat. Not, of course, the Maglite he'd used in his search for the missing telephone.

I tiptoed past the trash bags. A gym bag rested next to a bag of golf clubs. I knelt by the sleek plastic bag, edged the zipper open. Empty. I lifted it up. Nothing underneath.

A piercing voice demanded, "I don't think it's mice. Kathleen, do you have a rat? I swear that gym bag moved. It would take a rat."

There was a hurried shuffle as the Bible study group members moved away from the kitchen door.

Kathleen gave an unconvincing laugh. "Things have been moving about out on the porch. Maybe that's it." She was backing closer to the bags of cans, trying to interpose herself between me and the women. Abruptly, she pointed toward the chief. "Look, he's found something!"

I hoped her ploy was successful. In any event, I took advantage of the momentary distraction to plunge my hand into the golf bag. I tried not to rattle anything, but the clubs clattered together. Heads swiveled in my direction. I tried to still the quiver of the clubs. I pushed my hand deeper and felt the barrel of a small gun. My fingers closed around it.

Kathleen surged toward the screen door. "Someone's out there. I heard someone outside. Oh dear, should we check?

Oh, Chief, you said there'd been a crime. Do you suppose the criminal's come back?"

High gasps and startled cries rose from the church-women.

Chief Cobb moved fast for a big man. He was at the screen door and pushing it wide. The beam of his flashlight crisscrossed the yard. He plunged down the steps.

While everyone's attention was focused on the chief, I yanked the gun out. It seemed incredibly small to me, scarcely larger than the palm of my hand. However, had anyone glanced in this direction, the gun would have been instantly visible, apparently dangling in space. Quickly, I dropped my hand behind the golf bag. This could only be a temporary respite. Somehow I had to remove the gun from the porch before the chief completed his circuit of the back-yard.

I looked toward the kitchen, but the house offered no sanctuary. Once within, I would again face the conundrum posed by the physics of a nonmaterial being transporting a material object. Besides, it would be even more damaging to Kathleen if the gun were found in the house.

Chief Cobb banged onto the porch, his face creased in a forced smile. "Nothing untoward outside, ladies. Now I'll finish my search. Please feel free to return to your—uh—meeting."

Not a woman moved.

He looked from one to another, gave a short nod. I assumed he had a long acquaintance with women. He accepted inevitability with grace. He moved fast, perhaps regretting his visit and certainly not giving any indication he felt the search was going to be productive. He upended the rubber boots, gave each a shake. "This won't take much longer."

His audience observed him closely.

I studied this area of the porch. It was about six feet to the screen door. I had to put myself and the gun out into the night without anyone noticing. There had to be a way. I looked at the golf bag and at the trash bags filled with cans. I snaked my free hand back into the golf bag, yanked a head cover from a wood. It was a tight fit, but I managed to squeeze the gun into the head cover. Cautiously, I unzipped a side pocket and retrieved two golf balls. With the golf balls in my left hand and the lumpy head cover in my right, I slid above the floor close to the east wall.

I was almost to the screened door when Elise cried out, "Those golf balls. Where are those golf balls going? How are they going?"

It was no time to hesitate. I placed the head cover next to the door and stood. As I did, the golf balls rose.

Elise gave a sharp squeak.

With a mighty heave, I launched the golf balls at the sacks filled with discarded cans. One bag broke. Cans bounced onto the floor. Someone screamed. Chief Cobb thundered across the porch.

I reached down, grabbed the head cover, eased open the screened door, and slipped outside. I rose almost to the roof, the head cover well out of sight near the guttering.

"Who moved those cans?" Chief Cobb roared.

"A rat," Elise shouted. "I saw a rat. I know it was a rat."

"How did it open the back door?" the imperious woman with silver hair asked politely, her tone reasonable, puzzled, and verging on nervous.

"That door opens in the wind." Kathleen was studiously casual. I didn't think she had a future in acting, but she was doing her best. "It does it all the time. Don't give it a thought."

"The wind is out of the north," the reasonable voice observed. "How can it bounce open a door on the east? Chief, are you sure no one was out there?"

"Absolutely." His voice lacked certainty. He made a grunting sound. "Almost done. Let me see about that golf bag."

He stuck his hand into the bag and rattled the clubs. He checked the zippered side pockets. He stepped back, glanced up and down the porch, gave an irritated shake of his head. "There's no weapon here. Looks like we got a crank call." He nodded toward Kathleen. "I appreciate your cooperation, Mrs. Abbott. Please ask the reverend to call me tomorrow. I understand Daryl Murdoch spent a lot of time at the church. Maybe the reverend might have some idea why he was in the graveyard. I'll make another check of the backyard and be on my way."

As the screen door opened, I was up and over the guttering. I nestled the swaddled gun next to the telephone. Objects were accruing. I must deal with them. And with Kathleen. As soon as possible. But perhaps I'd better keep tabs on the investigation in case the murderer had other surprises in store . . .

CHAPTER 6

I lightly touched the meshed grille as the police cruiser turned east on Main Street. Riding in a police car was a new experience. I would have preferred to be in the front passenger seat, but it was occupied by a grease-stained sack from Braum's, a sixteen-ounce plastic malted-milk container, several file folders, a wrinkled windbreaker, and a can of mixed nuts. Chief Cobb lifted the yellow plastic lid of the latter, fished out a handful of nuts.

A sudden crackle and a voice spoke from the dashboard. "Chief, Anita." Her voice was low and hushed, her words quick. "Mrs. Murdoch just came home. I'd say she hasn't heard. Saw her face when the garage door opened. She looked tired, but no sign of emotion. She had on her uniform. She's a nurse. I'd guess she just got off duty. You'd think somebody would have called her on her cell, but maybe she has it turned off."

Chief Cobb's face was somber. "I'm on my way. Keep watch until I get there."

I sank back against the slick, plastic-sheathed seat. I'd not thought beyond saving Kathleen from her perilous predicament, but tonight marked trouble for others as well.

The cruiser picked up speed. We headed out Broad-

way. Everything seemed different. Littleton's Lumber Yard
was gone. There were a series of big buildings with fancy
signs—Home Depot, Wal-Mart, Circuit City. Parking lots
teemed with cars. Many of them seemed to be an odd hybrid
between old-fashioned pickups and sedans. About the spot
where I remembered the turnoff to a drive-in movie, there
was a cluster of houses. We passed more and more houses,
many with amazingly peaked roofs. High ceilings were obviously in vogue, but heating and cooling costs must be huge.

The cruiser turned in between two stone pillars. A dis-
creet sign on one pillar read KENSINGTON HILLS. The street
wound in a rambling fashion with offshoots every block
or so. A half mile into the hilly development, the cruiser
turned onto Laurel. We drove a half block, then slowed as
the chief pulled up beside another cruiser almost hidden in
deep shadow beneath a cottonwood. He pushed a button and
his window came down.

Officer Leland—aka Anita—who was in the second
cruiser, opened her door, stepped out. She bent to look
inside his car.

The chief grabbed at the stuff lying on the seat, pushed it
onto the floor. "Get in, Anita. I haven't had a chance to ask
about your trip. When did you get back?"

She came around the cruiser to the passenger door,
opened it. In the brief flash of the interior light, I had a
better glimpse of her face, somber blue-gray eyes, thin high-
bridged nose, pointed chin with the hint of a cleft. If she
smiled, she would be pretty in an old-fashioned, understated
way. She was a little older than I had realized, possibly her
late twenties or early thirties. She looked tired.

"Yesterday afternoon. Murray took my shifts while I was
gone. It's good to be back at work." She sounded distant and
I wondered if it was fatigue or if she was keeping some emotion under tight control.

The chief reached out, awkwardly patted one hand. "Guess the news wasn't what you'd feared."

She shivered. "Every time they turn up an ID that sounds like Vee, I think maybe this time I'll find her, know what happened to her. But it's always some other dead girl and I wonder where her family is, if anyone's looking. So"—she drew a deep breath—"Vee's still lost."

"You're worn out." His smile was kind. "You shouldn't have tried to come straight back to work."

"It's better to be busy." Her tone was strained. She clasped her hands, tight and hard.

"Well, I can sure use you. There's going to be plenty to do." He cleared his throat, was once again brisk. "Get word out to everybody to come in tomorrow morning, then knock off for tonight."

"You're sure you don't need me here?" She gestured toward a Tudor-style house. The light from living-room windows suddenly lessened as the drapes were drawn.

He shook his head. "It doesn't take two to bring bad news."

She nodded. "Good night, Chief."

He waited until she was in her cruiser, then eased his car down the street. He pulled into the driveway and parked.

I was right beside him when he reached the top of the bricked steps. He pushed the doorbell.

The porch light came on, brilliant as a stage spot, throwing the chief's face into hard relief, emphasizing the deep lines that grooved from lips pressed tightly together. He looked like a man bringing bad news.

The door opened. A stocky middle-aged woman looked out, her face inquiring. The RN badge on her wrinkled white uniform read JUDITH MURDOCH. Blonde hair braided coronet-style made her plain face look severe. She had an air of weary competence.

I was surprised. Even dead, there had been a sporty attitude about Daryl Murdoch. There was nothing sporty about the woman staring out with a puzzled face. "Yes?"

"Mrs. Murdoch? Mrs. Daryl Murdoch?"

She looked anxious. "Yes."

He pulled out his wallet, flipped it open to show his shield. "I'm Chief Cobb of the Adelaide Police. I regret having to inform you—"

"Has something happened to Kirby?" Her voice trembled. "Is my son hurt?"

"I'm here about your husband, Mrs. Murdoch. His body was found tonight in St. Mildred's cemetery." The chief's voice was gentle, but his eyes never left her face.

She looked dazed, uncomprehending. "Daryl's dead?" The words were slow and painful.

"Yes, ma'am." He spoke quietly. "His body was discovered near the Pritchard mausoleum. He died as the result of a gunshot wound, an apparent homicide. His body has been taken to the hospital. The law requires an autopsy. Is there someone I can call to come and be with you?"

"Daryl was shot?" Her voice was faint. "Who shot him?"

"We have not found any witnesses. We have secured the crime scene—"

I felt another qualm. Certainly the cemetery was not the actual crime scene.

"—and the investigation is proceeding. I know this is a hard time for you to answer questions, but I would appreciate a few minutes with you. I won't stay long. If you'll tell me someone to call . . ."

She held the door, moved like a sleepwalker to her right. She touched wall switches and bright lights revealed a rather stiff-looking living room with brocaded furniture, heavy red drapes, a red-and-blue Oriental rug, and a grand piano. She walked to a sofa, sank onto it. She gestured to an opposite chair with an overstuffed cushion and curly walnut legs.

Chief Cobb sat squarely, shoulders braced, hands on his knees. "To your knowledge, did Mr. Murdoch appear to be in fear for his life?"

"Daryl afraid? He was never afraid of anything." There was an odd tone in her voice.

The chief nodded. "Did Mr. Murdoch have any enemies?"

I stood by the piano, looking at family photographs. There was a long-ago wedding portrait of Daryl and Judith. She looked prim, but her shy smile had charm, her blue eyes were eager. Dark hair gleaming, he stood with his chest out, proud and confident. So many photos, documenting passing seasons, a little boy with a mop of dark hair on a tricycle, the same boy marching in a school band with a clarinet, diving from a platform, throwing a Frisbee high in the air.

I glanced at Judith. Her face was now flaccid with shock, but I doubted she'd had that eager look for many years.

"Enemies?" She made an odd, helpless gesture. "Sometimes Daryl made people mad. He always wanted things done his way."

The chief persisted. "Had he quarreled with anyone recently?"

"Not exactly quarrels." She took a deep breath. "Daryl didn't think a day was worth living if he didn't butt heads with someone. He wanted things done right. If they weren't, he let people know about it."

The chief's face was bland. "I understand. Some people are natural leaders."

"Daryl was always in charge." There was more sadness than admiration in her voice, and her eyes were empty. She drew her breath in sharply. "I have to find Kirby, tell him what's happened." She pushed to her feet.

Chief Cobb rose, too, looked around the living room. "Do you expect him home soon?"

Her hands came together, locked in a tight grip. "He's staying at a friend's house."

The chief's eyes glinted. "Where?"

She struggled for breath. "I don't know exactly. I'll be able to find him."

"You don't know where he's staying?" He raised an eyebrow.

Judith made no answer, looked away.

Chief Cobb rocked back on his heels, his face thoughtful. "When did he move out?"

Tears welled, spilled down her cheeks. Judith wrapped her arms tight across her chest. "Two weeks ago. He's nineteen and—" She broke off, looked worn and hopeless and bereft.

Chief Cobb's eyes were sympathetic, but the question was firm. "Were your son and his father estranged?"

She flung out her hands, looked at him earnestly. "It wasn't serious. Things would have worked out." Her tone was hollow. "It was about a girl. Daryl didn't like her. But Kirby wouldn't hurt anyone. Ever. He'll be very upset when I tell him. He and his daddy had so much fun when he was little, camping and fishing and hunting."

. . . when he was little . . .

I wondered if Judith realized the implication of her words. Father and son were close when Kirby was a little boy, ready to do what his father wished. Now Kirby was big and wanted to make his own choices . . . *hunting* . . . Kirby would know about guns. But that was not unusual. A great many Adelaide boys grow up hunting.

Cobb's eyes were intent. "What's the girl's name?"

"Lily Mendoza. She's a waitress at the Green Door."

Chief Cobb nodded. "Is Kirby in school?"

"He's a senior. Daryl wants—wanted him—to apply to OU, but Kirby wanted to stay here, go to Goddard."

Goddard is a wonderful regional college and the pride of Adelaide. I wondered if Daryl wanted his son to attend OU to get him away from what he saw as an undesirable romance.

"Well"—the chief's tone was genial—"don't worry, we'll find him for you. Who are some of your son's friends?" He pulled a small notebook from his pocket.

Judith rattled off names. "Bob Harris, Al Schuster, Ted Minter. I'll call them, try to find Kirby."

Chief Cobb said easily, "We'll get in touch with Kirby. Now, it will be helpful to know something about Mr. Murdoch's daily routine."

She answered quickly, eager to leave behind discussion of her son. "Daryl jogs . . ." A quick breath. ". . . jogged around six. After he showered and shaved, he went downtown for breakfast at Lulu's. He opened the office at nine." She looked inquiringly at Chief Cobb.

He nodded. "Murdoch Investments. Used to be Murdoch and Carey."

"He was here and there during the day, in and out of his office." She talked fast. "Daryl was on the vestry at St. Mildred's. That took a lot of his time. He often dropped by the church on his way home."

Chief Cobb made notes. "Was there any change in your husband's behavior in recent days? Was he worried about anything? Did he mention any concerns? Or fears?"

Judith frowned. "He was mad about something at the church."

"The church." The chief's voice had a curious tone. "That's where we found his car. If you don't mind, we'd like to take a closer look at it in daylight, though there didn't seem to be anything helpful when we checked it tonight.

We'll return the keys in the morning. Why did he go to the church this evening?" He held the pen poised over the pad.

I felt uneasy. Another link to St. Mildred's.

She stared down at the rug. "I don't know."

"He didn't tell you?" His voice was faintly surprised.

Judith's face tightened. "No." She spoke without expression.

Judith Murdoch's every word revealed more than she probably realized. She might as well have worn a placard announcing FAILED MARRIAGE.

The chief tapped the pen on the pad. "What was his schedule this afternoon?"

Judith turned up her hands, work-roughened hands. "I never knew." There was a world of emptiness in her voice. "I mean . . ." She struggled for composure. "Daryl didn't like to be pinned down." She stared at the floor.

"Where were you from four o'clock on?" His tone was matter-of-fact, but his gaze was sharp.

Something moved in her widened blue eyes. Was it in response to the time? A ripple of uneasiness? "Four o'clock?"

"Four o'clock to seven." The chief's voice was pleasant but determined.

She lifted a hand, smoothed back a tendril of faded hair that had escaped the coronet braids. "I'm a visiting nurse." She spoke slowly. "I see patients out in the country. I'd have to look at my book. I was at the Hillman place in late afternoon. From there, I went to the Carsons' and the Wetherbys'."

"Are you usually out this late on Thursday?" He nodded toward the porcelain clock on the mantel.

"Sometimes. I didn't hurry. I stopped and had dinner at the Pizza Hut on Gusher, then I decided to go to the show. When I got out, I stopped at the grocery."

I ached for her. A movie by herself. Maybe that was her

answer to Thursday night with no reason to come home. Bobby Mac and I always hurried home to each other. We never lost our laughter or our love.

The doorbell buzzed, then the door was flung open. Judith took a deep breath, looked toward the hall, fear evident in her strained posture.

Footsteps clattered on the tile. A little woman with fly-away dark hair framing sharp features burst into the living room. She was pencil thin and teetered on absurdly high heels. She looked at the police chief. "Oh God, Sam, is Daryl dead?"

"Yes. He was found in the cemetery. I'm glad you've come, Meg. I was going to call someone to help Mrs. Murdoch." He nodded toward Judith.

Meg moved rapidly toward Judith. "I was afraid it was true when I saw the police car. I had a bunch of calls about Daryl and I tried to get you but your cell didn't answer. Oh, honey, I'm so sorry."

Judith took one step, stopped. Her face crumpled. "Someone killed him."

Meg was pale. "As soon as I heard, I called Father Abbott. He's on his way over." The little woman swung toward the chief. "You go on now, Sam. I'll take care of Judith."

The chief pushed up from the chair, dropping the notepad in his pocket. "I'll be back in touch tomorrow. We may know more by then."

I watched him go, torn by uncertainty. If I went with the chief, there might be more to learn, but I wanted to meet— so to speak—Father Abbott.

The two women stood frozen as the chief moved heavily across the room. When the front door closed behind him, Judith whirled and ran from the room. Her face was unguarded, eyes staring, mouth working, a woman consumed by fear.

Meg was shocked. "Judith, wait. Let me help." But her call was unanswered.

Judith ran into a long room with a fireplace and easy chairs and two sofas and a pool table. She stumbled to the desk, grabbed up a telephone, punched numbers with a shaking hand. She leaned against a tall wingback chair as if her body had no strength.

Meg bustled up to her. "I'll make any calls—"

Judith slashed her hand for quiet, a harsh imperative gesture that brought Meg to a standstill. Finally, her words hurried and uneven, she said, "Lily, please, this is Kirby's mother. I have dreadful news. His father is dead. He was shot. When you get this message, tell Kirby to come home. I know he was with you this afternoon from four to seven. That's important. The police want to talk to him. Make sure he remembers to tell them that he was with you from four to seven." She clicked off the phone.

Meg slipped her arm around Judith's shoulders. "Do you want me to go over there, find him?"

"Oh yes, Meg. What if she doesn't get the message in time? You'll tell him—"

"I'll tell him. From four to seven."

They exchanged a look of perfect understanding.

"It's just to protect him. Kirby would never hurt anyone, but the police don't know him. When they find out Thursday is his day off, they'll want to know where he was." Judith's voice was metallic. "Someone might think the wrong things if they knew about everything."

Meg gave Judith a hug. "It might look bad. Bud and I used to bowl with Sam and Jewell. But after Jewell died, he stopped coming. Sam's a swell guy, but pretty black-and-white."

Their words were oblique, hinting at much I didn't understand. It was like seeing an old film with subtitles that left out most of the story, but I was a mother and I understood. Kirby and his dad obviously had quarreled ferociously, possibly in a public place, and Judith knew Chief Cobb would discover that fact.

The front doorbell rang. Meg whirled and hurried into the hallway. Her voice rang out: "Come in, Father Abbott. Judith's in the den."

Judith held tight to the back of the chair, trying hard to stand taller, smooth out her face, hide her fear.

Brisk steps sounded. Father Abbott stopped in the doorway, his face creased in concern. His sandy hair looked mussed, as if he'd forgotten to comb it. His priestly collar was slightly askew as if he'd tugged at it, his black suit wrinkled. His angular face sagged with weariness, but his dark blue eyes were kind and empathetic. "I came as soon as I heard." He walked to her, hands outstretched.

Judith sagged against the chair, her face crumpling, scalded by tears.

This was not a moment for me to observe. I looked away from Judith toward Father Abbott.

As I left, I carried with me an indelible memory of the man most important to Kathleen. Faces reflect character. Even in a quick glance, I saw grace and intelligence, purpose and commitment, sensitivity and determination.

I also saw deep fatigue, perhaps mental as well as physical. A slight tic fluttered one eyelid. His shoulders slumped with weariness. The immensity of life and death and the gulf between was mirrored in his eyes. He was there to offer solace and hope, peace and acceptance.

What a gift that was and what a burden to bear.

CHAPTER 7

I drifted deliciously between sleeping and waking, luxuriating in the comfort of the downy feather bed. I stretched and wiggled my toes. Heaven, of course, is always comfortable. Everything is in perfect harmony, so there is never a sense of mental or physical unease. On earth, minds fret, hearts grieve, muscles tire, bodies ache. Achieving the right balance is a never-ending quest.

My eyes popped open. Was I perhaps being too much of the earth? I flung back the covers and came to my feet. Quickly I imagined a rather formal blue flannel robe and slipped into it. Just in case. Gradually my tension eased. Wiggins wasn't here. After all, even Wiggins wouldn't frown on enjoying the moment. Joy is surely heaven-sent.

I gazed happily around the charming bedroom. I was sure—almost sure—that Kathleen would have been delighted to invite me to stay in the guest bedroom upon my return last night. I hadn't wanted to bother her and certainly morning was time enough to bring my presence to her attention.

Last night I'd prepared for sleep by envisioning pink satin pajamas. Comfortably attired, I'd slept the sleep of the just. I looked at the mirror. Oh, of course. I wasn't here.

I was uncertain how to dress for the day. Nothing too formal, but should I need to appear, should my actual presence be unavoidable and essential (Wiggins, are you listening?), it was important to be appropriately dressed. It wouldn't do to be garbed in the styles of my day, attractive though they were.

When I observed the church ladies last night, I was enchanted by the new fashions, although a little puzzled that most wore slacks. Their outfits were quite charming. Except for the shoes. The shoes appalled me, especially those with long upturned toes like an elf or blocky heels that brought Wiggins's sturdy black shoes to mind. I prefer jaunty shoes with shiny buckles or bright bows.

I wafted to the sewing room. It was rather cold. I rose and pushed up a register, welcoming a draft of warm air and the enticing scent of bacon. I was eager to reach the kitchen, but first I must dress.

I found a stack of clothing catalogs on a worktable. I would have enjoyed looking at everything, but I hastily made a selection, a double-breasted jacket and slacks in gray wool with a herringbone pattern and a Florentine-gold silk blouse. Matching gray leather pumps (with a reasonable heel) and small gold hoop earrings completed a tasteful ensemble.

I'd no more than made my choice when the door burst open and a slender form catapulted inside. Bayroo skidded to a stop halfway across the room. "I'm sorry. I didn't know you were here." Her quick smile was warm. "Your pantsuit is beautiful."

The child had excellent taste. "Good morning, Bayroo. Thank you." I smiled though I was disconcerted. Once again, even though I wasn't here, Bayroo saw me.

"I didn't mean to startle you. I need to get my costume out of the closet." She gestured across the room. "We're having our class Halloween parties today."

Bayroo would very likely mention seeing me when she went downstairs for breakfast. "Bayroo, can you keep a secret?"

She folded her arms in an X across her chest. "Sure. Cross my heart and hope to die."

"Your great-grandmother and I were very close"—I was counting on Bayroo having a very fuzzy idea of how long ago that might have been—"and I'm visiting here to lend your mom a hand, but it's a secret from everyone because it might be complicated to explain."

She stared at me, her gaze startled, then thoughtful, finally eager. She clapped her hands. "I know exactly who you are. There's a painting of you in the hall outside the parish hall. All the past directresses of the Altar Guild are there." She looked puzzled. "You were a lot older then. You have red hair just like mine. Mom told me you were my great-grandmother's sister. I'm named after you." She smiled, a curious smile that radiated mischief, excitement, and certainty. "You're a ghost and I guess you're young and pretty now because that's how you are."

Trust a child to understand. However, I had a conviction that Kathleen would not be pleased. I didn't even want to think about Wiggins.

She gave an excited hop. "This is so cool. How did you do it?"

"Do what?" I hoped for inspiration.

"Come back." She looked at me eagerly.

"On a wing and a prayer." Of course the reference meant nothing to her.

Bayroo nodded solemnly as if everything were explained. "Way cool. So"—she looked thoughtful—"you're here to help Mom? That's swell. She's been pretty blue lately. Dad's too busy to notice. You know my dad, don't you? He's the rector and he works all the time. He left before seven this morning. Men's early-morning Bible study. He has to do most everything and he only has a retired military chaplain to help out on Sundays and with some of the hospital visits and everybody on the vestry has plenty of ideas of more for Dad to do but there's never enough money and he's worried about the roof on the church and the winter heating bills. The heating bills are unbelievable—"

I heard the echo of parental discussion.

"—but the price of oil is great for Adelaide. Anyway, maybe you can help Dad, too."

"Bayroo?" Kathleen's call was faint.

"Mom's calling." My namesake flashed an apologetic smile. "I have to hurry downstairs for breakfast and finish my homework." She darted to the closet, banged inside, and came out carrying a plastic sword, a crimson smock, tall silver boots, and an eye patch. "I'm going to be a pirate. Do you think I should be Captain Hook or Blackbeard?"

"I'd be Captain Bayroo, a lady pirate who rescues captured sailors."

Bayroo's eyes gleamed. "What does she do with them?"

"She returns them to their ships and reaps wonderful rewards, gold and silver and rubies."

Bayroo saluted me with her sword—"Captain Bayroo, ready to sail"—and turned toward the door.

I called after her, "Remember, it's our secret. Your mom doesn't know I'm here at the moment. And, please, always pretend you don't see me unless I give you a thumbs-up."

She paused in the doorway, looked at me earnestly. "Don't worry. I had the lead in the fifth-grade play. I won't give a thing away. I won't tell a soul even though everybody'd be really pumped. A ghost in the house for Halloween! Way cool."

After Kathleen and Bayroo left for school, I heated two strips of bacon and a leftover frittata. I murmured a thankful grace and had a lovely breakfast. I was quite careful to be certain I was alone in the kitchen when I washed the dishes. I was enjoying a second cup of coffee when Kathleen returned.

She stopped just inside the door, stared toward the table. "You're here."

I took another sip, placed the mug on the table.

She shivered. "It's cold outside. The wind's picking up and the clouds look like old pewter. I keep thinking everything that happened last night is a bad dream, and I come home and that hideous coffee mug is in the air." She pointed with a shaking hand. "In the air."

I looked at the mug. It was bright pink with a flamingo-shaped handle. If she thought it was hideous, she should have discarded it. "I think it's cute."

She quivered. "All right. I hear a voice. You're here. Unless I'm imagining—"

Wiggins would have to understand that Kathleen's nerves were stretched. I needed to reassure her. I will confess I turned toward the mirror over the sink, not with any sense of vanity but simply to be sure my pantsuit was appropriate. In an instant the swirl of color resolved into my image. I brushed back a tangle of red curls. The cut of the jacket was exquisite. I would bring no shame on the rectory should I be observed.

Kathleen approached me, one hand outstretched, her gaze desperate and determined. She came within a foot, took a deep breath, reached out to grip my arm.

I lifted my free hand, patted her shoulder.

She went as rigid as a pointer sighting quarry. "You're here. You really, really are. But you weren't. Now you are. I don't understand."

"You worry too much, Kathleen. Relax and accept your

good fortune. First we must deal with Daryl's cell phone. Here's what I want you to do . . ."

My instructions were simple, but she repeated them, frowning as she muttered, ". . . at the end of the dock."

It would take only a moment to retrieve the cell phone from the roof. "I'll meet you there in half an hour."

Kathleen tossed her head like a fractious horse. "I have to pick up the cupcakes for Bayroo's homeroom Halloween party and visit Mrs. Mossman at the hospital and check on the shipment of candles for the Altar Guild. Can't you bring it here?"

I shook my head. "If that cell phone were found in the rectory, you'd be in big trouble. It won't take long. You'll have time for your errands."

She shivered. "It's awfully cold outside."

"Brisk, but secluded. Wear gloves." I finished the last sip of coffee.

"Gloves?" Her tone was wary. "Why do I have to wear gloves?"

I was amazed. Had Kathleen never read a mystery? Perhaps I could provide a reading list. I never missed a Leslie Ford novel. She gave such an interesting picture of wartime Washington. I'd read her latest, *Mrs. Latham's Primrose Path,* just before I visited the Department of Good Intentions. No wonder I was sent to assist Kathleen. "We don't want your fingerprints on Mr. Murdoch's phone. I'll see you there." I was fading from view when I realized that perhaps I should be clearer. "Actually, I'll see you, but you won't see me."

Kathleen stood at the end of the weathered wooden dock, hunched in a navy peacoat with a red-and-blue plaid scarf tied under her chin.

I settled on the railing, the telephone in one hand. I was quite comfortable in a gray lamb's-wool coat and gold cashmere scarf. I had forgotten how much fun it was to shop, although a catalog couldn't match going to Lassiter's. Lassiter's had been Adelaide's finest women's shop in my day. Of course Brown's in Oklahoma City had been my favorite store. I wrinkled my nose, remembering the scent in the bath-powder-and-perfume section.

Kathleen's face looked pinched.

The dock, understandably, was deserted except for us. Bulbous gray clouds looked as immovable as elephants at rest. A gusty wind corrugated gunmetal-gray water. Autumn-faded reeds rippled. The lake was in the center of the small nature preserve that adjoined the church property. The preserve on one side and the cemetery on the other provided St. Mildred's with a sylvan setting. Cedars and pines crowded the shoreline, providing a sense of remoteness. It was a perfect spot for our rendezvous, close to the rectory but at a safe remove.

Kathleen stared fixedly at the small telephone. "I'd better take it before someone sees it hanging there, although I don't know what kind of fool would come here on a day like this. But I'm here. It would be just my luck to have a nature class trot onto the dock. Or who knows? Maybe the Altar Guild will show up. Nothing would surprise me." She sounded despairing.

I was pleased to see that she wore soft leather gloves. I handed the phone to her.

She took it gingerly, flipped open the lid. It still reminded me of an oddly shaped compact. I moved to watch over her shoulder. The small screen suddenly glowed. A jaunty tune sounded.

Kathleen pushed and clicked. "See, you can take pictures." She held the phone up and suddenly wind-whipped water was in view on the tiny screen. Another click and the lake disappeared. "You can save them, too. Daryl kept a bunch. I'll do them in order." She clicked again. A picture appeared on the screen.

Kathleen looked puzzled. "How odd."

Pictured was a close-up of a shaky signature at the bottom of a printed page. I squinted to make out the name: *Georgia Hamilton.* I moved closer, the better to see, but Kathleen clicked and the image was gone.

Kathleen wriggled uneasily as if sensing my nearness.

I was sorry to crowd her, but I wanted a good view. "What do you think it means?"

"I have no idea. Georgia Hamilton almost died a few weeks ago, but she rallied and she's home again." Kathleen's tone warmed. "She's amazing. Ninety-five if she's a day and she never misses the early service. I suppose Daryl handles some of her investments."

Kathleen clicked again. She made a strangled noise in her throat.

The photograph was amazing in its clarity and detail. Kathleen sat on a puffy cream leather divan. Bright red-and-gold wrapping paper mounded near the open box in her lap. She held up a red satin nightgown, her eyes wide, her mouth agape.

"Daryl snapped the picture just as I opened the box." She glared at the screen. "I didn't know what was inside. How could I know? But how do I explain to anybody—especially Bill—why I was sitting in Daryl's cabin and opening what was obviously a present and pulling out a sexy red night-gown? When Daryl called Wednesday and asked me to the cabin, he said he needed a chance for a private visit with me about Raoul. He thought it was only fair—oh, his voice was so greasy—that he and I have a conversation before he spoke to Bill. Then he hung up. I called his cell and he didn't answer. I know he looked and saw it was me calling and of course he didn't answer. I was in a panic. I had to go. When I got to the cabin, he offered me a drink. I said no and he was all—oh, you know how it is when somebody's hitting on you."

I found the expression interesting. It was new to me, but I understood exactly what she meant.

"I told him what happened with Raoul. He pretended to be sympathetic, said he knew I'd been terribly lonely and Bill worked far too hard. Daryl said he was relieved there was nothing to this story that was getting around about me and Raoul, and since we'd cleared everything up, he had a small gift for me.

"I didn't see how I could refuse to open it. I'd just pulled out that hideous nightgown when he took my picture. I asked him what he thought he was doing. He said he liked to take pictures with his phone and this was such a good shot he should probably print out a picture for Bill or put it on the church Web site, but if I treated him nicely, he'd keep the shot for himself."

Kathleen's eyes blazed. "He said a good start would be for me to try on my new gown. He put the phone in his pocket. There was no way I could get it from him. I told him"—her voice was harsh—"exactly what kind of a louse he was and then I jumped up and threw the gown and the box and the papers in the fireplace and ran out of the cabin. He came after me, but I got in my car and locked it and got away." She jabbed at the phone and the picture disappeared.

Another click, a new picture. A man in his forties with thinning blond hair and sharp features hunched at a desk, writing on a piece of stationery. The sag of his head and the bleak emptiness of his expression spelled defeat, despair, hopelessness.

"Who is it?" But the picture was already gone and Kathleen shot me a mutinous glance. If she knew, she didn't intend to tell me.

Another click. An untidy middle-aged woman looked warily over her shoulder. She wore the blue smock of the Altar Guild. She held a collection plate. Behind her was the counter with the vested chalice for Sunday. A crucifix hung on the white wall above the counter. Walnut cabinets jutted into the room.

I knew at once that she was in the sacristy after a service, probably a weekday Communion since she was apparently doing the service alone. "She's counting the collection." Collection isn't formally taken at a weekday service, but the plate is left out for any donations.

Kathleen's brows drew down in a worried frown. "Maybe something startled her."

The woman in the photo's expression was oddly craven and wary.

I didn't doubt that Kathleen and I were considering the same unpalatable possibility. Was a member of the Altar Guild getting ready to filch from the offering plate?

Kathleen deleted that picture, retrieved another. "Oh dear."

A furtive hand tucked a handful of bills into the pocket of the blue smock.

"Oh." Kathleen's soft cry was a lament. "I can't believe it. I don't know what to do. But—" Swift clicks and that image, too, disappeared.

"Who was she?" I was sure Kathleen knew.

Kathleen pressed her lips tightly together.

"Kathleen"—an awful possibility struck me—"are those pictures gone forever?"

Her expression defiant, Kathleen looked toward the sound of my voice. "You bet they are."

I was horrified. "You've destroyed evidence that might help the police."

She lifted her chin. "I don't care. Let the police find out who killed him. I'm not going to get people in trouble, maybe ruin their lives, just because Daryl was nasty enough to take pictures of them when they were down. I know that's what he was doing. Sure, he may have been right to go after some of them, but let them get found out some other way." Her brows drew together in a worried frown. "I wonder if the rest of the pictures are like this."

She clicked twice. In one image, an elderly black man was placing cans of food in a brown grocery bag. In another, the police officer, Anita, her face impervious, was framed in an open car window.

Kathleen relaxed as the screen went blank. "Those last two don't amount to anything. That's Isaac Franklin, our sexton, and he's probably filling a sack from the food pantry for a needy family. The policewoman"—Kathleen's smile was satisfied—"was Daryl's bête noire. He saw himself as a macho man and drove like he thought he was Dale Earnhardt."

I was never a NASCAR enthusiast, but I remember Bobby Mac's excitement when Dale Earnhardt had arrived.

"She put a stop to that. Everywhere Daryl went, she seemed to be behind him. He got tickets faster than confetti spills. It was great to see him drive through town at thirty miles an hour. I loved it. I didn't even mind when she gave me a ticket a couple of weeks ago."

"You got rid of all the photos? For good?" I had to be sure.

"Every single one." Her stare, a trifle to the left of my face, was unabashed.

I understood Kathleen's reluctance to involve innocent persons in a murder investigation, but what if one of them was the murderer? I felt a civic responsibility. I had already complicated the police efforts by helping Kathleen move Daryl's body, though I still believed I'd made the right decision. Kathleen was innocent. Otherwise I wouldn't have been sent to her aid.

The cell phone was another matter. I had removed it from Daryl's body. The information it contained might make a difference in the search for his murderer. Somehow I had to aid that earnest police chief, though I wasn't sure what I could do. "Kathleen, we can't ignore what we've discovered."

She wasn't listening. She did something else with the phone, muttered, "Three saved messages. I called him back. I'd better check." *Click.*

"Thursday. Four-fifteen P.M.: 'I can't believe what you did.'" The voice was young, male, and anguished. "'I just found out from Lily.'" There was a silence, then a quick, choked, "'You'll pay for this. I swear you will.'"

Kathleen punched a button.

I sighed. One more piece of information, forever gone.

"Thursday, five-oh-seven P.M.: 'Mr. Murdoch—'" It was Kathleen's voice. "'There's been—'"

She punched.

"Thursday, eight-twenty P.M.: 'You got to call me.'" It was a woman's voice, young but hoarse. Bravado mingled with desperation. "'Listen, Daryl, I got to talk to you. You promised . . . Please. Call me.'"

Kathleen punched. "All gone. But"—she stared at the phone—"even though I erased the photos, there might be images somewhere inside." Abruptly, she raised her arm and flung the telephone far out into the lake.

CHAPTER 8

I knelt by the chimney on the rectory roof and picked up the head cover holding the gun. Kathleen's disposal of the cell phone was an unexpected complication. I had intended to convey both the phone and gun to Chief Cobb. Now the phone was gone.

I'd done my best to assist Kathleen. In fact, my mission appeared to be successful. Likely I would soon be recalled to Heaven, but I was uneasy. I had interfered with the proper investigation of a crime.

I looked Heavenward. Thick dark clouds obscured the horizon. Wind pushed at me. I was definitely still here. I took that as a clear indication that I should proceed. But proceed to do what?

Arrange for Chief Cobb to find the gun.

The thought was direct and breathtaking in its simplicity. Thank you, Wiggins. I pulled the gun out of the head cover. My new coat, the gray lamb's wool I'd selected from the catalog to go with my elegant pantsuit, had capacious pockets. I tucked the gun in my pocket. I was ready to depart for the police station, but fortunately I glanced down. I was invisible. My coat was invisible.

The gun was not invisible.

Even though the sky was overcast, someone might look up and note the flight of a gun through the sky if I swooped to the police station, especially since I didn't know where it was.

I pulled the gun out of the pocket, returned it to the head cover, and placed the bulging head cover beside the chimney.

I shivered. Despite the lamb's-wool coat, I was getting cold. It was time for a respite. In a flash, I returned to the rectory kitchen. I hung my coat on a coat tree, retrieved the flamingo mug from the dishwasher, and filled it with coffee. I found a notepad and a pen near the telephone. I settled at the table, positioning my chair where I would see anyone approaching the back porch.

I drew a gun on the notepad. I had to figure out a way to get it to Chief Cobb. Moreover, the information I'd gleaned from observing Kathleen with the cell phone might be essential in solving the crime. Quickly, I jotted notes:

PICTURES
1. Signature of Georgia Hamilton, apparently on a legal document of some sort.
2. A man in the depths of despair.
3. A member of the Altar Guild apparently stealing from the collection plate.
4. Isaac Franklin, the sexton.
5. The policewoman who showered tickets on Daryl Murdoch.

CALLS
1. He spoke of Lily. A young male voice. The caller had to be Daryl's angry son, Kirby.
2. A desperate woman begged Daryl to call her. However, the call was recorded after his death, which might indicate innocence. Or might not.

I sipped coffee, drew the face of a bloodhound with drooping ears and a worried expression. The cell phone was gone, but I knew what I had seen and heard. I was uncertain whether any of that information could—or should—be provided to the police. For now, I had recorded everything.

I looked around the kitchen, seeking a safe spot to keep my notebook. It was unfortunate that worldly objects, unlike my imagined clothing and coats, couldn't simply disappear for me. But they couldn't and didn't. I zoomed up to the ceiling and checked above the bottle-green oak china cabinet. I put the notebook behind the top molding.

I wondered if Chief Cobb was making progress. Last night, when I'd wished to be in the cemetery, there I was.

What if I wished to be at the police station?

The two-story cream-colored stucco building covered the northwest corner at the intersection of Lee and Tishomingo, one block south of Main Street. Old Glory and the Oklahoma flag with its sky-blue field fluttered in a stiff breeze from a slender white flagpole. Shallow steps led to a central doorway. On one end of the second floor, barred windows looked as gloomy as the overcast day. I studied the inscription on the cornerstone:

ADELAIDE CITY HALL
1994
DEDICATED BY MAYOR HARVEY KAMP

I remembered Harvey as a long-haired, sneaky friend of my son. Ah, the wonders of maturity.

I went inside and checked the directory. On the first floor were the mayor's office, city planning, water, public works, planning commission, and treasurer. Now the mayor was a woman, Neva Lumpkin. Chief Cobb, the police department, jail, city attorney, and municipal court were on the second floor.

Chief Cobb sat at his desk, studying papers. He emptied a packet of sugar into a steaming mug of coffee. Stark fluorescent light emphasized the deep lines that grooved his face. Moisture rings and scrapes marred the battered oak desk, but Matisse prints added color to one dingy beige wall. Large bulletin boards, a detailed street map of Adelaide, and a map of the county hung on the wall opposite his desk.

I was intrigued by a machine similar to a skinny television set that sat on a leaf jutting from the desk. A luminous green screen glowed. A flat keyboard sat in front of it. Chief Cobb swiveled in his chair to face the screen. He lifted his hands, frowned, shook his head. He punched the intercom button on his desk.

"Chief?"

"Yeah, Colleen. What's the password this week?"

A sibilant hiss sounded from the intercom.

He looked irritated. "Don't whisper. James Bond isn't crouched under your desk, waiting to hear the password so he can crack security for the Adelaide Police Department. Changing the password every week wastes everybody's time. Doesn't the mayor have enough to do without figuring out a silly rule like that? Who can remember a new password every week? I, for one, can't. And I forgot to write down the new one."

Colleen's voice was low. "Uh, Chief, the mayor suggests city employees write down a password and keep it in a desk drawer."

"That's secure?" He was sardonic. "Okay, okay. I'll write it down. What is it this week?"

There was a long pause.

The chief leaned back in his chair, suddenly amused, and I imagined he was picturing his secretary looking around to be certain no one was in earshot.

Colleen's voice was barely audible. "Cougar."

I perched on the edge of his desk, looked at the screen. There was a line for a password, followed by asterisks. Curious.

"Cougar." He made no effort to be quiet. "Thanks, Colleen." He lifted his hands to the keyboard, typed.

I'd been a first-rate typist. I followed his fingers. He typed *cougar* into the box with asterisks. A few more clicks and he was looking at a list of messages. He clicked the first one.

To: Chief Cobb
From: Jacob Brandt, M.D.
Subject: Autopsy Report Daryl Murdoch

Autopsy file attached. Cutting to the chase: Death resulted from gunshot to the left temple. .22 slug recovered, sent to OSBI laboratory. Probable time of death between 4 and 6:30 P.M. Preliminary survey shows no evidence of drug use. Definitive toxicology tests under way. Victim right-handed. No trace of gunpowder residue on hand(s) of deceased. Suicide improbable.

The chief clicked. Information appeared on the screen superimposed on the message, instructions on how to print. Another click. Paper edged from a small square machine on the floor. The chief clicked again. The message disappeared. I studied the legend to the left of the screen. Apparently, the messages came into an in-box. One click and they appeared. Another click, a message was printed. Another click, the message disappeared. The chief reached down for the sheet, placed it in a folder.

Who would have thought such marvels were possible? I remembered how excited I'd been to have an electric typewriter. To think Wiggins still depended upon a Teletype. I would have to bring him up-to-date.

Chief Cobb pressed a key and the message from the medical examiner disappeared. He swung a meaty hand toward his telephone, punched a couple of buttons, and leaned back in his chair.

I bent nearer the luminous screen. One *ping*. A line announced: *One message in your mailbox.*

Suddenly a dour voice sounded. "Lab." As I turned toward the sound, I accidentally touched the chief's shoulder.

Chief Cobb's head jerked. Looking puzzled, he lifted a hand and brushed his shoulder. He peered behind him.

I eased away.

The chief shrugged and spoke in the general direction of his telephone. "Sam here. What you got on the Murdoch slug?"

"Slammed into bone." A gloomy voice, turgid as a silt-laden river, emanated from the squat rectangular plastic box beneath the telephone.

Conversing over a telephone without picking up the receiver. Another wonder.

The chief wrinkled his nose. "Too damaged to make an ID?"

"Yeah."

"Twenty-two?"

"Yeah."

Cobb's eyes slitted. "You got anything helpful, Felix?"

"Some dust balls on the back of his suit coat. No dust balls in cemeteries." A hoarse chuckle. "At least, not above-ground."

"Dust balls?" Cobb glanced toward a register near the ceiling. Little clumps of dirt wavered between vents.

"Yeah. Like when you clean up an attic or closet. House dirt."

"Anything special about it?"

"Nope. Ordinary, everyday dirt fluff. Got some cat fur in it. He either wallowed around on a floor somewhere just before he got wasted or the body was moved to the cemetery. Look for a dusty floor and a black cat."

I pictured the rectory back porch. Certainly there could have been dust on the tarp. Perhaps it was a favorite spot for Spoofer to nap.

"Yeah." Chief Cobb grasped a pencil and drew a woolly blob. "Thanks, Felix." He reached forward, poked a button. His face was thoughtful as he turned to his desk. He pulled a notebook near.

I looked over his shoulder.

He wrote, *Dust???*

A brisk tattoo sounded on the hall door.

The chief called out, "Come in."

A ruggedly handsome man in a baggy red sweater and gray slacks moved toward the chief's desk like a fresh-launched torpedo. A cotton-top blond with slate-blue eyes, he was a shade under six feet tall and loose-jointed, with large hands and feet. His craggy face looked intense and intelligent. I liked him instinctively.

Cobb gestured toward a chair. "What you got, Hal?"

Hal pulled the chair back, dropped into it. He pulled a notebook from his pocket, opened it, talked fast as if he had much to say and too little time. "Daryl Murdoch's son, Kirby, moved out two weeks ago. Senior at Adelaide High. Swim team. Math whiz. Waits tables at Garcia's. He's been camping out and going to friends' houses to shower. His girlfriend is Lily Mendoza. His dad didn't want him to date Lily. Next-door neighbor Wilbur Schmidt said all hell broke loose a couple of weeks ago, Kirby and Daryl yelling at each other. Kirby slammed out of the house and took his stuff.

"I talked to a friend of Kirby's, Hack Thurston. Kept it low-key, asked the usual, how long he'd known him, school, hobbies, et cetera. Turns out Kirby likes to target-practice with a twenty-two revolver out on the river bottom near Schooner Creek on his day off. Gets Thursdays off. Murder occurred Thursday afternoon. Checked Murdoch house this morning. No one home. Officer Leland is hunting for him."

Cobb nodded. "Good work. Find the kid's twenty-two."

Hal nodded. "I surveyed the crime scene again, including the Pritchard mausoleum. Somebody tried to prize loose that marble greyhound. I checked the crowbar we found under a bush. It had traces of marble dust. We could figure some kids—the first tip call came from a kid, right?—were in the mausoleum and maybe Murdoch saw some lights there and went to investigate and it ended up him getting shot."

The chief drummed the fingers of one hand on his desktop. "So some kids out to heist a marble dog from the cemetery just happened to have a twenty-two with them, and when Murdoch showed up, they shot him instead of running like hell? I don't think so. No, I got a gut feeling it's a lot closer to the church. Look at the lab report." He shoved it across the desk to the detective. "I don't think Murdoch went to the cemetery and got shot. I think he was shot somewhere else and dumped there."

Hal swiftly read the report. He immediately understood the significance of the dust balls. "Murdoch's car is in the parking lot of the church. Probably means he got that far alive. So where does that leave us? From the dust, I'd say he was shot inside. Maybe the church?"

The chief looked thoughtful. "Maybe. I'll need more before I can get a search warrant. And"—he rubbed his nose—"do they keep a cat in the church?"

The young detective shrugged. "I wouldn't think so. How about the preacher's house?"

Chief Cobb's eyes glinted. "We got a tip the gun was on the back porch of the rectory." He frowned. "I can hear the judge right now. 'What's this? Warrant to search the rectory at St. Mildred's? Because of a dust ball?'"

The younger detective's mouth turned down in a grimace. "You got that right. You better have evidence on a silver platter before you take that one before the judge."

Cobb looked determined. "Get the crime van and check out Murdoch's car from top to bottom. We better be sure there's no cat fur in it before I try for a warrant. Also check the Murdoch house for a black cat. When that's out of the way, maybe it will be time to try for a search warrant."

Hal bounded to his feet. "On my way."

I toyed with the idea of getting to Daryl's car and placing some dust balls and cat fur inside. But perhaps creating fake evidence wasn't exactly what Wiggins had in mind. However, I was truly worried. It was beginning to look as though our removal of the body from the rectory hadn't solved Kathleen's problem.

The chief swung back to his machine and clicked on a message with a red exclamation point in the margin.

To: Chief Cobb
From: Dispatcher
Subject: Crime Stoppers Call re Daryl Murdoch

Call received from pay phone outside Wal-Mart, 1023 Snodgrass, at 9:07 A.M. Text follows:
"Crime Stoppers. Ask Kathleen Abbott about the red nightgown and her visit to Daryl Murdoch's cabin on Pontotoc Road Wednesday night."
Anonymous caller spoke in a husky whisper. Unable to

determine sex of speaker. Tape has been turned over to
laboratory for analysis.

As a ghost, thankfully I wasn't subject to physical
manifestations of distress such as palpitations or difficulty
breathing. Nonetheless, I was shaken by the realization that
Kathleen's involvement in Daryl's murder must have been
the calculated objective of his murderer. Of that, there could
now be no doubt. Daryl's demise on the back porch obviously had been planned from the start. Last night, a call
brought the police to the rectory back porch in search of the
gun. Now an anonymous call threatened to embroil her further. How had anyone known about the red nightgown?

No wonder I was still here.

Chief Cobb leaned back in his chair, lips pursed in a
soundless whistle. He reached toward the phone. His hand
dropped. He snagged a stenographer's-size notebook, flipped
to a fresh page. At the top, he wrote *Kath*—

A sudden knock sounded, and the door to a connecting
office swung open.

Colleen's voice rose. "Excuse me, Mayor Lumpkin, Chief
Cobb is in conference."

"Come now, my dear. We all know these little fictions." A
heavyset blonde appeared in the doorway. Pudgy, crimson-
nailed fingers laden with rings clutched the doorframe. Red,
green, and gold stones glittered. "I have a little bone to pick
with Sam." She swept inside.

Unseen by the visitor, a plump brunette with a pleasant
face looked at the chief and turned her hands up in mute
apology.

The intruder closed the door, strode majestically across
the room. She was flamboyant in a vivid purple blouse and
ankle-length purple skirt with orange geometric forms. The

scarf at her throat was in matching orange. The skirt rippled as she walked. Orange boots tapped on the tiled floor.

Chief Cobb came to his feet, face stolid, eyes glinting with irritation. "Good morning, Neva."

She ignored the lack of an invitation to sit down and pulled the straight chair around to the side of his desk. With a brilliant smile, she gestured to him as she gracefully settled into the chair. "You are such a gentleman, Sam. Take your seat." It was a command.

The chief backed to his chair, sat. He placed his hands on his knees as if ready to spring up in an instant. "I'm on my way out."

She gave him another smile, but her eyes were cold. "I am well aware that you"—she placed a special emphasis on the pronoun—"are devoted to protecting our liberties. I'm sure you agree that a foremost duty of your law enforcement personnel is to share that commitment."

The chief made no move in his chair, but I realized he was suddenly alert and wary.

The mayor toyed with the end of her scarf. "Your department should be committed to impartial law enforcement. Justice must be blindfolded or"—she looked as though she awaited applause—"there is no justice at all. I am here this morning to discuss this essential component of our liberties." Her voice dropped, a public servant confronting a momentous truth. "Personal liberties are at the heart of our nation. That is why I had no choice but to break through the defense of your secretary. I know you must have quiet time to execute your duties, but you should instruct Colleen that treating other city officials—"

The mayor reminded me strongly of the high school principal who'd booted me from the faculty. I might not have been tempted to do what I did had it not been for her ill-natured expression and pursed lips. How like a pig's snout.

A box of paper clips sat near the in-box on the chief's desk. I palmed a handful of clips and skimmed just above the floor, coming up behind the mayor.

"—as interlopers is hardly appropriate."

I delicately pulled back the rim of her blouse and dribbled several clips on her dowager's hump.

She shuddered with the grace of an ice floe cracking.

Chief Cobb looked at her sharply. "Neva?"

A meaty hand yanked at the back of her blouse. Her head jerked around.

I expected the pointy little clips were now lodged near her waist.

The mayor wriggled in her seat, took a deep breath. After another wary glance behind her, she waggled a chiding finger, zircon flashing. "You will recall"—her gaze was stern though her eyes slid uneasily from one side to the other—"that I spoke to you last week about Officer Leland and her unfortunate compulsion to persecute an outstanding citizen."

Chief Cobb looked ever more stolid. "Yes."

The mayor glowed with righteous indignation. "I know for a fact that Officer Leland ignored your instructions. You did instruct her?" The last was a sharp, flat demand.

I flung the rest of the paper clips high in the air. As they floated down, many landing in her beehive hairdo, I untied her scarf and tugged.

She came to her feet, holding on and gazing desperately about. "What's going on here? Where did those paper clips come from?" She gave the chief a suspicious glare.

I flapped the scarf.

The chief stood. To him, she appeared to be shaking the scarf in the air and lunging forward and back.

I let go.

She lost her balance and crashed down on her chair.

Shakily, breathing fast, she pulled the scarf around her neck and tied it, all the while looking sharply in every direction.

"Neva." He eyed her with concern. "Could I have Colleen get you a cup of tea?"

She shook her head, sputtered, "When did you speak with Officer Leland?" She lifted a hand to brush at the paper clips in her hair.

"Last week." His tone was irritated. "We straightened everything out. As Officer Leland made clear, Daryl Murdoch never contested the tickets. They were based on infractions of the speed limit and driving regulations. She admitted his attitude irritated her, and that's why she paid special attention to his driving. I told her she had to avoid the appearance of particularized enforcement and she agreed." Cobb moved impatiently. "Neva, it hardly matters—"

"Hardly matters?" The mayor's voice was shrill. She darted puzzled looks at the paper clips in her fingers. "Daryl Murdoch is a leading citizen, a strong supporter of good government, and a personal friend of mine."

In politics, as Bobby Mac often said, friendship is just another word for money. I wondered how much Daryl Murdoch had contributed to the mayor's last campaign.

Cobb frowned. "In view of what's happened—"

"Let me finish, please." A flush turned the mayor's sallow cheeks apple red. "I promised Daryl that your officer's witless pursuit of him would end. Yet"—she leaned forward, one hand chopping as fast as a sous chef's knife—"I personally saw her stop his car yesterday afternoon, lights flashing, everything but a siren."

The chief's dark brows bunched in a frown. "Yesterday? What time?"

The mayor looked triumphant. "Right after five o'clock. I was leaving our lot. I stopped and watched. She came up to his window and leaned down in a most menacing fashion."

I nodded. That explained the picture in Daryl's cell. Had he taken it intending to show his friend the mayor? It was too bad I didn't have the cell with me. I would poke it into the thickest portion of her beehive hairdo. I looked about for something that might work.

"Five o'clock." Chief Cobb's spoke in a considering tone. "Probably not close enough in time to be helpful."

"Helpful?" The mayor glared, all pretense of civility gone. "How can it be helpful when a police officer disregards her superior's instructions?" And, of course, made the mayor look ineffectual.

"Too bad she didn't follow him this time. It might have saved his life. But I'll talk to her, see if she picked up anything useful. Now . . ." He stood.

"Saved . . ." The mayor's mouth gaped, revealing two gold crowns.

"You miss the morning news?" His tone was bland.

Bobby Mac and I always started the morning with Channel 4 news and *The Oklahoman,* the Oklahoma City paper that was distributed statewide. *The Clarion,* Adelaide's only newspaper, was published in the afternoon.

The mayor lifted her rounded chin. "I avoid television in the mornings. I focus on the positive. The world pummels us with negative images, turning our citizens fearful and defensive. As a concerned citizen and a devoted public servant"—she raised a clenched fist—"I demand to know why—"

"Yeah. Like you said in your last campaign, Neva. How did you put it? Embrace the positive, shed the draining chains of negativity. I'd sure agree that skipping the morning news gives you a head start. But you missed out today. Somebody shot Daryl Murdoch last night. His body was found in St. Mildred's cemetery."

"His body?" The mayor's mouth gaped like a hungry fish.

I edged an adorable thumb-size porcelain dog toward the edge of the chief's desk, my eyes fastened on that tempting mound of bleached hair.

A massive hand clamped on my wrist.

I shrieked.

"Shhh." A warning growl.

The mayor's chair tumbled backward. She stood and stared at the small porcelain figure that was still cupped in my palm, clearly hovering an inch above the chief's desk.

The chief bounded to his feet, but he was looking at the mayor, not at his desk.

I opened my fingers and the little dog slid to the desktop.

Trembling, Mayor Lumpkin swung about and bolted heavily from the room.

Chief Cobb leaned forward, punched the intercom. "Colleen, you'd better let the mayor's husband know that she"—he paused—"isn't feeling well. Have the technicians check out the heating system. It made a strange noise. Kind of shrill. Then a whooshing sound."

He grabbed a notebook and pen. As he walked toward the door, he righted the chair and swept the room with a final, puzzled glance.

The minute the door closed, I heard a deep-throated rumble, not so distant this time and definitely not thunder. "Bailey Ruth."

If Wiggins had been visible, I feared his face might have that high red flush that used to be called apoplectic.

"Precept Six." His voice rose almost to a shout. "Precept Six. 'Make every effort—'"

My head swiveled as I followed the sound of his voice. Wiggins was pacing back and forth in front of me. Perhaps if I offered a cold compress . . .

"'—not to alarm earthly creatures.' And what have you just done?"

Nervously I picked up the little porcelain dog.

"There you go again." He was breathing heavily.

"I haven't gone anywhere," I protested, sure of that fact. I was still here. I hadn't moved—

"That dog! Put it down. Its levitation astounded that poor woman."

Served her right in my view, but, of course, I kept this thought to myself. I carefully eased the little dog to the desktop.

"Once again you have transgressed the Precepts. Moreover, you are Reverting!" His tone put the accusation on the level of gravest malfeasance.

"Reverting." I sighed. Yes, I'd been tempted and succumbed, unable to resist unnerving the pompous mayor.

"Oh." The exclamation was deep and mournful. I pictured Wiggins with his head in his hands. "This is what I feared, an emissary using our special gift to no good purpose."

I knew my duty. "I'm sorry, Wiggins." Then I lifted my chin. I can't stay down for long, and Mayor Lumpkin was odious. "Chief Cobb has better things to do this morning than deal with her."

"Bailey Ruth." Wiggins was obviously forcing himself to speak temperately. "I will accept your well-meant effort to free the chief from an unwarranted interruption—"

I should have felt remorse at deceiving Wiggins, but my back was against the wall. I mustn't be dispatched back to Heaven until I'd rescued Kathleen. Her straits remained dire.

"—yet I must object to your methods. We won't discuss the paper clips or that episode with the scarf, but I cannot countenance that dog hanging in the air by itself. You must refrain from moving objects about with no apparent means of locomotion. What do you suppose that woman is going to tell everyone?"

Since Wiggins couldn't see me, I didn't try to stop the mischievous curl of my lips, though I hoped my reply was suitably grave. "Wiggins, don't be upset. She won't tell anyone."

"Oh." It was almost a moan. Suddenly there was a pounding rat-a-tat on the desktop.

My eyes widened. Was Wiggins pounding on the chief's desktop?

"Chief—" Colleen stood in the doorway.

Abruptly it was quiet. Wiggins and I didn't move.

Colleen stepped inside, looked behind the door. "Chief?" Her eyes cut to the desk. She shook her head and turned away. The door closed.

The chief's chair scraped back. A subdued voice muttered, "Revert. That's always the fear. I thought I'd left it all behind me, losing my temper, giving in to anger."

I sidled nearer the desk, perched on the edge. "Wiggins, certainly you had provocation."

"The man in charge"—his voice was as heavy as lumps of coal dropping into a boxcar—"must always serve as an example. That's what leadership is all about."

Oh dear. It wouldn't do for Wiggins to lose his spirit. "Wiggins, I could not be more proud of you. Here you are, taking time from your station to help out a new emissary. Why, having you here has been"—how many demerits was I acquiring and what was the penalty for a bold-faced lie?— "heaven-sent."

Fingers drummed on the desk. I glanced toward the door. It would be unfortunate if Colleen returned. Gradually, the tattoo softened, finally stopped. "Do you think so?"

"Definitely." I moved behind the desk, reached down, and patted his shoulder. "I am inspired. Encouraged. You can

return to the Department of Good Intentions confident you
have communicated effectively. I shall take up my task and
the Precepts shall be ever on my mind." There was something about talking to Wiggins that stuffed my mouth full
of syllables.

With that, I was gone. I hoped I hadn't left him in a slough
of depression, but duty called.

The rectory kitchen was dark and quiet. I didn't bother to
call out. Obviously, Kathleen hadn't returned from her errands yet. Perhaps if I concentrated on Kathleen while picturing a bubbling pot on an unattended stove, she would feel
uneasy and be drawn home. Was ESP counter to the Precepts? Possibly, but I was desperate.

I was pacing back and forth when the chief's car pulled
into the drive. The church, of course, was very close to downtown. At this moment it was way too close. As he walked up
the path to the back porch, Kathleen's cream-colored Ford
station wagon rattled past the kitchen window.

If he reached Kathleen before I did . . .

In an instant I flowed into the front passenger seat of her
car. There was no time for a greeting. "Don't look panicked,
but we have a crisis."

The car jolted to a stop. Her head whipped toward the
passenger seat, eyes wide. Her fingers clenched on the steer-
ing wheel.

I talked fast. "Somebody called the police, told them to
ask you about the red nightgown—"

Kathleen hunched her shoulders.

"—and your visit to Daryl's cabin Wednesday night."

She watched the chief's approach as if he were a giant
squid wielding a blazing hatchet.

I was exasperated. "Don't look like that. You might as
well hold out your wrists for handcuffs. Smile, Kathleen."

Her lips stretched into a travesty of a smile.

The chief was perhaps ten feet away from the car.

So much to tell. So little time. Such an unpromising confederate. "Tell him you went to the cabin because Daryl called and asked you to come and help him plan a surprise thank-you party for the church secretary. You don't know anything about a red nightgown. You talked about gifts but—"

The chief rapped in the window.

Kathleen rolled it down. "Chief Cobb." Her voice was high and thin.

I reached over and pinched her smartly on the arm.

She flashed a startled look in my direction.

The chief followed her gaze to stare, bewildered, at nothing.

"I thought I heard—" Kathleen looked flustered.

I've always been a good mimic. I was locally famous for performing a dialogue between Lucille and Ethel—I did both parts—that left our friends in stitches. Of course they might have already had one or two of Bobby Mac's bourbons on the rocks.

"—my cell phone." I sounded just like Kathleen.

Kathleen looked haunted.

"Oh." Cobb nodded. "If you have a few minutes, Mrs. Abbott, I'd like to visit with you about Mr. Murdoch." He stepped back, an obvious invitation for her to get out of her car.

I gave her another pinch.

Kathleen's hand jerked to the handle. She opened the door, scrambled out to stand beside the car.

When she made no move to invite him into the rectory, Chief Cobb studied her, his eyes cool and thoughtful. "From information received—"

I was impressed at how official that sounded. It had

simply been an anonymous phone call. I wondered if he was being quite fair.

"—we understand you spent time at Mr. Murdoch's cabin on Pontotoc Road."

Kathleen was obviously surprised. "That's not true."

I gave her an approving pat on the shoulder. This time she didn't flinch. Good girl.

Cobb's stare was hard, his eyes suspicious. "Do you deny having been there Wednesday night?"

Kathleen looked blank for an instant, not too long but long enough to convey the recall of an unimportant memory. Perhaps Bayroo's acting talent was inherited.

"Wednesday night? Oh, that." Her tone was casual. "He asked me to drop by and help him plan a special surprise for the church secretary. Daryl was senior warden, you know."

"How long did you stay?" He pushed one hand into a pocket, tumbled coins in a muted jingle.

Kathleen looked confident. "Only a few minutes."

"Why did he ask you to come to his cabin?" Cobb's gaze was searching, his suspicions not totally allayed.

She turned her hands up. "I don't know. He didn't explain. I suppose he had something planned there and it was more convenient for him."

"Not very convenient for you. All the way to Chickasaw Lake."

"Chief Cobb." Her tone was dry. "The rector's wife exists to make life more convenient for the members of the vestry."

He wasn't done. "What about the red nightgown?"

Kathleen's eyes widened in classic puzzlement. Ingrid Bergman couldn't have done it better. "I don't know anything about a red nightgown."

"You and Daryl never talked about a nightgown?"

Her laughter almost sounded genuine. "No. In fact, I've

never talked to him about anything but church matters or OU football or the chances for the Adelaide Bobcats to win another state championship."

She could not have mentioned safer topics of conversation at any Oklahoma gathering. Football, both college and high school, was sure to be discussed in almost any social setting from a honky-tonk bar to the parish hall.

He inclined his head. "Appreciate your help, Mrs. Abbott." He glanced toward the church. "Might as well visit with your husband while I'm here." But as he turned away, he stopped and stared at the black cat strolling toward Kathleen.

Spoofer came closer, green eyes lifted to gaze at the chief.

Cobb pointed. "Your cat?"

"Yes." Kathleen reached down, stroked black fur that glistened reddish in the sun.

Cobb squinted. "He ever go in the church?"

Kathleen looked surprised. "Oh no. The vestry wouldn't approve."

Cobb gestured toward the rectory. "I saw him in your house last night."

Kathleen's glance at the chief was puzzled. "Yes."

Cobb nodded, gave Kathleen one final unsmiling look, and walked toward the church.

Kathleen stared after him. Spoofer twined at her ankles, but she paid no attention. When the police chief was almost at the church door, Kathleen whirled toward her car.

I caught her by the elbow, hissed in her ear, "You just got home. Go inside."

If Chief Cobb had looked back, he might have seen Kathleen walking on a tilt toward the back porch because she was trying to veer to her car and I was tugging mightily toward the house.

I won.

In the kitchen, she looked wildly about, glared at a spot near the door. "I've got to get to that cabin. My fingerprints are all over that gift package. I threw the gown and box and paper in the fireplace and ran out. I don't know if everything burned."

I poured coffee into my flamingo mug. "I'm over here."

She whirled toward the table. "Can't you ever do anything but drink coffee?"

It was hard to believe she'd begrudge a cup of coffee. Before I could point out that even a ghost, certainly one as active as I had been so far today, welcomed a brief moment of relaxation, she had clapped her hands to her head.

"I can't waste time talking to nobody. I've got to get to that cabin before—"

I upended the rest of the mug. "Kathleen, please. Don't you have any confidence in me? I was able to prepare you for the chief's questions. Now I'm going to the cabin." I glanced toward the back porch. I decided that she'd had as much stress as she could manage. I didn't think it was a propitious moment to tell her about the dust ball with Spoofer's fur on Daryl's suit jacket. I'd surely have time to sweep the porch and get rid of the tarp after I dealt with the red nightgown. "Everything will be fine." I put the mug in the sink, aware that her eyes followed its progress through the air as if it were utterly repellent.

I was ready to depart for the cabin to check on the status of the gift box and gown when I looked through the kitchen window.

Chief Cobb still faced toward the church, but he wasn't moving. He stood with his cell phone to his ear. Ah, he must have had a ring before he went inside. A moment later, he turned, thrusting the cell phone into his pocket, and strode toward his car.

He moved like a man with a purpose.

I felt a tingle of excitement. Something had happened.

Kathleen was pacing near the table. "Bailey Ruth, have you left? Are you there yet? Oh, dear Heaven, how can I talk to somebody who isn't—"

"I'm here." I was ready to leave, but I had a suspicion that Kathleen might be poised to put herself in a big jam. "Promise me you won't go anywhere near Daryl's cabin."

Kathleen's face might not have been an open book, but I had no trouble reading it. Consternation was succeeded by guilt. Obviously, she'd intended to make a foray there as soon as I was safely absent. I hadn't raised two redheaded children without discovering all there was to know about guile, deceit, and general foolhardiness.

I walked to the table, pulled out a chair.

Kathleen stared at the moving chair, then flung out her hands in defeat. "All right, Bailey Ruth. You win. I promise. Hurry. You've got to get there before the chief. If the police find that box, my life is ruined."

"They won't. Trust me, sweetie." I didn't see an iota of trust in the forlorn face turned toward me, so, of course, I didn't tell her I was going to make a slight detour. As long as the chief was otherwise occupied, the red gown in Daryl's cabin was not a threat to Kathleen.

I wavered for an instant. I could go to the cabin and attend to the red nightgown, or I could follow the chief, be in on the latest developments. However, I was sure that it was essential that I keep tabs on the progress of the chief's investigation. Certainly I wasn't succumbing to the siren song of curiosity.

Certainly not.

CHAPTER 9

Judith Murdoch fingered the faux pearls at the neck of her blue sweater. "Are we in danger? Maybe Kirby and I shouldn't stay here."

Chief Cobb shook his head. "I don't see a threat to you or your son. You weren't home." He gestured at the ransacked room. "Whoever broke in probably made sure you were gone."

Kirby stood protectively near his mother, his thin, dark face furrowed in a worried frown. "Everything was fine this morning. We were only gone about an hour. We went over to the cabin—"

The cabin! I almost willed myself there, but a break-in at the Murdoch house had to be significant.

"—to get it ready for some cousins who're driving up from Dallas this afternoon. We left the back door unlocked for the cleaning ladies."

Chief Cobb stood in the doorway and surveyed the shambles an intruder had left behind in Daryl Murdoch's study. Drawers from the mahogany desk had been emptied and flung aside. A cabinet behind the desk hung on wrenched hinges, the paneling scraped and gashed, files pulled out, papers tossed. Books had been yanked from shelves, thrown into uneven mounds.

The chief crossed the room, pulled aside heavy red drapes. Splintered glass in a French door marked the means of entry. The door stood ajar. He glanced toward Judith. "Alarm?"

She stared at the broken pane and mound of glass. "We only set the alarm at night."

"Always set the alarm when you leave the house." The chief's admonition was automatic. He gestured at the mess. "Can you tell if anything is missing?"

She spread her hands helplessly. "I wouldn't have any idea. This was Daryl's room." Off limits to her was the unspoken message.

"A technician is on the way to dust for prints. Don't touch anything until we're finished. Have you checked the rest of the house?" He nodded toward the hallway.

Kirby looked embarrassed. "I wanted to look around, but Mom made me stay with her."

The chief nodded in approval. "Smart move. I'll take a look."

A rap on the partially open French door brought a gasp from Judith.

"It's all right, Mrs. Murdoch. I asked Officer Leland to make a survey of the premises." He looked inquiring. "Officer?"

Officer Leland was careful not to touch the door. She looked crisp and competent, her French-blue uniform fresh and unwrinkled. "No one home on either side, sir. No trace of an intruder except for what appears to be a fresh footprint in a patch of mud near a path into the woods. The print isn't distinct. It looks as though a man—that's from the size of the print—was running and slid on a mound of leaves. It is possible that the intruder parked in the wooded area behind the house. Of course the print could have no connection to the break-in."

"Put tape up. Show the technician, then search the woods for fresh tire prints."

"Yes, sir." Officer Leland turned away.

Chief Cobb looked at Judith. "Let's check the rest of the house, see if anything else has been disturbed."

I zoomed ahead of them. Everything looked to be in perfect order. I doubted there was more for me to learn at the Murdoch house. It was time to honor my promise to Kathleen and deal with the red nightgown.

Years ago Pontotoc Road was on the outskirts of town. It circled Chickasaw Lake. Most of the original cabins were fairly ramshackle, masculine retreats for poker and fishing and booze. Now the road was paved, but it still dipped and curved through thick woods and up- and downhill.

Oklahoma weather was as coquettish as I remembered. The morning's cold wind and lowering clouds were gone. The sky was a soft fall blue, and the air was warming. The high temperature would likely edge near seventy this afternoon. I wished away my lamb's-wool coat. Bradford-pear leaves glowed bright as Burgundy shot through with sunlight. Red-and-gold maple leaves fluttered in the gentle breeze. A sturdy sycamore shed tawny leaves that were heaped, sculpted by the wind, near the Murdoch cabin's front steps.

The drive ended in a turnaround near the cabin. A small green pickup was parked near the steps. It likely belonged to the cleaning ladies. I expected that was where Daryl had parked Wednesday evening. Kathleen likely pulled in behind his car. The drive didn't circle behind the cabin. Parking must always be a problem, cars straggling along the drive back to the road.

When Kathleen fled, she'd jumped into her car, locked

the doors, made a tight turn, and sped up the drive to the
road. She'd made no mention of another car. There were no
offshoot lanes from the drive.

Where had the other car parked?

I knew there had been another car or some means of
transportation. Someone else must have been present that
evening to know about the red nightgown.

I heard the whine of a vacuum cleaner within the cabin.
Soon I would go inside and see about the nightgown, but
it was essential to understand what had happened here
Wednesday night.

Had Daryl told someone about the episode of the red
nightgown? Sexual bullies don't relish looking foolish. It
was not a moment for him to recount with pride to his bud-
dies, Kathleen tossing the nightgown into the fire and slam-
ming out of the cabin. Therefore, someone saw Kathleen
unwrap that present, fling it to destruction, and flee. The
front windows were uncurtained, the interior shutters folded
back, affording a clear view within. I glanced up the drive.
The house wasn't visible from the road.

I pictured the cabin in the gloom of approaching night,
Daryl inside, the fire burning. Kathleen arrived, tense and
upset, and somewhere outside someone watched.

I stepped close to the window on the right. A buxom
woman in a red T-shirt and jeans flapped a spread onto a
twin bed.

I moved to the first window on the other side of the porch.
The window was raised about an inch. A wiry cleaning
woman in a flower-patterned housedress pushed a sweeper
close enough to the window that we would have looked eye
to eye had I been there. The machine's shrill whine rose to
a shriek.

I looked past her, saw the cream sofa where Kathleen had
sat. A leather recliner faced the sofa. A sagging easy chair

was near the fireplace. From here an observer would have seen everything that transpired.

I glanced down. Sycamore leaves bunched up in a puffy mound. Shoes would leave no mark. If someone had watched through this window Wednesday night, I would find no trace here.

I wasn't following the progress of the vacuum cleaner. The sudden cessation of sound startled me. I looked into the room and realized the cleaning lady was bending toward the fireplace.

At once I was beside her, but I watched helplessly as she gingerly lifted up the singed remnants of the red silk nightgown and the gift box and wrapping paper. She lifted her voice. "Jenny, you won't never believe what I found. Come look at this. Don't you know there's a tale behind this here."

Kathleen was my charge and here was evidence that would link her to a murder and tarnish her reputation forever. If I had come directly from the rectory as I had promised, Kathleen would not be in jeopardy. It was my old sin of curiosity. With a dash of impulsiveness. Good intentions may indeed pave the road to hell, but if-onlys point the way to the slippery slope to despair.

I stared at the dangling remnants of the red silk gown. Kathleen's future hung in the balance.

The Precepts warned against alarming earthly creatures and certainly Wiggins found any such activity reprehensible, but I had no choice. In a flash, I shot to the kitchen, opened my mouth, and yelled. As my shrill shout rose and fell, I felt a moment of pride. The sound was unnerving. I didn't know I had it in me.

"Mabel, what's wrong?" The strangled call came from the bedroom. "Are you hurt?"

In the living room, Mabel shouted, "Somebody's gettin'

killed in the kitchen. Hurry, Jenny. Run. Get out the front door."

I screamed again, as loudly as possible, pulling breath all the way from my toes.

Pounding steps sounded in the living room. I moved back to the fireplace in time to glimpse heavyset Jenny plunging through the front door. Doors slammed. The pickup roared to life, tires squealing as it took off.

I didn't waste a minute. The police would be here soon. I found a box of matches on the mantel. I set fire to various portions of the gown, flaring up a brisk blaze. I made sure the cardboard box and paper burned as well as the nightgown, every last scrap. When the flames began to die down, I took a poker and stirred the ashes, mashed them into nothingness.

My heart was pounding. I'd almost been a day late and a dollar short. I was ready to depart, pleased with my quick thinking, when I heard that unmistakable rumble. I didn't hesitate. "Hello, Wiggins. You'll be glad to know everything's dandy. The red nightgown—I'm sure you know all about it—is destroyed and Kathleen is safe." If not a gold star, surely I deserved a silver. "Now, if you'll excuse me, I have to see about the cat fur."

I reached the roof of the rectory. It was a good five minutes before I heaved a sigh of relief. I had no invisible companion, rumbling with displeasure. Apparently Wiggins was cutting me some slack. At least for the moment, I was captain of my fate. However, I wished St. Mildred's was not quite such an active church. A half-dozen cars were parked in the lot. Women streamed in and out. All were, I'm sure, doing good works, but at the moment they hampered my movements. Moreover, not fifty yards away, the back of the crime van was wide open and I noticed a technician jump out, carrying a blue plastic hand vacuum.

Standing to one side of a silver Lincoln Continental was the energetic young police detective. He bent to peer inside. "Hey, Artie, don't think this'll take long. Looks like Murdoch kept it clean."

They wouldn't, I was sure, find a trace of cat fur. I had to hurry. I clapped my hands in satisfaction. If I couldn't work unseen, why, no problem. It was time to be in the world, however briefly. Surely Wiggins would approve this circumspect appearance.

I landed on the rectory back porch and appeared. My elegant pantsuit was not quite the attire for housecleaning. I topped it with a blue smock appropriate for the Altar Guild. Possibly it was an excess of caution, but I added a matching turban. If anyone noticed a helpful member of the Altar Guild busy at the rectory, it would be better if red hair wasn't part of her description. I smoothed the edges of the turban to be sure no red-gold sprigs peeped from beneath.

I always enjoyed housework. There's such a sense of accomplishment when everything is tidy. Heaven doesn't need dusting. The only tidying that remains is to continue growing in goodness, and goodness knows, for most of us there is always room for improvement.

I felt a moment's unease. Had my return to earth encouraged my tendency to be inquisitive, rash, impulsive, and forthright?

"Undoubtedly." Wiggins sounded resigned.

Although my breath caught, I was almost getting used to his sudden utterances. I was terribly aware that he was once again here and I was in deep Dutch.

"However"—even his rumble was subdued—"there are times when appearing will cause less turmoil than not appearing. Try hard"—his tone was plaintive—"to remain out of sight. If I'd realized you were quite so noticeable . . ." His voice faded.

I started to reply, then felt certain he'd once again departed. Obviously he agreed that I must address the pressing matter of a dusty porch and a tarp that must never be subjected to a police microscope. Did I have carte blanche?

I hurried inside and grabbed a broom and a dustpan from the closet in the kitchen. I took only a moment to glance in the mirror over the sink. Good. The turban was a success. I had a brief memory, thanks to Turner Classic Movies, of Carmen Miranda and a turban piled high with a tower of pomegranates, mangoes, and bananas and presto, gleaming plastic fruit appeared. Smiling, I returned to the porch and set to work, humming "Trite Samhita," and sweeping in triple time. I loved to samba. Occasionally I added a conga step for flair.

I dumped several full dustpans into a trash sack. Spoofer certainly shed a great deal of black fur, but soon the porch was shiny bright. I was especially thorough around, behind, and beneath the corner of the porch where the tarp lay. I carried the trash sack out to the garbage pail. All four doors of the Lincoln were open. Dark gray legs protruded from the floor of the back seat. The blond detective stood with hands on his hips, watching. I observed him with pleasure. Bobby Mac understood when I admired a manly physique because I always saved the last dance for him.

As I returned the broom and dustpan to the closet in the kitchen, I caught a glimpse of myself in the mirror and laughed aloud. Although it looked top-heavy, my turban was quite comfortable. I patted a bright yellow banana, gave a little back tap, and samba'd onto the porch.

All that remained was to dispose of the tarp. A coil of cord, likely left over from a clothesline, hung from a hook. I cut a six-foot length. In one corner, I found a stack of gunnysacks. I shoved the rolled-up tarp in the gunnysack, added three stacked pottery pots for ballast, and flicked out the length of cord.

A knock sounded on the porch screen door.

I broke off humming and, clutching the open gunnysack, turned to look.

Standing on the steps was the handsome detective, the sun turning his cotton top snow white. He held out an open wallet. "Detective Sergeant Hal Price. I'm looking for the sexton. Can you tell me where I might find him?"

I stared at him, my mouth agape. Before I could think—there I went again, impulsive to the bone—I clasped the sack to the bosom of the smock and made a sound somewhere between a squeak and a shriek.

"Pardon me, miss." His drawl was contrite and his eyes, for a brief instant, admiring, until professional coolness returned. "I didn't mean to startle you." He spoke gently as if to a shying filly.

"Detective Sergeant?" I clung to the gunnysack, which bulged awkwardly over the pots, and was furious at myself. He didn't know what I held. He had no idea. I forced my grip to relax, rested the sack casually on the floor. "Is something wrong?"

"Everything's fine." His smile was electric.

On the one hand, I was flattered. On the other, I was uneasy. I didn't want to be remembered, but there is that spark when a man admires a woman that can't be disguised. Detective Sergeant Price wasn't going to forget our encounter. If I were old, he'd have been polite, kept a mental record as a good detective should, but there would not have been this crackle of electricity between us.

"Can I help you?" I tried to sound cool, not quite unfriendly, but definitely not encouraging.

He glanced at my left hand, saw the gold band, and gave a

tiny shake of his head. "I'm looking for the sexton and at the church they told me he might be at the shed by the rectory. Can you direct me?"

I pointed at the flagstone path. "Follow the path past the old well and go around those weeping willows and you'll find the shed."

He stood a moment longer, then nodded. "Thank you. And you are . . ."

Attracted he might be. A detective he remained.

"Helen Troy." The moment I spoke, I regretted the name. But what can you do when a man makes his interest so plain? It happens, you know, an encounter, and each of you knows that had the time been different, circumstances altered, memories could have been made.

He nodded and turned away.

At the bend in the path, he looked back.

A very attractive man. As soon as he was out of sight, I yanked up the sack and raced to the kitchen. I tightly rolled the cord around and around the sack and tied it in my best sailor's knot.

I waited several minutes. Detective Sergeant Price didn't reappear. I eased out the kitchen door. Women continued to come and go in the church parking lot, but none veered toward the rectory. I strolled to the pines and slipped behind them.

I was torn. Violating the Precepts seemed to result in an automatic visit from Wiggins, but I was in a hurry. The sooner I dumped the tarp, the better, and I still needed to deal with the gun. I could zoom to the lake faster than I could walk. Surely Wiggins would applaud swift execution of my duties.

I disappeared and zoomed. The gunnysack, of course, dangled in the air. I darted from tree to tree so the sack appeared in midair only briefly. The sense of isolation and

peace increased the deeper I traveled into the nature preserve. When I sighted the sparkling blue water of the lake, I
felt as relieved as any ten-year-old hearing that old familiar
cry, "Ollie, ollie, oxen's free." Of course I had no idea at the
time we were shouting what was likely a phonetic imitation
of the German *Alle, alle, auch sind frei*. I hoped I might have
occasion to share this moment later with Wiggins, and he
would have an appreciation of my intellectual turn of mind.

Perhaps it was this thoughtful pondering that distracted
my attention from my surroundings. I rode a breeze out
toward the middle of the lake, imagining the surprise on
Wiggins's face when—

Abruptly, the bag was tugged from my hand.

Startled, I made a grab for it. Had a crow intercepted
me?

"Precept Six, Bailey Ruth, Precept Six." Wiggins's tone
was imploring.

I loosened my hold.

The lumpy gunnysack plummeted down.

I was exasperated. After all, he'd yanked the bag from
me. "Wiggins, I thought you had it."

"A gentleman never struggles with a lady." Clearly, in his
heart he found this custom a grave hindrance.

Water plumed upward as the sack splashed into the lake.

A hoarse shout sounded below. "Lord Amighty, look!"
An old man with a straggly white beard stood at the end of
the dock, pointing his bamboo fishing pole at the ripples in
the water. He wore a puffy jacket over bib overalls.

A lean woman with sharp features turned from a bait
cooler. "What's the matter with you, Pa?"

He waggled the pole. "Something big poked out of that
water. Bigger than any fish. I'm going to get the boat and go
out there and see."

If he poked his pole down, snagged the gunnysack, and

hauled it out, he'd be sure to tell his cronies at the feed store. If word got back to Detective Sergeant Price, as it very well might in a small town, he would remember the turbaned lady with the gunnysack on the rectory porch.

The fisherman lumbered toward the end of the dock. His boat wasn't in sight. That gave me a minute, perhaps two.

"Wiggins, that sack mustn't be found. There's no time to spare." At all costs, I must forestall a discussion. If Wiggins wouldn't play up, well, I looked down, it would be a long fall. "Quick, I'm going to reappear. Hold me up. I need my turban."

Below us, oars slapped through water.

I became visible. Just as I began to tumble down, strong hands gripped my arms, held me up. I snatched the turban from my head. My hair cascaded free. I threw the turban high. In a flash, I disappeared. I reached out to catch the turban. I didn't take time to ponder what I would have done had it disappeared, but I tucked away the knowledge that imagined items, once visible but separate from me, remained in existence.

I pulled free from Wiggins's grasp.

"Precept Six." Wiggins's despairing call followed me as I plunged down and poked the turban into the water, only the top of the artificial fruit protruding near the spot where the gunnysack had disappeared.

The boat came around a clump of reeds.

I eased the turban to the surface.

The woman leaned over the side. "Pa, it looks like a bunch of bananas."

He rowed with vigor, and the boat moved nearer.

"Hold up," she cried. "I can get it." She bent perilously far out, reaching.

I gave the turban a little push and it came easily into her hands.

Her weathered face softened. "Why, it's the prettiest thing I ever did see. I'll dry it out and it'll be good as new."

He frowned. "How'd that get out here, Effie?"

Effie didn't know or care. She carefully laid her treasure on the bottom of the boat. "Some old crow got it and decided it wasn't no use to him and dropped it down just for me, Pa."

He grunted and swung the boat around, heading back for the dock. He gave a final questioning look over his shoulder.

I shook the icy lake water from my fingers. I didn't bother to look about. Not that I would have seen Wiggins. I knew he was near. I wished I wasn't picturing him glowering, with arms folded.

"Precepts Three, Four, and Six flouted." His voice was gruff.

Did I hear the faraway whistle of the Rescue Express, dispatched to retrieve an errant emissary?

Silence.

Had Wiggins left? Or was he affording me quiet time in which I might ponder working behind the scenes without making my presence known, becoming visible only when absolutely essential, and refraining from alarming earthly creatures? Or, in the case of Detective Sergeant Price, attracting them.

A rumble sounded near enough that I cringed.

"Unfortunate. Extremely unfortunate." A heavy sigh. "However, though I am loath to endorse the concept of the ends justifying the means, it would be equally reprehensible to refuse to admit that sometimes desperate measures may be demanded."

That was good enough for me. "Thank you, Wiggins. I knew you'd be pleased."

"However, it appears"—a pause—"an unfortunate choice

of words." His displeasure was evident. "It is clear," he rumbled, "that you are far too attractive."

"Oh, Wiggins." If I could have seen him, I would have flashed him a wink. "Men like women. Women like men. Don't you remember?"

Suddenly a deep burst of laughter erupted nearby. "Oh, I remember. I certainly remember. But"—he was once again stern—"it is simply a reminder that you really must not appear, Bailey Ruth."

"I'll do my best." That might be ambiguous, but I meant it well. "Now I hate to hurry away, but I simply must deal with the gun."

If a shout followed me, I honestly didn't hear it.

St. Mildred's brimmed with activity. I stood on the rectory roof and nudged the lumpy head cover with the toe of my shoe. Any of the women scurrying into or out of the church could easily have tucked a gun in a purse and marched into the cemetery without anyone paying any attention.

I had made every effort to honor the Precepts despite Wiggins's perception of chaos. I pushed away the memory of my interlude with the very appealing detective sergeant and the tussle with the gunnysack above the lake. Did I dare appear again in another guise to take the gun to the cemetery? Time was wasting. That gun needed to be placed where the police could find it. It seemed amazing that I'd begun the morning with that intent, and here it was, almost noon, and the gun remained atop the rectory.

Moreover, I was hungry. I felt buffeted from my morning, my encounters with Wiggins, the shock of that anonymous call implicating Kathleen, my scramble to warn her before the chief caught her by surprise, my last-second heroics to snatch the nightgown from the cleaning lady, my samba-energized cleaning of the porch, and the challenges of dispatching the tarp. Nonetheless, I was determined to dispose of the gun before pausing for lunch.

My gaze skimmed the parking lot and the backyard. Three women, chattering cheerfully, were walking toward the church, their backs to me. Just below me, the Halloween decorations were much less ominous in bright sunshine than they'd been on my arrival last night, although it seemed to me that the huge spider's reddish eyes had an eerie glow and the bat was amazingly lifelike.

In an instant I was hovering beside the bat. The papier-mâché creature wasn't the almost cuddly, small furry creature I associated with barn lofts. This bat had a good six-inch wingspan. It was definitely big enough. I loosened the wires that held it to a dangling rope. With a quick glance around, I tossed the rope up around the tree limb.

With my help, the bat flapped its wings and rose to the roof. I doubted my bat was particularly batlike, but it would serve well enough. I took the gun out of the head cover, placed it on the back of the bat, where it was hidden from view below. Wiggins would applaud the ingenuity that made it unnecessary for me to appear at this moment.

The bat and gun and I sailed into the cemetery without incident. I went directly to the mausoleum, which was included within the yellow tape erected by the police to proclaim a crime scene. A moment later, the gun was tucked between Hannah Pritchard's tomb and the interior wall.

Sunlight spilled into the mausoleum. I wafted to the greyhound, smoothed the top of his head, would have sworn I heard a throaty yip, felt the warmth of skin. At Hannah's tomb, I stroked the cat whiskers.

I definitely felt lucky. Now all I needed to do was make an anonymous call to the police, inform them that the gun that had been used to shoot Daryl Murdoch was hidden in the Pritchard mausoleum.

My face furrowed in a frown. Making phone calls was definitely more challenging now than it had been when I'd lived in Adelaide. Obviously, there were means of tracing where calls originated. I needed a telephone that wasn't linked to the rectory or the church.

I was stymied for a moment. I didn't have time to zoom around Adelaide seeking a telephone. I needed a place where there were plenty of telephones and possibly one I could use without notice.

The library.

The solution came so swiftly I knew it was meant to be. Bobby Mac's sister Julianna had been a librarian for thirty years. Her passion was Latin. Julianna's thrill upon arriving in Heaven was meeting the poet Horace. As she had murmured to me: *Sic itur ad astra.* As always, she kindly translated: "Thus one goes to the stars," or more eloquently, "Such is the way to immortality."

I smiled and murmured Julianna's favorite from Horace: *Carpe diem, quam minimum credula postero!* It was my credo at this moment. I definitely intended to seize this hour and not trust some later day.

I was puzzled for a moment when I found myself in a rotunda with the state flag of Oklahoma in a bright mosaic on the floor. This wasn't the old red-brick Carnegie library on Second Street, but I approved of the lovely new building, nonetheless.

Three witches huddled around a cauldron. Bunches of red tissue simulated a bed of burning coals. Twists of silver tissue poked upward from the cauldron as coils of steam. To one side, a witch with a beaked nose held a decorated placard announcing: STORY TIME FOR LITTLE SPOOKS 10 A.M. SATURDAY. On the other side, a witch with bright red eyes held another sign: FRIENDS' MONSTER-SLIME DINNER 7 P.M. FRIDAY, COME AS YOU AREN'T!

Two bulbous-bodied cardboard tarantulas balanced on a giant black web that stretched over the door to the reading room. I stepped inside and a plastic skeleton extended a hand as a sepulchral voice intoned, "Welcome to thrills and chills."

Books filled rows of metal shelving, but a good portion of the near room was filled with the television-like machines. Patrons hunched at the keyboards. Colorful images flashed on the screens.

I looked covetously at the telephone on the main information desk. However, it was far too public for me to use. I wafted upstairs in a flash and through a locked door marked STAFF.

A narrow hallway led past four cubicles separated by partitions. Puffy paper pumpkins hung from the ceiling. Each cubicle held a desk and a chair with one of those machines with a keyboard and screen. Three were occupied. Telephones rang, chairs squeaked, voices rose in a hum.

I slipped into the unoccupied cubicle. The in-box held a green skull that glowed with phosphorescent paint. I admired the studio portrait of a little girl about seven. The desktop was neat, papers stacked, pens at the ready. I opened drawers until I found a directory. The first time I dialed, I got an automatic recording: "Dial nine for outside calls." I started over.

The call was answered on the second ring. "Adelaide Police."

I spoke softly. "I have information about the murder of Daryl—"

"Excuse me, ma'am. You'll have to speak up. I can't hear you."

I gripped the receiver, tried again. "I have information—"

"Louder, please."

This time I spoke loud and fast. "The gun used to shoot

Daryl Murdoch is hidden in the Pritchard mausoleum at the cemetery."

A chair on the other side of the partition squeaked. A round face framed by spiky black curls appeared over the edge of the partition. "Hey, Callie, what's—"

No more words came. A look of eager curiosity was replaced by the beginnings of a puzzled frown. "Callie?" She looked up and down, seeking what evidently wasn't there. "How come the phone's up in the air?"

"Let me connect you . . ." I slammed the phone into the receiver.

Abruptly the face disappeared. Feet thudded as the questioner bounded out into the aisle. She moved to the cubicle's entryway, peering inside. "Callie, where are you?" She looked up and down the aisle. "Where did you go?"

The phone on the desk rang.

As I zoomed out of her way, I knocked against the skull. It rolled from the in-box and bounced on the desk.

The puzzled librarian clutched at the partition.

The phone continued to peal.

Reluctantly, the librarian edged into the cubicle. Leaning away from the shiny skull, she yanked up the receiver. "Adelaide Library." Her voice was uneven, breathless. "How may I help you?" She warily watched the skull.

"Yeah. I heard part of it." She twined the cord around one finger. "No. It wasn't me. I don't know who called you. I mean, I heard it, but nobody's here." Her face folded in a frown. "I don't know a thing about a gun. Well, sure, send somebody over if you want to. But I can tell you now that nobody here knows a thing. And there's this skull that bounced . . ."

Kathleen spread mustard on thick slices of homemade white bread. She added lettuce, bread-and-butter pickles, and ham. I counted three sandwiches on the stoneware platter. One for me, possibly? She lifted a bowl of potato salad from the refrigerator.

I always like to help my hostess. "Would you like for me to set the table?"

She whirled toward the sound, though I'd moved to the cabinet and was reaching up for dishes. "How many will there be?"

She turned again. "Bill and me. But—" She glanced out the back window. "If you're hungry, I suppose you could eat first."

It wasn't the most gracious invitation I'd ever received, but it would do.

I opened the cabinet, picked out three plates, each in a different color, one of the charms of Fiesta pottery. I selected azure blue for Bill, pine green for Kathleen, sandstone red for me.

As I placed them on the table, she glanced through the window into the backyard and the path from the church, then demanded anxiously, "What about the nightgown?"

"Not a trace remains." I didn't think it was necessary to explain that the gown's destruction had been a near thing.

She leaned against the counter, holding the potato salad. "Thank you, Bailey Ruth."

"My pleasure." I took the bowl from her, carried it to the table, then lifted the platter of sandwiches.

Kathleen watched its progress through the air. "What frightens me is that I'm beginning to think that platters and bowls traveling through the air untouched by human hand is normal."

I would have been insulted, but she was stressed. I didn't bother to answer. It took only a moment more to add silverware and napkins.

She delved again into the refrigerator, added a plate of

deviled eggs bright with a dash of paprika, and cut celery stalks stuffed with pimiento cheese.

I pulled out my chair. "Since Father Bill's coming, you don't mind if I start?" I took a sandwich, scooped up a generous amount of potato salad, plucked a deviled egg and stalk of stuffed celery. The ham was delicious, the bread fresh and yeasty. The potato salad was my favorite, made with mustard, not drenched in mayonnaise. I murmured grace and lifted my sandwich.

"He's supposed to be here at noon." She sounded weary. She plunked ice cubes into glasses, brought them and a pitcher of iced tea.

I knew I was home in Oklahoma, where iced tea is the drink of choice year-round.

"Who knows if he'll come? Bill never does." She poured tea for us. "Maybe he will. Maybe he won't."

I wondered if she realized how forlorn she sounded.

Soon enough it would be time for me to demand information from Kathleen, but as my mama always insisted, "Mealtime is a time for happy faces." Deferring to the Precepts, I couldn't offer a smiling face to Kathleen, but I could focus on happy matters. "Will you help out at Bayroo's Halloween party this afternoon?"

Kathleen's smile was immediate. "It's going to be so much fun. I baked meringue in the shape of hearts and made an *X* on them with red licorice for 'X marks the spot.' And . . ."

I listened and murmured and smiled as she described the party plans. I forced myself to eat sedately, though, truth to tell, I was ravenous from my morning's exertions and could have devoured two sandwiches in the time I spent daintily consuming one. "Bayroo says she always wears a pirate costume."

Kathleen laughed. "With a gold eye patch, not a black one. Bayroo says her pirate is stylish."

We were absorbed in lunch and conversation. The sudden opening of the back door shocked us to silence. Kathleen looked in panic at my plate, with its obvious remnants of a meal at a place where no one sat.

I didn't hesitate, stealthily moving the plate and glass below the surface of the table. I put them on the floor, then reached up to grab the silverware and napkin, and dropped down again. However, a meal service is not a normal feature of a kitchen floor. I looked swiftly about. There was a space between the refrigerator and the counter. The area between wasn't visible from the table.

Two black-trousered legs stood between me and my goal.

"Kathleen." Father Bill's voice was grim.

I shot up to look.

A bleak frown combined with his clerical collar and dark suit made Kathleen's husband appear somber. He stopped, hands clenched at his sides. He should have been handsome, his shock of sandy hair cut short to disguise a tendency to curl, deep-set dark blue eyes, straight nose, stalwart chin with a cleft. Instead he looked haggard and worried.

"Bill?" Kathleen took a step toward him. "What's wrong?"

He took a deep breath. "The police chief came to see me. He told me you went to Daryl Murdoch's cabin Wednesday night." Father Bill jammed his hands into his jacket pockets.

Kathleen stood as if her bones had turned to stone.

Father Bill tried to smile. "That was some story you came up with. I know he didn't plan a gift for Mamie. He wanted me to fire her. But I told the chief surprises were right up Daryl's alley. That was certainly true. And the uglier the better." He looked even grimmer. "I know what happened. You went because of me, didn't you? Daryl said he had to talk to you about me."

Father Bill seemed to have no awareness of his surroundings. Now was the moment. Hovering just above the floor, I moved behind him with my plate and napkin and silverware. There was barely room to squeeze past.

Kathleen's eyes widened. Her gaze followed the table service moving a few inches above the floor. She looked stricken.

Father Bill's face softened. "That's what I thought." He moved toward her in a rush, pulled her into his arms, looked down into her face. "You shouldn't have gone there. Did he try to get you to tell him? What did you say?"

I reached the refrigerator.

Kathleen gave him a quick look, then her eyes veered down, drawn as if by a magnet to the retreating table setting.

I tucked everything out of sight.

She closed her eyes in relief.

"Kathleen." His voice was suddenly soft. "Don't be upset. You're wonderful." He gently took her chin, lifted her face. Her eyes opened and their gazes met. "It must have been horrible for you, the police chief demanding to know what you talked about and you trying to protect me. I'm sorry you had to go through that. Sorry about everything. But you're my wonderful brave girl, going to that cabin, staring him down. It was just like Daryl"—his voice was hard—"to try and pry information out of you."

"He was awful." Kathleen's eyes were dark with memory. "But I didn't say anything about you."

He loosed his grip, began to pace. "Of course not. I wouldn't tell you anything about—well, that's the problem, I can't tell anyone. That makes me suspect number one to the police."

Kathleen's hand clutched at her throat. "You? Bill, I don't understand."

He faced her. "It's simple enough. Daryl and I had a shouting match yesterday morning. Somebody must have heard and told the police. The chief wants to know what happened and why. I can't tell him. I don't know what Daryl may have said to anyone else on the vestry. If Daryl hinted at financial laxity, well, I may not be rector here much longer. An audit will show everything's absolutely as it should be, but if that kind of suspicion is raised, I'm done for. Everybody will think I was going to do something illegal and Daryl called my hand. If anyone has to be above suspicion, it's a priest."

Kathleen was distraught. "No one can ever say that about you. You're the most honest man in the world, the most honorable, the kindest, the best." If she'd had a sword, she would have brandished it.

Suddenly Bill's face re-formed, alight with laughter. "That's my girl."

She was distraught. "It's crazy for them to suspect you."

He forced a smile. "Don't worry. Things usually come right. And if they don't, we'll have done our best. Now"—he was brisk—"can you pack up some of that nice lunch for me? I'm late getting out to the Carson ranch. Juanita's having a bad day."

Kathleen shivered. "There can't be anything worse than losing a child. Tell her I put a flower on Josie's grave yesterday." It took her only a moment to put together a lunch, fill a thermos with coffee.

Bill took the brown bag, bent, kissed her lightly on the lips, but Kathleen held tight, kissed him with a desperate intensity.

Slowly they moved apart. He reached out to touch her cheek. "It's okay, honey." But when he reached the door, he looked back. "I hate it that you had to lie for me. If the chief comes back to you, tell him the truth, Daryl inveigled you to go to the cabin so he could quiz you about me, but you didn't know a thing. And you don't. Because"—his frown was ferocious—"I didn't like some of the chief's questions. He seemed to think you and Daryl . . . Well, I set him straight there. I told him you didn't even like the man, and much more to the point, you're my wife and you would never dishonor your vows."

Suddenly he was serious again. "I love you, Kathleen."

"Oh, Bill." She was in his arms. They clung to each other. Their lips met in a passionate kiss.

I left. Some moments are not meant to be shared.

When Father Bill came outside, striding toward his car, I returned to the kitchen.

Tears were streaming down Kathleen's face. She stumbled to the table, sank into a chair, sobbing.

I brought a box of tissues, placed it at her elbow.

". . . feel so awful . . . what would he think if he knew . . . and I went to Raoul's apartment . . . oh, Bill . . . I've got to tell him the truth . . ."

I poked her in the shoulder. "Do you want the chief to arrest him?"

She flung up her head, stared at me—well, in my general vicinity—in horror. "Bill? That can't happen."

"It could." I hated to make her day harder, but it was time to face facts. "The chief is already suspicious of Bill. If you suddenly tell the truth about your visit to Daryl, the red nightgown's enough to convince the chief that Bill had plenty of reason to shoot Daryl. Don't change your story." I handed her some tissues. I retrieved my plate and table setting from their hiding place, settled back at the table.

She swiped at her face. "What if the chief finds out Daryl wanted to fire Mamie? Somebody will know. Somebody," she said bitterly, "always knows in Adelaide."

That was small-town truth baldly stated. Someone always knew.

"That's news to you. All you can report is what Daryl said, so he must have changed his mind." I was sorry Kathleen had lost her appetite. Stress seemed to increase mine. I enjoyed every mouthful.

Kathleen clasped her hands. "All right. We talked about a present for Mamie. She loves to eat at fancy restaurants. I said I was going up to Oklahoma City next week to shop and I could pick up a gift certificate at Mantel's. She adores Bricktown."

I bustled to the sink with our plates. This time Kathleen didn't even complain about the airborne dishes. "Good. Now"—my crisp tone was a call to order—"it's time to talk turkey."

CHAPTER 10

I f possible, Kathleen looked even more stricken. "You're going to be here for Thanksgiving?"

Clearly I was not affording her comfort during a difficult time. It's lonely work to save someone who views you as just one more problem. I resisted the temptation to share my favorite turkey recipe. Instead I took pity on her obvious despair. "I expect to finish my task before then. That, of course, depends upon you."

"Me? What can I do?" She wadded damp tissues into a ball.

"Provide information no one else possesses." I'd never spoken truer words.

Her look of astonishment was genuine.

"Kathleen." I was patient. "An anonymous caller informed the police that you were at Daryl's cabin Wednesday night and"—here I spaced my words for emphasis—"you were holding . . . a . . . red . . . nightgown."

She waited without a flicker of comprehension.

"What does that tell us?" I remembered my long-ago teaching days and *Moby-Dick* and the student who couldn't see why everybody made such a big fuss about a whale.

Her face crinkled with effort. "Daryl told someone?"

"Very unlikely." I hadn't known Daryl Murdoch, but nothing I'd learned about him suggested a man who would reveal an episode that made him look foolish and, possibly worse, ridiculous.

She nibbled at her lower lip, knowing the answer, reluctant to voice a chilling truth. "Someone saw me open that box." Her eyes rounded in scared realization. "Someone was watching through a window."

"Try to remember everything about the cabin and the woods around it. When you arrived, it was getting dark. Did you see another car?"

"No." She was definite. "There was only one car, Daryl's silver Lincoln. Lights were on in the cabin. I could see inside, so the blinds weren't closed. Anybody could have seen us."

"The cabin is off the road. You didn't see another car. Yet someone watched through a window." I considered why a stealthy approach, which had included hiding either a car or bicycle, might have been made to that cabin. "I think your arrival gave Daryl one more day to live."

"One more day to live?" Her voice was faint.

"A visitor with innocent intent doesn't lurk outside and spy. The murderer stood there, gun in hand. When you opened the gift and quarreled with Daryl, the plan changed. Instead of shooting Daryl there and then, the decision was made to lure him to the rectory. The murderer's plan was for his body to be found on your back porch and your fingerprints in his cabin. Part of the gift box survived the fire until I burned every scrap. You would have been suspect number one."

Kathleen's eyes were huge. "That means the murderer knows me. Bailey Ruth, what am I going to do?"

I wafted up and retrieved the notepad from the top of the china cabinet.

Kathleen was too dazed to object to the airborne notebook and pen.

I sat down opposite her. "You won't be safe—and Father Bill won't be safe—until Chief Cobb solves the crime."

Kathleen frowned. "No one could honestly suspect Bill."

I looked at Kathleen's tear-streaked face. Was she too fragile to take any more shocks? Or could she be tough? "My dear." I spoke gently. "Father Bill may end up as the prime suspect. He and Daryl quarreled Thursday morning. Daryl was shot Thursday afternoon on the back porch of the rectory—"

Kathleen gripped the edge of the table. "No one knows that."

"The murderer does, and Chief Cobb has his suspicions." I described the cat-fur-laden dust balls on Daryl's suit jacket and the chief's plan to get a search warrant. ". . . but I've swept up the porch and gotten rid of the tarp."

Kathleen looked down as Spoofer strolled across the kitchen floor. "That's why the chief looked hard at Spoofer, isn't it?" Abruptly, she sat up straighter in her chair. "I'll tell the police about finding Daryl's body."

"Absolutely not." I was firm. "That would only increase the chief's suspicions of Father Bill."

A flush colored her cheeks. "There has to be something I can do. It's all my fault. If I hadn't gone to Raoul's apartment, Daryl wouldn't have been murdered here."

Kathleen was right, of course. Daryl would have been shot in his cabin as the murderer first intended. Mea culpas didn't matter now.

She looked ready to jump up and rush out, wanting to do battle for her Bill.

"There's a lot you can do."

Her face was eager.

"Daryl's cell phone."

She sagged back in her chair. "I'm pretty sure it's ruined, Bailey Ruth. Besides, I don't see how finding it would help."

"We don't need to find it." I was impatient. "Look at it, Kathleen. Why did he save your picture?"

"To cause me trouble." Her eyes narrowed. "I see. Anybody could look at my picture and say there was a motive for his murder. So maybe the other pictures—"

I patted her hand. "Exactly." I flipped open the notebook. "Let's take the photos in order. Why would Daryl keep a picture of Georgia Hamilton's signature?" I'd scarcely had a glimpse before Kathleen erased it. "Do you have any idea what kind of document it was?"

Kathleen looked thoughtful. "A contract of some kind. The thing that sticks in my mind is that the date wasn't recent and I wondered why he'd have a picture of it now."

A legal document? "Who was her lawyer?"

"Bob Shelton. Shelton, Shelton, and Shelton. He's the middle one. But there can't be anything there. Bob was the best senior warden we ever had, and he's honest to the core."

I wrote down *Bob Shelton*. "If he's an honest man, he'll be glad to help us."

I felt we were making progress. "Who is the blond man?"

"Walter Carey." Kathleen brushed back a tangle of dark hair, her gaze intent. "His wife's in my bridge group. Harriet's a sweetheart. Things have been tough for them lately. She's gone back to work and I know she wanted to be a stay-at-home mom."

I didn't have to tell Kathleen how disturbing that photo had been. If ever a man looked defeated, it was Walter Carey. "We'll hope he turns out to be innocent, for his family's sake, but we have to find out why Daryl took that picture. If you know why, you must tell me."

"Nobody knows exactly what happened, but Walter and Daryl quarreled. No one knows why. Maybe Walter wasn't bringing in enough money. He hasn't looked prosperous for a couple of years, while Daryl's cars got fancier and his clothes more expensive. The partnership broke up a week or so ago. Walter's opened an office in a seedy little strip shopping center on the edge of town." She looked in my direction. "There could be something there, Bailey Ruth. I heard Daryl kept all the clients." She stopped, looked surprised. "Georgia Hamilton was one of Daryl's clients."

And Daryl carried a picture of a contract with her signature in his cell phone.

Kathleen sniffed. "Georgia thought Daryl hung the moon. I guess maybe he was pretty good at what he did." She shrugged. "But Georgia was Daryl's client, not Walter's. I guess that wouldn't have anything to do with Walter. Anyway, about Walter, people have been gossiping—"

In a small town, gossip is the second favorite sport after football.

"—and some of them say there has to be something wrong with Walter and maybe he's been drinking too much. That may be true. He had way too much to drink last week at a party at the country club. Harriet's upset. She said Daryl didn't have to be so insulting."

"Insulting?" There can be bad feelings when a partnership breaks up, but what would be insulting?

Kathleen looked grim. "Daryl had the locks changed at the office. All of them, interior and exterior. They said Daryl had Butler's Locksmiths there the same day Walter moved his things out. And that's . . ."

I wasn't listening. Images popped in my mind: Walter's despair, a locksmith at work, Chief Cobb surveying Daryl's trashed den. I slapped shut the notebook. "Got to go. Hope I'm not too late."

I heard Kathleen's startled cry, was almost away, then whipped back to the table to zoom the notebook and pen to their hiding place. I called down, "Remember, don't change your story. Stay calm. And stay away from the people who were pictured in his phone." It could be dangerous for Kathleen to nose around. "Now I'm off. Back soon."

Daryl Murdoch's secretary replaced the telephone receiver with a bang and swiveled to her machine. Her fingers flew over the keyboard, and words appeared on the screen. She had short, crisp white hair, a long face, lips that pursed as she thought, and a decisive air.

The phone rang. She picked up the receiver with a grim frown. "Murdoch and—Murdoch Investments, Patricia Haskins speaking . . . Oh, thanks, Wanda." Her voice and face softened. "I've already had my coffee break. I'm staying in the office." She listened, then glanced at the clock.

It was ten minutes after two.

"I intend to put in a full day." Her tone was prim. "Mr. Murdoch left quite a bit of work for me to update. I was here at eight o'clock as usual and I'll leave at five. I want everything to be in good order for Mr. Murdoch's clients. I've made progress, but"—and now she sounded huffy—"it would be easier if the phone didn't keep ringing. Oh no, not you, Wanda. I've had a bunch of calls, the press and the police and some people who don't have any manners and think I'll tell them things I don't even know about when it's not my place to talk about Mr. Murdoch. Worst of all, during the lunch hour, there were five calls where someone hung up when I answered. I don't know what the world is coming to. The caller ID said 'Unknown.' Unknown and Unwanted." She sniffed in disgust.

As I wafted through the closed door behind her desk, I made a special note of her name: Patricia Haskins. Hired to do a job, she intended to do it whether anyone knew or not. She could as easily have painted her nails or closed the office early for a long and leisurely lunch.

I suspected that her old-fashioned sense of duty had spared this office a thorough ransacking. Unless I was very much mistaken, the lunch-hour calls had been made to determine whether the office was empty.

I left the secretary at work and sped through a closed door into Daryl's elegant and surprising office. Nothing was out of place. I felt a whoosh of relief. I had arrived before Walter Carey with the keys I suspected that he'd stolen from Daryl's desk this morning. I felt certain Daryl's study must have contained an extra set of keys to the office.

I'd tell Bobby Mac all about Daryl's office, red leather sofas, a rich burgundy desk, each wall a different shade of red, from carmine to rose to crimson to a purplish hue. The ridged and serviceable carpet was brilliant fire-engine red. A blue seascape above the faux fireplace was a striking contrast. The office was different, dramatic, and undoubtedly expensive.

The desktop was clear except for two folders. The in-box held several papers. The out-box was empty. A row of red lacquered wooden filing cabinets sat against an interior wall.

I started with the files, opening the cabinet marked G–I. I flipped past *Grindstaff, Grimsley, Gunderson* . . . I skipped faster. *Hadley, Hall, Hasty* . . . I backed up. Ah, here it was: *Georgia Hamilton.*

I plucked the file from the cabinet, settled into the luxurious comfort of the red leather sofa.

My eyes widened as I read the neat printing on the outside of an envelope appended to some kind of legal document:

*Enclosed within is Walter Carey's admission of guilt
in obtaining Georgia Hamilton's signature to the
sale of mineral rights to the Hamilton ranch with the
intention of skimming a portion of income.*

The simple sentence was followed by a legal description of the property. I opened the envelope, slipped out a piece of white stationery. This, too, was handwritten.

On April 16, 2005, knowing that Daryl Murdoch was out of town, I took a mineral deed to Georgia Hamilton and told her I was there on Daryl's behalf. I told her the mineral deed was an oil-and-gas lease covering the mineral rights to Hamilton ranch for a one-eighth royalty. Actually, it was a deed by which she sold all of the mineral rights to Horizon Development Corporation. I knew she was unable to read the contract because of macular degeneration. As the agent for Horizon Development, I leased the rights to Monarch Drilling for a three-sixteenths royalty. I kept half the bonus money that Monarch paid up front for the lease, and sent half to Mrs. Hamilton. When royalty income came in, I sent her a portion. I created fake royalty reports which I mailed to Mrs. Hamilton in an envelope with the letterhead of Murdoch and Carey.

Walter Carey

A second sheet contained the brusque notation:

All mineral rights held by Horizon Development to the Hamilton Ranch reverted to Georgia Hamilton on October 18, 2007.

Walter Carey
Authorized Agent Horizon Development

My eyebrows rose. Not at the confession. I knew there

had been chicanery and any Oklahoman knows that mineral rights can spell big money if the land overlies an oil-and-gas deposit.

The dates shocked me.

I was on the earth in the twenty-first century, quite a long time after Bobby Mac and I started out on our last big fishing trip. My, how time had flown, but of course there is no time in Heaven. In the everlasting communion of all souls and all saints, I enjoyed the presence of souls from all ages without the limitations of the temporal world. Still, the twenty-first century . . .

No wonder so many inventions were unfamiliar.

I wondered how Daryl had discovered his partner's double-dealing. Perhaps Mrs. Hamilton spoke to him of the oil-and-gas lease she thought she'd signed. Daryl knew he hadn't arranged for either the lease or sale of the mineral rights. It probably didn't take him long to discover the truth about Horizon Development, resulting in a confrontation with Walter and that cell-phone photo of a man in despair.

I returned the confession and the rights reversion to the envelope, but I didn't clip it to the document. I closed the folder, placed it in the G–I drawer. I still held the envelope.

A check of the windows revealed that they were solidly implanted within their frames. I couldn't raise a window, loosen a screen, and tuck the envelope there for later retrieval. The windows, walls, and door afforded no difficulty for my passage, but the envelope simply couldn't—

Patricia's brisk voice caught me by surprise.

I looked toward the door. It was opening. ". . . no one's been here, Chief Cobb, but I'm happy to show you."

The envelope dangled in the air. I dropped to the floor, the envelope darting down. I slid the envelope beneath the edge of an Oriental rug atop the red carpet.

". . . told Mrs. Murdoch I would check the office to make sure everything was all right."

Patricia Haskins drew herself up. "Is there any reason why the office should not be in good order?"

Chief Cobb was quick to reassure her. "Mrs. Murdoch said you would have everything well in hand, but there was an unauthorized entry at the home this morning and I wanted to be certain nothing had been disturbed here." He scanned the office. His face gave no hint of his attitude toward the bordello-red room.

"Oh." The secretary drew in a quick breath. "My goodness, that's shocking. No, everything's as it should be." She looked about the room with pride.

Chief Cobb walked around the desk, looked down at the folders. He gestured toward them. "Is there any particular reason why these two folders are out?"

"He was scheduled to meet with these clients today." She opened the first folder. "Mr. Murdoch had drawn up a list of underperforming stocks with a recommendation to sell in order to offset capital-gains taxes." She flipped open the second. "Mrs. Flint was a new client. Here's the financial plan he'd worked out." She sighed. "I suppose I might as well put them up."

I stared at Chief Cobb's right foot. The tip of his black shoe was perhaps an inch from the edge of the rug.

If I eased out one end of the envelope, then tapped on his shoe, he would look down, see the end of the envelope protruding. The chief would pick it up and Walter Carey would be exposed as a crook.

I touched the fringe on the rug.

". . . any change in his demeanor in recent days, Mrs. Haskins? I know you are very perceptive and possibly you can help us more than anyone else to determine Mr. Murdoch's state of mind." The chief's tone was warm and admiring. Obviously, he wasn't above using flattery to encourage confidences.

Mrs. Haskins preened. "Well, when you put it like that. But"—she looked disappointed—"I'm afraid Mr. Murdoch was just as he always was. In fact, he'd seemed in a very good humor recently."

That didn't raise my general opinion of Daryl, considering his activities.

Mrs. Haskins brightened. "The only thing—"

I scooted my fingers beneath the rug.

"—a little out of the ordinary was last night. Right after work. Oh." She clapped a hand to her lips, but her eyes were excited. "I suppose he died not long after he left here. Do you suppose . . . I hope not . . . but I saw his son." Her lips pursed in disapproval. "Kirby's been a real trial to Mr. Murdoch, taking up with a girl the family didn't care for. I was getting into my car when Kirby drove into the parking lot, his tires screeching. Mr. Murdoch was turning left into the street. That lady policewoman stopped him. Left turns are prohibited there. It's the middle of the block, you see, and they've had so many accidents there."

Chief Cobb looked impatient. "Mr. Murdoch started to turn left?"

"He pulled out and the police car came up behind him. The officer got out and talked to him for a minute, then she went off. I suppose she warned him. Anyway, he turned right. Now that I think of it, his son's car came out and turned right, too." Her eyes were huge. "Do you suppose . . ."

Chief Cobb was bland. "That may turn out to be helpful. Perhaps his son can give us some idea of the direction his father took. Did you know where Mr. Murdoch was going?"

"Why, yes." She was the all-knowing, competent secretary. "He had a meeting set up at St. Mildred's." She frowned. "He was found in the church by the cemetery, wasn't he? I wonder why he went there?"

"We don't know that he did." The chief's tone was judicious.

Clearly, Chief Cobb wanted to know why dust balls with cat fur had been found on Daryl's suit coat. The chief gave the secretary an encouraging look. "It's helpful to know he intended to go to the church. Would anyone else have known?"

Some knowledge flickered in the secretary's eyes, but her face was smooth and bland as she spoke. "I suppose that's possible."

Not only possible, but, I was sure, quite certain. Her indirect answer was truthful as far as it went. I wished I could tug on Chief Cobb's sleeve, remind him that truth isn't always complete, but he was glancing at his watch, moving toward the door.

I slid my hand away from the rug. Walter's confession was safe enough where I'd put it. I have no sympathy for swindlers, but I should afford Walter Carey a chance to explain his actions. If I was not very much mistaken, Walter would slip into this office tonight with his stolen keys.

I intended to be here.

The cuckoo clock warbled two-thirty. I stood in the middle of the rectory kitchen, hands on my hips. I hadn't asked Kathleen to await my return and, to be reasonable, she had no idea how long I would be gone, but I couldn't help feeling thwarted. I felt some urgency in deciding whether the individuals pictured or recorded on Daryl's cell phone should be revealed to Chief Cobb.

I retrieved my notebook and jotted down the information about Walter Carey and the Hamilton ranch mineral rights.

I felt calmer. After all, I now knew everything but the identities of the Altar Guild member who had stolen from the collection plate and the woman who had begged Daryl to call her.

"A church member . . ." I popped to my feet, opened drawers near the telephone, found the church pictorial directory. In a moment I had the Altar Guild member's name: Irene Chatham. Perhaps it was just as well that Kathleen wasn't here. She would have been reluctant to tell me. I added Irene Chatham's name to my list.

I still faced the challenge of identifying the woman with the desperate voice. But just as someone saw Kathleen enter the young professor's apartment and repeated that information, I was confident that the Adelaide gossip mill knew all about Daryl's extramarital adventures. All I had to do was find a source of information.

I pulled my chair nearer the table. I like making lists. It was time—

The back door banged open. Bayroo plunged into the kitchen. "Hi." Her voice was pleased.

I looked up with delight. It was lovely to feel warm and welcome and that's how I felt every time Bayroo looked at me. And saw me.

Her wide grin was as warming as a hug. "I've had the swellest day ever. Is Mom here?" She shrugged out of her backpack, tossed it into a wicker rocking chair, pulled off her pink jacket, and tossed it on a rung of the coat tree. "I can't wait to tell her about our party."

"She's not home—"

Bayroo's eager smile faded.

"—but why don't you tell me?" It is lonely to come home to an empty house.

Her freckled face once again glowed. "Okay. I'm starving. Won't you have a snack with me?"

"I'd love that." I flipped my notebook shut.

She hesitated, then asked quickly, "I don't know what to call you. I know you are my great-grandmother's sister, so should I say great-aunt?"

I laughed. "That sounds like a very distant relative. Why don't you call me Auntie Grand?"

"Auntie Grand." She listened as she spoke, then flashed me a smile. "Yes. You are Auntie Grand."

In a moment we had a feast on the table. Mugs with steaming-hot chocolate and graham crackers topped with melted chocolate and marshmallows.

Bayroo licked away a chocolate mustache. "We had a monster style show and everybody voted. My costume came in third. We had candied apples with black licorice stuck to the sides, dangling like jellyfish tentacles." She grinned and gave a mock shudder. "Mrs. Gordon showed a vampire movie in social studies and told us all about Bram Stoker. It was the most fun day ever. But tomorrow will be even better!" She wiped a smear of marshmallow from her chin. "The Spook Bash is going to be the most exciting party in the history of Adelaide. You remember how I told you last night that we met Travis Calhoun—"

When Bayroo had shared her news last night on the rectory back porch, I'd been much more attuned to the proximity of Lucinda to the exposed tip of Daryl Murdoch's black leather shoe.

"—and he said he would come. Well, his aunt's a teacher and she came by homeroom and told me Travis was really excited to be invited. It's all because I asked him and I was the one who saw him. Lucinda was scared to stay in the preserve. She was a scaredy-cat and went to the other end of the block and watched his aunt's house from Mrs. Berry's yard and I had to come and tell her after I actually talked to him. I did it all by myself and we would never have been able to run into him, you know, like it was a real accident, if I hadn't hidden behind the big cottonwood in the preserve and watched for him." Bayroo's eyes shone. A quick frown tugged at her eyebrows. "You won't tell Mom, will you?"

"Of course not." I munched another bite. "It sounds exciting. Who is Travis Calhoun?"

Her sandy eyebrows shot up. Her eyes widened. Her lips parted. "How could you not . . . Oh, sure. I guess you don't watch a lot of TV or go to the movies where you are. Anyway, he's really famous." She twined a strand of red-gold hair in her fingers. "Travis played Huck Finn on Broadway. He has freckles, too." She gave an impish smile. "Maybe that's why he liked me. He made movies when he was a little kid and now he's fifteen and he's the star of *Show Me the Way* on TV. Oh, you'd love his show. He got killed in a car wreck and now he's an angel and he comes back and he helps kids who are getting in scrapes."

I almost explained that in theological terms, Travis's character was a ghost. Angels are supernatural creatures and messengers of God. But it didn't really matter.

"My dad says he's a ghost, not an angel, and I guess you know that. But it is way cool and when the show starts he wears these big golden wings and I told Dad it's dramatic license." She nodded wisely.

Obviously, I didn't need to worry about Bayroo's religious instruction. Or her perception. "Where does he live?"

"In Hollywood." She breathed the name in awe. "In Beverly Hills. I saw a story about him in *People*. He lives in this big mansion that has a red-tiled roof and gardens and a swimming pool, of course. A chauffeur drives him to the studio in a Bentley." She looked at me. "That's a really fancy car. Wouldn't it be wonderful?"

A mansion in Beverly Hills. "What about his family?"

Some of the sparkle left her eyes. "His mom died when he was little, like maybe four or five. He lives with his dad, who's a big Hollywood director, and his stepmother. She's a movie star. He usually comes here and stays with his aunt on holidays because his dad and stepmom have lots of places to go and things to do. This time he's here for his birthday. I've already talked to the music teacher and she's going to bring the sixth-grade chorus and we're going to sing 'Happy Birthday' to him and I want to give him a special present." Her face fell. "But what could I give somebody like Travis Calhoun?"

I pointed at the oven. "Do you like to cook?"

Bayroo nodded.

"I'll bet no one ever makes him a homemade birthday cake." Fancy cakes are fine, but nothing ever tastes as good as homemade. "Why don't you call his aunt's house and ask him what his favorite cake is?"

She looked dubious. "That's no big deal."

"Try it and see."

Bayroo looked deep into my eyes. I don't know what she saw, perhaps a mother's memory of a child's face at a family birthday table. Each of mine had a favorite cake—lemon for Rob, burnt sugar for Dil.

Bayroo opened the directory, turned the pages until she found a number. She picked up the cordless telephone, shot me an anguished look.

I nodded firmly. "Courage."

She punched numbers. "H'lo." Her voice was high and quivery. "This is Bayroo Abbott. I invited Travis to the Spook Bash and . . . Hello. Hi, Travis." She took a deep breath and the words tumbled out. "I'd like to bake a cake for your birthday and I wondered what your favorite is, you know, the kind of cake you like best, but maybe you've already—white? With chocolate icing. That's my favorite, too. I make it from scratch, the icing, too. I'll bring it to your aunt's house in the morning but I can just leave it on the porch . . . Are you sure? That'd be great!" She hung up and whirled toward me. "He's really excited." Her voice was amazed. "I can take it over and he said maybe I'd come in and we'd have a piece together. Gosh, I'd better get to work. I'll go up and print out my recipe."

Print out a recipe?

Bayroo dashed from the kitchen. I followed as she raced up the stairs.

She darted through the third door on the right. I scarcely had time to appreciate the fresh brightness of Bayroo's room—one wall painted blue with a cresting white wave, bookcases crammed with books and hand-painted buffalo and sports trophies and dolls, and movie posters—when she thumped into a swivel chair and turned on a machine the twin of the one in the chief's office and those at use in the library and in each of the library staff cubicles.

She turned it on and the screen glowed. I looked over her shoulder. "What is it and what does it have to do with a recipe?"

"What is what?" She was clicking and moving the oblong on the pad next to the keyboard.

I reached out and touched the screen. "This! I see them everywhere."

"It's a computer, Auntie Grand."

"Computer." Another new word for me. "How does it work?"

Bayroo found what she sought, clicked again, and paper oozed from the machine on the floor.

By the time we reached the kitchen, Bayroo clutching the recipe and explaining computers, I was overborne with information about word processing (a fancy name for typing), e-mails, programs, printers, passwords, files, and mouses.

At least the next time I visited the chief's office, I wouldn't be so confounded. The next time . . . Should I go there now? But I wasn't ready to impart the information I'd gained from Daryl's cell phone. I had yet to talk to Irene Chatham. I sighed.

". . . I use butter. It makes all the difference—" She broke off. "What's wrong, Auntie Grand?"

I managed a smile. Dear, empathetic Bayroo. I suppose I looked gloomier than the nature-preserve lake on a January day. "I have a problem, sweetie, but there's nothing you can do about it. Go ahead with your baking." I tapped my pen on my notebook. I knew what I had to do, but I didn't see any way to accomplish my task.

"Maybe I can help." She came and stood by me, hands planted on her slender hips. "I know a lot about Adelaide. What do you need to know?"

I had no idea if she was aware of the senior warden's demise. In any event, she was much too young to embroil, even peripherally, in a murder investigation. Certainly I couldn't tell Bayroo why I needed to talk to people. But perhaps if I articulated my difficulty, a solution would occur to me.

I stood and gave her a hug. "You are a help just being my friend. Let's get everything out for your cake and I'll explain."

She pulled up a kitchen chair next to a counter. "You sit here, Auntie Grand. I can do it all by myself. I told Travis I'd make it." She bustled about the kitchen, retrieving a mixing bowl and measuring cups and spoons and cake tins. A moment later, she'd assembled her ingredients. She propped her recipe sheet on a stand.

I remembered my cooking days. I had a Betty Crocker cookbook that was dog-eared and stained. I settled on the chair. "I have some questions I need to ask some people."

She nodded and poured cake flour into the measuring cup.

"But"—I shook my head—"even if I could go and see them, they can't see me. And even if they could"—after all, I could appear if it was essential—"I can't see why they'd talk to me."

Bayroo looked thoughtful. "I can see you."

"I know. Other people can't."

She cut butter into the flour-and-sugar mixture. "Way cool. But I thought you could do something special and actually be here."

"Oh yes, indeed." Much to Wiggins's consternation. "I could be here if this were a big city. But in Adelaide, everyone would want to know about that redheaded stranger. You know how small towns are. If someone from the church saw me, they might walk down the corridor outside the parish hall and look at the paintings of the former directresses of the Altar Guild. That would never do."

"Oh." She was thoughtful. "I don't think they'd recognize you. You're a lot younger now." She said it easily, as if it made all the sense in the world. She shook her head, looked solemn. "But if anybody did recognize you, I guess, like Mom always says, the fat would be in the fire."

Kathleen had learned that old saying from her grandmother, my sister, Kitty.

Bayroo waggled the mixing spoon at me. "I know what to do. You can't be here as yourself, but you can be here as somebody else. You know, a disguise."

"A disguise?" I pictured a trilby hat and oversize spectacles.

"Sure." She stirred. "Like a nurse or secretary or census taker or social worker."

It was an interesting suggestion, but Walter Carey, Irene Chatham, Isaac Franklin, Kirby Murdoch, Kirby's girlfriend Lily, and the unknown woman wouldn't be likely to answer questions from a stranger unless they thought I had official status.

Official status . . .

"Bayroo." I sang her name. "You are brilliant. A disguise!" It was as if a door had opened. "Have fun with your cake. I'll see you later."

CHAPTER 11

Partitions separated six cubicles. Each held a computer. Voices rose and fell around us. Brisk footsteps and ringing telephones contributed to an atmosphere of intense activity.

Patrol Officer A. Leland's desk took up half the space in her cubicle. She hunched in her chair, apparently oblivious to her surroundings, and stared at an open notebook, her expression empty.

I doubted her eyes saw the writing.

Today her honey-colored hair was drawn back in a bun. A few curls escaped to soften the severity of the style. If she loosened her hair, let it frame her narrow face, and added a bit more makeup, she would be pretty. Her eyes were deep blue, her features fine—wide-spaced eyes, straight nose, gently rounded chin.

The police uniform was flattering to her fair skin, the long-sleeved shirt French blue, the trousers French blue with a navy stripe down each leg. The shirt bore an Adelaide police patch on each shoulder and a metal name tag—A. LELAND—and badge over the left breast pocket. The leather shoes were black, as were the socks.

It had been a sacrifice to shed my elegant pantsuit, but I

knew it was necessary. I envisioned my new outfit, found the shirt a bit scratchy. I needed a name for my tag. I couldn't appear as Officer B. R. Raeburn. Perhaps A. Great for Alexandra the Great? J. Arc for . . . No. That was not a happy ending and too presumptuous. N. Bly for Nellie Bly? If Wiggins had seen fit to send me to France, that might have been an option. There had to be the perfect name, a woman I'd admired . . .

I smiled. I would be M. Loy. I'd always tuned in for her Nick and Nora Charles movies on TV, although it seemed to me that she spent most of her time holding Asta the terrier on her lap and watching as William Powell detected. But Myrna Loy had style and that was enough for me.

Patrol Officer M. Loy was now ready to embark on her investigation. I debated adding a holster for a gun, decided that wasn't necessary. After all, I wouldn't be passing in review to make sure I met department regulations. I simply needed to appear official to those whom I wished to question.

The phone on Officer Leland's desk rang.

She picked up the receiver. "Officer Leland." She listened, her shoulders tightening. "Yes, Chief." A quick breath. "I stopped Mr. Murdoch at shortly after five P.M. yesterday. He was making an illegal left turn onto Main Street. Since you'd spoken to me"—she cleared her throat—"I didn't give him a ticket, just a warning." She picked up a pencil, rolled it around and around in her fingers. "No, I didn't follow him. He drove off, heading east. That's all I know. Yes, sir." She put down the receiver, looking drained.

She reached out to pick up a silver picture frame. She placed it on the edge of her desk, stared at the photograph of a young woman with soft brown hair, bright blue eyes, a devil-may-care smile, and a defiant tilt to her head. I saw a resemblance to Officer Leland, but she was a pallid version of the vibrant creature in the photograph.

Officer Leland's face crumpled for an instant, her hands gripping the sides of the silver frame. Slowly her face changed, from grief to stern resolve. She grabbed up the receiver, held it for a long moment until a buzz sounded. She replaced the receiver, her hand resting on it, then, with a deep breath, yanked it up, dialed.

"Chief, may I see you for a moment? There's something I have to tell you . . . Thank you." When she pushed up from her chair, it seemed to take a great effort, slightly built as she was. She walked down the narrow corridor between the partition-separated cubicles. Each foot might have been weighted with chains.

Whatever difficulty she faced, her problems were far afield from my tasks. I steeled myself against the sense that here, too, was someone in deep trouble. I couldn't take on everyone's problems. I was charged with aiding Kathleen and already I'd widened my concern to include Father Bill. I couldn't add Officer Leland to my list.

She paused at the doorway, gripped the knob, and opened the door. She squared her shoulders and stepped into the hall as if marching to her doom.

It was time for me to depart. I was now equipped to find out whether I needed to bring to Chief Cobb's attention any of those pictured or recorded on the dead man's cell phone. That was my clear-cut objective. But that burdened young woman . . . All right. I'd find out why she was upset, but I wouldn't tarry long. I wafted to the chief's office.

Chief Cobb was standing by a long rectangular table. File folders were ranged around the perimeter. Each bore a large square white label. All pertained to the Murdoch investigation. Chief Cobb's thick iron-gray brows knotted in a frown. Lines of fatigue creased his square face. He picked up a report.

I looked over his shoulder.

Persons of Interest:

Kirby Murdoch, son of victim—Estrangement over girlfriend. Target practice on the river bottom Thursday afternoon. Cannot produce gun. Claims it was stolen from his car.

The Rev. Wm. Abbott—Quarreled with victim Thursday morning, refuses to reveal cause. Was his wife involved with Murdoch? Story of her visit to Murdoch's cabin not credible.

Kathleen Abbott—A vestry member is worried that Mrs. Abbott is

A brisk knock sounded.

He replaced the report on the table, turned.

Officer Leland stepped inside, closing the door behind her. She was pale, but composed.

"What can I do for you, Anita?" His voice was formal, but the look in his eyes startled me, a mixture of gravity and longing.

Anita stood stiff and still. She looked young and vulnerable. She didn't meet his gaze.

Yet each was intensely aware of the other even though both were making every effort to pretend it wasn't so. They were linked by that magic sensitivity that spells desire and uncertainty and hope.

She moved to the end of the table, stood with her hands in tight fists. "I may have information that could be important in the Murdoch case."

He frowned. "You followed him yesterday?"

"Oh no." The denial was swift. "It isn't that. It's . . . I have to go back a long way to explain. You remember two years ago when you came out to my brother-in-law's farm, the night he shot himself."

"I remember." His steady gaze was filled with pity.

"You were kind." Her eyes mourned. "You tried to help us. Then, when Vee ran away, you did your best to find her."

His jaw tightened. "She shouldn't have left you to deal with it."

Anita's shoulders sagged. "She never could face up to things. Never. I don't think she's still alive, you know. I keep thinking someday word will come, but every time it's like this last trip. The description matches—young woman, un-identified, found dead. But it isn't Vee. Anyway"—she made a sudden impatient gesture—"I don't know if you ever knew the man Vee was involved with."

He rubbed one cheek. "It didn't need to be part of the record. When a man shoots himself, leaves a note, that's all an investigation needs."

"I know. But now I have to tell you." She flexed her fingers, shook them. "She was having an affair with Daryl Murdoch."

Chief Cobb looked startled. "Murdoch?"

"Vee should have known better." Anita spoke in a mono-tone. "She was always wild, even when she was a kid, taking chances, thinking she was special, and when somebody like him went after her, I guess she thought she'd have a chance to marry a rich man and she told Carl she was leaving him. When he shot himself, she called Murdoch and he hung up on her. Like everything else in her life, when things got rough, she quit. She took all the money in the house and left town."

"Is that why you followed him around?" His voice was sharp.

Anita stared down at the tips of her shoes, her face working. "The first time I stopped him, I didn't know who it was. He couldn't believe I was actually going to give him a ticket. The second time I knew his car. I guess I liked stopping him. He didn't know I was Vee's sister. No reason why he should have. After that, I kept an eye out for him." She lifted her face. "I know I shouldn't have, but I didn't see why he shouldn't have to follow the rules. So"— her gaze was defiant—"I followed him around and that's what I have to tell you about. It might be important. He always has a girlfriend. He's been seeing a woman who lives on Olive Street for about a year now. Cynthia Brown, 623 Olive. But he hadn't gone there for about a week." She reached up, touched her name badge. "If you want to fire me, I'll understand." Tears filmed her eyes. "I hate to disappoint you, Chief. I tried hard to be a good officer. You're the reason why I changed my major to criminal justice. I've never forgotten the night Carl died . . . I wanted to be able to help people the way you helped me."

"Speed laws are supposed to be enforced." His voice was gentle. "Your surveillance of Murdoch may turn out to be key to solving the case."

She reached up, wiped her eyes with the back of a hand. "I had to tell you even if it meant my job."

"Your job's okay." His tone was abstracted. He turned away, paced along the table. "I've been meaning to tell you. There's an opening in the security office at the college."

Anita watched him with a stricken look. "I see."

He stood, staring down at the folders. "If you're interested, I'll give you a top recommendation. Then, if that works out, maybe some Saturday . . ." He swung to face her. "Maybe we could go up to Oklahoma City, have lunch at Bricktown, take a ride on the canal, maybe drop by Bass Pro." His gaze was hopeful.

Her eyes lighted. "That sounds wonderful." The words came on a ragged breath. "I'll apply Monday."

I smiled. My presence hadn't been necessary. Everything looked positive for the widowed chief and the young woman he had inspired. I was glad to see the beginnings of happiness. Moreover, I now had the last piece of information I needed. Unless I was very much mistaken, the woman who had desperately wanted Daryl Murdoch to call her lived at 623 Olive Street.

It was time for Officer M. Loy to begin her investigation.

Olive Street was four blocks north of Main. Most of the small frame houses were in various stages of disrepair, window screens missing, front porches sagging, paint peeling. Weeds choked the abandoned train tracks that intersected Olive near number 623.

The middle front step to 623 had buckled in the center. The window shades were down. No light glimmered in front. I circled the house. Light shone from a high kitchen window. I looked inside, drew my breath in sharply.

A young woman with a mass of dark curls and a round face sat at a battered kitchen table. Slowly she raised a gun to her temple. Tears streamed down a face blotched from crying. She gulped and sniffed, her eyes dull with misery.

There was no time to knock, no time to arrive in customary fashion. I was at her side at once. Reaching out, I gripped her arm, forced the gun to one side. I willed myself present, saw my image, unfamiliar in the blue uniform, in a cracked mirror over the sink.

"No." I spoke sternly.

Her hand sagged. The gun clattered to the floor.

Now I knew that my detour through Chief Cobb's office had not been on behalf of Anita Leland. I relinquished my grip, reached down to pick up the gun. I broke it open, spilled out the shells in my hand. Bobby Mac taught me how to handle a gun a long time ago.

She stared at me. "How did you get in?" She brushed back dark curls. "You're the police?"

I pulled out a chair, sat opposite her. "That doesn't matter. I'm here to help you." I smiled. "Tell me, Cynthia."

"No one can help me."

"God will help."

She stared at me uncertainly. "You sound as if you know." She shook her head almost angrily. "What can you know? You aren't any older than I am."

I wished suddenly I could shout it aloud: *Don't judge anyone by age, not the young and not the old. It's who they are and what they've done and what they know in their hearts that matters, always and forever.* No one would listen. The world would go on its merry way, adoring youth for the wrong reason, ignoring those in the winter season.

Instead, I looked deep into her eyes.

She looked into mine.

Slowly her face changed.

I've known sorrow and fear, loss and trouble, sat at the bedside of the dying, tried to help the lost, struggled to find my own way. Bobby Mac and I were happy, but no life is untouched by heartbreak and pain. That was part of me and that was what I offered to Cynthia.

"Your eyes . . . They're like my mother's eyes. Oh, if only she hadn't died. She would have kept him from hurting me. He'll hurt me so bad I'd wish I was dead, so I might as well do it myself."

I took her hand, felt its clammy coldness. "Who will hurt you?"

"My dad. He's hurt me a lot and if he finds out I'm pregnant—" She clapped her hand to her mouth.

"Daryl Murdoch?"

The emptiness of her face told its own story. "I told him about the baby and he didn't care. He said I should have been more careful."

"When did you tell him?"

She massaged her head as if it hurt. "I called him and he didn't call back. I went to his office yesterday. I told him when he came out to his car. He pushed me away and left. Now he's dead. I saw it on the morning news. He's dead and there's no one to help me, no one at all."

"Yes, there will be help. Go to Father Bill at St. Mildred's Church. Do you know where that is?"

She nodded, her hand clinging to mine.

"Tell him you need help to go away to a safe place to have your baby. You can go and stay. They'll help you find a job, and when the baby comes, they'll find a home. Will you do that?"

"Yes." The word was a sigh.

But I had to ask. "Did you follow Daryl when he left his office last night?"

"No." Her eyes flared in alarm. "I didn't shoot him."

I felt cold. "How did you know he was shot?"

"It was on TV this morning. I didn't do it. I swear."

I picked up the gun. "Where did you get this?" It was a .22 pistol.

"I stole it from my dad's house. He has lots of guns."

"I'll take it with me." I kept the shells in my hand, tucked the gun in my waistband.

She shivered. "I don't want it." Her look was young and earnest. "I won't do that again. I'll go to the church in the morning."

I looked around the cold kitchen, spotted a gas stove, found matches, lit the flame. "When did you last eat?" I moved to the refrigerator.

"I don't know." Her voice was dull.

I fried bacon and scrambled eggs with milk, seasoning salt, a half teaspoon of Worcestershire sauce, and a dash of brown sugar. I fixed toast and poured a glass of milk.

I placed the plate in front of her. She pushed the eggs with her fork, finally took a bite, then with a look of surprise and gratitude eagerly ate. "These eggs are good. I didn't know I was so hungry."

I debated what to do, then made up my mind. "This won't be the only visit you'll have from the police." Chief Cobb would be sure to explore what he'd learned from Anita.

Cynthia put down her fork, her young face once again frightened and vulnerable.

I chose my words carefully. "Don't mention my visit here. We'll pretend it didn't happen. Tell them you wanted to see Daryl, so you went to his office last night, but he'd already left. Don't say anything about the baby."

Her eyes crinkled in puzzlement. "Why are you helping me?"

Honest truth is sometimes best. "Because you are alone." And lost. And frightened.

"All right." Her eyes were luminous. "Thank you. I hope"—she looked anxious—"you don't get in trouble."

I was already in trouble. Wiggins was likely despairing of me at this very moment. "Everything will work out." That was surely the most positive of thinking. I had no reason to think anything would work out and I seemed to go from bad to worse when it came to meddling with Chief Cobb's investigation. "There's nothing you can do to help the police." Officer Leland had stopped Daryl as he turned out of the lot, leaving Cynthia behind. Certainly he was alive and well then. "So it's better not to say anything more than you have to."

She drank a gulp of milk. "All right."

I left her finishing her light supper, looking worn but at peace. I hoped I'd done the right thing to encourage her to refrain from telling the chief that she'd seen Daryl Thursday evening, but I couldn't help wondering. She'd said her father's house had many guns. Had I carried one of those guns to the Pritchard mausoleum for the police to find?

Once outside, I took my latest acquisition out of my pocket, disappeared, and wafted to the top of an old oak. I tucked the gun in the crook between a branch and the trunk, too far above ground to be noticeable. Then I zoomed down to the street, found a manhole cover, and dropped the shells inside.

Daylight was fading fast, the shadows deep and dark on Olive Street. I didn't expect Walter Carey to slip into his former partner's office until darkness fell, so I didn't feel rushed. Instead of going directly to Murdoch Investments, I strolled toward Main.

I wasn't surprised when I heard that rumble nearby. "Although becoming visible is never desirable, in some instances it is acceptable." We moved along in silence, then a soft harrumph. "That dear girl. Good work, Bailey Ruth."

Wiggins left as quickly as he'd arrived.

I was smiling when I reached Main Street. I took a moment to look up and down. The Bijou marquee was dark and the front looked boarded over. The corner where our drugstore sat now advertised CORNUCOPIA TEA SHOP, NATURAL FOODS. What other kinds were there?

Then I saw the red neon of Lulu's. In a flash, I arrived in the narrow entrance to the café. I suppose it was impulsive of me, but I hadn't had a Lulu hamburger and fries in, well, it was a lifetime ago. I was greeted by a delectable scent of hot grease.

Every stool at the counter was occupied as well as the four booths. Lulu's hadn't changed a whit in all these years and it was packing in the customers as offices and stores closed. A tall blond waitress and a lanky teenage boy served the counter and the booths. She was quick and efficient. He was more lackadaisical.

It took me only a moment to figure out the system. To-go orders in sacks were placed on a tray near the cash register to await pickup. When the boy put down his order pad to fix a chocolate soda at the fountain, I tipped over a menu to cover the pad and quickly scribbled a to-go order for Myrna: cheeseburger with onions, mustard, and pickles, and fries. When everyone seemed occupied, I pinned the order up for the cook.

I wafted through a door marked EMPLOYEES, found the fuse box. When my sack was ready, I peered closely at the menu, and almost let out a yelp when I saw the prices. How could a hamburger and fries cost four dollars and fifty cents! However . . . I imagined a five-dollar bill, a shocking sum, and hovered over the tray with the to-go orders.

When no one was near the cash register and everyone behind the counter was fully occupied, I took the check from the sack, slid it and the five-dollar bill slowly toward the cash register, then wafted to the fuse box and flipped a series of switches. The power went off. The café went dark and voices called out.

I felt my way out into the dining area. There was enough light coming through the plateglass window from street-lamps to make it easy to reach the front counter. I grabbed my sack and hurried to the front door. Unfortunately, since I'd had no need to open the door upon my arrival, I hadn't realized a bell sounded.

The bell tinkled. A flashlight beam swept toward the front, spotlighting my white sack as it moved briskly through the air.

"Wait a minute." The waitress's shout was angry and determined. "Hey you, stop." As the lights came back on, the waitress plunged out onto the sidewalk, heavy flashlight in hand. She started to yell, then froze as the sack, dangling from my unseen hand, sped up the sidewalk.

I looked back.

She backed toward the door to Lulu's, her face slack with disbelief.

I reached the corner, swerved out of her sight. I was terribly aware that I had violated Precepts One and Six, but certainly it was inadvertent. I clutched my sack tighter, felt warmth through the paper, and darted from shadow to shadow, not wishing to cause any further distress.

"Bailey Ruth." Wiggins's voice was as emphatic as the stamp of a jackboot.

I wobbled on the top step of Murdoch Investments. "Did you serve in the military, Wiggins?"

"The Rough Riders, San Juan Hill, July first, 1898." His pride was evident.

"Wiggins, that's wonderful. I can't wait to hear—"

"Bailey Ruth." Exasperation warred with an evident delight in recalling his days with Teddy. "This is not the moment."

I sensed movement and curled my arm around that Heavenly scented sack. I had no intention of yielding my hamburger to Wiggins. "I need sustenance, Wiggins. I have a big evening facing me." I determinedly kept my tone light. I wouldn't be guilty of whining. Nonetheless, facts are facts. "And there's no getting around the fact that when I carry an actual physical object, I can't pop from here to there in an unobtrusive fashion."

"There is food at the rectory." The reproof was clear.

"Wiggins, that was my first thought." How many fibs was I piling up on my record? Would they even let me back in Heaven without a stint in Purgatory? "But even if I popped there and back again, there wasn't enough time. I must take up my post inside"—I bent my head toward the building—"before darkness falls." Twilight was settling around us.

"I see." A pause. "Bailey Ruth, you always seem to have an answer. It's quite confounding. And I do have other emissaries to oversee. Very well, carry on."

Thus justified, my fingers tight on my sack, I oozed to the rear of the office building. I placed the sack on the top step and wafted inside. In only a moment I had opened the back door, retrieved my supper, and locked the door. A moment later I was inside Daryl Murdoch's office. I drew the drapes, then turned on a lamp near one end of the red leather sofa.

In a small refrigerator behind a curving bar, I found a Dr Pepper. That thrill could only have been topped by discovering a Grapette. Not, of course, that I was particular.

I spread out my feast on a tiled table in one corner and offered a very thankful grace. I enjoyed every mouthful. The onions were sautéed in a tasty brown tangle and the fries fresh, crisp, and salty. The taste of Dr Pepper brought memories of lazy summer picnics and fishing trips with Bobby Mac. However, I didn't linger and cleaned up quickly, depositing the sack in the kitchenette wastebasket.

I turned off the lamp and opened the drapes. The glow from a streetlamp seeped inside, providing some light. I stretched out on Daryl's exceedingly comfortable and luxurious leather couch and promptly began to worry about the notations in the chief's notebook concerning Father Bill and Kathleen. I wished I'd had a chance to read the rest of his comments before Anita arrived in his office. Perhaps I—

The door to Daryl's office swung slowly in.

Even though I was expecting a visitor, my throat felt tight. I swung upright, pushed to my feet, willed myself present.

A dark form slipped across the room. The drapes were drawn. A click and light spilled over the end of the room from the lamp. Walter Carey never glanced toward me.

He went straight to the filing cabinets, pulled out the G–I drawer.

"Are you looking for your confession?" My voice sounded overly loud in the stillness of the night-shrouded office.

He froze, one hand gripping the steel side of the drawer. Slowly, still holding to the drawer as if for support, he turned and stared at me. His lips parted. His haggard face was pasty white.

"It isn't in there." I looked into eyes glazed with shock. "It's in a safe place."

He took a step toward me. "How did you know?"

"When Daryl's study was the only room searched this morning and I was told that he changed the locks after you moved out of the offices, the answer seemed obvious. The intruder—you—wanted his keys. And here you are. There's one thing that puzzles me."

He stood with his chin sunk on his chest, shoulders slumped, hands thrust deep into his pockets.

"What happened to the money you stole from Georgia Hamilton? I understand you and your wife are having financial problems, have had for some time. She's gone back to work."

He lifted his head. "I wasn't really stealing. I borrowed the money. Just for a while."

" 'Borrowed.' " My tone was judicious.

He flushed. "I was paying everything back. I swear to God. Pretty soon I was going to make up a contract with Mrs. Hamilton buying back the mineral rights and then she would receive the royalty reports directly from Monarch. I was within twenty thousand of making up what I'd borrowed." His voice shook with intensity. "I told Daryl. He didn't care. Damn him to hell."

"All right. Let's not call it stealing. Certainly it was fraud. Why?"

He stared down at the tips of his shoes, his face weary. "The stock market went to hell—" "The Beer Barrel Polka" interrupted. He yanked a cell phone from his pocket, frowned. His glance at me was apologetic. "It's my wife. She'll worry if I don't answer."

"Answer by all means." I glanced down at the rug. He stood within a foot of where the confession was hidden.

"Yeah? . . . Catching up on some work . . . Father Bill's wife?" He sounded puzzled.

I was suddenly attentive.

"No, she's mistaken. I wasn't near the church last night. It must have been somebody else's car . . ."

Oh dear. Kathleen had ignored my warning and set out to investigate on her own. I was delighted at her initiative and concerned for her safety. If I had any idea where she was or what she was likely to do next, I'd go there. But for now, I must discover what I could from Walter.

". . . I doubt it means anything. She's probably just curious. Like everybody else in Adelaide." His tone was bitter. "Don't worry, honey. No. I can't come home yet." His look at me was pensive. "I'll call if . . ." A deep breath. "If anything delays me. Yeah. Love you." He clicked off the phone, slid it in his pocket.

"The stock market," I prompted. I understood stock-market drops. Apparently the twenty-first century was no different from the twentieth. What goes up must come down, which many investors learn to their sorrow. He assumed I was aware of some recent financial debacle.

"I'd put the money into too many tech stocks." He didn't explain, apparently assuming I would understand. "I fudged things, made them look better. I guess I didn't want to admit I'd made some big mistakes. But I made good on everything. I was paying Mrs. Hamilton back and I'd even added money for interest."

"So you stole for pride, not gain." Men won't ask for directions and they never want to admit to mistakes. "How did Daryl find out?"

He almost managed a sardonic smile. "Mrs. Hamilton may be in her nineties, but she's a sharp old dame. A couple of weeks ago, Daryl dropped by to see her and she told him how pleased she was about the oil development on the ranch and how smart he'd been to set it up and how much she'd enjoyed having a chat with me when I brought her the papers to sign. He didn't ante to her, but he knew damn well he hadn't handled any leases. He found the recorded deed to Horizon Development at the courthouse and figured out what had happened. That's when he kicked me out of the office, all high-and-mighty even though I know he's cut corners. He was holier than a prayer book when he called me into his office, but not too holy to stop from blackmailing me."

"Blackmail?"

"He had me over a barrel. He kept my share of the partnership. As long as he had that confession, I had to agree to anything he wanted." He shoved the file drawer shut, faced me. There was no fight in him. His shoulders slumped, his hands hung loosely at his side.

"You had to make sure he didn't turn you in." The confession resting beneath the Oriental rug was surely reason enough for murder. "How did you lure him—" I broke off. I'd almost said *to the rectory*.

Walter's head jerked up. "Wait a minute. I didn't take him to the cemetery. You think I shot him? That's crazy. I hated him, that's for sure, but I knew he wouldn't use the confession. He wouldn't want Georgia Hamilton to know she'd been cheated."

I folded my arms, looked at him skeptically. "If you knew

he wouldn't use it, why did you let him have money that belonged to you?"

"I couldn't take the chance." He looked at me earnestly. "But I swear I didn't shoot him. You've got to believe me."

I didn't have to believe him. But I did. I saw a man who had gambled and lost, but there wasn't an iota of threat in him. And he'd said "take him to the *cemetery*." Or was that simply a clever murderer taking advantage of the mysterious transfer of Daryl's body?

How could I know? But whatever the truth in regard to Daryl's murder, surely I wasn't going to gloss over Walter's chicanery. The thought didn't catch up with my swift impulse to reassure him. "If you didn't shoot him, there's no reason for the financial problems to be aired."

His stare was incredulous. "You mean nobody will ever know?"

"If you didn't shoot him," I spoke firmly, "the matter is closed. When Chief Cobb contacts you, say that you and Daryl disagreed over the future of the business. As for what you've lost, you might consider it a penalty for dishonesty."

"What about the confession? As long as it exists, I can never feel safe." He still looked hopeless.

"I'll take care of that." One way or another.

"Who are you? Why are you doing this?" He was suddenly suspicious.

I was about to ignore another Precept, but circumstances alter cases. "You might consider me your conscience."

I disappeared.

Walter's face went slack. His head swiveled slowly around the room. He breathed in short, tight gasps.

I had his attention. I made my voice crisp. "Swear you will never again mishandle any financial matter."

Once again, he looked around the room, seeking the source of the voice. But there was no place where a slender red-haired policewoman could be hidden. He stared at the closed door.

He knew the door hadn't opened. He knew there was no other exit.

Slowly, he lifted a shaking hand. "I swear."

CHAPTER 12

I popped to the rectory. A lamp shone in the kitchen and another in the front hall, but no one was home. Where was Kathleen? Why couldn't she follow instructions? Perhaps I now had some inkling of Wiggins's distress when I improvised. How could I blame Kathleen? She was trying to save the man she loved, but I wished I were at her side.

I popped back to the parking lot outside Daryl's office. The starry night was crisp and cold. I looked Heavenward. If there were a cosmic scoreboard, it might read HOME TEAM 14, VISITORS 0. So far I'd yielded all the points to Daryl's mistress and his ex-partner. I'd set out to discover whether Cynthia Brown or Walter Carey had motives for murder. The obvious answer was yes.

My original plan had been to provide Chief Cobb with any information he might find relevant. I didn't doubt the chief would find Walter and Cynthia legitimate suspects—if he knew.

Whether he ever knew was up to me.

Had I been too impulsive? Was Wiggins even now scratching through my name as a future emissary from the Department of Good Intentions? I welcomed the cool fresh breeze and waited. Wiggins didn't come. Perhaps once again he was willing to accept a good result or, at the least, wait and see the outcome. Perhaps another emissary, hopefully one far distant, was embroiled in difficulties.

Impulsive or not, I needed to keep going, as fast as I could. The night was young. There were others to seek out. I'd never wallowed in introspection when I was of the earth. This was no time to start.

I stood in the parking lot outside Daryl's office. I found a stall with his name painted in red: RESERVED FOR DARYL MURDOCH. He'd brushed aside a desperate girl, driven to the exit onto Main Street, and been stopped in an illegal turn by Officer Leland. About this time his son arrived.

I remembered the high young voice, cracking in anger, that had been recorded on Daryl's cell phone: *I can't believe what you did . . . I just found out from Lily . . . You'll pay for this. I swear you will.*

What had Daryl done?

The small sign in the front yard was tasteful: THE GREEN DOOR. I recognized the old Victorian house. In my day, it had belonged to Ed and Corrine Baldwin. Now it housed a dinner restaurant. I stood on the porch and looked through sparkling glass panes. Old-fashioned teardrop crystal bulbs in a chandelier shed a soft light over a half-dozen circular tables with damask cloths and rose china. Small tap-dancing skeletons flanked centerpieces of orange mums.

A slender young woman was serving orange sorbet in tall crystal glasses at a near table. A scarecrow hung in the doorway to the entry hall.

It might be awkward for Lily Mendoza if a police officer arrived demanding to see her. I didn't want to jeopardize her job. I thought for a moment, nodded. I glanced around the floor of the living room, noted styles of purses. When I wished myself present, I held a small blue leather bag.

I opened the front door and stepped into the nineteenth century. Panels of gleaming mahogany covered the lower walls. Heavily patterned wallpaper in a rich shade of burgundy rose above the wainscoting. Geometric tiles glimmered in the pale light from hanging stained-glass lanterns. Ferns trailed from a huge wicker basket. A gimlet-eyed parrot peered from a brass birdcage. As I entered, it gave a piercing squawk and spoke in a rough throaty voice, "Ahoy, matey. Avast. Begone."

A waitress, who looked trim and athletic despite being dressed in a hoop dress with a daisy pattern, pushed through a door at the end of the hallway, carrying a tray with two entrées. She paused when she reached me, glanced at my uniform, but asked politely, "Do you have a reservation?"

I shook my head, held up the purse. "I'm here with a lost purse. May I speak to Lily Mendoza?"

"Lily doesn't work here anymore. Mrs. Talley"—a pause—"let her go."

Let her go? Why? "When?"

The girl's gamin face squeezed into a frown. "Yesterday. Anyway, if you want to take the purse to her, she has an apartment in the old Blue Sky motel near the railroad tracks." She moved toward the living room.

I kept pace. "Where's Mrs. Talley?"

The girl gestured down the hallway. "In her office." She moved swiftly into the dining room.

I walked past a whatnot with a bust of Homer and a collection of Dresden shepherdesses. I gave a quick knock on the door, stepped inside a library that now served as an office, though the mahogany bookcases still held leather-bound volumes. Austen, Trollope, and Thackeray, no doubt. To my left was a blue Chinese vase as tall as I was. The red-and-blue Oriental rug was worn and frayed.

An angular woman with frizzy gray hair piled atop her

head sat behind a massive walnut desk, staring at a glowing screen. The computer looked out of place in the carefully done Victorian room. She heard my step, turned to see. Prominent collarbones detracted from her décolleté blue silk gown with puffy sleeves. She frowned, making her porcelain-white face querulous. "Yes?"

"Good evening, Mrs. Talley. I'm here about Lily Mendoza and Daryl Murdoch." I closed the door behind me.

She drew in a sharp breath, stood. "You don't think Lily had anything to do with what happened to him?" She lifted a hand, clutched at the thick rope of amber beads.

"We have to check it out." I looked stern.

She held tight to the necklace. "She was upset, but she wouldn't do anything like that. She's a sweet, sweet girl."

I frowned at her. "What did she say?"

Mrs. Talley stared at the hollow bust of Homer. "I hated doing it. But I didn't have any choice. Daryl held the mortgage on the house and he'd given me a break on payments while I'm getting the Green Door up and running." She swung toward me, her face haggard. "We're doing real well. I can make a go of it. I have to since Johnny died and there isn't any money and I have to be home during the day with my mom—oh, you don't care about all that. But you see my position. Daryl insisted I fire her, said he'd call all the payments due immediately if I didn't." She looked at me with shamed, sad eyes. "I told her I had to cut back on staff, but she knew that wasn't it. She'd seen Daryl leave my office and I guess she figured it out. She said, 'Mr. Murdoch made you, didn't he?'" Mrs. Talley's eyes glistened with tears. "She came up and hugged me and told me it was all right, I mustn't worry. Don't you see? She's a good girl."

Blue Sky Apartments was a fancy name for a seedy former motel. Units ran lengthwise behind the office with two shorter sections on either side. I found Lily's apartment, number seventeen, by walking from door to door, checking the nameplates. An old Dodge with one flat tire listed in the drive on one side of the building. Through thin walls, a television blared. On the other side, a rocking horse and playpen sat next to two motorcycles. A baby's cry rose. Lily's front curtain was drawn, but light seeped around the edges.

I knocked.

Through the thin door, I heard running steps. The door was flung open. For an instant her heart-shaped face was open and eager, dark eyes luminous. "Kir—"

I understood why Kirby Murdoch cared. She was lovely, dark-haired, slim, vibrant, but more than that, she had an aura of kindness as warming as a blazing fire on a snowy night.

"Miss Mendoza, I need to speak with you about the murder"—I let the word hang in the cold night air—"of Mr. Daryl Murdoch."

Her face was abruptly still and shuttered. "I don't know anything about it."

I forced myself to be brusque. "May I come in? Or would you rather go down to the station?"

She backed away, held the door for me.

The room had been provided with a small kitchenette. There was a small camp bed, a sofa with a red-and-black-checked throw, two chairs that had seen better days. A gooseneck lamp stood by a card table with a small computer. Textbooks were stacked on the floor.

She gestured toward the sofa, took one of the chairs, sat stiff and straight with her hands folded in her lap. She looked small in an oversize maroon sweatshirt with the emblem of Goddard College.

I looked at the books. "Are you in school?"

"I go part-time."

"Are you putting yourself through school?"

"Yes."

There was an admirable story here, a student without a family to help, making her own way, trying hard to build a better life. If Daryl Murdoch had been here, I would have told him he was a fool. I liked this girl, admired her, hoped she and Kirby would have the happiness they both deserved. But . . .

"You told Kirby his father got you fired. Kirby was furious. He called his father, threatened him, said he would pay for what he'd done."

She didn't say a word, stared at me with dread.

"He threatened his father, went to his office."

Lily jumped up. "Kirby didn't talk to him. He was too late. His father had left."

"Kirby's car was seen turning after his father's."

"Kirby didn't follow him. I called Kirby, got him on his cell, told him to come here. He did. We were here. I promise."

Were they together at her apartment before—or after—Daryl Murdoch was shot?

Chief Cobb's information indicated Kirby's gun hadn't been found. "Where did Kirby keep his gun?"

She hesitated, reluctantly said, "In the trunk of his car."

"Did you know it's missing?" I watched her closely.

She lifted a hand to her throat. "It can't be. Kirby went out for target practice Thursday afternoon."

"Kirby claims someone stole it."

Lily jumped to her feet. "If Kirby said it's gone, it's gone."

The gun was gone, but did it disappear before or after Daryl Murdoch died?

I smelled cake when I entered the rectory kitchen. I smiled. It was the first time I'd smiled in hours. Tramping around in the cold, finagling information, was draining. I lifted the plastic cover from the stand. If Bayroo's cake was as delicious as it looked and smelled, Travis Calhoun was going to be very happy. I wondered if I would be here to attend the Spook Bash tomorrow and see this famous young man.

Very likely yes. I didn't seem to be making any headway in my task. Or tasks. I'd uncovered multiple motives for murder, but I was unwilling to implicate Cynthia Brown or Walter Carey or Lily Mendoza.

Maybe I wasn't cut out for detecting. Was I naive? I bristled at the thought. I may have been a small-town girl, but I knew a Galahad from a Cardinal Richelieu. However, and I felt perplexed, perhaps I was too empathetic.

. . . impulsive . . .

I looked toward the ceiling. If Wiggins wanted my attention, he would have to be more direct. I didn't dwell on the fact that I'd certainly been visible this evening, but now that I was at the rectory, I was properly invisible. Perhaps that would soothe Wiggins. In fact, he should be pleased at my progress.

Had I been hoodwinked by Cynthia or Walter or Lily? Possibly. In the end, I might feel compelled to reveal to Chief Cobb what I'd learned about one or all of them.

I replaced the cake cover without filching even a tiny swipe of the rich chocolate icing. Perhaps I'd find a snack in the refrigerator.

The rectory was silent. Where was everyone? Especially Kathleen? It was a quarter to nine. The Abbotts were certainly a busy family. I supposed Father Bill was out on parish duty. I remembered that Bayroo was going to a skating party tonight. As for Kathleen, I felt uneasy. Obviously, she'd tried to stir things up with Walter Carey. What else had she done?

The porch door slammed.

I was ready with a cheery greeting when the kitchen door opened and a black-robed witch stepped inside, carrying a scruffy broomstick. Her conical hat tilted forward. Sticky-looking strands of green hair protruded sideways. A squashy red boil disfigured the wrinkled, putty-colored face. A hand swept up, lifting the hat with attached hair and mask. Kathleen dropped her purse onto the table and slipped out of the robe.

"What a stunning outfit." Almost horrid enough to destroy my appetite. Almost.

Kathleen drew in a sharp breath. "Hello, Bailey Ruth. I didn't know you were here. How could anyone know?" The last was a mutter. "Isn't the mask neat?" She sounded more cheerful. "It's fun to wear a mask. No one can see you frown. Did you know it's against the rules for a rector's wife to frown?" She smoothed her ruffled hair. "I was at the Friends of the Library dinner. If I didn't show up in costume, I'd be fined. That's twenty-five bucks I can use to buy groceries. But"—her face lightened—"I got in some good work. Bud Schilling's the junior warden. He's got a houseful of kids and he's always wanted the church to build a family center. I told him I knew there'd been some concern on the vestry about Daryl's saying he was going to talk to Bill about a financial matter. I told Bud Judith Murdoch called me and she said she was sorry Daryl got mad at Bill because of the new plans Bill had for the family center." Kathleen beamed.

"Clever." I looked at Kathleen with new respect. The junior warden would tell the rest of the vestry. No one would ever bring up the matter with Judith Murdoch out of kindness. Kathleen had very likely rescued her husband's career.

Kathleen's smile faded. "How about you? Do you have anything important to give to the police?"

"Not yet." I opened the refrigerator door, found some Cheddar cheese. "Walter Carey's wife called him and told him you'd been to see her."

Kathleen whirled toward the refrigerator. "How did you know?"

"I was there." I was already at the cabinet. I opened it, lifted down a box of Ritz crackers.

"Do you eat all the time?" She didn't wait for an answer. "I know you told me to sit tight. I can't. I'm scared to death for Bill. I had to do something. Harriet's scared. That seems suspicious to me. Did you find out anything?"

"Possibly. I don't think Walter's the murderer. Nonetheless, Kathleen, you should leave it to me to investigate the people who were on the outs with Daryl. I'm already dead."

She shook her head sharply. "Bill's in trouble. I have to find out everything I can. I wish I hadn't thrown that phone in the lake. But I'll get that information to the police chief someway. I've figured out why Bill won't tell the chief anything. He's probably protecting Irene Chatham. She's—"

I interrupted. "The light-fingered member of the Altar Guild." I enjoyed Kathleen's look of awe, but felt compelled to reveal my source. "I checked the church pictorial directory."

Kathleen paced. "In between working at the church, I've looked everywhere for Irene."

"She's on my list, Kathleen." My tone was reproving. Had I learned it from Wiggins?

Kathleen ignored me. "Every time I tried to talk to Isaac, he was surrounded by people wanting him to carry something or move something."

I topped the crackers with cheese slices and carried my plate to the table.

She watched disapprovingly. "One of these days somebody's going to walk in and see dishes up in the air and the fat will be in the fire."

I smiled and enjoyed my snack. "That may be." Food soothes me and my tone was equable. "Kathleen, sit down and relax. We'll find out more tomorrow."

She continued to pace. "Tomorrow I have to help get everything ready for the Spook Bash. I won't have a free minute."

I felt great relief. I didn't want Kathleen to stir up the quiescent tiger. "I'll see to everything."

She'd paused by the cake stand, lifted it to look in surprise at Bayroo's cake.

I explained about the birthday gift and her face softened in a smile. Then once again she looked worried. "I'm going to try again to catch Irene." She walked toward the phone, but stopped to stare at a slate on a stand next to the telephone. A message was written in red chalk:

7:45 p.m. Urgent. Dad, call Isaac. He's upset.
Something about a wheelbarrow and the police.
Gone to skate with Lucinda. Home about nine-thirty.

"Oh." Kathleen looked faint.

I lost my appetite.

She ran for her car. I was already in the passenger seat, waiting.

The brick bungalow's front shutters gleamed with recent paint in the porch light. Late-blooming pansies added color to the front flower bed. A red candle burned brightly in a toothy jack-o'-lantern on a front step. A skeleton in a pink tutu dangled from a planter hook in the porch ceiling. An engraved nameplate by the doorbell read ISAAC AND EVELYN FRANKLIN.

Kathleen rang the doorbell. She'd insisted that she be the one to talk to Isaac. I insisted I would accompany her, though unseen.

The door opened. Isaac Franklin was on the shady side of fifty, lined dark face, silvered hair, but he looked muscular and fit. The minute he saw Kathleen, his grim expression altered. "Come in, Mrs. Kathleen. You come right in."

Kathleen stepped inside. "Isaac, what's this about your wheelbarrow?"

He folded his arms, frowned. "I don't hold with taking a man's work tools. Like I said, if a body can't report mischief without stirring up a hornet's nest, I don't know what the world's coming to."

A plump pretty woman bustled to his side. She was stylish in a pale violet velvet top and slacks and white boots.

I especially liked the boots. I'd remember them and perhaps another time . . .

She took Isaac's arm in a firm grip. "Papa, you can't be on your high horse when there's been a murder. Come in, Mrs. Kathleen, and Isaac can tell you what happened."

Kathleen was offered the most comfortable chair in the den. Evelyn put the TV on mute. Isaac joined his wife on the divan, clamped his hands above his knees. "I'll tell you, Mrs. Kathleen, I never been so surprised. First thing this morning, I saw somebody had been fooling around in my shed. I don't leave things any old which way. Everything has a place and everything is in its place. So when I found the wheelbarrow jammed up next to the shovels—"

It had never occurred to me to quiz Kathleen about her return of the wheelbarrow to the shed. I understood her panic and haste, but that hurried dumping of the wheelbarrow might be her undoing.

"—I checked to see if anything was missing. I can tell you I know what's where." He looked puzzled. "I looked real good and nothing was missing. Everything else was there and where it should be, but, like I told that officer this afternoon, somebody'd had my wheelbarrow out and I know that for sure because there was some mud on the wheel and I'd just greased it good the other day and I don't put anything away dirty." He nodded three times for emphasis. "Somebody took my barrow out and did I don't know what with it. I'd guess kids, but I don't see how they got into my shed. It was locked up like always when I left yesterday afternoon and locked again this morning, but somehow somebody got that barrow out and put it back. That seemed mighty odd to me. I went over to tell the rector, but he wasn't in his office. When I came home for lunch, Evelyn told me she'd heard on TV about Mr. Murdoch being found shot in the cemetery. I called the police because it seemed to me they should know there was something odd going on around the church." He glowered. "I didn't take kindly to it when that officer asked me about how Mr. Murdoch and I had words outside the parish hall on Monday. Turned out Mamie Pruitt couldn't wait to tell the police about me and Mr. Murdoch, but I told that officer to go and talk to Father Bill. Father Bill took my part just like he should. I got those groceries out of the pantry for the Carter family that live down the block from us. Mr. Carter, he's in the hospital, and Mrs. Carter, she lost her job, and there's five kids and no food for the table. Father Bill said of course I could take food for folks in need, but that mean-hearted Murdoch didn't want help going to anybody but people approved by some committee or other. And the policeman badgered me about keys. Who had keys except for me? Well, like I told him, there are keys here, there, and everywhere. The rector, he has keys to everything, and so do the senior warden and the junior warden and the Sunday school superintendent and the head of the Altar Guild. So it isn't like I was the only one that has keys.

Then he wanted to know where I was between five and seven last evening and I told him it wasn't no business of his." His eyes glowed with outrage.

Evelyn patted his stiff arm. "Now, Papa." She turned bright eyes toward Kathleen. "Isaac was with me. He got home right on schedule at a quarter after five and we had a quick supper then we went over to our daughter Noreen's and took care of Ikie and Sue so Noreen and Bobby could go to a show."

Kathleen's smile was reassuring. "I'm sure the officer didn't intend to offend you when he asked where you were yesterday. They ask everybody who might have been in the area."

"See, Papa?" Evelyn patted his arm.

Isaac still frowned. "I don't hold with that policeman taking my barrow away. He gave me a receipt. I told him I needed my barrow with all the stuff I'll be hauling away after Halloween's over, pumpkins and bales of hay and what all. I need my barrow. Mrs. Kathleen, can you get me my barrow back?"

Kathleen hunched over the wheel of her car. "If the police link that wheelbarrow to Daryl, Bill will be arrested." She turned toward me, though, of course, the passenger seat appeared empty. In the wash of a streetlamp through the window, her face looked pale and desperate.

I agreed. Father Bill was definitely at risk. I was very much afraid for him. If only we knew where the chief's investigation was headed. There might be a way to find out if I were clever enough to remember what Bayroo had told me about computers. "I'll go to the police station and see if I can work the chief's computer. Bayroo showed me this afternoon."

Kathleen's glance at me was pitying. "I don't think so,

Bailey Ruth. You have to know the password and it takes some skill to find files."

Files? I didn't want to ask Kathleen what that meant. I pictured a gray steel cabinet. "I know the password. Cougar."

Kathleen's eyes narrowed. "If I could get in, I can find out what we need to know." She pressed fingers tight against her temples for a moment. Her hands dropped. She asked quickly, "Where is his office?"

"City hall. Second floor."

"Do the windows open?"

"I'll find out." Before she could exclaim, I was in the chief's office. The windows were old-fashioned, with sashes. Back in the passenger seat, I reported, "Three windows on the south side. They open."

"That's all I need. Here's what we'll do . . ."

It was a good plan, a daring plan. I hoped it wasn't a foolhardy plan, but Kathleen was already shoving the car into gear and speeding toward the rectory and the supplies we would need.

The chief's office was chilly. I remembered my days in the mayor's office and the way he turned down the thermostat when he departed for the day. He never arrived until a good hour after the staff, so he wasn't concerned in winter with how long it took for the offices to get warm. I'd arrived to a frosty workplace often enough that I learned to nudge the thermostat up as soon as he was out the door. Now I found the thermostat, pushed it to seventy. I turned on the light.

At the window, I lifted the sash and leaned out.

Kathleen stood in the deep shadow of an old cottonwood. In her witch's robe, she was simply a darker splotch in the shadow.

I held out my hands. I missed the tennis ball on her first

try. The second time I caught it. A cord was taped to the ball. Swiftly, I pulled hand over hand and the cord lifted the rope ladder she'd retrieved from the Boy Scout troop's storeroom in the church. I placed the hooks over the sill.

Kathleen wasn't even breathing hard when she climbed through the window to join me.

"Well done," I praised.

"I did a rope course last summer." She spoke softly. She glanced about, with one furtive look toward the door, and strode to the chief's desk. She slipped into his chair. In a moment the screen was bright.

I pointed at a little picture on the screen. "That one."

Kathleen clicked, found a file for Murdoch, and in a moment we were looking at a list that included interviews with Mrs. Murdoch, Kirby Murdoch, Kathleen Abbott, Father Bill Abbott, and Isaac Franklin.

Kathleen clicked on *Isaac Franklin*. It was essentially the same information she had gained tonight but there was an addendum:

Det. Sgt. Price took custody Friday of the wheelbarrow from the shed behind St. Mildred's rectory. Sgt. Price noted cedar needles in a clump of mud on the wheel rim. There are no cedars on church property. Cedars are plentiful in the cemetery, where the victim was found. Moreover, an inspection of the barrow revealed dust balls that might correspond to those found on the decedent's suit coat. These discoveries suggest that the body was transported to the cemetery in the wheelbarrow from the vicinity of the church. Saturday morning a thorough search will be made of the church grounds and cemetery for any trace of the wheelbarrow's passage.

Kathleen moaned. "What if the wheelbarrow left tracks when I brought it back?"

I patted her shoulder. "I'll take care of it in the morning." I'd be there at first light, but if I missed an impression, suspicion was going to be focused on Father Bill or Kathleen.

The little arrow darted up. The file went away. She opened the file on Father Bill.

Rev. Abbott refuses to reveal the reason for his quarrel on Thursday morning

A door banged open. Footsteps pounded across the floor toward Kathleen. A deep voice shouted, "Hands up."

Kathleen scrambled out of the chair and raced toward the window.

Holding his gun straight ahead, gripping it with both hands, a policeman thudded after her.

I shoved the chair with all my might. It slammed into him and he fell, the gun clattering to the floor.

Grabbing the gun, I raced to the window, tossed it far into the night.

The policeman scrambled to his feet. He shoved the chair out of his way.

Kathleen reached the ground. I unhooked the rope ladder, dropped it down. I pulled down the window with a resounding smack.

The policeman stopped and gazed in disbelief at the closed window.

I swooped past him to the glowing screen. It would be disastrous if the chief knew we'd been into those files. I didn't have time to figure out how to turn it off. I reached the back of the machine, saw a dizzying array of cords. Perhaps if I pulled out one . . . or several . . .

The machine made a noise like a fish swallowing.

But it would certainly be apparent that someone had meddled. Quickly, I reinserted plugs.

Crackle. Hiss. There was an odd sound as if the machine quivered in its depths.

The policeman swung toward the computer. I applauded his bravery as he pelted around the desk, then jerked to a stop. He stared. At nothing, of course.

He looked at the small empty space between the back of the computer and the wall.

I wasn't there. I stood staring at the computer. I felt true distress when I saw the black emptiness of the screen. I hoped the damage was not irreversible.

The policeman backed away from the empty space, then whirled and pounded toward the door.

I touched the black screen, but there was no flicker of color.

Perhaps I'd done enough for tonight.

CHAPTER 13

I tried to be quiet as a mouse." Bayroo sat on the petit point ottoman with her knees tucked under her chin. "I hope I didn't wake you up. I brought breakfast." She pointed at an enameled tray. "Blueberry muffins and oatmeal. Mom thought I fixed it for me and she didn't see me add a mug of coffee and an extra bowl and plate. She's really frazzled. The Spook Bash is today, and she's already over at the church." Bayroo grinned. "I've been thinking wake-up thoughts, like 'Auntie Grand, it's almost eight o'clock and I'm so excited I feel like I could fly if I tried.' "

She jumped up, closed her eyes, scrunched her face. "Maybe if I hold my breath and flap my arms." She lifted from the floor, thumped down. "I jumped," she confessed, "but I still feel like flying."

Eight o'clock. Chief Cobb had ordered a search of the church grounds and the cemetery this morning. I swung upright in a panic, rushed to the window. No police cars were parked in the back drive or—I craned to see—the visible portion of the church parking lot.

Bayroo was at my side, her face concerned. "Is something wrong?"

"Everything's fine. But I have to go out soon." I smiled

and gave her a good-morning hug, then held her at arm's length. "My, you look nice."

Her cheeks turned bright pink. "Do I look too special?" She fingered the top button on her crisp blue-striped blouse. Navy corduroy slacks were tucked into soft white boots.

I liked Bayroo's white boots, just as I'd liked the ones I'd seen yesterday. They added a bright note to a cloudy fall day. "You look perfect. Casual but nice."

She brushed back a swath of fiery-red hair. "I hope Travis doesn't think I'm a carrottop like that awful Jason Womble. He sits behind me in math, and whenever he has to pass a paper or anything he says, 'Here you are, Carrottop. Better watch out for monster rabbits.'"

I laughed.

Bayroo didn't join in. Her eyes flashed. "Jason's mean."

I reached over, gently touched a flaming curl. "Next time tell him he's color-blind. You aren't a carrottop, you're a Titian redhead, and there are paintings to prove it."

"Titian?" She looked at me doubtfully.

"Titian," I said firmly. "The famous Italian painter. He loved to paint models with red-gold hair just like yours. Check out an art book from the library, show Jason what's what."

"Titian. Oh, I'll do it. Thank you, Auntie Grand." She was at the table, lifting the covers from the cereal bowls. "I brought real cream. Mom says her family always had real cream with oatmeal. And lots of brown sugar."

We sat down and I continued the family tradition by spooning two tablespoons of brown sugar and pouring a generous splash of cream. "Thanks for bringing up breakfast." It was an auspicious beginning to the day. Everything was certain to come right. I felt it in my bones. Or would have, had I had bones. In any event, being with Bayroo was a good start.

I poked a chunk of butter into the warm center of the blueberry muffin.

Bayroo clapped her hands. "I love watching a muffin float in the air."

I was starved. "Not for long." I finished the muffin. "You look excited."

Her thin face was eager but uncertain. "I have the cake ready to take to Travis's house. He said I could come this morning and I want to go there more than anything. But what if he thinks I'm one of those irritating fans who won't leave celebrities alone? I mean, I don't really know him and he's here to visit his aunt and maybe I should just put the cake on the porch with a note. Would that be better? Then he'll know I really think he's swell, but I'm not trying to horn in. I mean, he has to know Lucinda and I were hanging out around his aunt's house. Lucinda was at the other end of the block and I was in the pine grove." She looked at me earnestly. "Don't tell Mom. We aren't supposed to go in the preserve by ourselves—girls, I mean, especially after dark. But it wasn't quite dark and I had to have somewhere where I could watch for him and Lucinda didn't see him because he came from my direction." She finished in a rush. "I don't want him to think I'm a hanger-on."

Bayroo had no inkling how beautiful she was, her red-gold hair shining in the sunlight, her freckled face kind and hopeful, bright and fresh in what were almost certainly her newest casual clothes.

"He'll think you're a nice new friend who wants his birthday to be special. It wouldn't be at all friendly to leave the cake with a note. You march right up to his aunt's front door and knock on it." I raised my hand in a fist, pretended to knock. "I promise you it's the right thing to do."

"You're sure?" She looked at me as if to a fount of wisdom.

"Positive." If only I were as positive of my course this morning.

"Okay. I'll do it. If I can hide in the preserve when it's getting dark"—for an instant her eyes were wide with memory that surely wasn't pleasant, then they shone again with happiness—"I can do anything." She absently spooned her oatmeal in a dreamy reverie.

I finished my muffin, hurriedly drank coffee, delighting in the bitter undertone of chicory. It was time to go to work. I scarcely gave a thought to my costume. Well, perhaps that wasn't quite accurate. I took a quick peek in one of the catalogs I'd brought from the sewing room and chose a royal-purple velour jacket and slacks with a rose silk blouse and purple scarf. And white boots. No one would see except Bayroo, but a woman has to feel at her best when she sets out to destroy evidence.

I went straight to the cemetery. Thursday night we'd followed a gravel path, then crossed the end of the paved church parking lot. However, we'd trundled over a patch of dirt to reach the pavement near the mausoleum. Last night I'd used a pine bough to erase those tracks. Had I missed any?

The breeze was chilly though the sun shone brightly. I thought of a short white cashmere coat with oversize purple buttons and immediately felt much more comfortable as well as stylish.

Despite a bright blue sky, the cemetery was shadowy beneath the overhanging limbs of sycamores, maples, sweet gums, and Bradford pears. Some leaves still clung, but mounds of red and gold and purplish leaves were banked against headstones by the erratic wind. Three big cedars lined the path near the mausoleum.

I found a wheelbarrow trail a few feet beyond the spot where we'd left Daryl. Quickly, I smoothed over the narrow furrow, my fingers brushing against cedar needles. I'd just satisfied myself that the area near the mausoleum was clear of wheel tracks when three police cars pulled up and stopped on the other side of the mausoleum.

Hurriedly, I zoomed in ever-widening circles until I reached the fluttering yellow tape that marked the crime scene. So far so good.

Anita Leland and the young man who had helped secure the scene Thursday night led the way. "I'll check inside the tape. Jake, start outside the tape, look between here and the church. Harry, go fifty yards east, then fifty west." The search party fanned out, scanning the ground.

Stocky Jake began his search just past the breeze-stirred tape, head down, expression intent. I sped ahead of him. Jake and I spotted a deep gouge in a depression about twenty yards from the marked-off area. The track was on a straight line from the mausoleum to the church parking lot. "Yo," he shouted. "Found it."

Immediately Anita and Harry joined him. Anita sighted a line leading to the church parking lot. "Okay, one of us on each side, move slowly, take your time . . ." She stuck small yellow flags on either side of tracks as they were found. The search party took on an Easter-egg-hunt atmosphere, excited shouts erupting as the unmistakable path of the careening barrow was discovered.

I hovered overhead, but there was no opportunity to erase the damning evidence. I'd not worried about the wheelbarrow when Kathleen assured me she'd returned it to the shed, but I hadn't calculated the path she'd taken when she dashed away from the mausoleum. Unfortunately, Kathleen had ignored the gravel path and headed straight for the rectory backyard.

Anita's fair face was flushed with excitement. She hurried across the parking lot. Perhaps most damning of all was the intermittent trail in the rectory backyard leading directly to the shed. Flags sprouted. Anita stood next to the shed and used her cell phone. "Send the crime van. We've got a fresh path, clear as can be."

I envisioned a grim sequence of events: the rectory wheelbarrow tagged in evidence, the wheelbarrow linked to the crime scene, further consideration of the unexplained dust ball laden with cat fur, Father Bill questioned again, now with greater suspicion.

If Kathleen hadn't flung Daryl's cell phone into the lake, Chief Cobb would have many more suspects. Walter Carey committed fraud. Irene Chatham stole from the collection plate. Kirby was furious with his father over his treatment of Lily Mendoza. Cynthia Brown was pregnant and desperate. I suspected that Daryl's secretary knew more than she had revealed about her boss's departure for the church. But perhaps most significant, last night when I'd talked to Kirby's lovely Lily, she'd been shocked that his gun was missing.

Where was Kirby's gun? When had it gone missing?

The windowed alcove overlooked a backyard that would be spectacular in the spring, dogwood and redbuds surrounding a pond with water lilies. A breeze stirred autumn leaves that fluttered to the ground.

Judith Murdoch peered out the window. She wore a black blouse, dark gray slacks, black shoes. She stood stiff and straight.

A barefoot Kirby hunched over his plate at the breakfast-room table. His gray sweatshirt and pants were fuzzy and ragged. A stubble of beard shadowed his face. Uncombed hair bunched in tangles. He held a mug of coffee, but the Danish on the plate before him was untouched. Red-rimmed eyes stared forlornly at his mother. "Mom, I want to talk to you about Thursday."

Judith turned to face him. Fear flickered in her eyes, fear and grief and despair. "You were with Lily Thursday night."

He put down the mug. "Mom, I saw—"

She broke in, her voice harsh. "Kirby, promise me you'll tell the police you were with Lily."

The doorbell rang.

Judith looked toward the hall, wavered on her feet.

Kirby pushed back his chair. "I'll take care of it, Mom. I'll take care of everything." He was at her side, gripping her arm.

The bell pealed again.

Kirby steered his mother to the window seat. "Sit down and rest. I'll see about it." He gave a worried backward glance as he hurried into the hallway.

When the door opened, Chief Cobb's deep voice easily carried to the breakfast room. "Good morning, Kirby. If you have a moment, I have some questions about your movements Thursday."

Judith pushed to her feet, rushed to the hall.

I followed and stood by the waist-tall Chinese vase near the entry to the living room.

Judith clasped her hands so tightly the fingers blanched. "He's told you everything he knows. Can't you leave us alone? We have family coming. We have to plan the funeral. There's so much to do."

Kirby glanced from the frowning chief to his mother. "It's okay, Mom. Go upstairs and rest. I'll talk to the chief." Kirby touched her arm. "Please."

Judith glared at the chief. "Kirby doesn't know anything about what happened to his father. Nothing." Her voice was shrill.

The chief rocked back on his heels, his heavy face determined. "Sorry to intrude, Mrs. Murdoch, but I have a duty to investigate your husband's murder. He was shot with a twenty-two." Cobb turned toward Kirby. "You were target-practicing with a twenty-two Thursday afternoon on the river bottom." It was a statement, not a question.

Kirby jammed a hand through his tangled hair. "Yeah. I shoot most Thursdays. When I finished, I put the gun in the trunk of my car."

"Where is the gun now?"

Kirby didn't answer.

Chief Cobb pressed him. "Yesterday you said it must have been stolen from the trunk of your car."

"Yeah." He stared at the floor.

I felt a chill. He was trying not to look at his mother. Kirby thought she'd taken the gun. Why did he suspect her?

The questions came fast.

"What time did you put it in the trunk?"

"About two-thirty."

"Where was the car between two-thirty and five?"

"Parked in the lot next to my girlfriend's apartment."

"Locked?"

Kirby gnawed at his lower lip. He started to speak, stopped, finally spoke. "Yeah. It was locked."

His mother drew in a sharp breath.

Chief Cobb was somber. "Where were you shortly after five P.M. Thursday?"

Judith took two quick steps, stood between the chief and her son. "He was with his girlfriend. He's already told you."

"He can tell me again. Here or downtown. This time he can tell me the truth. He was seen outside his father's office shortly after five o'clock." Chief Cobb's gaze was cold. "Your choice, son."

Kirby swallowed. "Yeah, I was there."

Judith gave a strangled cry. "You can't do this. I'll call our lawyer."

Chief Cobb's eyes narrowed. "I'm seeking information, Mrs. Murdoch. I'm not making an accusation. It looks like you think your son had something to do with his father's death. Are you afraid of what your son is going to say?"

Judith looked tortured. "You're twisting my words."

Kirby jammed his hands into the pockets of his sweatpants. "I went to Dad's office because I had to talk to him."

"You followed him out of the parking lot?"

Kirby's face ridged. He took a deep breath. "Yeah. I started after him." He shot a desperate, grieved look at his mother, moved uneasily on his feet. "Dad drove to the church." He put out the words with effort. "I waited until he parked. I caught him just outside the church. I told him what a louse he was for getting Lily fired from her job. It was a rotten thing to do. He said he'd make sure she never got another job."

Cobb waited.

Kirby shuddered, again stared at the floor. "We were yelling, and when I looked up we'd walked into the cemetery. I got madder and madder and he shoved me and I shot him."

"What happened to the gun? Did you put it in the trunk and somebody stole it?" The chief looked sardonic.

"No. I threw it away in the cemetery."

Cobb pursed his lips. "Nobody stole it?"

"No. I threw it away." Kirby's expression was dogged.

Chief Cobb studied Kirby. "I am taking you into custody for questioning. We'll go downtown and arrange for a lawyer to be present."

Judith threw out her hands. "He didn't do it." She was frantic, her voice rising. "He's lying. He didn't shoot his father. I did. Kirby didn't follow his father."

Chief Cobb turned on her. "How do you know that, Mrs. Murdoch?"

Judith looked oddly calm when she spoke. "I was there. I was waiting in my car. I followed Daryl. He was alone in his car." She looked at Kirby, her face stricken. "You saw me, didn't you?"

"Mom, don't." Kirby's voice was anguished.

Cobb looked at her intently. "Why did you follow him?"

Judith's face was bleak. "He's been cheating on me for years. I finally had enough. I followed him to the church. I'd already gotten Kirby's gun out of his car. He never locks his car. That was another lie. I drove by his girlfriend's apartment and saw his car Thursday afternoon. That's when I got the gun."

Chief Cobb folded his arms. He looked from one to the other. "I want to speak to each of you separately. Kirby, let's step outside for a moment." He nodded at Judith. "Please wait in the living room."

Judith clasped her hands. "Kirby didn't shoot his father."

Kirby didn't look toward Judith. "Mother didn't do it. I swear. She doesn't know how to shoot a gun. I did it."

Chief Cobb folded his arms. "I can take you both into custody, interview you separately. So take your choice. Here. Or downtown."

Kirby jerked a shaking hand toward the door. "Let's go outside." He turned away. The chief followed. Judith stood rigid, staring after them.

When the front door closed, I was at the chief's elbow.

Cobb gave Kirby a hard look. "Take it from the first. You got to the church. What happened?"

"I caught up with him outside the church. We started arguing. We were making a lot of noise. He grabbed my arm, pulled me toward the cemetery. We walked for a few minutes and we were yelling at each other and I pulled out my gun and shot him."

"Which gate did you take into the cemetery?"

Kirby looked wary. "How should I know? It was just a gate."

Cobb rubbed one cheek. "The main road curves to the south. Were you near that curve?" The Pritchard mausoleum was a good hundred yards from that curve.

Kirby moved uneasily, but he managed a straight stare. "I guess. Yeah. That sounds right."

Cobb gestured as if he held a gun. "You pulled out the gun and shot him. Did the bullet hit him in the chest?"

Kirby thought fast. He knew guns, especially knew .22s. To be deadly, a small-caliber bullet had to strike a vital area. "Yeah. His heart. Right on."

"What did you do with the gun?"

Kirby hesitated an instant too long, then said quickly, "I went over to the nature preserve and threw it into the lake."

Cobb's face furrowed in irritation. "You've got a new story every time. First, somebody stole the gun. Then you threw the gun away in the cemetery. Now you tossed it in the lake. You're lying. One way or another, you're lying. You don't know where the body was found. You don't know where he was shot. Or maybe"—his gaze was cold—"you're clever as hell and you know the answers but you're lying your head off. Wait here." He slammed into the house.

Kirby called after him, "Mom's trying to protect me. She didn't shoot him."

Cobb strode into the living room.

Judith waited by the fireplace. The flames crackled but she shivered. "Kirby's trying to protect me. I'm sorry." She looked like she would collapse, then drew herself up. "I'm ready to go to jail."

The chief nodded. "Just a few facts, Mrs. Murdoch. Where were you standing when you shot your husband?"

Her eyes flared. "I was"—she hesitated—"facing him.

We'd quarreled. He came toward me. I pulled the gun out of my purse and shot him."

"Where were you?"

"In the cemetery."

"Where in the cemetery?" His gaze was sharp.

Judith clutched at her throat. "I don't know exactly. I don't remember where we were. I was too upset."

"Did you enter by the south gate or the west gate?"

I thought rapidly. Kathleen and I had used the wheelbarrow to enter through the north gate. The main gate was on the west side of the cemetery. There was also a gate to the south. I had the distinct sense Judith was desperately trying to guess the right answer. Logically, if she and Daryl had walked from the church, they would have entered through the west gate.

She fluttered her hands. "We came in through the west gate."

"Where did you go?"

She shrugged, looked puzzled. "I don't know. We were walking and talking. I wasn't paying any attention. I don't know exactly where we were. I can't say exactly. I shot him and then I ran. I don't know where I was."

"You were facing him as you fired the gun." Chief Cobb made it a statement.

"That's right." She watched him carefully.

"The bullet struck him in the chest." Another statement.

She made no answer.

"Chest or face?"

"I didn't look. I pressed the trigger and turned and ran away."

I shook my head. Judith obviously had never hunted, never listened to men who did. Hitting any target is difficult. Shooting blind was almost a guarantee of a wild shot.

Cobb's expression was skeptical. "Where's the gun?"

Now she looked triumphant. "In the backyard. I buried it in the flower bed behind the third rosebush from the walk."

His eyes narrowed. His gaze became intent and speculative. "Show me."

She hurried to a patio door, flung it open. The chief was right behind her.

Cobb found the soft mound of dirt behind the third rosebush. He knelt and gingerly scraped away loose soil, piling dirt to one side. He scraped until the ground turned hard. He looked up at Judith, his face grim.

She bent forward, anxious and uncertain. "It was there. I buried it there."

Cobb pushed up from the ground, grimacing as he straightened one knee. "If you did"—his tone was cold—"it doesn't seem to be there now, Mrs. Murdoch."

"Someone's taken it." She twisted her hands together.

"Just like somebody took it from the trunk of your son's car. Or didn't take it, depending on who I ask." He glared at Judith. "I'm telling you and you can tell your son that I intend to find out who killed your husband, with or without your help."

The patio door opened and Kirby came out.

Cobb looked at him. "Maybe you took the gun out of its hole."

Kirby said nothing, though he cut his eyes toward his mother.

Cobb brushed the dirt from his hands. "I'll be in touch."

When he disappeared around the edge of the house, Kirby strode toward his mother. "What did you tell him?"

"I told him I shot your dad. He didn't believe me."

Kirby jammed a hand through his hair. "He didn't believe me either."

Judith's face was ashen. "What did you tell him?"

He blinked, holding back tears. "I didn't tell him I saw your car when we came out of the parking lot. I never will."

"You saw my car?" Suddenly her face looked years younger. "You saw me following your dad? So you turned away, didn't you? Oh, Kirby, when I realized your dad was going to the church, I came home."

"Then what happened to my gun? It should have been in my car."

Judith began to laugh and it turned into a sob. "I was so afraid when they said he was shot with a twenty-two. Friday morning I went out and looked and found it in your trunk. I picked it up and smelled it—"

He looked shocked. "I was target-practicing Thursday afternoon. That's all. Did you think I shot Dad?"

"Of course not. But I was terrified the police would think so. I buried the gun in the backyard, but now it's gone."

"Gone?" For an instant, satisfaction lighted his face. "Maybe that's a good thing. Let's hope it never turns up. We know it didn't have anything to do with Dad getting shot, so good riddance."

Chief Cobb moved quietly away from the side of the house where'd he stood and eavesdropped. His face was grim as he climbed into his car. "Damn fools?" he muttered to himself. "Or is one of them crafty as hell?"

A musical peal sounded.

The chief yanked out his cell phone. "Cobb." He listened. "A clear match?" His smile was grim and satisfied. "Yeah. I'm on my way to the church now."

CHAPTER 14

Father Bill picked up a small Dresden shepherd, but his gaze was abstracted, the gesture automatic. The glaze of the shepherd's coat was worn away. I suspected Father Bill often held the figurine, turned it in his hand when dealing with troubles of body and soul. His face furrowed. "You're certain the tracks were made by the rectory wheelbarrow?"

Chief Cobb was in a familiar posture, sitting upright in the straight chair that faced the rector's desk, hands planted firmly on his legs. He looked overlarge in the shabby office with its full bookcases and old-fashioned wooden filing cabinets. The chief's gray suit was wrinkled, his tie loose at the neck. He looked tired. "No question. There are traces of mud and cedar needles from the cemetery on the wheel. There are no cedars in your backyard. Moreover, the wheel rim has a gash in it that makes the tread unmistakable."

"I can't explain it." Father Bill's thumb slid up and down on the faded porcelain. "Daryl's keys would open the shed, although I don't see why he would have wanted a wheelbarrow or, if he wanted one, why he would take it to the cemetery."

The chief's gaze was sardonic. "I don't think Mr. Murdoch took the wheelbarrow. We have to wait for confirmation from the lab, but right now it looks like his body was placed in the wheelbarrow and transported to the cemetery. The barrow was returned to the shed. Murdoch may have been shot here."

"Here?" Father Bill looked shocked. "In the church?"

Chief Cobb nodded. "Here or near the church or the rectory. Murdoch left his office, right after five, headed this way." He moved nearer the edge of the chair. "Where were you Thursday evening, Reverend, from five o'clock to six-fifteen?"

"At the hospital. Ted Worsham was dying." His face was weary. "Not unexpected, but his wife was very upset."

The chief asked quickly, "Did you leave the hospital at any time between five and seven P.M.?"

Father Bill's face was somber. "I got there around four, but I came back here a little while later. I don't know exactly when."

"You left the bedside of a dying man. Why?" His eyes never left Father Bill's face.

Father Bill rotated the Dresden shepherd around and around. "Daryl paged me around five. I called him. He said he wanted to see me in a few minutes at the church. I hurried here. I waited half an hour, but he didn't come."

Cobb's face was grim. "You didn't say anything about this yesterday. Don't you think it might be important to a murder investigation when the body is found next door to the church to tell the police the victim had planned to be at the church around five o'clock?"

Father Bill said nothing, his face as unyielding as the chief's.

Cobb frowned. "You and Murdoch argued Thursday morning. You won't say why. Now you claim he pages you Thursday afternoon, you call him, he asks you to come to the church, and you leave a dying man's bedside to come. What was so urgent that you would do that, Reverend? Did Murdoch ask you? Or did he order you?"

Father Bill's gaze was level. "It concerned the matter we'd discussed Thursday morning. I had to be here to make sure—" He broke off.

"What matter did you and Murdoch talk about, Reverend?" The chief's glare demanded an answer. "What was so important you left a dying man to come and see Murdoch?"

Father Bill slumped back in his chair, his face weary. "It was a parish matter that I am not at liberty to discuss."

Cobb snapped, "What did he have on you, Reverend?"

"It did not concern me personally." Father Bill's hand tightened on the statuette.

"Didn't it?" Cobb stared at him. "I talked to a couple of members of the vestry yesterday. Murdoch had contacted them, called a special meeting for Sunday afternoon to address, as he put it, 'a fiduciary matter.'"

Kathleen's chat with the junior warden at the Friends' dinner last night was probably enough to salvage Father Bill's reputation with the vestry, but Chief Cobb might not be convinced.

"That was the warden's prerogative." Father Bill's face looked pinched.

Cobb demanded, "What will you tell the vestry?"

Father Bill's voice hardened. "Nothing."

Cobb let silence build. Finally, he stood.

Father Bill came to his feet, realized he was holding the shepherd. He glanced at it in surprise, placed it on the desk. "Chief, I regret that I can't answer your question. However, I'm sure the matter has no connection to Daryl's murder. If I felt otherwise, I would take action." His face was solemn. "I swear before God that I did not see Daryl Murdoch at any time Thursday afternoon or evening. I have no knowledge of his murder."

Cobb gave a short nod. "I'll be back in touch, Reverend."

When the door closed behind Cobb, Father Bill walked, frowning, head down, to his desk. He settled into his chair, reached for a yellow legal pad, the page filled with dense writing. He took a breath, picked up his pen, began to reread his work. Abruptly, he flung the pen down, along with the pad. He retrieved the parish directory, opened it.

I looked over his shoulder.

His finger ran down the page, stopped at the number for Irene Chatham. He picked up the receiver, then slowly replaced it, shaking his head.

It was obvious that Father Bill intended to continue to protect Irene Chatham's good name even though his own reputation was at risk. Even worse, he might be arrested on suspicion of a murder he had no motive to commit.

Not if I could help it . . .

The small houses on Whitlock Street ranged from well kept to dilapidated. Purple and yellow pansies bloomed in profusion in the front bed of a neat brick bungalow on the corner. Next door was a frame house painted dark purple. A jacked-up, tireless pickup looked as though it had been in the rutted drive for years. A too-thin black-and-tan dog with droopy ears was tethered to a railing on the sagging porch. His head came up. He lifted it and howled.

I veered toward him. He backed away as far as he could until the rope held him fast, body rigid. I dropped to one knee. "It's all right, old fellow. They aren't taking very good care of you, are they?" I stroked his head. Slowly, he relaxed. I ran my hand over his back, felt his spine and ribs. "I'm sorry, Jack," I murmured. My son, Rob, always called

228 CAROLYN HART

his dogs Jack. "I'll come back, I promise, and see what I can do."

Irene's house was the third from the corner. It needed paint and a new roof. Overgrown bushes rose midway to the windows. The flower bed was a mass of leaves. Brown weeds poked from ridges and cracks in the cement walk.

Inside the house, I sniffed in distaste at the living room's stale, airless smell, potpourri mingling with dust. Irene stood in front of the fake fireplace, digging frantically into a shapeless crocheted bag. She yanked out a clear plastic change purse, upended the contents on the dingy white mantel. She counted aloud. "Ten—twenty—thirty-four." She swept the bills and assorted change back into the purse and dropped it into the crocheted bag. She moved toward the front door, eyes feverishly bright, long face drooping in misery.

A woman's clothes announce to the world how she sees herself. Whether she chooses the latest fashions or prefers plain and sensible, each choice tells its own story. I shook my head at Irene's dress. One cuff was torn, a spot of grease stained a front panel, part of the hem sagged. She was a walking testament to despair. She needed fresh makeup and a good wash and brush of her straggly gray hair, but she plunged toward the door, obviously in a tearing hurry to go somewhere, do something.

In a flash, I was on the porch and became visible. I changed, reluctantly, from dashing velour into the crisp Adelaide police uniform. I was absorbed in the transformation and didn't realize until I heard a sound behind me that I wasn't alone. I swung about to look into the startled face of a postman.

He shifted the heavy bag, peered at me in astonishment. "You had on one outfit, now you're in a uniform. That's what I saw." He was belligerent. "Where'd you come from, anyhow?"

His question was understandable. I stood with one finger poised to jab the doorbell. When he climbed the steps, he couldn't have missed seeing me. I pushed the bell, gave him a reassuring smile. "I know how it is. Sometimes our minds are a million miles away. Isn't it a beautiful day?"

The postman jammed mail into the box, turned, and fled down the steps.

I looked after him in concern. I hoped the rest of his day went better.

The door opened. Irene gasped and took a step backward, eyes wide with shock.

"Mrs. Chatham, may I have a moment of your time?" I looked at her sternly. "I'm Officer Loy. I need to speak with you about a matter concerning St. Mildred's."

Irene's lips moved, but no words came. She opened the door with a shaking hand. She led the way into the frowsy living room, gestured at an easy chair. She sank onto the divan, clutching her purse and coat, and stared at me with desperate eyes. "Father Bill promised he wouldn't tell anyone."

"Father Abbott has not discussed you in any manner with the—uh—with us." I must remember that I represented Adelaide's finest. "Our information came from Daryl Murdoch's cell phone." Indeed it had. "You recall the photographs he took?"

Irene wrapped her arms tightly across her front.

"You do recall?" I imitated the chief, bent forward, looking stern. "Two photographs. In one, you held the collection plate. In the second, you took money and stuffed it into the pocket of your Altar Guild smock."

"I don't know what you are talking about." She took shallow breaths.

"Come, come." I doubted my response exemplified effective interrogative technique. I tried again. With a glower. "Mrs. Chatham, you were photographed stealing money from the collection plate. This would not be a serious matter from the police standpoint except for the fact that Father Abbott and Mr. Murdoch quarreled. Father Abbott has refused to explain the reason to the police, saying only that it is a parish matter which must be kept confidential."

Watery brown eyes regarded me sullenly.

I didn't mince words. "Father Abbott's silence has made him a prime suspect in the murder investigation."

Something flickered in Irene's eyes. Hope? Relief? "I don't know anything about a disagreement between Father Bill and Daryl. Daryl was"—her voice shook—"always complaining about something at church." Her gaze slid away, sly as a fox easing into a chicken house.

Craven self-interest should never come as a surprise, but I'd been confident I could easily prove Father Bill's lack of motive and make Chief Cobb realize that the answer to Daryl's murder didn't lie in the church.

Perhaps it did.

I looked at Irene in a different, more searching light. Her expression was vacuous. Deliberately so? "Mrs. Chatham, the police are not interested in internal matters at St. Mildred's. They—we—are investigating a murder. If you explained that Father Abbott was defending you and not engaged in a personal quarrel with Mr. Murdoch, it would direct the investigation away from Father Abbott."

The fingers of one hand plucked at the collar of her coat. Irene lifted her eyes, watched me carefully. "Those pictures make it look bad, but it wasn't that way. I'd put money in the plate earlier and then I realized I had to pay some bills and I took it back." Her voice was stronger as she spoke, realization dawning that no one could prove otherwise. Daryl was dead. "That's all there was to it. But Daryl wouldn't listen and he went around to Father Bill and told lies about me, called me a thief."

"If you don't speak out, tell the truth, Father Abbott may be arrested." Surely she would explain when she understood the seriousness of his situation.

Irene's sandy lashes fluttered. She stared at the floor, didn't say a word.

I waited.

She jumped to her feet. "I've got things to do. I was on my way out. I'm sorry I can't help."

I stood and blocked her way. "Where were you Thursday between five and seven P.M.?"

Panic flared in her face. "I didn't even—" She clapped a hand to her lips.

"What didn't you do?" My tone was sharp.

"Nothing. I was here. I was here the whole time." She shrugged into her coat, took a step toward the door. "You can't prove I wasn't."

Irene Chatham was terrified and in her fear was willing to say and do anything to protect herself.

Why?

If I could find the answer, I might know everything I needed to know about Daryl Murdoch's murder.

I moved ahead of her to the door. "We'll be back in touch, Mrs. Chatham." As soon as I could figure out how to set Chief Cobb on her trail.

She slammed the door behind us, clattered down the front steps. She was almost running to reach her car, a shabby green coupé.

I was glad that she didn't take time to realize there wasn't a police car parked on the street and that Officer Loy was no longer behind her, but sitting beside her as the car lurched around the corner.

Irene drove too fast, lurching across Main as the light turned red. She ran another red light and careened around corners. On the outskirts of town, she pushed even harder on the gas pedal. The car swooped up and down hills, squealed around curves. We'd gone perhaps ten miles from Adelaide when a billboard on the right announced:

BUCKAROO CASINO
FUN AND MONEY
MONEY, MONEY, MONEY FOR EVERY HONEY

The billboard sparkled with gold coins spewing from a slot machine, piling into a glistening mound.

As she found a parking space in a crowded lot, I craned for a better view of the low-slung stucco building with a crimson neon outline of a slot machine on the near wall.

Irene slammed out of the car and hurried in stumbling eager steps up the broad cement walk with images of green shamrocks and diamond rings. She pushed through the door, turned immediately to her right. She stood in a short line, pushed over the money for a bag full of change.

The huge crowded room was dimly lit except for the flash of neon. Music blared loud enough to hurt my ears. An electric guitar echoed, drums thumped, and a hoarse-voiced man shouted lyrics. Clouds of cigarette smoke turned the dim air dusky.

Irene dashed to a line of slot machines, began to feed quarters. She yanked the lever, watched, stuffed in another coin. One quarter after another. Squeals of excitement sounded from a buxom blonde at a nearby slot machine. A croupier's call rose above the mutter of voices.

I'd obviously returned to an Oklahoma quite different from the one I'd departed. If anyone had told me, a lifetime ago, that there would be a gambling casino right outside Adelaide, I would have said, "When little green men arrive from Mars."

Perhaps that had happened, too.

Now I understood why Irene Chatham was a thief. All I needed to know was whether she was a murderer, too.

Jack gave an eager snuffle. I rubbed behind a black-and-tan ear. "Told you I'd come back, boy." I untied the rope from the railing, gave a tug. He obediently trotted alongside. We were almost to the street when a woman's voice cried out, "Shelly, look at that dog. Look at his rope. It's up in the air as if someone's holding it."

Behind a well-kept white picket fence, a woman bent toward the ground. A silver-haired woman with bright eyes pointed toward Jack. "That dog's rope is straight out like a comet's tail."

I dropped the rope.

A young woman, balancing a baby on one hip, rose from picking up a pacifier. The baby wailed. "Every time he spits it out, he wants it back. That rope's on the ground, Mama."

"It was in the air." Her voice was insistent.

I darted behind an oak, appeared, then strolled out. I picked up the rope and smiled at the neighbors. "Good morning."

The older woman continued to look puzzled.

The young mother spoke over the baby's cry. "Are you taking that dog? Thank Heaven."

The young mother's response was more appropriate than she would ever realize.

She patted the baby's back. "I've called the city a bunch of times to complain about how the Dickersons treat him. He's a stray and they kept him, but half the time they don't put any food out. I've been giving him kibble and water. You can't talk to the Dickersons." Her nose wrinkled as if she smelled rotten fish. "Mostly they're drunk, both of them, and yelling so much in the middle of the night it wakes

Tommy up." She gave the baby a swift kiss. Then she looked distressed. "Are you taking the dog to the pound? They put them to sleep after three days."

Jack gave a little yip.

"Absolutely not. He's on his way to a new home." I hoped Kathleen was up to a new family member. "Though"—I was realizing I had some challenges facing me—"I wonder if you could help out. We have volunteers who take care of dogs while we find a new home. It's a new program. But I don't have time to get any dog food. I'm on duty." Much as I wanted to help Jack, I had no time to shop. "Could you possibly give me enough kibble to take care of him for a couple of days?"

The older woman nodded. "Of course. I'll dash in and get some."

The young mother jounced the wailing baby on her hip. "Did you leave them a notice?"

My rescue mission was getting ever more complicated. I tried to appear chagrined, which wasn't difficult. "I didn't have a notice with me. If you would have some paper, perhaps . . ."

She called after her mother. "Bring out a pen and paper, Mama."

In only a moment, I was jotting in capital letters on an 8-by-10 white notecard:

NOTICE OF ANIMAL RESCUE
*Neglect of a domestic dog is prohibited in Sect.
42, Para. 12 of the Adelaide City Statutes. Under
the authority vested in me as a sworn officer of
the law, I herewith and hereby take custody of
one malnourished mixed-breed dog from the front
porch at*

I glanced toward the house.

817 Whitlock Street. Inquiry may be made at the Adelaide Police Station.

Signed this 28th day of October.

I wrote *Officer M. Loy* with a flourish.

I doubted the Dickersons would rush to call the police. I used the tape provided by my new friends to attach the message to the front door of Jack's former residence. As I passed by the picket fence, I paused. "We had a call out here on Thursday. A car ran the stop sign"—I pointed toward the corner—"and almost hit a bicyclist. By the time we got here, there was no trace of the car and the rider was too upset to give us a good description. I don't suppose either of you"—I looked inquiring—"happened to be outside around five o'clock Thursday evening? It was cold and windy."

The older woman clapped her hands. "I'll bet it was Irene Chatham. She's a hazard behind the wheel. I get off work at four-thirty and I get home about a quarter to five. She almost hit me coming out of her drive." She pointed at Irene's house. "I'll bet she ran right through that stop sign."

I got the particulars, the make and year and color of her car, then tucked the bag of food under one arm, took Jack's rope, and off we went. I hoped it didn't occur to the bungalow's residents to wonder why Officer Loy was afoot. I didn't look back.

We'd gone only a few steps when I heard that familiar rumble.

"Precepts—"

I finished for Wiggins, "Three and Four."

Jack gave an eager snuffle, came up on his back legs, his front paws in the air.

"Good fellow." Wiggins spoke with delight.

Jack's chin went up and I knew Wiggins was stroking his throat.

Jack dropped down.

A genial harrumph. "Although becoming visible is best avoided, you handled this chap's rescue very nicely. The official notice was well done. There will be no cause for the observers to suspect that anything unusual has occurred. However"—a heavy sigh—"the episode last night at the police station was highly irregular. Awkward. A blot upon the bright shield of the department."

I was puzzled. "The police department? I thought the policeman did as well as could be expected."

"Not a blot on the police department." Now Wiggins was roused. "A blot on the fine reputation of the Department of Good Intentions."

"Wiggins." I handed him the leash. "If I've failed, I'll resign at once."

The leash was back in my hand immediately. Just as I expected, Wiggins would never desert Jack and I was taking him to a new and good home. I had a sudden picture of Wiggins as a little boy, minus the walrus mustache, a hound eagerly licking his face as he laughed in delight.

"Don't be hasty, Bailey Ruth." Wiggins's voice was a bit farther away. "In the face of adversity, you protected Kathleen last night. Moreover, Kathleen is growing in courage. Keep up the good work."

Jack's head turned, and I knew he was watching Wiggins depart.

I tugged on the leash. "Jack, old buddy, let's go faster."

He answered with a little woof.

When we reached the church, Jack and I moved from tree to tree because there were a half-dozen cars parked behind the rectory and more cars and pickups in the church parking lot. Teenage boys were hefting bales of hay and monster pumpkins. Girls giggled and held the door to the parish hall. I was glad Kathleen was occupied with setting up for the Spook Bash.

As soon as Jack and I were safely on the porch, I disappeared. In the kitchen, I found some plastic bowls, filled one with water, the other with a small portion of kibble, brought them to the porch. Jack noisily drank, then devoured the food. He looked up expectantly.

I smoothed the top of his head. "I know you're still hungry. But we'd better start off slow."

Jack stared for a moment more, then wagged his tail, as if to say, *Sure thing,* and began to explore the porch. I stepped back into the kitchen and printed on the message blackboard:

> *Stray dog in need of a good home. Name: Jack. Will bring good fortune. BR*

I was sure of the latter. If it weren't for Jack, I wouldn't know one important fact: Irene Chatham had lied when she claimed to be home from 5 to 7 P.M. Thursday evening. In fact, she'd screeched from her driveway in a tearing hurry at about a quarter to five. I was almost sure I knew where she was going, but I needed proof. I suspected that Murdoch had called Irene from his office, intending to force a showdown with her and the rector, and Murdoch's secretary was aware of that call. She was the kind of secretary who always knew what the boss was doing.

I found the telephone directory. In only a moment I had the address for Daryl Murdoch's secretary. I checked the parish directory. Patricia Haskins was also a communicant of St. Mildred's. I found that very interesting, but not, given my speculations, surprising.

* * *

The stucco apartment building was built around a patio with a pool and benches. I checked the mailboxes near the office. A neatly printed card in 307 read: *Patricia Haskins*.

I reappeared when I stood outside her door. The wooden shutters were closed in the front window. I knocked. No answer. I looked around, saw no one, disappeared, and wafted inside.

The living room was exquisitely clean, the walls pale blue, the overstuffed furniture in soft white faux leather. A tiger-striped cat on a cushion near the kitchen lifted his head, studied me with enigmatic golden eyes. I had no doubt he saw me.

I knelt, smoothed silky fur. "Nobody home?"

The cat yawned, revealing two sharp incisors and a pink tongue.

I popped up, made a circuit of the living room. No dust. No muss. No casual disarray. One wall of bookshelves held biographies, books on bridge, and Book-of-the-Month club titles. On another wall were three framed Edward Hopper prints.

A small walnut desk sat in one corner. I found her checkbook in the right-hand drawer and a box of checks as well as stubs neatly bound with rubber bands. I hunted for an engagement calendar, found an address book. There was an entry for Irene Chatham. It was a link, but this was a small town. I needed more.

The bedroom yielded nothing of interest but a collection of family pictures in neat rows atop a bookcase and on a dresser. It was cheerful to see that the rather formal Mrs. Haskins was also a mother and grandmother. In a Christmas scene, her eyes soft, her smile beatific, she was reaching out to touch the dark curls of a chubby little girl.

The kitchen was immaculate. A neat white cardboard

bakery box was open. It held three dozen sugar cookies shaped like pumpkins with big chocolate eyes and curlicues of orange frosting. I edged one out, ate it neatly. I was turning to go when I saw the large wall calendar with notations in several squares. And yes, she'd marked this Saturday:

8 A.M. PICK UP TWILA, OKC
4–8 P.M. MADAME RUBY-ANN/SPOOK BASH

I understood the first entry only too well. Patricia had picked up a friend and gone up to Oklahoma City, probably for a couple of hours of shopping and lunch. The second entry gave me hope that she planned to return in time to attend St. Mildred's Spook Bash this afternoon. But who was Madame Ruby-Ann?

I planned to attend the Spook Bash. I wanted to see Bayroo's new friend. Now I had another excellent reason to be present. I was counting on Patricia Haskins telling me the name of someone who'd called Daryl or whom Daryl had called to set up a meeting at St. Mildred's.

I wondered if Chief Cobb had picked up on Patricia's careful reply when he'd asked whether anyone else might have known Daryl's destination . . .

CHAPTER 15

The chief sat at a circular table near his desk. He frowned, wrote swiftly on a legal pad. Folders surrounded him. A cordless telephone was within reach.

The chief's desk was pushed out from the wall and a bulky figure squatted behind the computer that had suffered unfortunate trauma last night. I was disappointed to see that the screen was still black. The oblong box next to the screen had been opened. The interior looked like so much honeycomb to me. I moved around the desk. Cords lay in a limp row on the floor.

The man staring at the computer shook his head. His orange ponytail swung back and forth. White stitching on the back of his blue work shirt read COMPUTER WHIZ. "Chief, you gotta know this had to be deliberate."

My heart sank.

A chair scraped. The chief came behind the desk. "Last night Sergeant Lewis found the light on. He saw an intruder."

"You don't say," Computer Whiz marveled. "How'd some joe break into the cop shop?"

Chief Cobb hunched his shoulders. "There wasn't a

break-in. No alarms sounded. The electric keypad on my office door didn't record an entry."

Computer Whiz rocked back on his heels. "So nobody came in but somebody came in. Did the cop get a good look?"

Chief Cobb folded his arms. "Sergeant Lewis thinks it was a woman."

A snicker. "He doesn't know one when he sees one?"

Chief Cobb was short in his answer. "All he saw was a witch's costume. When he came after her, she went out the window."

The repairman glanced toward the windows. "Second story, Chief. Was she was flying on a broomstick?"

"Whoever it was got away. Somehow." The chief, too, glanced at the windows. "Lewis is a good man, but he claims he was running toward her when a chair tripped him and he dropped his gun and the window slammed down. His gun's gone. We haven't found any trace of it. That's when he saw a flash and heard popping sounds and the computer went black."

"Somebody"—Computer Whiz pointed with an accusatory finger—"jammed this cord here and that cord there. Nobody ought to take out plugs and put them back in the PS2 ports when the monitor's up and running. It blew the fuses on the motherboard and the whole system crashed."

Cobb frowned. "Sergeant Lewis claims no one was near it."

Computer Whiz looked skeptical. "Maybe Sergeant Lewis imagined pops and crackles and somebody'd already done the deed. Or maybe it's like he said, he walks in and the system blows. In that case, invisible fairies must have been playing pin the tail on the poor damn computer. Take your pick, but somebody did it."

The chief looked morose. "Can you fix it?"

"Yeah." The repairman sounded cheerful. "It'll take a while."

Cobb's face wrinkled. "How long? I'm in the middle of a murder investigation." He pointed at the legal pad. "I'm having to write stuff out by hand."

Computer Whiz shrugged. "I've done all I can do today. Got to order some parts from Oklahoma City. When I get them, it'll be two days minimum. If all goes well."

Chief Cobb grunted, returned to his table. When the door closed behind Computer Whiz, Cobb blew out a spurt of air, scrawled on his pad:

Screwy stuff re Murdoch case

> *Victim's cell phone missing from the crime scene. Had it in my hand, something poked me in the rear, I dropped it. It has never been found despite thorough search.*
>
> *Anonymous call claimed murder weapon was on the back porch of the rectory. During search, golf balls thudded into a black trash bag full of cans. How did the golf balls get out of the bag? No one standing by bag.*
>
> *Tip received that preacher's wife got a red nightgown from victim at his cabin. Call made at three minutes after 8 p.m. Thursday from pay phone outside Shell station on Comanche. Cleaning lady Friday claimed she found a burned portion of a red silk nightgown in the fireplace. She picked it up and a woman screamed in the kitchen. The cleaning ladies fled. There was no trace of a nightgown when Det. Sgt. Price investigated. Nothing but ashes. Who was in the kitchen?*

Tip came in Friday from library that murder weapon was in the Pritchard mausoleum. Librarian in next cubicle looked over. Phone was in the air, slammed into receiver. Nobody there. Gun found as promised.

Fake police officer interviewed Joyce Talley, owner of the Green Door, Friday night. Impersonation discovered when Mrs. Talley called the police to insist Lily Mendoza had nothing to do with Murdoch murder. When contacted, Mendoza related she also was interviewed by a redheaded policewoman with a nameplate reading M. Loy. Described her as attractive redhead in her late twenties, about five feet four inches tall and slender. Corresponds to description given by Mrs. Talley.

I'd left rather a trail across Adelaide. Hopefully Officer Loy need not need appear again.

More screwy stuff possibly related to Murdoch case

Friday afternoon Det. Sgt. Price spoke to a woman on the back porch of the rectory. Said she was drop-dead gorgeous.

I remembered looking into slate-blue eyes . . . I shook myself back to the present.

Wore a wedding ring. Expensive clothes under one of those blue cover-ups church ladies use. Hair covered by a turban with a bunch of fruit on it. Wonder if she was a redhead? Gave her name as

Helen Troy. No Troys at St. Mildred's. No one of that
name is listed in any directory in the city or county.
Description: Late twenties, about five feet five inches
tall. Fair skin with a spattering of freckles.

I felt rather breathless. It didn't take a badge to see the
direction of Chief Cobb's thoughts. Who was the unknown
Mrs. Troy? Why was she cleaning the back porch of the
rectory? I was afraid I'd erected a signpost reading CRIME
SCENE.

Chief Cobb scrawled:

> *Intensify search for Troy.*
> *To-go sack taken from Lulu's Friday evening.*
> *Front door opened, sack sped down sidewalk,*
> *nobody there. However, cash left on the counter with*
> *the check. Order for M. Loy.*
> *Fake police officer M. Loy took custody of a*
> *black-and-tan dog from 817 Whitlock Street. Next-*
> *door neighbor called to commend police department*
> *on its new policy to rescue abused animals.*
> *Description of Loy corresponds to those given by*
> *Talley and Mendoza.*
> *Loy? Troy? Some meaning there?*
> *Computers blew Friday. Sgt. Lewis saw light on*
> *in my office, suspected intruder. Unlocked door,*
> *entered. Insists he surprised a witch at the computer*
> *who fled, climbing out of the window. He was*
> *tripped, gun disappeared, window slammed shut,*
> *then computer whined, popped, and flashed, screen*
> *went dark. Nobody was in the room.*

Cobb shook his head, flipped to a fresh page.

PERSONS OF INTEREST
1. *The Rev. William Abbott, rector St. Mildred's.*
   Quarreled with Murdoch Thursday morning.
   Refused to reveal reason for disagreement.
   Claimed privileged matter. Murdoch had called
   vestry meeting for Sunday afternoon to consider
   fiduciary irregularity. Motive: Possible financial
   wrongdoing. Opportunity: In church when crime
   likely occurred.
2. *Kathleen Abbott, rector's wife. Lied about reason*
   for visit to Murdoch cabin Wednesday

I drew in a sharp breath.

Cobb started. He looked around, stared at his closed door, frowned.

I edged away from his shoulder. The man had hearing like a lynx.

He resumed writing.

I returned, breathing delicately.

evening. Junior Warden Bud Schilling said Murdoch
was determined to see church secretary fired,
under no circumstances would have planned to
purchase a birthday gift for her. Motive: Unclear.
Cabin visit and phone call re red nightgown
suggest sexual liaison, but Murdoch was having
an affair with Cynthia Brown. No evidence exists
that Mrs. Abbott was involved with Murdoch.
Moreover, she appeared to dislike him. Possibly
she quarreled with him in defense of her husband,
but that doesn't explain the red nightgown.
Opportunity: Her whereabouts during critical
period unknown.

He reached for a file, flipped it open. He picked up his telephone, punched numbers. "Mrs. Abbott?" He listened. "Do you have a cell number for her?" He wrote quickly on the outside of the folder. "Thank you."

No doubt Bayroo had answered. I hoped the delivery of the cake had gone well.

Cobb clicked another number. "Mrs. Abbott? Chief Cobb. Where were you from five to seven Thursday evening?" He scrawled a thumb-size question mark on his pad. "Oh, at the rectory. Did you see anyone near the shed at the back of the property?"

I hoped Kathleen was keeping her cool.

"A witness observed you returning a wheelbarrow to the shed." He looked as predatory as a cat toying with a mouse.

I gasped. Aloud.

His head jerked every which way.

I didn't regret worrying him. Wasn't it against the law for a policeman to lie? Why, his very own notes made it clear he didn't know where Kathleen was when Daryl was shot.

He gripped the phone tighter. "You didn't mention that earlier."

What was Kathleen saying? It was time I went to the parish hall. If only I were in time . . .

The parish hall looked like a combination rummage sale and carnival. Huge posters announced:

ANNUAL SPOOK BASH
4–8 P.M. SATURDAY OCTOBER 29
ST. MILDRED'S PARISH PUMPKIN PARTY
ALL GOODS, SERVICES, AND ENTERTAINMENTS DONATED
PROCEEDS DESIGNATED FOR ADELAIDE FOOD BANK

Big fans in the corners of the room were tilted toward the ceiling, rippling orange and black streamers that dangled from oak beams. The wail of a winter wind moaned from the sound system. Black trash bags were taped to the windows, making the room dim. Cardboard skeletons with arms akimbo and one leg in a high kick were pinned on either side of each window. Decorated gourds, Thanksgiving centerpieces, pumpkin ceramics, assorted collectibles, homemade cakes, candies, breads, and jams filled trestle tables around the perimeter. Apples bobbed in large zinc pails. Cardboard signposts advertised FACE PAINTING, MADAME RUBY-ANN'S FANTASTIC FORTUNES, MYSTERIOUS MAZE, GHOST BUSTERS TENT, PUMPKIN PALETTE, and DINAH'S DEE-LICIOUS DINER.

Orange T-shirts with SPOOK BASH in topsy-turvy black letters identified volunteers. Teenagers arranged pumpkins and struggled with bales of hay. Voices, high and low, young and old, reverberated. ". . . over here, Pete, over here . . . be careful or it'll fall . . . put all the chocolate on one table . . . can't stand that noise . . . Suzie, those angel cards are precious!"

Kathleen stood near the maze made from stacked hay bales, clutching her cell phone. She looked as wary as a kayaker in a swamp teeming with alligators, but she sounded untroubled. "Oh, that. I never thought about mentioning it. I saw the wheelbarrow out in the yard and thought I'd better—"

I yanked the cell phone from her hand—"bring it in the house."

"In the house? You mean the shed." The chief sounded puzzled.

"Did you say Fred?" My voice was an excellent imitation of Kathleen, but that was easy, she sounded so much like my sister, Kitty. "It's awfully noisy here. I think I'm misunderstanding you." I held the phone up in the air as the wind noise reached a high pitch and a teenage girl shrieked, "Eeeek, there's a snake in the hay. Tommy said so."

"What's going on?" Cobb snapped.

I spoke loudly. "We're getting ready for the Spook Bash. It starts at four o'clock here in the parish hall. We have baked goods and hot dogs and chili and collectibles and games and a contest to paint faces on the pumpkins and—"

A little girl's piercing voice demanded, "Mama, Mama, look at the cell phone up in the air."

I glanced down. Curious brown eyes stared at the cell in my hand. Of course there was no hand visible. Drat.

Kathleen moved fast, placing her hand over mine.

I struggled to hear.

Chief Cobb interrupted. "Okay, Mrs. Abbott. I saw the posters when I was at the church this morning. But I want you to explain why you put the wheelbarrow in the shed Thursday evening."

I grabbed Kathleen's shoulder, pivoted her so that she was between me and the little girl who was tugging on her mother's T-shirt. "Wheelbarrow?" My voice rose in surprise. "What wheelbarrow?"

Kathleen tilted to one side, valiantly held up her hand, but there was a gap between it and the cell phone.

Chief Cobb was impatient. "The wheelbarrow that is kept in the rectory toolshed. You were observed returning it to the toolshed."

The little girl's voice rose. "Mama, that cell phone's up there by itself."

Her plump mother, chattering to an animated volunteer, reached down, swooped her up onto one hip. "Don't interrupt, Mindy."

I dropped down behind a bale of hay. "I don't know anything about a wheelbarrow." I combined innocence, amusement, and a hint of impatience. Myrna Loy was such a good influence. "The sexton takes care of all the lawn equipment and tools and he does a wonderful job. Someone's made a mistake. Certainly I had nothing to do with a wheelbarrow at any time. I only went out into the yard for a minute Thursday to get the teal arrow. I know people get rushed, but even a volunteer should be responsible. There it was, simply propped up by the back steps, and you know how uncertain the weather's been and I was right in the middle of dinner and scarcely had time but I dashed out to bring it inside—"

"Bring what inside?" He sounded confused.

"Why, I told you." I oozed patience. "The teal arrow. A donation for the collectible table. That's what I thought you were asking about. The teal arrow." I enunciated clearly.

"Teal arrow." He might have gnawed the words out of concrete.

"That's right." My tone was congratulatory. "Teal arrow. Just the prettiest shade of blue. Quite striking."

Cobb tried again. "I'm talking about the wheeeeeel bar-rrrrow."

"You'll have to ask the sexton. Perhaps he can help you."

The little girl's head poked above the hay. She peered down.

I swooped up, thrust the phone at Kathleen. I hissed in her ear. "Teal arrow. Keep it up. Invite him to the Bash. Find a teal arrow."

I settled in the chair across from the chief. I was relieved when he finally said a brusque good-bye to Kathleen. Obviously, she'd held her own and continued to talk about the teal arrow.

Chief Cobb clicked off the phone. He glared at his tablet, scrawled:

> *Admitted seeing wheelbarrow, then changed her story. Something about a teal arrow. Slippery as*

an eel. She's hiding something. That anonymous
phone call claimed the gun was on the back porch.
Something funny went on when I was searching the
porch. And a black cat lives there. Murdoch got
that dust and cat fur somewhere. Maybe it's time
to call the judge, see about a search warrant. But
the porch was cleaned! Who was the woman in the
turban? Who's running all over town pretending
to be an officer? It all ties up with the rectory.
Could Mrs. Abbott have found the body on the back
porch, used the wheelbarrow to move it? She isn't
big enough to handle the body by herself. Maybe
a friend helped her. Maybe her husband helped.
Opportunity: Yes.

   Judith Murdoch. Motive: Jealousy. Aware of
husband's infidelities. Originally claimed she went
to a movie, but has now admitted she was near
her husband's office as he left. She followed him
to church. Offered confession but cannot describe
actual crime scene or body. Fearful of son's
involvement (see below). Took gun from son's car,
claims she hid it in the backyard but the gun wasn't
there. Opportunity: Yes.

   Kirby Murdoch. Motive: Anger over father's
treatment of girlfriend. Admits target practice
with a .22 pistol that afternoon, could not produce
gun. Followed his father's car as he left his office.
Also confessed. Couldn't accurately describe crime
scene or body. Possibly deliberate misinformation.
Opportunity: Yes.

   Lily Mendoza. Motive: Remove obstacle to her
relationship to Kirby Murdoch. Never known to
have met the victim. No expertise with guns, but
could have taken .22 from Kirby's trunk. Claims to

*have been home alone during critical period. No
corroboration. Opportunity: Yes.*

*Cynthia Brown. Refused to confirm relationship
with victim although she admits trying to contact him
after work Thursday. Claimed he drove away and
she went home. Opportunity: Yes.*

*Walter Carey. Insisted breakup of partnership
with victim was Carey's decision. Knowledgeable
business leaders indicated Carey has been in
financial distress for several years, and certainly
the termination of the partnership wasn't positive
for him. Obvious hard feelings as the breakup was
sudden and Murdoch immediately replaced the
locks at his office. Carey said he was working late
Thursday. No corroboration. Opportunity: Yes.*

*Isaac Franklin, sexton St. Mildred's. Motive:
Victim confronted him over removing food from the
church pantry for the needy. Sexton supported by
rector. Sexton's report on wheelbarrow led to search
of cemetery and church grounds. Discovery of tracks
suggests murder occurred at or near the church.
Use of the wheelbarrow likely would not have been
otherwise discovered, which supports sexton's lack
of involvement. Arrived home at a quarter after five.
Arrived at daughter and son-in-law's home at six.
Confirmed by wife and daughter and son-in-law.
Collusion unlikely. Opportunity: Unlikely.*

Cobb frowned at the tablet. He pushed away from the
table, wandered to his desk, his gaze abstracted. He opened
the drawer, found a sack of M&M's, poured out a half dozen,
tossed them in his mouth. He glanced at the wall clock, gave
an abrupt nod. He punched his intercom. "Hal, if you've got
a minute, I'd like to see you."

"Be right there."

The chief punched another button. "Anita, I can use your help if you're free."

"I'm on my way."

He was standing with his back to the table, munching M&M's.

I resisted the impulse to filch a few. I picked up his pen, delicately loosened a clean sheet from the table. The chief stood with his back to me. I printed in block letters:

IRENE CHATHAM STOLE FROM THE COLLECTION PLATE AT ST. MILDRED'S. MURDOCH HAD PROOF. HE INSISTED FATHER ABBOTT CALL THE POLICE. FATHER ABBOTT REFUSED. THEY QUARRELED.

The chief's door opened. I wrote a little faster:

THIS IS THE FIDUCIARY MATTER MURDOCH INTENDED TO REPORT TO THE VESTRY.

"Chief." Anita's voice was puzzled. "How's that pencil moving by itself?" She stood in the doorway, one hand pointing.

I eased the pencil to the table.

Cobb whirled, approached the table. He picked up the pencil, shrugged. "Optical illusion, I guess. Anyway—" His gaze stopped. He reached for the sheet with the printed message. "Where'd this come from?"

Anita came up beside him. "One of the folders?" She waved at the laden tabletop. She looked fresher today, less tired.

"I know everything in every folder." He thrust the sheet at her. "Who did this?"

She read, shook her head. "I suppose it was part of someone's notes."

"Block letters?" He scrabbled through the nearest folder, pushed it aside, checked one after another.

Anita spread out her hands. "Somebody wrote it."

He closed the last folder. "Yeah. Somebody did." He stared at the sheet, his face perplexed. "I would have sworn this wasn't in any of the files."

The door opened. Detective Sergeant Price hurried to the table. He moved fast, as if there was much to do and too little time.

The chief held out the sheet. "Take a look at this, Hal. Do you know anything about it?"

Hal read it, raised an eyebrow, returned the sheet. "News to me."

Chief Cobb slapped it on the table. "There are too many weird things about this case. But"—he jabbed a finger at the sheet—"wherever it came from, we have to check it out. It's too specific to ignore. Anyway, I can use some help this afternoon."

He described his conversation with Kathleen Abbott. "She claims she misunderstood, didn't mean a wheelbarrow, that she went out into the backyard to retrieve some donation for the collectible sale at the church. It's part of the big Halloween bash that starts"—he checked his watch—"in about fifteen minutes. I want us to show up. I want people to get the idea we're there to look things over. I'm going to track down the vestry members, see what I can find out about the padre and the vestry. And talk to this"—he tapped the printed message—"Irene Chatham. Hal, find Mrs. Abbott and insist she show you the teal arrow. Anita, check with some of the church ladies, see if you can get a get a line on this Helen Troy. Hal, describe her."

"Nefertiti."

The chief blinked. Officer Leland looked puzzled.

I kissed my fingers, blew a kiss toward my favorite police detective.

A slight flush pinked his cheeks. "Classic bone structure. She's a knockout. It shouldn't be hard to find her."

"Shouldn't be if she's such a hottie." The chief looked amused. "But nobody's pointed the way yet."

Hal looked thoughtful. "Not the kind of gal you see at the grocery. The kind of woman who'd look good in a sleek black dress and I think she had a helluva figure from the look of her legs. She was wearing fancy gray heels."

I nodded with approval.   •

Officer Leland was intrigued. "Of course churchwomen will do anything to help, but she doesn't sound like someone who spends much time cleaning porches. So I wonder what was so important about the porch."

I looked at her sharply, realized her eyes were shrewd and intelligent. She'd figured out what mattered.

The chief was looking at her with admiration. "That's the point. She cleaned the porch. Maybe she knew there'd been a body there." He suddenly looked formidable. "I want to know if she was a redhead. Maybe she likes to impersonate the police. Keep your eyes open for a good-looking redhead."

In the church parking lot, Kathleen stood outside a big plastic contraption with clear plastic panes on all sides. The green top was shaped like a dragon. A machine blew air to keep it inflated. Inside, a half-dozen boys yelled and rolled and jumped on the bouncy plastic bottom.

Kathleen lifted a flap and yelled, "No kicking. Absolutely no kicking or wrestling. Two more minutes and it's the girls' turn."

I had to speak loudly for her to hear, but the boys were

making so much commotion I didn't worry about being overheard. "What is this? What's going on?"

Kathleen lifted a finger to indicate she'd be with me ASAP, then turned her thumb toward the contraption, yelled, "Jupiter Jump, only three tickets. Girls next for the Jupiter Jump."

I suppose she thought that was a sufficient explanation. I wished I had time to go inside and bounce. What fun! However . . . I shrieked into her ear. "The police are coming. We have to find a teal arrow. They'll want to see it."

Suddenly the shouts inside the inflated plastic plaything turned angry. ". . . off my back . . . stop that . . . gonna shove you . . ."

Kathleen lifted the flap at the entrance, poked her head inside. "That's enough, boys. Time's up. Out. Out. Out."

Boys ranging from six to midteens tumbled through the opening. The last one was scarcely gone before the girls clambered inside.

I tugged on Kathleen's jacket sleeve. "A teal arrow. You've got to find one. The police will be here any minute and you have to show it to them."

A sudden screech and a burst of tears sounded inside the jump. Kathleen held up a hand, once again pulled aside the flap. "Abigail, don't pull Teentsy's braids. Let go. Pronto. Abigail, you get in that corner. Teentsy, come bounce by the door."

When a semblance of harmony was restored, she gripped the edge of the opening flap, looked around.

"I'm over here. Come on, Kathleen, we don't have much time."

"I'm all alone. Sally Baker didn't show up. I can't leave the jump. I'll tell them—"

I gripped her arm. "Don't tell them anything. I'll take care of it."

*   *   *

I zipped to the rectory. A teal arrow. I closed my eyes. Perhaps I might look in the attic and find some arrows. Our vigorous rector had been quite an archer. A piece of wood and I would be in business.

I opened my eyes. Lying on the kitchen table was a two-by-four-foot weathered wooden plaque. Mounted on it was an arrow. The shaft was a bright teal.

I clapped my hands. "Thank you, Wiggins." I looked out the window. Three police cars turned into the far end of the church lot. Not a minute too soon, but miracles always seem to happen that way.

I looked critically at the plaque. Wiggins had done a fine job, but I felt it needed a tad more pizzazz. I rummaged in the craft drawer and found a large gold sticker that had an official appearance. I added it beneath the arrow. I used a red marker and inscribed in looping script:

Authenticated By Hackworth Antiques, St. Louis, Mo

In the same ornate handwriting, I wrote on a plain sheet of stationery:

Genuine arrow once owned by Daniel Boone

For good measure, I added a seal to the bottom of the sheet. I turned the board over, taped the sheet to the back.

As I started down the back steps of the rectory, I realized, with an unhappy memory of the upright dog leash, that the arrow could not arrive apparently self-propelled. I'd half appeared when I looked down and saw slate-blue trousers. This was no time for Officer Loy to surface. A quick transformation into my purple velour and I hurried toward Kathleen.

"Mrs. Abbott?" I looked at Kathleen inquiringly.

Kathleen looked past me and gasped.

I turned and came face-to-face with Detective Sergeant Price. It was too late to wish for a scarf.

We looked at each other across time and space. I saw strength and honor in his eyes and more.

I don't know what he saw in mine.

I took a step back and gave him an impersonal smile, a smile that I hoped was cool and distant and yanked up the drawbridge between us. I rushed into speech. "Isn't this a lovely event? I can't resist church sales. You never know what you are going to find." I swerved toward Kathleen. "Hello, Mrs. Abbott. You probably don't remember me. Helen Troy. I've just transferred my membership from All Souls' in the city. I'm making friends with some of the church ladies and I was so glad to help out yesterday with a little sweeping at the rectory, but you weren't home. I found this adorable teal arrow at the collectible sale and they said you could tell me about this donation. Is it really"— my voice was hushed— "an authentic Daniel Boone arrow?" I turned the board over, handed it to her.

Sergeant Price came a step nearer, staring at my undeniably flaming-red hair.

Kathleen balanced the board in one hand, then the other, looked at the front, peered at the back. Now it held her fingerprints.

I was pleased with myself. I felt as buoyed as a poker player drawing an inside straight. That moment of pride lasted until I looked across the church parking lot and saw Chief Cobb heading toward us. Purposefully.

Kathleen sounded buoyant. "Teal arrow. Yes, indeed, here's the teal arrow. We certainly hope it's genuine, but I don't know who donated it. Someone left it propped up against the back steps of the rectory Thursday night."

"I see. Perhaps I'll not take a chance on it, then. But thank you." I began to back away.

Detective Sergeant Price moved toward me. "Mrs. Troy, I'd like to speak with you for a moment."

"Oh, my son Billy's waiting for me at the fortune-teller booth. I'm really in quite a hurry." I swung on my heel and headed for the church. I sped in front of a large family. Red-heads.

"Wait. Wait, please." The detective dodged around a group of Cub Scouts.

I used a group of teenage boys as a screen and ran for the church. On the church steps, I risked a backward glance.

Detective Sergeant Price stood by Chief Cobb and Officer Leland, pointing, then they started toward me, moving fast.

I yanked open the door, plunged inside. The hallway was crowded. A half-dozen children giggled and pushed as they hurried toward the parish hall.

The door opened. I saw Officer Leland's slate-blue sleeve.

I disappeared.

CHAPTER 16

Chief Cobb gestured up the hallway. "Let's find her. I'll check the main hall, you two take a look in classrooms, offices." He raised his voice. "Coming through." The authoritative tone parted the mass of children.

I hovered near the ceiling of the parish hall. The lights had been dimmed on the north end. Flashing orange, red, green, and yellow spots played across the ceiling and walls. Somber organ music evoked specters tiptoeing through a graveyard. Occasional high screams and banshee wails shrilled from a tent. A crooked sign on the front of the tent identified it as SPOOK HOUSE. ENTER AT YOUR PERIL. 5 TICKETS.

Children of all ages painted pumpkins lined up on trestle tables. Thumpy music blared from one corner where sheet-draped children bent and swayed and hopped and chanted in an odd combination of dance and calisthenics. Lights blazed over a small stage at the south end of the hall. Almost everyone was in costume except for Sunday school volunteers in orange T-shirts.

A long line stretched from Madame Ruby-Ann's tent out into the hall. I dropped inside. An orange turban, dance-hall makeup, and flaming cerise robe transformed Patricia

Haskins into a fortune-teller. She bent near a crystal ball, touching it lightly with her fingers. Eyes closed, she crooned to a wide-eyed teenage girl in a peasant costume, "Beware the dark stranger. Turn aside, reach out to the blond Galahad. The familiar may seem ordinary, boring, pedestrian, but the crystal never lies. Your future belongs to a young man whom you've overlooked. He awaits you." A shudder. Her hands fell away. She pressed a palm to her head. "The crystal demands much. Make way for my next appointment."

The girl looked dreamy. "Is the blond boy's name Jeff?"

Mrs. Haskins picked up a small fan, opened it, hiding her face. "Jeff, Jeff, I think it is Jeff."

I materialized in my Officer Loy uniform directly behind the girl. "Did I hear you say you were ready for me?"

"Oooohh. Jeff." The girl bounced to her feet. "I can't wait to tell Amy."

"Go the most direct way," I urged. "Duck out over here." I held up a side of the tent.

Madame Ruby-Ann frowned. "Wait a minute. Why send her out that way?"

I'd learned a thing or two when I worked in the mayor's office. If a question isn't welcome, ignore it. "Mrs. Haskins, I'll be quick and to the point. You weren't altogether frank when you spoke to Chief Cobb yesterday. You are, in fact, withholding important information." I stalked, which was difficult in the limited space, to the card table and bent down to place my hands on either side. "Someone contacted Mr. Murdoch just before he left his office. Who was it?"

Fingers laden with costume jewelry toyed with the fringe on the brocade cloth covering the card table. "That call didn't have anything to do with what happened to him. Irene Chatham's in the Altar Guild and she probably called to check something with him."

"Did you overhear their conversation?"

"Only a little. I opened Mr. Murdoch's door and heard him say, 'I'll be at the church in fifteen minutes.' So I suppose"—Patricia's tone was defiant—"that even though technically it's true that Irene was aware he was going to the church, she could never be a suspect. She's terrified of guns. Anyway, you can go ask. She's in charge of the hip-hop ghosts."

"Hip-hop?" This was new to me.

"Kids love hip-hop. The nice kind," she explained hastily. "No dirty lyrics or gang stuff. They do a musical review at the far end of the parish hall. They're dressed in sheets with white paint on their faces. They have a great time."

I ducked out of the tent.

A growl greeted me. "No more appearing, Bailey Ruth. I have reached the limits of my patience."

A volunteer in an orange T-shirt stared at me. "What did you say, Officer?"

No one stood near us and I knew she was trying to locate that deep, undoubtedly masculine, and obviously irate voice.

Wiggins might soon embroil us in more public notice than he would wish.

"I heard that, too. An echo, I suppose." Wiggins could mull that over. "Perhaps sound bounces off the ceiling." I looked up. "Heavens, aren't the chandeliers interesting? They're very unusual. Different colors. I particularly like the red one." I pointed up to the chandelier in the center of the parish hall.

The volunteer slowly nodded, managed an uncertain smile, and moved away.

As soon as she walked around the fortune-teller's tent, I disappeared and wafted up to the red chandelier. I perched on the rim. It was easier than it sounds. Three massive wooden chandeliers shaped like wheels hung from the parish-hall ceiling. There was plenty of room to sit on the outer rim.

I felt a sudden lurch.

"Bailey Ruth." Wiggins was adamant. "No more appearing. It simply won't do. Now, I'll admit that was good work with the dog and I understand you felt it essential to speak with several people. But, enough is enough."

It was time for an end around, as Bobby Mac always advised when nose to nose in an altercation. "Wiggins, look at the children. Isn't that adorable?"

Irene Chatham, her lugubrious face transformed by a bright smile, energetically led a troupe of sheet-clad, starkly white-faced kids in an energetic—and to me most peculiar—performance. She, too, wore a sheet, which flapped as she moved. Madame Ruby-Ann called it a dance, so I supposed it was.

Irene lunged to her right, one arm extended, and chanted in concert with the dancers, "Shake a leg," a lunge to the left. "Watch the ghosties flop. Witches' brew can't get you," a lunge to the right. "Shake a leg. Halloween's hot, school's not. Hey baby, hey baby, hey baby . . ."

"My goodness, how active," Wiggins observed. "I suppose you're waiting for a moment to confer with Kathleen. Remember, Bailey Ruth, work quietly in the background."

The chandelier rocked as he left.

I'd made no reply to Wiggins. I could not later be accused of perfidy because I knew full well I would appear again. I was determined to confront Irene. At the moment the presence of Chief Cobb kept me aloft. He was in the center of the room, face grim, looking, looking, looking.

I drifted down, stood a few feet from Irene.

Chief Cobb gave a final searching glance at this end of the hall. He shook his head, moved toward Detective Sergeant Price, who stood near the pumpkin-painting station. The hip-hop dance concluded and the ghosties ran toward a lemonade stand. Irene turned off the music. She swiped at her flushed face.

I dropped down beside her, hoped I was hidden by the milling crowd, and appeared in my French-blue uniform, fresh, crisp, and stern-faced. "Mrs. Chatham."

Irene's mouth opened, rounded in an "oh" of dismay. She took a step back, one hand grasping at her neck, panic flickering in her brown eyes.

I folded my arms, hoped my posture was intimidating. "From information received, we are aware that you spoke with Mr. Murdoch shortly before five P.M. Thursday. You met him at the church. It will be necessary for you to describe what happened or I'll have to take you to the station." My eyes were cold, my voice gruff.

She gulped, desperate as a goldfish out of water.

I lifted one hand to shake a finger at her, then stopped, feeling my own sweep of panic. Chief Cobb came around a corner of the Mysterious Maze and saw me. His face twisted in a scowl. He plunged into the swirling crowd, elbowing his way.

"Mrs. Chatham, you were seen. What happened?" I wished I could grip her scrawny shoulders and shake.

"I didn't meet him. I swear I didn't. When I saw—" She stopped, clapped shaking fingers to her mouth. "I didn't stay. I don't know anything and I've got to get the next number started." She whirled around, shouted, "Middle school hip-hop. Time."

Chief Cobb was momentarily slowed by two burly high school boys maneuvering a dolly piled with cases of Cokes.

I had only seconds left. "What did you see? Quick?"

She flung out her arm, shooing the gathering ghosties into place. She bent, touched a button, and the throbbing beat blared. The children began their gyrations, shouting, "Boy say, boy say, boy . . ."

Chief Cobb loomed just past Irene, shouted, "Stop there, lady. I got you now."

What could I do? An abrupt disappearance violated Precept One: Avoid public notice. And possibly Precept Five: Do not succumb to the temptation to confound those who appear to oppose you. However, I had no choice.

Chief Cobb ducked around a cotton-candy machine, hand outstretched.

I disappeared.

I didn't move fast enough to evade Wiggins's clipped order. "The chandelier."

I sat on the chandelier and felt a bump as Wiggins joined me.

Below us, the chief grasped at air. His face creased in astonishment. His big head jerked from one side to the other, his eyes seeking an answer. There was an empty circle where I'd stood and talked to Irene. Irene, eyes huge, trembled, still mouthing in a hoarse whisper, ". . . brew can't get you . . ."

Cobb plunged nearer, glared down at her.

She gasped.

"Where is she?" he shouted over the music.

She looked back and forth. "Who?"

"That . . ." He swallowed, forced out the words. "That cop. That redheaded cop."

"I don't know." Her tone was numb. "She was here and she went away."

Cobb's hands clenched. "There isn't any place to go."

The beat continued and the ghosties pranced. ". . . hey say, hey say, watch the ghosties flop . . ."

Irene blinked. "Maybe she went behind the cotton-candy machine."

Cobb took a few steps, peered behind the churning froth

of pink sugar. Impatiently, he strode back. "What did she talk to you about?"

"I told her I didn't know anything about anything." Irene's voice rose. "She threatened me, said she'd take me to the police station, and here I am, trying to help out at the church." Her voice wavered in a sob. "I told her I was busy and couldn't talk now."

Cobb made a growl of frustration in his throat. "That woman's going to jail just as soon as I get my hands on her. Impersonating a police officer is a serious crime."

"Impersonating . . ." Irene had her goldfish look, eyes huge, mouth open.

"If she comes around again, call us." Cobb frowned. "Who are you, ma'am?"

Irene murmured, "Chatham. Irene Chatham."

His question came hard and fast. "Are you the one Daryl Murdoch accused of stealing from the collection plate?"

She grasped at her throat, eyes bulging. "That was a mistake. Absolutely a mistake. I just needed to make change. There's not a word of truth to it." Her lips folded in a tight line.

He was unimpressed. "When did the incident occur?"

Her face was mulish. "There was no incident."

Cobb's eyes narrowed. "Did Murdoch take his accusation to Father Abbott?"

She stared at him wide-eyed. "I wouldn't have any knowledge about conversations between Mr. Murdoch and Father Bill."

"That's not an answer." His look was scathing. "Are you the one Abbott's protecting?"

Her hands clenched. "Ask Father Abbott."

I was furious. She knew Father Bill would protect her.

Cobb stared at Irene. "Did that redheaded woman ask you about stealing?"

Irene's eyes flickered away. "I didn't understand what she wanted, but she was unpleasant. Now you say she's a fake. The police department shouldn't let people go around pretending they are officers and acting rudely."

His face was grim. "I'll be back in touch, Mrs. Chatham." He turned on his heel, began a slow, measured survey of the hall.

I wasn't done with Irene Chatham. She might think she'd seen the last of me, but she hadn't. We'd have a tête-à-tête she wouldn't forget as soon as she left the parish hall. If, of course, I managed to elude Wiggins.

Now the rumble was deep and full-throated. "Bailey Ruth, I've reached the end of my patience. The Rescue Express is en route. You will board shortly."

I held tight to the rim. "No."

"No?" He was dumbfounded.

Was I the first emissary to mutiny? Was Purgatory my destination? I took a deep breath, tried to keep my voice steady. "I've not finished my job. And I have to say"—I felt the sting of tears down my cheeks and my voice wobbled—"I've never had anyone treat me this way. Give me a chance, Wiggins. Leave me alone. Stop looking over my shoulder every minute. I can handle everything by myself."

"Oh." He sounded chagrined, a kindhearted man daunted by the sniffles that indicate tears. "Possibly I have been too much here. After all, it's your responsibility. Very well. Do your best." He didn't sound as if he had the faintest hope that I would manage with any success.

The chandelier swung.

I wiped my cheeks and felt liberated. No more Wiggins looking over my shoulder, frowning and grumping and harrumphing. I would be in charge. I would do very well by myself, thank you very much.

A drumroll sounded, *da-dum, da-da, da-dum, da-da, da-dum*. A trumpet blew. Lights blinked on and off.

At the base of the steps to the small stage, Marie Antoinette was impatiently adjusting a white-gold wig. A pirate—oh, it was Bayroo!—waved a sword aloft in time with the drums. She looked eager, excited, and, to Auntie Grand, absolutely lovely, Titian hair gleaming, fine features alive with delight. A sandy-haired boy in a blue pullover sweater and faded jeans grinned at her. Freckles splashed his angular face. He gave a thumbs-up. A towheaded Robin Hood thudded up the steps.

Father Bill joined Robin Hood on the stage. For once, Father Bill didn't look pressed or weary. His smile was bright and glad and proud.

From the audience, a peasant girl yelled, "Go, Jeffie."

Robin Hood flapped a big hand. He went to the mike, thunked it. "Sound on?" His voice reverberated. "Welcome to St. Mildred's annual Spook Bash."

The drummer pounded in a frenzy. Cheers rose.

Robin Hood grinned. "Thanks for coming and supporting the youth group outreach to Adelaide. I'm Jeff Jameson, youth group senior high president. We'll begin our program with a prayer from Father Bill."

Father Bill shook Jeff's hand, then took the mike. He bowed his head and prayed in thanksgiving for the youth group and their hard work to raise money for the food pantry. Before he handed the mike back to Jeff, Father Bill grinned at the revelers. "How about a cheer for the youth group?"

The roar from the audience was almost equal to the welcome given to Adelaide's Bobcats when they took the field on a Friday night.

Jeff took the mike. "Thanks, everyone. We've worked hard, but it's been so much fun and now we have a wonderful turnout, so all the effort was worthwhile. This year's Bash offers more fun and prizes and scary thrills than ever before. Most amazingly, we have a very special guest who's come to help us make this the best Spook Bash ever. Everybody please welcome Travis Calhoun."

The lanky boy in jeans reached the platform, one hand held high in greeting.

Girls squealed and hugged one another. It reminded me of the bobby-soxer days when teenage girls swooned over Frank Sinatra.

Robin Hood gestured toward the trestle tables laden with pumpkins. "Travis has agreed to judge the painted-pumpkin faces and present the awards. He's in Adelaide to visit his aunt and there's a special story behind his appearance here. Lucinda Wilkie, middle school president, wants to tell us how she and Bayroo Abbott met Travis and invited him to join our party. Come on up, Lucinda." He clapped. "And Bayroo."

Marie Antoinette bustled onstage. Bayroo followed, but she looked surprised. She glanced from Robin Hood to Marie, a frown tugging at her face.

Marie Antoinette righted her wig, pushed her glasses higher on her nose, and stepped to the mike. "Everybody in the world knows Travis Calhoun—"

Lucinda was guilty of exaggeration. I'd never heard his name until she and Bayroo arrived on the rectory porch Thursday evening. Of course I had to remember that I was *in* the world, not *of* the world.

"—who stars in *Show Me the Way,* Emmy Award-winning TV series now in its third season. Travis has the lead in a feature film, *Gotcha Covered,* to be released in November. He plays the role of a teenager who has to turn detective when his mom, a bank president, is kidnapped during a holdup. He's here this afternoon to spend time with us and we want to thank Bayroo Abbott, who made this possible. Bayroo heard at Safeway that Travis was in town to visit his aunt and she wanted him to know we'd love to have him at the Spook Bash. His aunt lives across from the entrance to the nature preserve." Lucinda pointed vaguely to her right. "Anyway, it was Thursday and just getting dark and kind of a spooky night." She leaned close to the mike. Her wig tilted. She pushed it upright. "We decided we'd wait at each end of the block so we'd know when Travis got home and then we'd go up and introduce ourselves. There's a busy parking lot next to the house and Bayroo wasn't sure she'd see him because of cars coming in and out. She realized she'd have a better look at the house if she waited in the nature preserve."

Bayroo reached out, tugged at Lucinda's puffy sleeve.

Lucinda shook her off, increased her volume. "Bayroo's trying to hush me. Her folks told us never to go in the preserve by ourselves and of course we don't, but this was a special exception for a very good cause and it's brought more people here today than ever before and that means we are raising more money for the Adelaide food pantry for the homeless. But"—her tone was breathless—"Bayroo had a really scary time. She heard leaves crackling and somebody was walking through the woods not too far from her and she just about had a heart attack. She hunkered down behind the stone pillar at the entrance. A little later, she heard sounds again and she was really glad when she saw Travis getting out of the car and she dashed across the street and said hello and said we all think he's swell and we'd like to make Adelaide fun for him while he was here and he was so nice and he invited us in and we met his aunt and we told him about the Bash and here he is. Travis Calhoun!" She held out the mike.

He moved with the ease of a seasoned performer, flashed

a good-humored smile. He gestured for Bayroo to join him. "Sounds like you could star in a Nancy Drew film."

Bayroo's face was as red as her hair. She glanced uneasily around the hall. "It didn't amount to anything. Lucinda's making up a good Halloween story."

Travis held the mike down to pick up the sound of his shoes as he stealthily slid them on the flooring, lifted it again. "Footsteps of doom." His voice was sepulchral. He intoned, "Bayroo Abbott, what frightful denizens of darkness dwell within the haunted preserve?"

Bayroo looked uncomfortable. "Honestly, we never go in the preserve alone."

I suspected she was hoping to avoid searching questions from Kathleen and Father Bill.

She managed a bright smile. "Sure, it was scary, but as soon as I saw the car, I knew everything was all right. Anyway, nobody cares about that. Everybody wants to know who the winners are." She picked up a burlap sack. "We have them right here." She handed an embossed diploma-size sheet to Travis.

Travis held it up in the air for all to see. "Neat, isn't it? Everybody who painted a pumpkin face gets one. You know, that's nice." He was suddenly serious. "It gets pretty old to see kids try their hearts out and not get any notice. I'd like to congratulate the Pumpkin Patch committee for making everybody a winner." He looked at Bayroo. "And for making me feel like a winner here in Adelaide, where I didn't know a soul, and now I feel like I belong." He swung back to the audience. "You know what Bayroo did?" He waved to encourage the audience's questions.

"Hey, what?" "Did she scare up a ghost in the preserve?" "Bet she gave you a Bobcat T-shirt."

Travis shook his head. "I'd like to have a T-shirt. But this was even better. She baked me a birthday cake, my favorite,

white with chocolate icing, and she brought it over and gave
it to me this morning and I've already eaten half of it. It's the
first homemade birthday cake I've ever had."

Oh, that dear boy. Living in a mansion may be fine and
fun. Living in a loving family is better than a mansion any
day.

"So"—he turned his hands up—"when she asked if I'd
mind judging the contest, I said sure. I had a blast looking at
the pumpkin faces. All of them were great. We have prizes
for everything from the meanest face to the sweetest, the
scariest to the friendliest, the happiest to the grumpiest. As
your name is called, please pick up your pumpkin and bring
it to the stage to receive your award. Our first award goes to
Emily Howie for . . ."

A sweet-faced little girl carried a dainty pumpkin toward
the stage.

Travis continued to call out prizewinners. Bayroo slipped
down the steps, looking relieved to be out of the spotlight.

I surveyed the hall, spotted Chief Cobb in the doorway, face somber, eyes still scanning the crowd. While I'd
watched the presentation on the stage, the hip-hoppers had
disbanded. Irene Chatham was nowhere to be seen.

I zoomed back and forth, seeking Irene. Kathleen was
working fast at the cash desk for the collectibles. Father Bill
stood in an alcove, arms folded, head bent, as he listened to
a sharp-featured woman who gazed up at him searchingly.
Walter Carey, his face gentle, knelt to listen as a dark-haired
elf whispered in his ear. Isaac Franklin helped an old lady
with a cane as she tapped toward the bake sale.

I found Irene in a far corner that had been turned into a
temporary old-fashioned diner. She sat at a table with several other women, sipping a Coke, listening intently.

I swooped down, caught fragments of conversation:

"They say Father Bill's had to talk to the police several

times. Why do you suppose?" The plump woman's bright brown eyes darted about the parish hall.

A lean blonde with a horsey face was adamant. "There's nothing to it. Apparently Father Bill happened to be in his office around the time Daryl was killed."

"What was Daryl doing"—the voice was freighted with innuendo—"in the cemetery?"

The blonde smothered a giggle. "Maybe Judith faked a call from his current mistress, hid behind a tombstone, and blew him away. That's what I would have done. I can't imagine why she's . . ."

I retreated to the nearest chandelier, intent upon keeping Irene in view. It was a relief to know the general populace had no inkling that Kathleen and Father Bill were high on Chief Cobb's suspect list. I was sure the women below had heard everything generally known in Adelaide about Daryl's murder and the investigation. But Kathleen and Bill faced more and harder scrutiny from Chief Cobb.

I'd tried to deflect the chief with the block-letter note implicating Irene. I felt sure he'd follow up on that inquiry, but Irene's bland response and refusal to admit to wrongdoing would likely protect her.

I had to find a way to inform the chief what I now knew for fact. Irene had been aware that Daryl was going to the church and she'd sped recklessly from her driveway at shortly before five o'clock.

What were the odds she'd driven straight to the church? I felt it in my bones. When I had bones. But . . .

I stared down. Irene listened, her gaze darting from face to face. She looked complacent. There was no trace of her earlier panic when I'd confronted her. She nibbled at a Baby Ruth. No one ever appeared less murderous. She'd removed her hip-hop sheet. Her green print dress had seen better days, as had her limp brown cardigan. She was frowsy, down-at-heels, possibly sinking into marginal poverty. But murderous?

A desperate creature can be driven to desperate measures.

I wondered if Chief Cobb understood the enormity of her situation. She had to have money to fund her gambling. Daryl threatened what had likely been a steady source of cash. Perhaps even worse, he threatened her respectability, Irene Chatham, member of the Altar Guild, churchwoman in good standing.

Men have surely been killed for less.

Irene licked a dangling bit of chocolate and peanut from one finger.

Had this woman stood in the flower bed Wednesday evening peering into Daryl's cabin? Had she seen Kathleen fling the red nightgown into the fire and coolly plotted a murder on the rectory back porch? Had she met Daryl at the church Thursday evening and marched him to his date with death? Had she called the Crime Stoppers line and said the murder weapon was on the back porch? On Friday, had she called again to describe the red nightgown? Were her stubborn denials of theft the product of lucky stupidity or cunning dissembling?

Irene? I moved impatiently. The chandelier began to swing. I oozed away.

The horsey woman glanced up. "The chandelier—"

I put out a hand, stopped it.

She blinked, shook her head.

The dark-eyed woman said slowly, "It looked like someone gave it a push, then reached out and stopped it. Some spooky things have been happening around the church. That chandelier shouldn't have moved. And did you hear about the cell phone Virginia Merritt saw up in the air Thursday night in the church parking lot?"

"Thursday night! That's when Daryl was shot in the cemetery. I heard his cell phone's missing. Do you suppose . . ."

The women hunched nearer the table, talking fast.

I repaired to the chandelier. I hoped the church wasn't in serious danger of achieving a reputation as a haunted place. However, a ghost has to do what a ghost has to do. Despite my ups and downs, I'd accomplished quite a bit. I knew more than anyone about Daryl Murdoch's murder, yet I couldn't name the murderer. Chief Cobb may have learned some facts to which I wasn't privy, but not many, and surely I knew everything that mattered.

I knew Kathleen and Father Bill were innocent.

I knew the true suspects and their motives:

Judith Murdoch. She'd set out to confront her husband over his latest mistress. Had she really turned away at the church?

Kirby Murdoch. He was estranged from his father because of Lily Mendoza and furious about her job loss. His .22 pistol had been shot that day. During target practice, he said. When he saw his mother's car, had he turned away, driven to Lily's? Wouldn't he have been more likely to follow? Perhaps his mother had ended up at the church to confront Daryl. Or perhaps Judith turned away but Kirby followed his father.

Irene Chatham. Daryl was threatening to expose her as a thief.

Cynthia Brown. Was her near suicide the product of despair? Or guilt?

Walter Carey. He had motive and to spare. He certainly had broken into the Murdoch house to get the keys to Daryl's office. He would be ruined if the truth ever came out.

Isaac Franklin. Was an insult to his pride—Daryl treating him with disrespect over the groceries—reason enough to kill?

It had to be one of them but—

A fire alarm shrilled. The undulating shriek blared, high, harsh, shocking.

The lights went out.

ries and shouts rose. "Jan, where are you?" "Wait for me." "Get out, everybody, get out." "Paul, find Buddy, I've got Leila." "Don't push, please."

"Quiet." Father Bill's shout was commanding. He was on the platform. "Evacuate in an orderly manner. Form lines."

The black trash bags covering the farthest window were yanked down and light spilled inside. The next window was uncovered.

Father Bill called, "Good work, Jeff."

"Travis and I will get the bags down." Jeff was breathless.

"That's enough light. You and Travis help the children get out." Father Bill pointed toward the doors. It was possible to see, if dimly.

Chief Cobb's deep voice boomed from the south door. "Police Chief Cobb here. Remain calm. Everything's under control. Take your time. We're going to get everyone out. There's no smoke. Take your time." The surge toward the two exits slowed, became more orderly.

Father Bill peered out at the moving throng. "Thanks, Chief. Good job, boys. Kathleen, lead through the north door and out to the parking lot. Go to the far side near the rectory. Assemble by Sunday school classes."

Abruptly, the main lights came on. Glad cries came as mothers scooped up children. Long lines, now four abreast, moved swiftly through both exits.

Fire engines rumbled into the parking lot, the sirens ending abruptly. It seemed only an instant and firemen in white hats and bulky yellow coats were thundering inside. One shouted, "Where's the fire?"

Father Bill jumped down from the platform, worked his way through the diminishing crowd. "It must be the roof. There's no smoke inside." He looked anxious, kept checking to see if the evacuation was continuing. "Are flames visible outside?"

"No flames. No smoke. We'll check it out." The fireman turned away, gestured to his men. Firemen left the parish hall in a heavy run, thudded out into the main hallway. Chief Cobb followed. Muffled shouts could be heard. "Anybody smell smoke? Check those closets."

The tall golden lights of the parking lot dissipated the gloom of dusk. Car headlights added their bright gleam. Families searched for missing children, came together in thankfulness.

Father Bill was the last person out of the church. He stood on the steps, gazing out at the surging mass of evacuees. His voice was strong, reassuring. "Firemen are looking for a blaze and making certain no one remains inside. We'll stay here until there's an all clear sounded."

Breathless and shaking, the sexton burst out the door, reached Father Bill. "The fuse box was messed with. Somebody threw the switches. That's why the lights went off. The fire alarm by the nursery was yanked plumb out. Father Bill, I don't think there's a fire. There's no smoke, nothing hot. I looked everywhere. The firemen are up in the attic and down in the furnace room, but they don't see anything wrong. Somebody played a mean trick on us."

278   CAROLYN HART

"No fire." Relief made Father Bill look years younger.

The door swung open and Chief Cobb and the fire chief stepped outside. Firemen filed down the steps, returning to their engines. Chief Cobb held up a hand. "There is no fire. The alarm had been pulled, but there is no trace of fire anywhere in the church building. If anyone has any information regarding this incident, please contact me or one of my officers. It is against the law to trigger a fire alarm without cause."

Voices rose and fell. "A false alarm." "No fire after all." "Thank God." "If it was a Halloween prank . . ."

Kathleen pushed through the crowd bunched near the foot of the stairs. In the stark light at the entrance, her face was white and strained. "Bill, where's Bayroo? I can't find her anywhere."

Father Bill was impatient. "She's out there." He gestured at the several hundred dark figures moving in no coherent pattern. "She was with the young people." He called, "Bayroo?"

Kathleen ran to the top of the steps. She whirled to face the parking lot. She stretched out her hands. "Bayroo." Her call rose above the sounds of the crowd, the shuffle of feet, the rumble as the fire engines pulled away. "Bayroo, where are you?"

Silence fell. No one moved. No one spoke.

"Bayroo?" Kathleen clutched Father Bill's arm.

No answer.

Father Bill held Kathleen tight, stared out at the lot. He shouted. "Bayroo! Bayroo!"

Marie Antoinette, one hand clamped to fake curls to keep her wig in place, dashed up the steps. "She was right with me. We were helping the little kids in the Mysterious Maze and we got outside and Jimmy Baker was sick at his stomach. He always throws up when he gets excited. Somebody turned on a flashlight. It was shining right at Bayroo and a voice called out, 'Bayroo Abbott, this way please.' I had to help Jimmy and then everybody was moving across the parking lot and I didn't see her again." Tears rolled down Lucinda's face, smearing the dramatic makeup. "I even looked in the house." She pointed toward the rectory. "She wasn't there. Nobody's there. Oh, Mrs. Abbott, where can Bayroo be?"

Kathleen clung to her husband. "She's gone, Bill. She's gone. Somebody's taken my baby."

Father Bill's voice shook. "We'll find her. We will, Kathleen. Please, God." It was a father's shaken prayer.

Chief Cobb cupped his hands to his mouth. "Bayroo Abbott. Bayroo Abbott."

Murmurs of sound rose, but Bayroo was gone. In the melee, no one had noticed her departure.

Kathleen darted down the steps. "I'm going to get flashlights."

Father Bill turned to Chief Cobb. "We have to have help. We need search teams. Can't you get some dogs to help track?"

Chief Cobb looked stolid, but his brows pulled down in a worried frown. "Perhaps she was frightened by the false alarm. There's no evidence she's been abducted."

Father Bill gripped the chief's arm. "Bayroo would never run away and leave the children. Never."

Chief Cobb held his cell phone. "No one saw her leave under duress."

Father Bill's voice was husky. "Our senior warden was murdered not far from here. Now Bayroo's in danger. You've got to help us."

Kathleen returned with flashlights. "I'm going to look." Her eyes were hollow, her face desperate. "Maybe in the preserve, maybe . . ."

Father Bill gripped her arm. "They're setting up teams. The Boy Scouts are coming. We'd better stay here."

Kathleen pulled away. "I can't stay." She started out into the night, calling, calling.

Chief Cobb stared after her, then punched his cell phone. "All officers are to report to St. Mildred's Church . . ."

St. Mildred's happy Spook Bash was transformed into a crime scene. Chief Cobb knew it wasn't regulation to assume so soon that a missing child had been abducted, but the memory of Daryl Murdoch's body in the cemetery had to be dark in his thoughts.

The parish hall was the heart of a rescue effort. I was aware of the bustle and effort under way. Walter Carey stood in one corner, using his cell phone to contact the Boy Scouts, calling them to come and help. Dogs arrived, barking and snuffling. Names were taken, information sought.

I understood Kathleen's need to search. I would have joined a team, but they didn't need me. I forced myself to remain. I had to think. I knew well enough that Bayroo had never left of her own accord. She'd been taken. But why and by whom?

The first necessity was understanding why Bayroo was taken. The alarm was pulled, the fuses thrown, firemen summoned, all to provide an opportunity to kidnap Bayroo. Only a sense of dire urgency would have prompted such an elaborate charade. The kidnapper could not afford to allow the passage of time. Bayroo had to be snatched immediately.

What peril could Bayroo pose to anyone?

There was only one possible answer. Bayroo knew something she must not tell. What secrets did Bayroo have? She had been upset when Lucinda described her sojourn in the nature preserve Thursday evening. The girls were forbidden to go into the preserve. Everyone knew danger lurked for unaccompanied young girls in remote and untrafficked areas.

Bayroo had ignored that rule and something—someone—frightened her. But she'd reassured everyone—was she speaking to her parents?—and said she'd been scared, but as soon as she saw the car, she knew everything was all right.

She saw a car late Thursday afternoon as dusk was falling, a car hidden in the preserve. Whose car? Did she recognize that car?

Within minutes of Bayroo's arrival in the preserve, the murderer marched Daryl Murdoch at gunpoint to the rectory and shot him on the back porch. His murder was planned. The murderer would not park in the church lot and certainly not behind the rectory. Instead it would be so easy to drive into the nature preserve, leave the car hidden behind pine trees or willows. That meant the murderer knew Daryl was en route to the church, knew it beyond question.

Bayroo had been kidnapped by Daryl's murderer. I almost dropped to the floor, determined to accost Chief Cobb. But he might brush me aside. After arresting me, of course, banishing me to jail. That would not be a problem for me, but I had to know enough, be emphatic enough, that he would listen.

The solution was obvious now. Of all who had reason to wish Daryl ill, only Walter Carey, Irene Chatham, and Isaac Franklin had been in the parish hall to hear Lucinda's artless revelations. Judith and Kirby Murdoch were not present. Nor was Lily Mendoza. Or Cynthia Brown. Walter was organizing the Scouts into a search team. The somber sexton hovered near Father Bill.

Irene Chatham. She knew Daryl was coming to the church. Her rackety old car had squealed from her drive in time to arrive at the preserve, be hidden before Daryl reached the parking lot.

Irene—

I stared down.

I saw Irene Chatham shoving a serving cart with two

coffee urns against the wall nearest the south exit. She lifted Styrofoam cups from a bottom shelf, arranged packets of sugar and creamers. It was a churchwoman's immediate response to a gathering.

If I'd suddenly tumbled from a mountaintop and turned end over end through space, I could not have been more shocked. Irene Chatham was innocent. Her presence here was proof. She was innocent and she had not abducted Bayroo. Then who . . .

I gripped the wood rim of the chandelier, held on as if its concrete reality would anchor me to facts. These things I knew:

1. DARYL MURDOCH HAD TOLD IRENE CHATHAM HE WAS ON HIS WAY TO THE CHURCH.
2. IRENE'S CAR HAD SPED FROM HER DRIVE AT SHORTLY BEFORE 5 P.M.

The conclusion seemed inescapable: Irene came to the church. I pressed my fingers against my temples. She was at the church, but it wasn't her whom Bayroo had seen or her car that Bayroo recognized. However, Irene told me, *"I didn't meet him. I swear I didn't. When I saw—"* She'd broken off, claimed she hadn't seen anyone. I thought she was lying. Irene had a talent for lies.

Irene had seen something. Or someone. I had to get the truth from her. I would do whatever I had to do. Time was racing ahead. How long had Bayroo been gone. Twenty minutes? Half an hour? How much time did Bayroo have left?

Irene bent into the freezer in the kitchen. When she spoke, as she reached for a large tray, her voice sounded hollow. "I'll get some cookies out, heat them up. It would be nice if we had a snack for everyone."

Another volunteer was bustling out of the kitchen with

baskets of chips. She called over her shoulder, "Good idea, Irene. Be back in a minute."

Irene moved to a big oven, turned it, set the temperature. She looked absorbed, almost cheerful. She liked being helpful. She might be a compulsive gambler, a thief, and a liar, but she enjoyed helping people and working with children and keeping the Lord's house immaculate and holy.

I appeared. I spoke gently. "Irene, we need your help."

She whirled, backed against the stove. "You." It was a gasp. "I'll call the police chief."

"We'll talk to him in a minute." Please God, yes, with a name and the hope and prayer that Bayroo was still safe.

Irene glared. "He said you were a fake. I don't have to talk to you. I don't have to say a word."

"Bayroo Abbott's been kidnapped. You are the only person who can save her."

Her sallow face flushed. "That's crazy. If you're accusing me of hurting Bayroo, I never, never would."

"Irene, listen closely." She was one of those women— Bobby Mac believed this to be true of all women—who never hear any statement without taking it personally. "Daryl Murdoch's murderer kidnapped Bayroo. Bayroo was in the preserve Thursday evening and saw a car. We have to find out what car she saw."

"I didn't see any car except—" She clapped a hand to her mouth. Panic flickered in her eyes.

"You were here at the church." I felt a surge of triumph.

Her shoulders tightened in a defensive posture. She stared at me, fear mixing with stubbornness.

"What did you see? Was it Kirby Murdoch? Judith?" Even as I asked, I was unconvinced. Neither had been in the parish hall during the Spook Bash.

Irene's eyes jerked toward the door into the parish hall. She tried to slide away.

I blocked her escape. "Bayroo's been gone a long time now." I heard the tremor in my voice.

Her face crumpled. "If I admit I was here, they can say I killed him and I swear I didn't. I got here and I saw him, and when I saw the policewoman I thought he was going to have me arrested and so I left."

My hand closed on her arm. "Policewoman?"

Her face drooped in remembered fear. "She was walking toward him."

"Are you sure it was a police officer?" I struggled to understand.

"Of course I'm sure." She sounded angry. "I may be in trouble, but I've got eyes that see. She had on that uniform, just like you do, but I know she's a real police officer. She gave me a ticket once. Officer Leland."

"Anita Leland." Anita Leland, who had often followed Daryl Murdoch, knew his daily routine.

Irene's eyes were empty. "There wasn't any reason for him to have a policewoman come to the church." Her lips quivered. "Except for me."

Her voice was so low I could scarcely hear. She flung up her head and the words came fast as rocks thrown by an angry crowd. "If I'd had a gun, I would have been glad to shoot him. Father Bill was going to let me pay everything back. I would have. Somehow. But Daryl wanted everyone to know. He wanted me to go to jail. I hated him. I turned and ran to my car. I was afraid to go home. I drove around for hours and finally I was so tired, I drove up my street and the houses were dark and no one was waiting for me. And now . . ."

I heard Irene's bitter tirade while the puzzle pieces slotted into a perfect pattern. I'd tried to jam the wrong shapes together, poking a weak-willed woman into the role of a quick-thinking, opportunistic, coolheaded adversary.

Anita Leland hated Daryl Murdoch. Anita blamed Daryl for her sister's husband's suicide and her sister's disappearance. Anita had planned to shoot Daryl Wednesday evening at his cabin, but she looked through the window and saw Kathleen and the red silk nightgown. Anita changed her plan, decided his death on the rectory back porch would provide a ready-made suspect.

Anita had been warned to stop her ticketing campaign against Daryl. Thursday evening she stopped him as he left his office. She didn't give him a ticket, so why . . . Maybe she told him there had been trouble at the church, a break-in, and he told her he was on his way there, would meet her in the parking lot.

Anita didn't park in the church lot. She hid the police car in the nature preserve, walked the few hundred yards to the parking lot, met Daryl. Perhaps he had been told the problem was at the rectory and he walked willingly with her to the back door and onto the porch.

Anita shot him. Did she tell him who she was when she held the gun to his head? She shot him and slipped through the gathering gloom, seen by no one. She must have felt very safe when she reached the preserve. Bayroo heard the crunch of leaves. Was it at the time of Anita's departure for the church or at the time of her return? Whichever, Bayroo had been frightened until she saw the car. A police car. This afternoon, Bayroo turned away the story of her derring-do, saying she'd been scared until she saw the car.

Anita Leland could not let Bayroo describe that car.

I looked at the clock above the stainless-steel sinks. A quarter to seven. Now the shadows were falling, dusk turning to dark. And Bayroo . . . My throat ached.

". . . you want me to tell that policeman I was there." Irene was talking again. "He knows about the money. What if he won't listen? He won't think a police officer could be involved. Oh"—she choked back a sob—"I have to tell him. Do you think we can save Bayroo?"

I blinked back a tear. Irene Chatham was an unlikely heroine, downtrodden, frightened, querulous, selfish, yet kind at heart, wanting to do right but failing and falling as we all so often and easily do. I gave her a swift hug. "You can do it. You're strong, Irene. This will put a star in your crown."

She looked startled. I resisted an urge to reassure her that Heaven was all and more than she could ever imagine and someday all despair would be gone for her, all sadness and tribulation.

I grasped her elbow and turned her toward the entrance to the parish hall. "I'll be right there with you." In a manner of speaking.

Irene struggled for breath, gave a short nod.

When we reached the door, I disappeared.

Irene's gaze darted uneasily around the hall, stopped on Chief Cobb. Lucinda was huddled in a chair drawn up to one side of the central table, where he sat with a mass of papers and an array of phones. People clustered in one corner, waiting to speak with detectives.

Lucinda no longer wore the bouffant wig. Her Marie Antoinette gown looked bedraggled. She lifted a hand to wipe away tears that spilled from reddened eyes.

Irene slowly approached the table, stopped a few feet away.

Chief Cobb spoke gently. "Don't cry, Lucinda. You're doing a good job. Try to remember what the voice sounded like."

Lucinda's face squeezed in misery. "I wasn't paying attention. I barely heard it. I thought maybe her mom or dad wanted her to come help them somewhere. It was a grown-up. A woman. But"—she shook her head—"it could have been a man with a high voice." Fresh tears flooded.

I gave Irene a little push.

Her head swung toward me. She blinked in utter surprise. She glanced down at her arm, which I held in a firm grip. "Where . . ." It was a strangled whisper.

"I'm here." I spoke softly. "You can't see me. Don't worry."

She wobbled unsteadily, the beginnings of panic in her face.

"This is no time to faint." I squeezed her arm. "I'm here on earth to help Bayroo. That's all you need to know. Now it's time for you to do your part."

She tried to pull away.

I urged her forward. "Don't think about me. Think about Bayroo." Bayroo and the desperate woman who had taken her away.

I pulled her up to the table. It was crowded with papers, phones, a radio set, and maps.

". . . and that was the last time you saw her?" Chief Cobb's expression was bleak.

"Chief Cobb?" I managed a credible imitation of Irene's voice.

He glanced up. "Yes?" He was brusque.

Irene stood mute, her breathing quick and shallow, trembling like a poplar in a high wind.

I whispered, "Start with the parking lot."

Her eyes slid sideways, where I should have been. She gulped for air. "I was at the church Thursday evening. I saw Daryl walking to meet that policewoman. Officer Leland."

Chief Cobb frowned. "Officer Leland?"

Lucinda wiped her teary face, sniffled. "Was she the one who put the police car in the preserve?"

Chief Cobb looked from Irene to Lucinda. His look of incredulity slowly faded. Shock drained the ruddy color from his face, made him look old and gray and unutterably weary.

"Bayroo was scared to pieces in the preserve until she saw the police car. Then she knew everything was all right. And now . . ." Lucinda dissolved in sobs.

Cobb stood up so quickly his chair crashed to the floor of the hall. The sudden clatter brought silence.

Father Bill swung around from the portable television set that was blaring the story of Bayroo's abduction, the call for volunteers, the progress of the investigation. He took a step toward the chief, stopped as if his legs had no strength. He reached out a shaking hand.

Walter Carey turned toward the chief's table, holding up a hand to quiet a muscular scout's rapid speech.

The chief's eyes scanned the faces in the room, searching, hunting, hoping. Abruptly, he called out, "Where's Anita? I thought she'd gone with one of the search parties."

No one spoke.

Once again I spoke in Irene's wavering voice. "Can you call her car?"

Cobb shot Irene a look of surprise, then bent over the table, punched at the radio set. "Calling Car Six. Calling Car Six . . ."

Just then, Walter Carey plunged through the crowd, frowned down at Cobb. "GPS?"

Chief Cobb looked up. His voice was level. "I wanted to equip each car with a GPS. It was voted down by the city council. Unnecessary expense. Like the mayor said, 'How could we lose a police car?'" He bent again to the radio.

"Calling Car Six. Calling . . ."

CHAPTER 18

My eyes adjusted to the almost impenetrable darkness. Slowly shapes formed, dark shadowy bunches of trees, tangled shrubs, branches that let through scarcely a glimmer of cold moonlight.

I heard an eerie echo of Chief Cobb's voice, tinny and distant. "Calling Car Six. Calling Car Six." I moved nearer the sound, bumped into metal. Anita's cruiser was parked alongside a tall stand of cane. I ran my hand along the side of the car, found an open window. I poked my head inside.

". . . report immediately. Calling Car Six, report . . ."

Taking a quick breath, I opened the door. The light flashed on. I glanced front and back. Nothing. No one. I had feared what I might find, but Anita had taken Bayroo with her. I closed the door and walked through crushed grasses to the gravel road.

Branches creaked in the ever-stirring Oklahoma wind. I faintly discerned the road. Obviously, I was out in the country, some remote and untraveled area.

Was I too late? My heart twisted. Dear, sweet, fun Bayroo, where are you? I had to search, move as quickly as possible. I rose high, looking for a light, a sign of movement.

Whatever Anita planned, let me be in time. It seemed an eon and yet I knew only seconds had passed.

Below me were woods and beyond the trees an overgrown field, dark and quiet in the moonlight. A ramshackle barn loomed perhaps twenty feet away, silhouetted against the night sky. A derelict combine lay on one side amid a jumble of trash, coils of barbed wire, rusted milk cans, the frame of a windowless jalopy, lumber scraps in a haphazard pile. An owl suddenly rose from the barn roof, hooting, his wavering mournful call a warning of trespass.

Light flickered from a hayloft, a brief, dancing dart. A spear of light through the wide window illuminated the dark and leafless limbs of a huge maple. A wooden shutter creaked into place and the vagrant gleam was gone.

The hayloft . . .

I arrived in the filthy, junk-filled loft.

A Maglite lay atop a battered wooden table. In its beam, Anita struggled to push an old chest of drawers against the shutter, throwing a monstrous shadow against a stack of galvanized tubs.

Bayroo's frightened eyes followed Anita's every move. Bayroo's face was pale, her wrists manacled, her pirate costume torn at one shoulder. She was a few feet behind Anita. As Anita shoved the chest, the wood grating on the loft floor, Bayroo edged toward wooden steps that descended into a black void.

The handcuffs clanked.

Anita whirled. She clamped her hand to her holster, drew out the gun, whipped it level with Bayroo's head.

If I rushed her, the gun might fire. I was poised to move, knowing a desperate struggle would ensue. Anita was young and fit, trained to overcome attackers.

Anita held the gun steady with both hands. "How old are you?" Her voice was thin.

"Eleven." Bayroo's green eyes were wide and staring.

I wished I could take her in my arms, tell her she was going to be safe, that someday she would look back and understand she'd been caught up innocently in the ugly aftermath of dark passions, that anger and murder and violence would not touch her life, take her life.

Bayroo had not yet seen me. Her eyes, young, vulnerable, defenseless, questioning, never left Anita's ashen face.

Anita's lips trembled. "Eleven. Vee was eleven when Mama died. I raised her up. She was always beautiful. You're beautiful, too." Her haggard face was heavy with remembered grief and love.

"Thank you." The words hung between them, Bayroo's polite response automatic. How often must Kathleen have said, "Always say thank you when you are complimented."

"Eleven." Slowly the gun sank until the muzzle pointed at the dust-laden floor, streaked now by footprints.

The moment had passed, the awful moment when Anita had chosen between life and death for Bayroo.

"Why did you have to be in the preserve?" Anita's voice shook. "Why? If you hadn't been there, if you hadn't seen me, everything would be all right."

Bayroo looked puzzled. "Weren't you supposed to be there?"

Anita ignored her. She jammed the gun into her holster, flexed her fingers as if her hand ached.

Bayroo shivered. "I'm cold. Are we going to stay long? My mom and dad will be worried about me. Why did you bring me here?"

"Don't talk, kid." Anita's voice was gruff. She swallowed hard, her features drawn in a tight frown as she studied the loft. Her face was pale, remote, distant. I saw no trace of the young woman whose tremulous glance had spoken of love to Sam Cobb.

Bayroo looked up and saw me. Her eyes widened in amazement, in joy, in relief.

I placed a finger to my lips, shook my head.

Bayroo's green eyes glistened. Tension eased from her stiff frame, terror erased.

Please God, her faith would be justified. Yet I had no surety of success. Even if I were able to find a weapon—that scythe in one corner? the ax handle without a head?—there was no guarantee I could wield an awkward tool quickly enough to forestall a gunshot.

I glanced toward the stairs. A push? I felt a bone-deep chill. I could defend, yes. I could protect, yes. But could I be the instrument of injury or worse?

The loft was cold, cold with my foreboding, cold with the chill of a late October night, cold with the emptiness of an abandoned building. The loft was a repository for discarded household goods. Cotton wadding poked from holes dug by mice or rats in an old sofa and a stained mattress. A refrigerator door lay next to a rusted plow. The ax handle leaned against a worn saddle. Thick dust covered everything.

Anita gave an abrupt nod. "Come here, kid."

Bayroo reluctantly took one step, another, came nearer, the handcuff links clinking.

Anita gestured at the mattress. "Sit down."

Bayroo's face wrinkled in distaste. "It's dirty."

Anita gave her an odd look. "Dirt won't hurt you."

Bayroo glanced toward me.

I nodded, made a tamping-down gesture, hands outstretched, palms down.

Obediently, Bayroo sank down. She sat with her knees hunched to her chin, her body drawn tight.

Anita moved fast. She dragged the refrigerator door to the mattress, knelt next to Bayroo. In an instant she loosed the handcuff from Bayroo's right wrist, snapped it in place around the door handle. She pushed up from the floor, strode to the table, reached for the flashlight.

As she started for the stairs, Bayroo cried out, "Please, don't leave me in the dark." Her young voice quavered.

I stood at the top of the stairs. Slanting steps plunged into gloom.

Anita came even with me; her face looked old and empty. She hesitated for an instant, hunched her shoulders, started down.

I raised my hand. If I caught Anita in the middle of her back, pushed with all my might, she would tumble head over heels.

My hand slowly fell.

The light went with her, fading as she thudded down the wooden steps, her hurrying feet pounding. The golden glow diminished, less and less, and then was gone. Blackness, thick and heavy, enveloped us, pressing down with the weight of the unseen.

"Auntie Grand!" Bayroo's thin voice rose in a wail.

I whirled, went to Bayroo, wrapped her in my arms. She sobbed, hiccuping for breath, her body shaking in uncontrollable spasms. ". . . hate the dark . . . always hated the dark . . . mean things . . . awful things in the dark . . . Oh, Mom, I want my mom."

"Hush, dear child." I pressed my cheek against her sweet-scented hair, held her tight. "We'll find a way. She's gone now. I'll open the loft window and it won't seem so dark." I loosed my hold, started to get up.

Immediately her fingers closed tightly on my wrist. "Don't leave me."

I squeezed her shoulders. "We're fine." I kept my voice easy. "I'll get us out of here."

"What did I do wrong?" Bayroo cried harder. "I just hid so I could watch for Travis."

"You didn't do anything wrong." I held her tight. "Not a single thing. It's Mr. Murdoch's murder. You see, she shot him and she'd hidden the police car there."

Bayroo gasped. She sat up straight, her breaths coming quickly. "She did? He was the senior warden. I read all about it in the paper, but Mama wouldn't talk about it. Why did she do that?"

"Anger. 'Anger is a weed; hate is the tree.'" The words came readily. I'd learned that and much more in a recent class I'd taken with Saint Augustine. "She was angry for things he'd done and she let anger take over her life." There would be, please God, time and enough to try to explain to Bayroo the noxious growths that can squeeze out love and forgiveness and grace from our lives.

"Now she's mad at me?" Bayroo's voice was small, but no longer shaken by sobs.

"Not you." Not at a child, a pretty girl who baked a special cake for her new friend, a beloved daughter, a friend. "At what's gone wrong in her life." At the loss of choice and hope and a future.

Bayroo moved uneasily. "What is she going to do?"

"I don't know." Had murder been in Anita's heart when she enticed Bayroo away? I feared so. She had come close, desperately close, when the gun was aimed at Bayroo. What would she do now? Her only chance was to make a run for it, perhaps drive to Dallas, lose herself in that sprawling city. For now, she'd left Bayroo alone.

I needed to make haste, find a way for Bayroo to escape. "You can help me figure out how to get you out of here."

"Out?" She moved and the links of the handcuff clinked. "I'm fastened here." Her voice wobbled.

I spoke easily. "Let's get a little moonlight. That will help. I'm going to move that chest away from the loft window, open the shutter. I'll be right back." I gave her a reassuring pat. Her body stiffened, but she made no complaint.

I pulled the drawers from the chest, placed them to one side. I gripped the sides of the chest, edged it away from the shutter. The bottom scraped against the floor. I paused to listen. Would Anita hear the noise, return to discover the source? Or did she feel confident that Bayroo was stuck and noise didn't matter? No sound came from the stairs. In a moment I'd shoved the chest to one side.

The shutter was harder to manage. I didn't know if Anita had wedged something to keep it in place or if an old hinge had jammed. I pulled and struggled and finally, with a desperate yank, the shutter splintered and gave way. I tumbled backward.

Moonlight splashed into the loft. Night air swept inside, cool swift air threaded with wisps of smoke.

"I smell smoke." Bayroo's voice was puzzled.

I smelled smoke, too, thicker and stronger. Now that it was silent in the loft, the scrapes and bangs and screeches ended, I heard a faint crackling sound, the insidious rustle as flame devoured desiccated wood. Now a rustle, the fire would soon be a roar.

"Auntie Grand!" Bayroo yanked her arm. The bracelet rattled against the handle. "I can't get loose." In the spill of moonlight, she was a small, dark shape jerking frantically.

In a sudden, frightening rush, hot, oily smoke clouded the loft, obscuring the moonlight, turning our world dark again with no glimmer of light from the loft window. Bayroo began to cough. "Auntie Grand, look at that funny glow."

Orange-tinted smoke swirled into the loft, rising from the barn floor. Flames could not be far behind.

"Auntie Grand, did she set fire to the barn?" Bayroo's voice was stricken.

"Yes." Away from Bayroo's young face, Anita Leland had made a fatal decision.

Bayroo choked and sputtered, words coming in short gasps. ". . . stuck . . . can't move that door . . . chest hurts . . ."

"I'm coming." I pictured the ax shaft and I was beside it, my grasping hand tight on its splintery handle. Bayroo was not far away. I dropped down beside her.

Thin arms reached out, clung to me. Bayroo breathed in quick, desperate gasps. Acrid fumes clogged our throats.

"I'm here." I wedged the shaft into the space between the handle and door, used the ax handle as a fulcrum, and applied my weight. I pushed and pushed and pushed. Abruptly the refrigerator door handle snapped. The ax shaft went flying and I fell in a heap, but I was laughing and crying and hugging Bayroo. "The window," I shouted. "We've got to get to the window."

Bayroo wobbled to her feet. I clutched her arm and we blindly moved forward. How far? Ten feet, perhaps twelve. Blessedly, the smoke thinned in time for me to see the opening. Bayroo hung her head out, drawing in deep breaths. The rush and hiss of flames crackled ominously.

Moonlight spread its glory over the barnyard, making the branches of the huge old maple distinct against the night sky.

The nearest branch was only fifteen feet away. Not many feet to walk or run, too many feet to jump. I looked down and saw the moonlight spread across the dirt so far below. The loft window was at least thirty feet above the ground.

Behind us the fire flared and heat pulsed toward us, flames curving and twisting, reaching to the roof.

Bayroo looked down. She clung to the side of the loft. "Auntie Grand, I can't jump down and the tree's too far!"

Despair curled in my heart. Beloved Bayroo was doomed. I would try, but I knew, even as I slipped my arm around her shoulder, that I would not be able to carry her to the tree.

I'd never felt more alone. I'd insisted to Wiggins that I wanted no more interference, that I was capable of completing my task. Pride had prompted my outburst to him, and now Bayroo would pay a dreadful price because of me.

I bent close to her cheek, shouted over the roar of the flames. "We'll make it. Jump toward that lower branch, Bayroo. I'll be with you."

We jumped. I clutched Bayroo and held tight and struggled, but she was too heavy, slipping from my grasp, her cry rising in the night.

"Steady, now." Wiggins's deep voice was as strong and loud as the clack of train wheels. "I've got you both. Here we go," and we reached the tree.

The refrigerator door handle dangling from the handcuff banged against Bayroo, but her grasping fingers locked onto a branch. She swung for a moment, pulled herself up, and clung to the trunk, pressing her face against the bark, her back heaving as she struggled for breath.

I landed beside her.

"Auntie Grand." Her voice was faint. "I thought I heard a deep voice."

I started to answer, then heard a faint cautionary rumble. Dear Wiggins, determined to the last that proper procedure be followed. I reached out until I found his hand and squeezed it in thankfulness.

"The fire's making noises." And it was. The old barn seemed to groan and cry. "Shh. We'd better be quiet." I peered down at the uneven ground, seeking any trace of Anita. "Just in case."

Fire poked through the roof, a darting, angry tongue of red.

Suddenly a shout sounded from the loft. "I'm coming. I'll get you out. I'm coming."

Bayroo and I stared at the loft window. Smoke whirled and curled, orange and black and gray. A single light stabbed through the swirls. "Where are you? I've got the key for the handcuffs—" A whooshing sound marked the collapse of the loft. The voice was lost in the burst of sound. Flames whirled skyward as the walls crumpled, turning the night sky crimson.

Stainless-steel handcuffs, soiled with dirt and oily smudges, lay on Chief Cobb's desk. He jerked his head toward them. "The kid's story has to be true. Those handcuffs prove every word. That and the scrapes on her arms. It beats everything how she got herself free. It sounds like a Houdini trick, working in the dark, using an ax shaft to prize away the refrigerator handle, jumping out to catch the tree."

Detective Sergeant Price slumped in the chair across from the chief's desk. "Anita." He spoke the name in sadness, in grief, in farewell.

Cobb's face was gray and drawn. He stared at the handcuffs. "Right from the first, I should have looked at her. Anita told me about her sister, Vee, and Daryl. Anita knew all about Murdoch, where he went, his girlfriend. But I never thought . . ." His hand shook as he touched a folder on his desk. "I checked on the girl whose body she went out to California to see. This came in just a little while ago." He read in an empty voice: "'Re inquiry unidentified body found Huntington Beach, female approximately midtwenties, blonde, DOA drug overdose, positive ID made: Virginia Leland Durham.'" Cobb pushed the folder away. "It was Vee. Anita lied to me."

The detective pushed back his chair. "Sam, can I take you home?"

Chief Cobb sounded remote. "I've got stuff to see about. I'll go in a little while."

The detective came around the desk. His voice was gruff, but firm. "Anita tried to save the kid, Sam."

Chief Cobb was stern. "Anita set that fire."

"Yeah. But she came back, tried to save her." He placed his hand for a moment on the chief's shoulder, then walked away, his steps slow.

When the door closed, Sam Cobb folded his arms on his desk. He bent forward, rested his head. "Anita . . ."

A log crackled in the fireplace. Kirby Murdoch poked and flames spurted. He was smiling.

His mother stood in the doorway to the den. Judith Murdoch still looked worn and weary, but peace had smoothed away the tight and anxious lines from her face. She looked toward the plaid sofa and the slender young woman with a tortoiseshell cat in her lap. "Lady Luck likes you, Lily."

Lily Mendoza smoothed the angora cat's fluffy fur. "That's a great name."

"She's a great cat." Kirby replaced the poker. He settled beside Lily and Lady Luck, smoothed his hand over the distinctive brown and yellow and black fur. "You know, Mom, that's how I knew you'd buried the gun. Lady Luck was rolling in the fresh dirt, and when I went over, I thought it looked funny, and since somebody'd broken in, I thought maybe they'd hidden something and so I dug up my gun."

Judith gasped. "What did you do with it?"

"I shinnied up the drainpipe and hid it on the roof. I'll get it down tomorrow. But it won't matter since the case is closed."

There was no light in the small bedroom at the home for unwed mothers, but moonlight flowed in a golden stream through a window. Even breathing indicated that the occupant of the near bed was deep in sleep. I still wore Officer Loy's uniform. I hesitated, decided that she could make her final appearance. I became visible and stepped quietly to Cynthia Brown's bed.

"Cynthia, it's Officer Loy. I wanted to see how everything is going for you."

She struggled upright. "Oh, I didn't hear you come in." She sounded drowsy, but relaxed. She reached out, took my hand. "Everybody's been so nice to me. Father Bill helped me come here. They're going to help me find a job and I can stay here and have my baby. And then—" Her hand tightened on mine.

"And then?"

She took a deep, uncertain breath. "I don't know. I haven't decided. I could keep my baby, but they have families who want babies and will love them and be good to them. What do you think I should do?" Her voice was young and trusting.

"Do what is in your heart. God bless." I bent down, lightly touched her cheek with my lips. "Sleep now." I squeezed her hand, stepped away from the bed.

She sank back onto the pillow, and in a moment her eyes closed.

I smiled a farewell. Officer Loy faded away.

The frowsy living room blazed with light. Irene Chatham ate a macaroon and watched, eyes wide, as the TV newswoman swept the beam of a huge flashlight across smoking rubble. "Nothing remains of the abandoned barn where an Adelaide child was held hostage tonight, barely escaping with her life. Her captor was Adelaide police officer Anita Leland. Leland, who perished in the blaze, is considered the prime suspect in the murder of well-known Adelaide businessman Daryl Murdoch, whose body was found Thursday evening in the cemetery adjoining St. Mildred's Church. Irene Chatham, a church member, is credited with setting officers on the right track. Earlier tonight, Chatham spoke with reporters."

A film clip showed Irene, vivacious and voluble, lank gray hair stirred by the breeze, clutching her brown cardigan against the night chill, standing on the side steps at St. Mildred's: "So glad I was able to help. Just the most fortunate circumstance." Her cheeks glowed bright pink. "I'd been to the church Thursday evening, some things to check for the Altar Guild, and I saw Daryl Murdoch and that police officer and I had no idea until tonight that . . ."

I was smiling as I appeared. I chose my purple velour. After all, it was one of the final times I would enjoy it.

Irene froze, sat stiff as a cardboard skeleton. "You're here." Her voice shook. "You're not here. You're here."

I settled beside her on the sofa. "Just for a moment." I took a shaking hand between mine, held it tight. "You saved Bayroo. You were very brave."

Her eyes blinked. Some of the fear seeped away. "That's what everybody's been saying and it makes me think, maybe things work out the way they should. I mean, if I hadn't taken the money from the collection plate, he wouldn't have caught me and got those awful pictures. I still don't know where those pictures are, and if anyone ever sees them they'll know I'm a thief even though Father Bill said I could pay the money back."

I was emphatic. "The pictures were destroyed." As Irene said, maybe things happen for a purpose. I had been upset when Kathleen flung the cell phone into the lake. Now I was glad.

"Destroyed?" Her lips were tremulous. "I don't have to be afraid?"

"You don't have to be afraid." I gave her hand a final squeeze, stood. "Everyone's proud of you."

She waved a hand in dismissal. "You saved Bayroo. I'm sure of that. I know what everyone's saying, that she was clever and managed to get free, but I know you were there and you asked her not to tell."

"I was there only because you made it possible." I was fading away.

"You're going, aren't you?" Irene called after me. "I'm going to pay the money back, and I won't ever gamble again."

The Rescue Express would be here soon. I'd almost completed my rounds. I actually felt a little thinner, as if I weren't quite here. Of course I wouldn't be here much longer. Any minute now I expected the Express to barrel across the sky, sparks flashing from its smokestack, wheels thrumming.

I zoomed to Daryl Murdoch's office. Once inside, I turned on the light. After all, I don't see in the dark and I had to find Walter Carey's confession. I'd promised him it would be destroyed if he had nothing to do with his former partner's murder.

I lifted the rug, picked up the envelope, and, once again, faced that pesky law of physics, the impossibility of wafting a concrete object—the letter—through walls with the ease I enjoyed.

It was a minor impediment. I opened the office door, stepped into the secretary's anteroom. I found Walter Carey's address—619 Cherry Street—in the directory on Patricia's desk. Now all I had to do was deliver this material. Walter would be exceedingly relieved and my duties would be nearing completion. I opened the door to the hall.

Brrrng. Brrnng. Oooh-wah. Wah-oooh.

The cacophony almost startled me into my skin. Flashing

lights joined the wails and rings. Heart thudding, I was at the end of the hall. I yanked on the door, almost fainted when it refused to open. I scrambled to release the lock, yanked the door open, and flew outside.

"Halt or I'll shoot!" The shout was harsh. "Stop! Police."

A patrol officer stood at the base of the steps, gun aimed at the door.

I rose into the sky. When I looked down, the officer was staring upward for a last glimpse of the letter rising above him. His head swiveled to the open door through which no one had emerged.

I listened hard. Was that the shriek of the Express in the distance?

Fortunately, Cherry Street was only a few blocks from downtown. I circled the Carey house. Light splashed out on a stone terrace from a room at the back. I looked through the window.

Walter Carey was writing steadily on a legal pad. He stopped to raise his arms above his head, stretch, massage a spot on his back.

A distant *whoooo* brought my head up. I had to be quick. I tapped on the French door.

He looked toward the terrace, frowned.

I tapped again. I became visible, once again choosing the purple velour outfit. My image was indistinct in the glass.

Walter unlocked the French door. His lips parted. No sound came.

I thrust the envelope at him. "Here it is. The confession. You did a good job tonight. With the Scouts."

His fingers closed on the paper, held it tight. He managed an odd, lopsided smile. "You get around, don't you?"

I smiled in return. "Sometimes. Good-bye, Walter. Good luck." And I disappeared.

Only a few minutes remained. I must take my return ticket and board the Express. But there was one more stop I had to make.

Father Bill was stirring dark chocolate into hot milk. A tray held three mugs and a plate full of oatmeal cookies.

Upstairs, in Bayroo's room, Kathleen sat beside her bed. Bayroo's Titian hair, shining clean, tumbled over the shoulders of her soft white nightgown. Propped up against a bolster, Spoofer curled against her side, purring with a happy rumble. Bayroo held her mother's hand. "I'm okay, Mom." Bayroo's smile was drowsy. "I'm all right. I—" Then, eyes shining, she rose on one elbow, looked where I stood had I been there to see. "Auntie Grand, I told Mom you saved me."

Kathleen stood up so quickly her chair fell to the floor. "You're here? Oh, Bailey Ruth, thank you. I wish we could tell the world—"

I touched a finger to her lips. "It's our secret, Kathleen. I came to say good-bye."

The wheels clacked, the Express thundering toward the rectory, just as it had on Thursday evening. I had no time left.

"Good-bye." I threw a kiss to Bayroo. "Good-bye. I love you."

I rushed outside, hurrying up to grab the handrail, and was swept up into the Express. I looked down at the lights below, watched until I could see them no longer.

Good-bye, dear Adelaide. Good-bye.

CHAPTER 19

The Rescue Express thundered into the familiar red-brick station. I was the last passenger to disembark. The other travelers seemed to follow a well-known drill, dropping their ticket stubs down a chute attached to the office, gathering their luggage, and hurrying away, faces shining, voices merry.

I slowly crossed the platform, passing carts laden with luggage ready for other departures. I'd not had time to pack even a satchel when I'd jumped on board on my way to help Kathleen. Perhaps the haste of my departure would excuse my mistakes.

Except there had been so many. I pushed away memories. Certainly I had intended to honor the Precepts.

Wiggins strode toward me.

My steps were lagging. I looked here, there, everywhere, admiring the dash of gold in the arch of clouds, the trill of birdsongs, the sweet scent of fresh-mown grass, the sound of a faraway choir with voices lifting in joy.

Foreboding weighed upon me, heavy as midnight gloom.

Wiggins boomed, "Bailey Ruth, where's your get-up-and-go?" He sounded genial.

I risked a look.

Wiggins's stiff cap was tilted back atop his bush of curly brown hair. His round face was bright and eager, his muttonchop whiskers a rich chestnut in the sunlight. His high-collared white shirt was crisp, his gray flannel trousers a bit baggy, but his sturdy shoes glowed with bootblack.

"Welcome home." His voice was warm. He gestured toward the station. "A few formalities, then you'll be free to go."

Would I be free to return to the Department of Good Intentions?

We passed a crystal wall and I glimpsed my reflection. I'd given some thought to my appearance. I wanted to appear businesslike. Not flighty. I was confident the gray wool pantsuit was appropriate and the Florentine gold of the silk blouse and small gold hoop earrings and crimson scarf almost matched the glow of Heaven. Here I was, Bailey Ruth Raeburn, red hair curling softly about my face, green eyes hopeful though uncertain, home in Heaven.

We walked together into his office. I settled on the bench as he hung his cap on a coat tree. He settled into his oak chair and slipped on his green eyeshade.

I looked out the bay window, admired the shining tracks. Finally, I forced myself to look at him. His eyes were grave.

"I'm sorry to say—"

My heart sank.

"—that never in my experience as stationmaster have I encountered a rescue effort so fraught with—" He stopped, apparently at a loss for words.

I twisted a gold button on my jacket.

He appeared perplexed and muttered to himself, "A flying crowbar. The airborne cell phone. That shocking episode with the mayor. Destruction of the police station's computer system, and"—a heavy sigh—"Officer Loy."

I started to rise. It would be easier for all concerned, especially me, if I slipped away, left him to regain his composure.

He made a swiping gesture with his hand.

I sank back onto the chair.

His brows beetled in a frown. "However." He cleared his throat.

That rumble was familiar. Just so had he prefaced our many encounters on earth.

His tone was judicious. "As I should have recalled from my earthly days, good often comes out of difficult circumstances. I returned to earth and do you know what happened?"

I feared I knew all too well.

"I Reverted." His roar capitalized the verb. Wiggins slammed his fist on the desktop. "So how can I be critical when an emissary caught up in the stress of the moment makes unfortunate choices?"

I hoped this was a rhetorical question.

He swept ahead. "There's no denying your shortcomings."

My nod was heartfelt.

"You were inquisitive." It was a pronouncement.

I twined my scarf in my fingers.

"Impulsive." He made a chopping motion with one large hand.

My collar felt tight.

"Rash." A shake of his head, this thick brown hair quivering.

Was the wool of my lovely suit irritating my skin?

"Forthright." His tone was thoughtful.

I sighed.

"Daring." He spoke with finality.

I awaited dismissal.

Suddenly his generous mouth spread in a huge smile, his brown eyes glowed. "God bless, Bailey Ruth. You saved Kathleen and dear Bayroo. When you thought of me, knew you needed help, why, I was able to come in time. If it had not been for you . . . However"—he stood and waved an admonishing finger, though kindly—"I feel that your status as a probationer must continue."

Continue?

"Before another mission can be considered, I suggest you spend time in contemplation of the Precepts, especially Precept One." His thick brows drew down. "And Three." A head shake. "And Four. And Six. My goodness, that's a shocking number of Precepts you haven't mastered. However, if you study hard"—he looked at me doubtfully—"perhaps next time—"

My heart raced. Next time. Oh, dear Heaven, there might be a next time. I might still be on probation, but the door had not been closed.

"—events will proceed in a more orderly manner."

"I'll learn the Precepts by heart. Of course," I was quick to reassure him, "I already know them. It was simply that things happened. Everything will go much better next time. Oh, Wiggins." I jumped up and gave him a hug.

Next time . . .

Turn the page for a sneak peek at Carolyn Hart's next
Bailey Ruth mystery,

MERRY, MERRY GHOST.

*Available in hardcover November 2009
from William Morrow.*

B*ailey Ruth, honey, always wait to be invited."*
     I edged a little nearer an arch of clouds suffused with gold and rose. Once around that cumulus corner, I knew what awaited, softly rolling hills, a red-brick train station, and shining silver rails stretching to the horizon.

I wanted to break into a run, yet I couldn't quite dismiss the memory of my mother's caution when I was a child. Certainly, I didn't want to impose myself upon anyone even though in Heaven I'd always found welcome everywhere.

Heaven?

Do I detect skepticism?

That's fine. Avert your eyes from beauty. Ignore love. Yawn at the splendor of the universe. Insist that the world is nothing more than rollicking atoms. Someday you'll see.

I always knew there was a Heaven, even before Bobby Mac and I met our demise when our cabin cruiser went down in the Gulf of Mexico as Bobby Mac pursued a tarpon on a fatefully stormy day. There's nothing like going out with a big splash. I recalled with pleasure the Adelaide, Oklahoma *Gazette* and the front page story with a picture:

Oil Wildcatter,
Mayor's Secretary
Perish in Gulf Storm

Robert MacNeill (Bobby Mac) Raeburn II, 54, and his

wife Bailey Ruth Raeburn, 52, of Adelaide were pre-
sumed lost at sea following a storm in the Gulf of
Mexico. Their capsized cabin cruiser *Serendipity* was
discovered yesterday off the coast of Texas. Despite a
massive sea-air search, no trace has been found of the
Adelaide natives and well-known civic leaders.

Raeburn was a successful oilman . . .

The photograph on the *Serendipity* had been taken in
sunshine, unlike the lowering black clouds and driving
rain we faced that final day. It was an especially fine picture of Bobby Mac with his dark hair, dark eyes, and daredevil smile. He held a rod bent against the pull of a tarpon.
I lounged against a railing, red hair tangled by the breeze,
smiling freckled face lifted to the sun. I remembered that
lime-green blouse. The color was a nice contrast to crisp
white shorts.

On impulse (I'm afraid I often succumb to impulse), I
envisioned myself in an identical blouse and shiny white
cotton shorts and espadrilles. I paused and took a peek at
my reflection in a sheet of crystal. Of course, I abjured
vanity in Heaven. I was simply enjoying a memory. There I
was, a youthful and lively ethereal me with red curls bright
as flame, narrow eager face spattered with freckles, and
curious green eyes. I smoothed my hair, beamed at the reflection. In Heaven, no matter our age at death, we are seen
at our best, whenever that was. I'd enjoyed all my days, but
twenty-seven had been a very good year. Occasionally, I
was reflective, not, I will admit, a usual state for me, and
then I might appear a confident forty, but twenty-seven was
my age of choice.

The *Gazette* story told all about Bobby Mac and me and
our families, and son, Rob, and daughter, Dil, and their children and spouses. I was described as "the vivacious red-

headed secretary who added a lively element to the mayor's office and was known for her frankness."

Frankness.

I sighed, came to a full stop. Frankness was a nice way of saying I often spoke without thinking. That's why I was uncertain of my welcome around the cumulus corner that was now close enough to touch. I reached out, stroked the soft wall of cloud, filmy as springtime fluff from a cottonwood tree. We had lots of cottonwoods in Adelaide.

Frankness.

Okay. I'm forthright. Quick to act. Some might say hasty. *All right. All right.* I spoke aloud in admission.

I wanted to go around that corner.

All right, around that corner I would go. All Wiggins could say was no.

My heart would be broken.

Before I could change my mind, I strode around the cottony column touched by streaks of pink and gold and there was the adorable, old-fashioned country train station, silver tracks stretching into the blue sky. DEPARTMENT OF GOOD INTENTIONS was emblazoned on a golden arch. Wiggins, who ran the department, had been a station agent when on earth. Since a well-run station was his sense of Heaven, here he was, in charge again, sending out emissaries to help those in trouble. On earth I'd often felt I was the beneficiary of celestial grace. Giving back is one of earth—and Heaven's—greatest pleasures.

This wasn't my first visit to the department. I'd been eager to return to earth to help someone in a tough spot and, truly, I'd done the best I could on a previous mission. All emissaries are issued a parchment roll inscribed with the Precepts for Earthly Visitation. I'll admit I'd run afoul of Wiggins's rules a few times.

To be accurate, I had transgressed a great many times.

I drooped. If Wiggins listed my infractions, they'd run a page or more.

Yet when I had made my final report, Wiggins had clearly said I might be used again as a Heavenly agent though, he'd hastened to add, I would still be on probation. Had Wiggins decided I was too unsuitable? Was even probationary status not possible for me? Was that why I'd had no summons from him for another adven— mission?

Possibly he'd simply neglected to consider me for a task. Mama told us kids not to invite ourselves, but I remembered quite a few instances when being bold paid off. The squeaky wheel and all that.

In the distance, I heard the clack of wheels on the rails and the poignant wail of the train whistle. The Rescue Express was nearing the station. Clearly, Wiggins would soon be dispatching earthbound travelers or welcoming home those whose journeys were done.

I was shot through with a hot flash of sheer envy.

Oh, dear. How small-spirited of me. Certainly, I was delighted that others had found favor in Wiggins's eyes and been dispatched for adventure . . . Scratch that thought. Adventure was never the goal of a well-behaved emissary. Certainly, I wasn't seeking fun and thrills.

Well, maybe a little bit.

Okay, okay, I loved excitement and, whether Wiggins wanted to admit it or not, being dispatched to earth to help someone in dire need was a grand adventure.

If Wiggins was aware of my unworthy feelings, surely he understood I was only revealing the depths of my desire to be helpful.

I filled my mind with a vision of the parchment roll and the Precepts and mounted the station steps two at a time. It was only as I was passing into the station that I realized I was still in a blouse and shorts. Fortunately, a new wardrobe occurs in an instant of thought.

By the time Wiggins looked up from his desk, I was in a drab black jacket dress with white trim on the jacket and plain black leather shoes. My hair was subdued in a chignon with only a few unruly red curls. I affected a reserved expression.

Wiggins rose at once, a look of surprise on his florid round face. He was just as I remembered, stiff black cap riding high on reddish-brown hair, bristly eyebrows, spaniel-sweet brown eyes, thick muttonchop sideburns, walrus mustache, crisp white shirt, suspenders, gray flannel trousers, and shiny bootblacked shoes.

"Bailey Ruth." Big hands enveloped mine in a warm grip. Suddenly he frowned. "You look different."

Was he remembering the lavender velour pantsuit I'd enjoyed on my previous earthly adven— mission? If I were fortunate enough to serve on earth again, I could find out about the latest fashions and enjoy them. I was confident that pleasure in beauty, whether of nature or couture, was God-given. At this moment, I was determined to appear studious and contemplative, a role model of an emissary, the sort who popped to earth, worked unobtrusively, and left without notice.

Unlike my previous experience.

I gave a cool smile. "It's the new me. I've been studying Zen."

"Oh?" He blinked in surprise.

"The better to serve as an emissary." I remembered not to even hint at the word ghost. Wiggins loathes the term. Although as far as I'm concerned calling a spade a digging implement doesn't make it not a spade. If you know what I mean.

"Zen." He raised a brushy eyebrow.

"Zen." I tried to sound authoritative.

"Zen?" His tone invited elucidation.

"Zen. Meditating on paradoxes." I dredged that from a long ago memory of my son Rob's Zen phase when he was in college.

"Indeed." His smile was kind. "Does that assist you in remaining in the moment?"

He might as well have been speaking Greek. If he had been speaking Greek, I would have understood. In Heaven we all understand each other whether we speak Cherokee, Yiddish, or Mandarin. Or Greek.

Zen in any tongue was beyond my grasp. It was manifestly unfair that Wiggins, who'd departed the earth long before I, had obviously been attending Zen classes in Heaven.

"I don't know a thing about Zen." In admitting defeat, I hoped to demonstrate my core honesty.

His smile was huge. "Oh, Bailey Ruth. You always manage to surprise me."

I blinked back a tear. "That's the problem, isn't it? I don't do things by the book." I meant by the parchment roll, but he understood. "Is that why you haven't summoned me for a new adven— mission?"

Wiggins tugged at his mustache, then gestured to a bench beside his desk. He settled into his chair, and after a quick glance through the bay window at the tracks, he faced me, his genial face perplexed. "You have been in my thoughts."

Was this good? I was determined to believe so. I beamed at him. "I'm glad. Perhaps my coming here today was meant to be." I leaned forward. "Clearly, there's a problem on earth that I can solve." That put the ball in his court. Hopefully my I-can-do attitude was attractive.

Instead of an answering smile, he looked thoughtful. "You do have a special qualification."

Better and better. "Whatever the project requires, I am ready."

"Undoubtedly you have a qualification." His tone was reluctant, as if an admission wrung under duress. "However, you lack the calm and reserve of a Heavenly emissary. You are," he ticked off the offenses one by one, "inquisitive, impulsive, rash—"

I completed the litany. "—forthright and daring."

We looked at each other, I with fading hope, Wiggins sorrowfully.

I was tempted to change back into a blouse and shorts and waft to Bobby Mac and the *Serendipity*, riding in crystal clear blue waters for another eternal day. Yet Wiggins had thought of me for a mission. There had to be a reason. "My special qualification?"

His florid face relaxed into warmth and delight. "Bailey Ruth, you always loved Christmas."

Christmas . . . Oh dear Heaven, Christmas was the most special season of the year. Cold and gray outside? When I listened to the jingle of the Salvation Army kettle, I felt warm as toast. Jammed among sharp-elbowed shoppers in a suffocatingly hot store? That cashmere sweater was perfect for Aunt Mamie. A broken oven and twenty-three expected for Christmas dinner? Bobby Mac pulled out the grill, bundled up against a forty-degree north wind, and that day's ribeye steaks were ever after celebrated in family history.

My eyes sparkled as I recalled some of my favorite things:

Sugar cookies shaped like stars and iced in red.

Main street ablaze with green and red lights and plenty of tinsel.

Strings of holly.

Carolers on a crisp starlit night.

Cutting down our very own Scotch pine out in the country.

Bobby Mac holding Rob in one arm, Dil in the other, and small hands reaching up to place a wobbly star atop the tree.

Presents wrapped in bright red-and-gold foil.

Crimson poinsettias massed behind the altar and on the ledges by the stained-glass windows and in the narthex.

The exquisite peace and hope of Mother and Child in the manger.

I was swept by that wonderful feeling of the season when workaday cares recede and we glimpse a world bright with love. "Ooh. Christmas." Every Christmas Eve, Bobby Mac (a robust tenor) and I (an energetic soprano) entertained Rob and Dil with our duet of "Rudolph, the Red-Nosed Reindeer" as we pulled a sled laden with gifts into the living room. A two-foot tall stuffed reindeer with a shiny red nose was harnessed to the sled.

I came to my feet, quickly attired in my best Mrs. Claus suit and floppy red Santa hat, and belted out my most spirited version of Rudolph. Tap was popular when I was young and the wooden floor of the station a perfect venue . . . Four slap ball changes, four shuffle hop steps, a shuffle off to Buffalo . . . Sweeping off my Santa hat, I ended with a flap cramp roll and a graceful bow.

Flushed with success, I lifted my gaze to Wiggins.

He sat, brown eyes wide, expression bemused.

Had the man never seen a hoofer before? Had I blown any chance for adven—to be of service? Had my impetuous nature once again landed me in trouble?

His lips curved in a broad smile. His eyes shone. "That takes me back. Indeed it does. I saw Bojangles in Chicago in 1909. I never miss any of his shows."

I made a mental note to check the jazz schedule for Bill Robinson's next starlit performance. You haven't lived until you've seen a show with the Milky Way as spots.

"Only you, Bailey Ruth, would remember Christmas with a tap dance." Wiggins's tone was admiring.

I think.

Abruptly, he gave a decided nod. "That's why your dossier kept reappearing." He reached out, pulled a candy-cane striped folder close to him, flipped it open.

I craned to see. There was my picture, a sea breeze stirring my flaming hair as the *Serendipity* breasted swells.

Wiggins patted the top sheet. "You have the true spirit of Christmas and that is what I need here, despite your impetuous nature." He turned and thumbed through a stack of folders in various colors. He opened a black one.

I didn't dwell on his qualifying phrase. Christmas spirit I could supply in plenty.

His face was grave when he faced me. "This situation," he tapped the folder, "is murky. Your previous task was clear cut: a lovely damsel visited with a body on her back porch. Of course, I didn't expect the action you took . . ." Some of his enthusiasm seemed to drain away. He gave a quick shake of his head. "I don't know if the department should take a chance again. But," hope lifted his voice, "possibly in this instance nothing will be required of you except calm overseeing." He nodded decisively and repeated with vigor, "Calm overseeing," as if I might have trouble hearing.

I decided not to be offended.

"On balance, you might be perfect for this visit. You love Christmas and you have a youthful heart. I was especially touched that you spun stories for Dil and Rob about Santa's workshop and who might need a particular toy. You helped them feel the spirit of giving. Whatever happens, you can beam love on a dear little boy, an orphan whose future is uncertain." Wiggins tone fell to a puzzled mutter. "Surely Keith's protector has the best of intentions. She is kind and caring." He pulled a map close, marked a path in red, muttered, "Adelaide obviously is her goal. However, no contact has been made at the house."

"The house?" I figuratively rolled up my sleeves. This time around Wiggins could give me the background, prepare me for my task. I pushed away the uneasy sense that no matter how prepared I might have been on my previous mission, I would have been tempted to flout the Precepts if I felt the need. This time, however, I would be on my best behavior.

For starters, I would avoid appearing. The rich swirl of colors that preceded my transformation from spirit to earth-bound creature had an unfortunate effect on viewers.

I would remember that carrying discrete objects while not in the flesh was equally unnerving to them.

I would be particularly careful not to speak aloud when I wasn't there.

I wasn't concerned about the Precept prohibiting consorting with another departed spirit. Whatever my mission, it couldn't possibly involve a departed spirit. It would be easy to observe this stricture.

However, I felt a qualm. Other of the Precepts could easily pose a challenge. The life of a spirit is fraught with opportunities to transgress—however unintentionally—the Precepts.

I came back to the moment—perhaps I did have a penchant for Zen—to realize that Wiggins had been discoursing.

" . . . though the decorations are up, and I will admit they are spectacular, the heart of Christmas left Pritchard house when Susan Flynn received word of her son's death. So much sadness."

"Pritchard house?" I pictured a grand home high on Chickasaw Ridge. Only one house in Adelaide was red brick with two huge bay windows on the first floor, half-timbered and stuccoed and balconied in English Tudor with Gothic accents on the second story.

Wiggins tapped my folder. "I assume you know the Pritchards."

"Everyone in Adelaide knows the Pritchards." Growing up in Adelaide, I could count on these verities: My family loved me, the sun rose in the east, St. Mildred's Episcopal Church was our spiritual home, the wind blew mostly from the south, and two families comprised Adelaide's small-town aristocracy, the Pritchards and the Humes.

Paul Pritchard, cool-eyed and remote, came west from Boston in 1912 to establish Adelaide's first bank. The Pritchards were formal, reserved, elegant, and supportive of the community, often hosting charity teas in their Chickasaw Ridge home. The Humes—ah well—the Humes were another story altogether, boisterous, sensation seeking, sometimes scandalous. Their drink of choice had a bit more punch than tea.

"The Pritchards did everything perfectly."

Wiggins slowly shook his head. "Dear Bailey Ruth, don't be blinded by worldly success and social position."

I flicked the fluffy ball on the tail of my Santa hat over my shoulder. Woe be to me if Wiggins decided I was naive. I added hastily, "In their support of St. Mildred's." Paul and his wife Jane had been founding members of St. Mildred's and subsequent generations continued generous financial support to the church. "Hannah and Maurice Pritchard furnished the money for the chapel and cloister." I'd been in awe of Hannah on earth, but here in Heaven she was in one of my book clubs and I thoroughly enjoyed her gentle wit.

Wiggins's smile was avuncular. "How appropriate that your first thought would be of St. Mildred's. I commend you."

My face flamed. That is a redhead's hazard, scarlet cheeks when attempting a fib.

Fortunately Wiggins was looking at his folders. Again

he appeared uneasy. "It's unfortunate that I am not certain of Keith's arrival at Pritchard House. Yet I see no other purpose for the trip. The car appears to be en route to Adelaide. In any event, time is fleeting for Susan."

I blinked in surprise.

Wiggins is perceptive. "In the natural order, we know when to expect new arrivals. Susan suffers from congestive heart failure, but she isn't due here until June 15. Yet," his brow furrowed, "I am definitely worried. Call it a hunch." His tone suggested the word was not one he commonly used. Possibly hunch wasn't au courant until much after Wiggins's time on earth. Could he have picked it up from an emissary? Indeed, he looked embarrassed at his suggestion and said defensively, "I've been doing this over the course of many years as understood in earthly time—"

Time does not exist in Heaven, but I am no more able to explain this verity than to expound on Zen.

"—and sometimes I have a feeling of impending danger, almost as if a darkening cloud is blotting out the sun. That's why I think—"

A frantic *clack clack clack*, sharp as Rudolph's hooves on a Mission-style roof, erupted from the telegraph sounder on Wiggins's desk.

Wiggins quickly removed his stiff cap, clamped on a green eyeshade, and grabbed a sheet. He wrote furiously, murmuring, "Oh dear, what can this mean? Steps must be taken!"

The clacking reached a peak, abruptly subsided.

Wiggins tapped a response and came to his feet, all in one hurried motion. He gestured to me as he grabbed a bright-red ticket from a slotted rack. "No time to stamp. Red signals emergency. The conductor will understand. I'll pull down the signal arm for an emergency stop of the Rescue Express. Run, Bailey Ruth."

In an instant, I was racing toward the platform, ticket in hand, Wiggins pounding behind me. What a grand turn of events. I tried to hide my excitement. Wiggins would frown upon overt delight in being dispatched to earth. That might underscore his concern that I had, in my previous adven— mission, found it difficult to remember that emissaries are *on* the earth but not *of* the earth. This Precept evoked an emotional response from Wiggins, who deplored the possibility of an emissary reverting to earthly attitudes instead of exhibiting Heavenly virtues. This time would be different. I would most nobly remember at all times that I was *on* but not *of*. I would make Wiggins proud.

Despite my effort to remain suitably grave—hard to do when running full tilt—I felt my lips curving in delight. I, Bailey Ruth Raeburn, was once again ticketed for the Rescue Express. Watch my dust!

As the train screeched to a stop and a porter reached out to pull me aboard, Wiggins looked unhappily at the folder he clutched. " . . . no time for you to study the reports . . . find out everything about those who surround Susan Flynn . . . won't do for you to take the folder . . . existing matter would be a burden since of course this time you will not appear. I'm sure you won't."

I thought his tone rather pitiful.

" . . . shocking turn of events . . . I should have sent you sooner . . . such an unexpected act . . . protect that dear little boy . . ."

...uzzlers
from award-winning author

CAROLYN HART

THE HENRIE O MYSTERIES

DEATH IN LOVERS' LANE
978-0-380-79002-9
When one of her gifted journalism students is found
dead, Henrie O is determined to find the killer.

DEATH IN PARADISE

A fra... ...s...e Henrie O to San Antonio to investigate
the disappearance of her friend's devoted granddaughter.

RESORT TO MURDER
978-0-380-80720-8
Henrie O joins her grandchildren at an elegant oceanfront
hotel and is soon embroiled in a deadly puzzle.

SET SAIL FOR MURDER
978-0-06-072408-5
When her old friend Jimmy Lennox is accused of murder, Henrie O
must pursue a clever killer who may strike again.

Visit www.AuthorTracker.com for exclusive
information on your favorite HarperCollins authors.

Available wherever books are sold or please call 1-800-331-3761 to order.

CHH 0108